S0-DXO-685

# THE WILD ONE

He was sprawled, full-length, along a tree branch just outside her window . . .

"Just what on earth are you doing, Lord Gareth?"

He gave Juliet his most devasting grin and said, "Why, I have come to rescue you, of course. May I please come in and talk?"

"Of course not! I cannot have a man in my bedroom!"

"Why not, my sweet? I had you in mine."

"Really, Lord Gareth . . . You should go home. After all, you're the son of a duke, and I'm just a—"

"—beautiful young woman with nowhere else to go. A beautiful young woman who should be a part of my family. Now, do collect your things. I fear we must make haste, if we are to marry—"

"Marry?"

"Well, yes, of course. Surely you don't think I'd be hanging out of a tree for anything less, do you?"

*Other* **AVON ROMANCES**

CAPTAIN JACK'S WOMAN *by Stephanie Laurens*
HIGHLAND BRIDES: THE LADY AND THE KNIGHT
*by Lois Greiman*
MOUNTAIN BRIDE *by Susan Sawyer*
A PRINCE AMONG MEN *by Kate Moore*
STOLEN KISSES *by Suzanne Enoch*
TOPAZ *by Beverly Jenkins*
A TOUGH MAN'S WOMAN *by Deborah Camp*


*Coming Soon*

A DIME NOVEL HERO *by Maureen McKade*
A ROSE IN SCOTLAND *by Joan Overfield*


*And Don't Miss These*
**ROMANTIC TREASURES**
*from Avon Books*

BRIGHTER THAN THE SUN *by Julia Quinn*
TO LOVE A STRANGER *by Connie Mason*
WALTZ IN TIME *by Eugenia Riley*

---

Avon Books are available at special quantity discounts for bulk purchases for sales promotions, premiums, fund raising or educational use. Special books, or book excerpts, can also be created to fit specific needs.

For details write or telephone the office of the Director of Special Markets, Avon Books, Dept. FP, 1350 Avenue of the Americas, New York, New York 10019, 1-800-238-0658.

# The Wild One

## Danelle Harmon

AVON BOOKS ◆ NEW YORK

This is a work of fiction. Names, characters, places and incidents either are the product of the author's imagination or are used fictitiously. Any resemblance to actual events, locales, organizations, or persons, living or dead, is entirely coincidental and beyond the intent of either the author or the publisher.

AVON BOOKS
A division of
The Hearst Corporation
1350 Avenue of the Americas
New York, New York 10019

Copyright © 1997 by Danelle F. Colson
Published by arrangement with the author
Visit our website at **http://www.AvonBooks.com**
Library of Congress Catalog Card Number: 97-93788
ISBN: 0-380-79262-1

All rights reserved, which includes the right to reproduce this book or portions thereof in any form whatsoever except as provided by the U. S. Copyright Law. For information address Lowenstein Associates, Inc., 121 West 27th Street, Suite 601, New York, New York 10001.

First Avon Books Printing: December 1997

AVON TRADEMARK REG. U.S. PAT. OFF. AND IN OTHER COUNTRIES, MARCA REGISTRADA, HECHO EN U.S.A.

Printed in the U.S.A.

WCD   10  9  8  7  6  5  4  3  2  1

If you purchased this book without a cover, you should be aware that this book is stolen property. It was reported as "unsold and destroyed" to the publisher, and neither the author nor the publisher has received any payment for this "stripped book."

This book is dedicated to my editor, Christine Zika—
with gratitude for her enthusiasm, the lovely cover,
and of course, for suggesting I write this book
(and series) in the first place.
Thanks, Christine—you're brilliant!

# Acknowledgments

Many thanks:

To Lauren Bourque, for your patience, wisdom, inspiration and friendship. Thank God we ran into each other in Waitrose that day and I asked you about the sandwiches! [[[hugs]]]]

To Andrea Coursey, another platinum friend; thank you for your help with the manuscript, for always being there for me—and for encouraging me to "paint dreams" when I found my heart so painfully divided between the two countries I love so much.

To Antony Stone, whose Solutions are not just in Software; thank you for the time you spent on the manuscript, and for ensuring I got those certain Britishisms exactly right. You've shown me that life is not about irreversible decisions, but choices—and that nothing is ever cast in stone. You deserve every rose petal in the Antonial Shrine and then some.

To Julie Pottinger, aka Julia Quinn—I could buy you a hundred Friendly's sundaes and it still wouldn't be enough to thank you!

To Nancy Yost, my agent—your insight and advice are invaluable!

To Roscoe, who grudgingly sacrificed walks when I was on deadline.

And especially to Chris, my dear, sweet husband. How you can put up with me, I'll never know!

Thanks, everyone—for being who you are, and for being part of my life. I love you all.

# Prologue

Newman House, 18 April 1775

My dear brother, Lucien,

It has just gone dark and as I pen these words to you, an air of rising tension hangs above this troubled town. Tonight, several regiments—including mine, the King's Own—have been ordered by General Gage, commander in chief of our forces here in Boston, out to Concord to seize and destroy a significant store of arms and munitions that the rebels have secreted there. Due to the clandestine nature of this assignment, I have ordered my batman, Billingshurst, to withhold the posting of this letter until the morrow, when the mission will have been completed and secrecy will no longer be of concern.

Although it is my most ardent hope that no blood will be shed on either side during this endeavour, I find that my heart, in these final moments before I must leave, is restless and uneasy. It is not for myself that I am afraid, but another. As you know from my previous letters home, I have met a young woman here with whom I have become attached in a warm friendship. I suspect you do not approve of my becoming so enamoured of a storekeeper's

1

*daughter, but things are different in this place, and when a fellow is three thousand miles away from home, love makes a far more desirable companion than loneliness. My dear Miss Paige has made me happy, Lucien, and earlier tonight she accepted my plea for her hand in marriage. I beg you to understand, and forgive, for I know that someday when you meet her, you will love her as I do.*

*My brother, I have but one thing to ask of you, and knowing that you will see to my wishes is the only thing that calms my troubled soul during these last few moments before we depart. If anything should happen to me—tonight, tomorrow, or at any time whilst I am here in Boston—I beg of you to find it in your heart to show charity and kindness to my angel, my Juliet, for she means the world to me. I know you will take care of her if ever I cannot. Do this for me and I shall be happy, Lucien.*

*I must close now, as the others are gathered downstairs in the parlour, and we are all ready to move. May God bless and keep you, my dear brother, and Gareth, Andrew, and sweet Nerissa, too.*

*Charles*

Sometime during the last hour, it had begun to grow dark.

Lucien de Montforte turned the letter over in his hands, his hooded gaze shuttered, his mind far away as he stared out the window over the downs that stood like sentinels against the fading twilight. A breath of pink still glowed in the western sky, but it would soon be gone. He hated this time of night, this still and lonely hour just after sunset when old ghosts were near, and distant memories welled up in the heart with the poignant nearness of yesterday, close enough to see yet always too elusive to touch.

But the letter was real. Too real.

He ran a thumb over the heavy vellum, the bold, elegant script that had been so distinctive of Charles's style—both on paper, in thought, and on the field—still looking as fresh as if it had been written yesterday, not last April. His own name was there on the front: TO HIS GRACE THE DUKE OF BLACKHEATH, BLACKHEATH CASTLE, NR. RAVENSCOMBE, BERKSHIRE, ENGLAND.

They were probably the last words Charles had ever written.

Carefully, he folded the letter along creases that had become fragile and well-worn. The blob of red wax with which his brother had sealed the letter came together at the edges like a wound that had never healed, and try as he might to avoid seeing them, his gaze caught the words that someone, probably Billingshurst, had written on the back. . . .

*Found on the desk of Captain Lord Charles Adair de Montforte on the 19th of April 177 , the day on which his lordship was killed in the fighting near Concord. Please deliver to addressee.*

A pang went through him. Dead, gone, and all but forgotten, just like that.

The Duke of Blackheath carefully laid the letter inside the drawer, which he shut and locked. He gazed once more out the window, lord of all he surveyed but unable to master his own bitter emptiness. A mile away, at the foot of the downs, he could just see the twinkling lights of Ravenscombe village, could envision its ancient church with its Norman tower and tombs of de Montforte dead. And there, inside, high on the stone wall of the East chancel, was the simple bronze plaque that was all they had to tell posterity that his brother had ever even lived.

Charles, the second son.

God help them all if anything happened to him, Lucien, and the dukedom passed to the third.

No. God would not be so cruel.

He snuffed the single candle and, with the darkness enclosing him, the sky still glowing beyond the window, moved from the room.

# 1

*Berkshire, England, 1776*

The Flying White was bound for Oxford, and it was running late. Now, trying to make up time lost to a broken axle, the driver had whipped up the team, and the coach careered through the night in a cacophony of shouts, thundering hooves, and cries from the passengers who were clinging for their lives on the roof above.

Strong lanterns cut through the rainy darkness, picking out ditches, trees, and hedgerows as the vehicle hurtled through the Lambourn Downs at a pace that had Juliet Paige's heart in her throat. Because of Charlotte, her six-month-old daughter, Juliet had been lucky enough to get a seat inside the coach, but even so, her head banged against the leather squabs on the right, her shoulder against an elderly gent on her left, and her neck ached with the constant side to side movement. On the seat across from her, another young mother clung to her two frightened children, one huddled under each arm. It had been a dreadful run up from Southampton indeed, and Juliet was feeling almost as ill as she had during the long sea voyage over from Boston.

The coach hit a bump, became airborne for a split

second, and landed hard, snapping her neck, throwing her violently against the man on her left, and causing the passengers clinging to the roof above to cry out in terror. Someone's trunk went flying off the coach, but the driver never slowed the galloping team.

"God help us!" murmured the young mother across from Juliet as her children cringed fearfully against her.

Juliet grasped the strap and hung her head, fighting nausea as she hugged her own child. Her lips touched the baby's downy gold curls. "Almost there," she whispered, for Charlotte's ears alone. "Almost there—to your papa's home."

Suddenly there were shouts, a horse's frightened whinny, and violent curses from the driver. Someone on the roof screamed. The coach careened madly, the inhabitants both inside and out shrieking in terror as the vehicle hurtled along on two wheels for another forty or fifty feet before finally crashing heavily down on its axles with another neck-snapping jolt, shattering a window with the impact and spilling the elderly gent to the floor. Outside, someone was sobbing in fear and pain.

And inside, the atmosphere of the coach went as still as death.

"We're being robbed!" cried the old man, getting to his knees to peer out the rain-spattered window.

Shots rang out. There was a heavy thud from above, then movement just beyond the ominous black pane. And suddenly without warning it imploded, showering the inside passengers in a hail of glass.

Gasping, they looked up to see a heavy pistol— and a masked face just beyond it.

"Yer money or yer life. *Now!*"

*   *   *

It was the very devil of a night. No moon, no stars, and a light rain stinging his face as Lord Gareth Francis de Montforte sent his horse, Crusader, flying down the Wantage road at a speed approaching suicide. Stands of beech and oak shot past, there then gone. Pounding hooves splashed through puddles and echoed against the hedgerows that bracketed the road. Gareth glanced over his shoulder, saw nothing but a long empty stretch of road behind him, and shouted with glee. Another race won—Perry, Chilcot, and the rest of the Den of Debauchery would never catch him now!

Laughing, he patted Crusader's neck as the hunter pounded through the night. "Well done, good fellow! Well done—"

And pulled him up sharply at he passed Wether Down.

It took him only a moment to assess the situation.

*Highwaymen.* And by the looks of it, they were helping themselves to the pickings—and passengers—of the Flying White from Southampton.

*The Flying White?* The young gentleman reached inside his coat pocket and pulled out his watch, squinting to see its face in the darkness. Damned late for the Flying White . . .

He dropped the timepiece back into his pocket, steadied Crusader, and considered what to do. No gentlemen of the road, this lot, but a trio of desperate, hardened killers. The driver and guard lay on the ground beside the coach, both presumably dead. Somewhere a child was crying, and now one of the bandits, with a face that made a hatchet look kind, smashed in the windows of the coach with the butt end of his gun. Gareth reached for his pistol. The thought of quietly turning around and going back the way he'd come never occurred to him. The thought of waiting for his friends, probably some three miles behind thanks to Crusader's blistering speed, didn't occur to him, either. Especially when he saw one of the bandits yank open the door of the coach and haul out a struggling young woman.

He had just the briefest glimpse of her face—scared, pale, beautiful—before one of the highwaymen shot out the lanterns of the coach, and darkness fell over the entire scene. Someone screamed. Another shot rang out, silencing the frightened cry abruptly.

His face grim, the young gentleman knotted his horse's reins and removed his gloves, pulling each one carefully off by the fingertips. With a watchful eye on the highwaymen, he slipped his feet from the irons and vaulted lightly down from the thoroughbred's tall back, his glossy top boots of Spanish leather landing in chalk mud up to his ankles. The horse never moved. He doffed his fine new surtout and laid it over the saddle along with his tricorn and gloves. He tucked the lace at his wrist safely inside his sleeve to protect it from any soot or sparks his pistol might emit. Then he crept through the knee-high weeds and nettles that grew thick at the side of the road, priming and loading the pistol as he moved stealthily toward the stricken coach. He would have time to squeeze off only one shot before they were upon him, and that one shot had to count.

"Everybo'y out. *Now!*"

Holding Charlotte tightly against her, Juliet managed to remain calm as the robber snared her wrist and jerked her violently from the vehicle. She landed awkwardly in the sticky white mud and would have gone down if not for the huge, bearlike hand that yanked her to her feet. Perhaps, she thought numbly, it was the very fact that it *was* bearlike that she was able to keep her head—and her wits—about her, for Juliet had been born and raised in the woods of Maine, and she was no stranger to bears, Indians, and a host of other threats that made these English highwaymen look benign by comparison.

They were certainly not benign. The slain driver lay facedown in the mud. The bodies of one of the guards and a passenger were sprawled in the weeds nearby. A shudder went through her. She was glad of the darkness. Glad that the poor little children still inside the coach were spared the horrors that daylight would have revealed.

Cuddling Charlotte, she stood beside the other passengers as the robbers yanked people down from the roof and lined them up in front of the coach. A woman was sobbing. A girl clung pitifully to the old man, perhaps her grandfather. One fellow, finely dressed and obviously a gentleman, angrily protested the treatment of the women and without a word, one of the highwayman stuck his pistol into his belly and shot him dead. As he fell, the wretched group gasped in dismay and horror. Then the last passengers were dragged from the coach, the two children clinging to their mother's skirts and crying piteously.

They all huddled together in the rainy darkness, too terrified to speak as, one by one, they were relieved of their money, their jewels, their watches, and their pride.

And then the bandits came to Juliet.

"Gimme yer money, girl, all of it. Now!"

Juliet complied. Without a sound, she handed over her reticule.

"The necklace, too."

Her hand went to her throat. Hesitated. The robber cuffed it away in impatience, ripping the thin gold chain from her neck and dropping the miniature of Charlotte's dead father into his leather bag.

"Any jewels?"

She was still staring at the bag. "No."

"Any rings?"

"No."

But he grabbed her hand, held it up, and saw it: a promise made but broken by death. It was Charles's signet ring—her engagement ring—the last thing her beloved fiancé had given her before he had died in the fighting near Concord.

"Filthy lyin' bitch, give it to me!"

Juliet stood her ground. She looked him straight in the eye and firmly, quietly, repeated the single word.

"*No.*"

Without warning, he backhanded her across the cheek, and she fell to her knees in the mud, cutting her palm on a stone as she tried to prevent injury to the baby. Her hair tumbled down around her face. Charlotte began screaming. And Juliet looked up, only to see the black hole of a pistol's mouth two inches away, the robber behind it snarling with rage.

Her life passed before her eyes.

And at that moment a shot rang out from somewhere off to her right, a dark rose exploded on the highwayman's chest, and with a look of surprise, he pitched forward, dead.

*Only one shot, but by God, I made it count.*

The other two highwaymen jerked around at the bark of Gareth's pistol. Their faces mirrored disbelief as they took in his fine shirt and lace at throat and sleeve, his silk waistcoat, expensive boots, expensive breeches, expensive everything. They saw him as a plum ripe for the picking, and Gareth knew it. He went for his sword.

"Get on your horses and go, and neither of you shall be hurt."

For a moment, neither the highwaymen nor the passengers moved. Then, slowly, one of the highwaymen began to smile. The other, to sneer.

"*Now!*" Gareth commanded, still moving forward

and trying to bluff them with his display of cool authority.

And then all hell broke loose.

Tongues of flame cracked from the highwaymen's pistols and Gareth heard the low whine of a ball passing at close range. Passengers screamed and dived for cover. The coach horses reared, whinnying in fear. Gareth, his sword raised, charged through the tangle of nettle that grew dense at the side of the road, trying to get to the robbers before they could reload and fire. His foot hit a patch of mud and he went down, his cheek slamming into the fiery stinging nettles. One of the highwaymen came racing toward him, spewing a torrent of foul language and intent only on finishing him off. Gareth lay gasping, then flung himself hard to the left as the highwayman's pistol coughed another spear of flame. Where his shoulder had been, a plume of mud shot several inches into the air.

The brigand was still coming, roaring at the top of his lungs, already bringing up a second pistol.

Gamely, Gareth tried to get to his feet and reach his sword. He slipped in the wet weeds, his cheek feeling as though he'd just been stung by a hundred bees. He was outnumbered, his pistol spent, his sword just out of reach. But he wasn't done for. Not yet. Not by any stretch of the imagination. He lunged for his sword, rolled onto his back, and, raising himself to a sitting position, flung the weapon at the oncoming highwayman with all his strength.

The blade caught the robber just beneath the jaw and nearly took his head off. He went over backward, clawing at his throat, his dying breath a terrible, rasping gurgle.

And then Gareth saw one of the two children running toward him, obviously thinking he was the only safety left in this world gone mad.

*"Billy!"* the mother was screaming. "Billy, no, *get back!"*

The last highwayman spun around. Wild-eyed and desperate, he saw the fleeing child, saw that his two friends were dead, and, as though to avenge a night gone wrong, brought his pistol up, training it on the little boy's back.

*"Billeeeeeeee!"*

With the last of his strength, Gareth lunged to his feet, threw himself at the child, and tumbled him to the ground, shielding him with his body. The pistol exploded at close range, deafening him, a white-hot lance of fire ripping through his ribs as he rolled over and over through grass and weeds and nettles, the child still in his arms.

He came to rest upon his back, the wet weeds beneath him, blood gushing hotly from his side. He lay still, blinking up at the trees, the rain falling gently upon his throbbing face.

His fading mind echoed his earlier words. *Well done, good fellow! Well done. . . .*

The child sprang up and ran, sobbing, back to his mother.

And for Lord Gareth de Montforte, all went dark.

# 2

"**H**elp him!" Juliet cried. She thrust Charlotte into the other mother's arms, picked up her skirts and ran headlong through the weeds toward the fallen gentleman. "Dear God, he saved us all!"

Still in shock, the other passengers stood milling around like sheep; but Juliet's words penetrated their daze, and before he could flee into the woods the last highwayman was subdued, and a horde of people was charging through the weeds after Juliet.

"Is he all right?"

"Bless him, he saved that little boy, that dear, sweet little boy—"

Juliet reached him first. He lay on his back, half-concealed by a canopy of dripping nettles—broken, bleeding, still. She plunged to her knees beside him and grabbed his hand—so lifeless, so smooth—and shoved her finger beneath the lace that draped it, trying to locate a pulse.

Others came rushing up behind her.

"Is he dead?"

"Sure seems like it to me, poor fellow—"

Juliet looked up at them over her shoulder. "He's not dead, but I fear he will be if we don't get help, and soon!"

Ignoring the commotion behind her, she squeezed his fingers, willing him to hold onto life as more

13

people came running to his assistance. She saw the blood soaking through his fine clothes, the paleness of his cheek beneath the crescent of dark lashes that lay against it. Wet stinging nettles were crushed beneath the other. Tenderly, Juliet reached down, flinching as those same fiery weeds stung her own tender skin, and lifted his head so that his face was clear of them.

His cheek was already puckered and angry. Juliet looked up at the circle of faces above. "Someone, please give me a coat, a cape, anything!"

His breath smelled of spirits. His head was a heavy, lolling weight in her hands, his damp hair coming loose from its queue to spill in soft, tumbling waves over her fingers. Someone thrust a jacket beneath him, and she gently eased his head back down to it as more people came hurrying toward them.

"Let's get him out of these nettles and into the coach," Juliet said, instinctively taking charge. Thank God her upbringing in Maine's wilderness had prepared her for situations such as this! "You, take his feet. You there, help me take his shoulders. Hurry, let's go!"

Their fallen savior was a tall man, lean and honed with muscle, a dead weight as they struggled to lift him. They rushed him across the road to the coach, where two people were already spreading a blanket on the grass for him while another hastily began clearing the vehicle's interior of broken glass. The other mother stood nearby, pale and silent, trying to quiet Charlotte while her own children, seeing the injured man, hid their faces in her skirts.

Juliet shut her mind to her baby's distress. "Right here. Easy with him. He's been hurt, badly."

People pressed close, eager to help. This gallant gentleman had saved their lives, and everyone seemed to want to touch him. Hands reached out to support him beneath his arms, his body, his legs, though so many were not needed and only got in the way. Gently, they lowered him to the blanket while the coach was made ready for him. Kneeling beside him, the other passengers crowding around and above her, Juliet quickly loosened the flawlessly knotted, elegant spill of lace at his throat. Then she began unbuttoning his waistcoat, her fingertips going wet and slippery with blood as they neared the wound in his side.

*You can't die,* she willed him, working furiously now and calling for some light. *Not after what you've done for us!*

Charlotte, still in the stranger's arms, began to wail, only adding to Juliet's sense of urgency.

Someone found a candle and flint. Suddenly, feeble light danced over worried faces and threw Juliet's shadow across the injured man. As she gingerly undid the last button, his head began to move weakly on the blanket. He groaned in pain, his skin as white as chalk, his eyelashes fluttering.

"The child . . ." he said, thickly.

"The child's fine. Be still. Relax. You're going to be all right." Out of the corner of her eye, Juliet could see movement, shadowy and silent, as the dead were placed side by side and covered with a blanket. *Please God, don't let this poor gentleman be joining them.* She slid her fingers beneath his waistcoat, peeling it away from his blood-soaked shirt and feeling a wave of nausea at the sight that met her eyes. In the dim glow of the candle, blood was everywhere.

"Oh, dear God, I'm going to faint," murmured one of the woman passengers, who was quickly escorted away from the grim scene before she could.

And all the while Charlotte's piercing wails rang in Juliet's head.

She shut her mind to her bawling daughter. She shut it to the last highwayman, his hands tied to a nearby tree, his mouth cursing them in language horrible enough to make her toes curl. She shut it to the people breathing down her neck, to her own queasiness, to her fear that this man was dying and there was nothing that she or anyone could do for him.

"I need a knife," she said, anxiously looking up at the faces above. "Does anyone have one?"

A small blade was produced, and Juliet deftly slit the injured man's shirt all the way to his breeches. The fabric was soaked with blood. Gently, she eased it open where the ball had gone in. In the feeble light, it was impossible to tell how badly he was hurt, but there was an awful lot of blood.

"We need to get help immediately," she said, ripping a length of cotton from her petticoats and packing it into his side in an attempt to stop the bleeding. "I don't want to move him for fear of making his injury worse. Does anyone know where we are, how close the nearest village or town might be?"

"I think we're almost into Ravenscombe."

"Is there a doctor there?"

"Don't know. If not, might be one back in Lambourn, I should think...."

Juliet shook her head. "We can't go charging all over England with him while we're looking for a doctor. It would be better if one of you rides for help and brings one back." Glances were exchanged. "*Now!*"

Her sharp word jolted everyone into action. Two men ran to the nervous coach horses, but another was already leading a well-bred chestnut steed from out of the surrounding darkness. "Here, take his instead, it's saddled and ready."

"I'll go!"

"No, let me, I insist!"

After a brief debate about who would do the honors, someone swung up onto the tall hunter and the animal was away, thundering off down the road.

And then the little group was alone. Both Charlotte and the highwayman had finally quieted, and now there was nothing but the soft rustle of the wind through the copper beeches, the sound of rain pitter-pattering into the puddled ruts. It was falling harder now, and two of the women stretched a coat over the injured man, trying to protect his face from the wet as Juliet tore another strip from her petticoats and bound it tightly around his torso.

There was nothing to do but wait. In the deep silence of the night none of the passengers spoke, each remembering the shots, the highwaymen, the deaths—and this unknown gentleman's selfless sacrifice. They gathered close to him, protectively surrounding him, the rain falling softly in the grass verge, the hedgerows, and the field of young wheat beyond.

"Oughtn't take more than ten, fifteen minutes to bring back help," someone nervously whispered.

"Aye, fifteen at the most."

"Provided Hawkins finds a doctor, that is. . . ."

A small sound came from the injured man. He was stirring again, groping for the wound in his side and trying to gauge the extent of his injury. Juliet caught his hand, lacing her bloodstained fingers through his. It was a smooth, elegant hand, white as the lace that framed it, a gentleman's hand. Yet the skill with which he had handled his pistol had been deadly.

He groaned, and his head moved on the wet blanket. "Done for . . . oh, hell . . . the child . . ."

"Easy, there," Juliet murmured, smoothing the hair back from his forehead. "Help is on the way." With her other hand, she urgently beckoned the other mother forward. If their noble rescuer was dying, before he left this earth Juliet wanted him to see proof that he had indeed saved the boy.

"The child," he whispered, persistently. He opened his eyes—long-lashed, beautifully shaped, romantic eyes that looked oddly familiar—and looked dazedly about him. "Tell me the little one is all right. . . ."

"He's fine and with his mother," Juliet said softly, just as the man's searching gaze found the small boy, huddled against his mother's skirt and staring at him with huge, frightened eyes. Their savior smiled, at peace now, and Juliet did not protest when he carried her hand to his face and laid it against the angry red flesh of his cheek. "You saved his life," she murmured. "You're a hero."

"Hardly. I was just . . . in the right place at the right time, I think." His eyes closed, but nevertheless his mouth remained curved in the faintest of satisfied smiles. He turned his head so that his lips were in Juliet's palm. They moved softly, sending wanton little thrills rushing unexpectedly down her spine. "Heroes do not make bumbling . . . fools of themselves, as I have done."

"I think we'd all beg to differ on *that*, sir," Juliet said firmly, and was joined by a hearty chorus of agreement from those around them. "Can you tell us your name? Where you live? Your family will be worried and must be notified."

"My family won't—"

But his weak reply was buried beneath distant shouts, laughter, and the sound of hoofbeats rushing down on them from out of the night. Riders were coming from the south, and they were coming fast.

"Hail them!" Juliet cried, raising her head to stare down the still-empty road.

Suddenly, galloping horses burst into view, their riders spurring them to reckless speeds in what was obviously a race.

"*Stop!*" The grandfatherly passenger ran forward, waving his arms. "We've an injured man here!"

"Whoa!" The nearest rider hauled on his reins, sending his lathered horse skidding in the mud and rearing in protest. *Whoa!*"

"What the devil's going on here—"

"Good God above!"

They were a group of carefree young rakehells, all splendidly dressed, all riding neck or nothing, all obviously in their cups to one degree or another. One by one they vaulted from their mounts and ran forward, eager to lend what assistance they could.

"Bloody hell, it's Gareth!" cried the nearest, the tail of his fine Ramillies wig bobbing as he fell to his knees before the elegant gentleman. "What the devil happened to you, man? 'Sdeath, I've never seen so much blood in my life!"

"Shot. And watch your language, Chilcot . . . there are women and children about."

"Bugger my language, Gareth, tell us what happened!"

Juliet raised her head and looked this Chilcot in the eye. He, like their injured savior, didn't look much older than herself, but it was obvious that she had more sense than the lot of these spirited young bucks combined. "Can't you see your friend is in a bad way?" she admonished. "Pray, don't make him talk any more than he has to. Now, if you must know what happened . . ." She quickly told them about the highwaymen, the other passengers adding pieces to the story.

One of the young scapegraces pulled a flask of spirits from his coat, lifted his stricken friend's head, and held the flask to his mouth. "You mean Gareth took a bullet meant for one of the little ones?"

"He did indeed. He saved all of our lives."

"*Gareth?!*"

"Don't look so surprised, Cokeham," the tallest of the lot drawled, surveying the scene with a lordly gaze and pulling out a snuff box. He took two pinches, then snapped the lid shut with a casual flick of his fingers. "Hasn't he always been the one to walk out of cockfights, rescue puppies, shun the use of spurs? Don't just stand there gawking at him. Go get help. *Now!*"

"Oh, for God's sake, Perry," their fallen friend murmured, obviously embarrassed. He tried to move, and through his teeth, sucked in his breath on a gasp of pain. "Now, help me up, would you? Somebody?"

He tried to sit up, but Juliet put a hand on his chest. "You're staying right there, Mr. Gareth who-ever-you-are, until help arrives."

"Ooooh! Listen to the lady, Gareth! Plagued with petticoats you are, and she isn't even your wife!"

Juliet, impatient and growing angry, directed a glare toward the one who had spoken. "I assume you *boys* are his friends?"

He snickered. "We're the Den of Debauchery."

Juliet looked at Perry, tall, lounging and elegant—and the only one of the lot who seemed sober. "And you, I assume, are its . . . leader?"

"No, ma'am." He sketched her a bow, then indicated his friend beneath her restraining hand. "Gareth is."

"Well, then. Instead of standing around making him miserable while he bleeds to death in the rain, why don't you help us get him into the coach? Now that you're here and must know where a doctor can be found, *you* can bring us straight to help yourselves."

Perry's eyes widened, and his lazy insolence vanished. He straightened up, looking with new respect at the slight young woman with the twangy, unfamiliar accent who knelt beside his friend. And then he gave a slow smile of acknowledgment and touched his hat to her. "The girl is correct," he said, turning to his companions. "Hugh, you ride for the doctor and have him meet us at the castle. Cokeham, you stay here with these people and keep them safe until we can send someone back for them. I will drive the coach." His voice was grim. "We're taking Gareth to the duke."

"Now see here," the elderly man said huffily, his face angry as he seized Perry's silk sleeve, "he doesn't need a duke, he needs a damned doctor!"

But Perry merely smiled and arched a brow. "What, don't you know who your noble rescuer is, then?"

Once again, the injured man tried to sit up. "Perry—"

But Perry's eyes sparkled with private amusement. He stretched out his arm, sweeping it down and forward with a dramatic eloquence that caused his friend's eyes to flash with impatience and anger. "May I present Lord Gareth de Montforte . . . leader of the notorious Den of Debauchery, third son of the fourth Duke of Blackheath, and black-sheep brother of Lucien, the present and fifth duke." He straightened up. "Now, do take care. *I*, for one, have no wish to be held accountable to His Grace should anything happen to him."

Someone let out an exclamation of disbelief.

Lord Gareth de Montforte cursed beneath his breath.

And Juliet Paige went as white as the chalk mud in which she stood.

Their gallant savior wasn't just the *duke's* brother.

He was Charles's brother, as well—and the uncle of her baby daughter.

# 3

**A**s the passengers argued with Gareth's friends about where to bring him, Juliet got to her feet and walked a short distance away, trying to regain her composure and hide the shock that must've been written all over her face.

She ran her palms down her cheeks. *Dear God. This man is Charles's brother. He looks so much like him . . . how could I not have known?*

Her back to the commotion behind her, she drew several deep breaths, stared blankly into the darkness for a moment, then shut her eyes in a silent prayer for strength. Finally she rejoined the others, where she took Charlotte and retrieved her miniature from the highwayman's leather bag. Perry took her arm; at his insistence, she climbed into the coach to ride along with Gareth.

Wrapping Charlotte in a blanket, she angled herself into one corner of the small back seat, set the baby beneath her elbow, and reached for the injured man as his friends brought him in after her. Nobody noticed how her hands shook. Nobody noticed how her entire *body* shook. They settled him on her seat, positioning him so that his head and shoulders lay cradled in her lap, his eyes, glazed with pain, gazing up at her. And then the door was shut, Perry climbed up on the box, and the coach shot past the

22

worried faces beyond the window as Perry sent the
team off with a shout and a crack of the whip.

*Charles's brother.*

His weight was warm and heavy and solid. She
averted her gaze from his and found she could not
speak.

Not yet.

And as the vehicle moved through the lonely English night, Juliet leaned her cheek against the cold
window and let her thoughts drift back in time ...
back to that cold winter day in Boston when she'd
first seen Captain Lord Charles de Montforte.

He had been the stuff of a young woman's
dreams.

The memory was as near as if it had all happened
yesterday ...


She was minding the counter in her stepfather's
store, stuffing logs in the little stove; outside, the
cold morning air was as brittle as glass. The day was
like any other of late, with rinds of frost on the windowpanes and one or two customers who still had
any money left to spend walking up and down the
wide-planked aisles as they browsed the shelves.
And then she heard it: the steady rattle of musketry,
brisk commands, the ringing clatter of a horse's
hooves over frozen, crusty cobbles.

A flash of scarlet passed just outside. Tossing the
last log into the stove, Juliet rushed to the window
and, with the heel of her hand, cleared a spot in the
frosty pane. And there he was, sitting high atop his
horse, his coattails splayed over the animal's powerful brown haunches, his fair hair queued with a
black bow beneath his tricorn—a King's officer, capable and dashing, reviewing his troops on Boston
Common.

Her hand went to her suddenly fluttering heart.
She'd thought a handsome man in uniform was just

that—a handsome man in a uniform—but this one was different. His red tunic stood out against the fresh snow like the plumage of a cardinal, and even from a distance of some thirty feet she could see that he was well-bred, untarnished, something special. Back as straight as a steeple. White-gloved hands firm but gentle on the reins. A man above squalor, above indecency, above common, everyday things. From the elegance of his leather smallclothes to the sword at his thigh, from the whiteness of his breeches to the glossy mirror of his boots, he'd been a gentleman. A god. She couldn't have cared less whether he was a soldier or a colonial. She couldn't have cared less about anything. She fell in love. Right then and right there . . .

"Fancy that, the troops parading in our common as though they own the place. Pompous asses! Despicable louts!"

Old Widow Murdock, one of the customers in the store that morning, saw immediately what had caught Juliet's interest.

"Yes . . ."

"Juliet? I'd like a half dozen eggs. Mind you give me the brown ones, not the white this time. And no cracked ones, ye hear? Juliet! Are you listening to me? *Juliet!* . . ."

The coach hit a bump, jarring her rudely back to the present. Juliet closed her eyes, desperately trying to hold on to the memory, that sweet, sweet memory, but it faded back into the murky arms of time and she was once again in England—three thousand miles from home, from the memories, from a Boston that was torn apart by war.

Three thousand miles from that mass grave near Concord, where the single red rose she had left would long since have been blown away by the wind.

Her throat suddenly ached and she stared off into the night, her eyes stinging with unshed tears.

And here he was, Charles's brother, faintly familiar and thus already beloved, his very likeness to his dead sibling resurrecting all those memories Juliet had locked up inside herself, relegated to their proper place, since that horrible day last April. He lay heavily across her lap, his head cradled in the crook of her arm and his pale face just visible in the gloomy shadows of the coach. She should have known, of course. They both had the same romantic eyes, the same lazy smile, the same curve of the cheek and cut of the mouth, the same height, same build, same bearing. Only the hair color was different. Where Charles had been a gilded blond, his younger brother's hair was a few shades darker. It was probably tawny brown, Juliet thought. Somewhat fair in daylight. But not now.

The coach hit a rut and she heard him catch his breath in pain. Gingerly, she gingerly rested her arm across his chest to better steady him against the swaying rock of the coach. His blood, warm and sticky against her skin, had soaked through her skirts, her stomacher, her bodice. His eyes were closed, but she suspected he was conscious and merely drifting in his own private hell of pain and fear. She ached to speak to him, yearned to ask him all about Charles, tell him just who she—and Charlotte—really was. But she did not. It didn't seem quite right to intrude upon his thoughts when he might very well be dying, and so she remained quiet, cradling his head and now, seeking his hand in the darkness to assure him that he was not alone.

His fingers tightened immediately over hers, dwarfing them, and sudden tears stung her eyes as she gazed down at him.

*Dear God, he reminds me of my beloved Charles. . . .*

The ache at the back of her throat became un-

bearable. Her nose burned and she blinked back the
gathering mist in her eyes. *Damn these tears. These
weak, foolish, useless tears.* She squeezed her eyes shut
and tried not to think of Charles and his cavalier
smile, the hardness of his body and the way his
mouth had felt against her own. Instead, she tried
to see the dim shapes of trees passing just outside in
the darkness, to concentrate on the squeak and rattle
of the coach, to lull her mind into numbness and
keep at bay the huge waves of emotion that threatened the dam of her self-control.

And then her gaze fell on the baby, still swathed
in the blanket and nestled in the tiny space between
Gareth's head and the padded side of the coach.

Charles's daughter.

She didn't realize she was weeping until the
brother's pained whisper broke the choking silence.

"Are they for me?"

Her nose was running now. She sniffed, sniffed
again, flashed a smile that was too quick, too false.
"Are what for you?"

"Why, your tears, of course."

*Oh, Lord.* She shook her head, not trusting herself
to speak for fear she'd give in to the great, wracking
pain that threatened to burst from her. This man,
suffering so quietly, so bravely, did not deserve to
see tears; he needed hope, comfort, encouragement
from her, not an appalling display of weakness. She
suddenly felt selfish and ashamed—and guilty, too.
After all, the tears were not even for him, poor man.
They were for Charles.

"I'm not crying," she managed, dabbing at her
eyes with the back of her sleeve and staring out the
window to hide the evidence.

"Really?" He gave a weak smile. "Perhaps I
should see for myself."

And then she felt them; his fingers, brushing her
damp cheek with infinite softness and concern, trac-

ing the slippery track of her sorrow. It was a caress—achingly kind, gentle, sweet.

She stiffened and caught his hand, holding it away from her face and shutting her eyes on a deep, bracing breath lest that dam of her self-control break for good. She managed to get herself under control, and when she finally dared meet his gaze, she saw that he was looking quietly up at her, at her distressed face and the tears she was trying so valiantly to hold back.

"Is there anything I can do to help?" he asked gently.

She shook her head.

"Are you quite certain?"

"Lord Gareth, you're the one who's hurt, not me."

"No. That is not true." His eyes searching her face, he touched her other cheek, the one the highwayman had cuffed, his whole manner one of such gentle, selfless concern that she wanted to lash out at someone, something, for this injustice that had been done to him. "I saw that . . . that scoundrel strike you. If I could kill him all over again for that, I would. Why, your poor cheek still bears the mark of his hand. . . ."

"I am fine."

"But—"

"Dear heavens, Lord Gareth, must you keep at it so?"

The words had come out angrier than she intended. She saw the sudden shadow of confusion that moved across his eyes, and a sharp pang of remorse lanced her heart for having put it there. Her anger was not directed at him, but at the fates that had taken first one of these dashing brothers and would now, most likely, take another. It wasn't fair. It just wasn't damned fair. And here he was worried about her cheek, her silly, stupid cheek, when his life's blood was oozing all over her skirts and onto the seat, and his flesh was feeling colder and clammier by the moment. She wanted to cry. Wanted to put her head in her hands and bawl until all the grief and pain and rage and loneliness still locked inside her was purged. But she did not. Instead, she took a deep breath and met his questioning gaze.

*Same romantic eyes. Same kindness in their depths, same concern for other people. Oh, God . . . help me.*

"I'm sorry," she murmured, shaking her head. "That was unfair. I didn't mean to snap at you. I'm so sorry. . . ."

"Please, don't be." He smiled, weakly. "Besides, if those tears *are* for me, I can assure you there is no need to waste them so. I shall not die."

"How confident you sound! I—I wish I shared your convictions."

"Well, I simply *cannot* die, you see?" Again that slow, lazy grin that sought to reassure her even when the hot, tinny smell of his blood could not. "My brother Lucien would not allow it."

"And is Lucien a god whom even death obeys?"

"But of course. He is the Duke of Blackheath. A deity unto himself, I am afraid. . . ."

His eyes had closed. He was growing weaker, his voice little more than a thready whisper now, yet even so, he tried to inflect a certain jaunty humor to his tone that tore fiercely at Juliet's heartstrings. How brave he was. How totally selfless. She gazed down at him, and shook her head in growing despair. "Save your strength, my lord. I know you're just trying to bolster my confidence that you will indeed survive."

"Perhaps." He opened his eyes and looked guilelessly up at her. "But as I'm trying to bolster my own as well, what harm is there in it?"

She sought his hand. Laced her fingers through his and squeezed. A long moment passed between them, with neither saying a word as they held hands in the darkness and the coach bounced over the night-lonely road.

"Why did you do it?" she finally asked, her voice breaking. "Why, when you could have just turned your back on all of us and gone safely back in the direction from which you'd come?"

His eyes widened in blank surprise, as though he was confused that such a question even needed, let alone deserved, an answer. "Why, 'tis my duty, of course, as a gentleman. There were women and children amongst your lot. . . . I could not have turned tail like a coward and left you all to perish, now, could I?"

"No," she murmured, sadly. "I suppose not."

She pulled her hand from his to make sure the strip of cloth with which she had bound his wound was still in place. Her fingers came away wet with blood. Fresh dread coursed through her and she surreptitiously wiped her fingers on her cloak, stilling her expression so as not to alarm him.

He was not fooled, though. She could see it in his eyes. But he knew she was already upset, and was too kind to distress her further. Like the gentleman he was, he changed the subject.

"Speaking of those children . . ." He tried to turn his head within the curve of Juliet's arm so that he could look at Charlotte. "It appears that one of them . . . is yours."

"Yes, my daughter. She's just over six months."

"Will you lift her up so I may see her? I adore children."

Juliet hesitated, thinking that sleeping babes were best left alone. But it was not in her to deny the wishes of a man who might very well be dying. Carefully, she picked up the infant and held her so that Gareth could see her. Charlotte whimpered and opened her eyes. Immediately, the lines of pain about Gareth's mouth relaxed. Smiling weakly, he reached up and ran his fingers over one of the tiny fists, unaware that he was touching his own niece. A lump rose in Juliet's throat. It was not hard at all to imagine that he was Charles, reaching up to touch his daughter.

Not hard at all.

"You're just . . . as pretty as your mama," he murmured. "A few more years . . . and all the young bucks shall be after you . . . like hounds to the fox." To Juliet he said, "What is her name?"

"Charlotte." The baby was wide awake now and tugging at the lace of his sleeve.

"Charlotte. Such a pretty name . . . and where is your papa, little Charlie-girl? Should he . . . not be here to . . . protect you and your mama?"

Juliet stiffened. His inadvertent words had sent a bolt of pain slamming through her. Tight-lipped, she pried the lace from Charlotte's fist and put the infant back down beside her. Deprived of her amusement, the baby screwed up her face and began to wail at the top of her lungs while Juliet stared out the window, her mouth set and her hand clenched in a desperate bid to control her emotions.

Gareth managed to make himself heard over Charlotte's angry screams. "I am sorry. I think I have offended you, somehow. . . ."

"No."

"Then what is it?"

"Her papa's dead."

"Oh. I, ah . . . I see." He looked distressed, and remorse stole the brightness that Charlotte had brought to his eyes. "I am sorry, madam. I am forever saying the wrong thing, I fear."

Charlotte was now crying harder, beating her fists and kicking her feet in protest. The blanket fell away, tumbling to the floor. Juliet attempted to put it back. Charlotte screamed louder, her angry squalls filling the coach until Juliet felt like crying herself. She made a noise of helpless despair.

"Here ... set her on your lap, beside my head," Gareth said at last. "She can play with my cravat."

"No, you're hurt."

He smiled. "And your daughter is crying. Oblige me, and she will stop." He stretched a hand toward the baby, offering his fingers, but she batted him away and continued to wail. "I'm told I have a way ... with children."

With a sigh, Juliet did as he asked. Sure enough, the instant she was beside him, Charlotte quieted and fell to playing with his cravat. Silence returned to the bouncing coach, with only the rattle and squeak of the springs, Perry's occasional shout, and the sound of the horses galloping over the darkened roads intruding upon the quiet within.

His hand on her back, Gareth steadied the baby so that she would not fall. He looked up at Juliet. "You have done much for me," he said at last. "Will you honor me by confessing your name?"

"Juliet."

He smiled. "As in Romeo and Juliet?"

"I suppose." *Though my dear Romeo lies cold in his grave, an ocean away.* She looked out the window once more—anything to avoid gazing into those romantic, long-lashed eyes that reminded her so much of Charles's, anything to avoid watching his hand, so strong and large against Charlotte's little back and possessing the same graceful elegance that the baby's father's had had. Coming here to England, she now knew, had been a mistake. A dreadful mistake. How on earth could she bear this pain, this constant reminder of all she had lost?

"You have an accent I do not recognize," he was saying. "'Tis certainly not local. . . ."

"Really, Lord Gareth—you should rest, not try to talk. Save your strength."

"My dear angel, I can assure you I'd much rather talk to you than lie here in silence and wonder if I shall live to see the next sunrise. I . . . do not wish to be alone with my thoughts at the moment. Pray, amuse me, would you?"

She sighed. "Very well, then. I'm from Boston."

"County of Lincolnshire?"

"Colony of Massachusetts."

His smile faded. "Ah, yes . . . Boston." The town's name fell wearily from his lips and he let his eyes drift shut, as though that single word had drained him of his remaining strength. "You're a long way from home, aren't you?"

"Farther, perhaps, than I should be," she said cryptically.

He seemed not to hear her. "I had a brother who died over there last year, fighting the rebels. . . . He was a captain in the Fourth. I miss him dreadfully."

Juliet leaned the side of her face against the squab and took a deep, bracing breath. If this man died, he would never know just who the little girl playing so contentedly with his cravat was. He would never know that the stranger who was caring for him during his final moments was the woman his brother had loved, would never know just why she—a long way from home, indeed—had come to England.

It was now or never. "Yes," she whispered, tracing a thin crack in the squab near her face. "So do I."

"Sorry?"

"I said, yes. I miss him, too."

"Forgive me, but I don't quite understand. . . ." And then he blanched and stiffened as the truth hit him with debilitating force. His eyes widened, their lazy dreaminess fading. His head rose halfway out of her lap. He stared at her and blinked, and in the sudden, charged silence that filled the coach, Juliet heard the pounding tattoo of her own heart, felt his gaze boring into the underside of her chin as his mind, dulled by pain and shock, quickly put the pieces together.

Boston.

Juliet.

*I miss him, too.*

He gave an incredulous little laugh. "No," he said, shaking his head and grinning foolishly, as though he suspected he was the butt of some horrible joke or worse, knew she was telling the truth and could not find a way to accept it. He scrutinized her features, his gaze moving over every aspect of her face. "We all thought . . . I mean, Lucien said he tried to locate you. . . . No, I am hallucinating, I must be! You cannot be the same Juliet. Not *his* Juliet—"

"I am," she said quietly. "*His* Juliet. And now I've come to England to throw myself on the mercy of his family, as he bade me to do should anything happen to him."

"But this is just too extraordinary, I cannot believe—"

Juliet was gazing out the window into the darkness again. "He told you about me, then?"

"*Told* us? His letters home were filled with nothing but declarations of love for his 'colonial maiden,' his 'fair Juliet'—he said he was going to marry you. I . . . you . . . dear God, you have shocked my poor brain into speechlessness, Miss Paige. I do not believe you are here, in the flesh!"

"Believe it," she said, miserably. "If Charles had lived, you and I would have been brother and sister. Don't die, Lord Gareth. I have no wish to see yet another de Montforte brother into an early grave."

He settled back against her arm and flung one bloodstained wrist across his brow, his body shaking. For a moment she thought the shock of her revelation had killed him, and the jerky movements of his body were the reflexes that follow death. But no.

Beneath the lace of his sleeve she could see the whiteness of his grin, and Juliet realized that his convulsions were not those of death, but of giddy, helpless mirth.

For the life of her, she did not see what was so funny.

"Then this baby"—he managed, sliding his wrist up his brow to peer up at her with gleaming eyes—"this baby—"

"Is your niece."

# 4

**M**y niece!

But at that very moment Perry whipped up the team, sending them charging through Blackheath's great gates and down the long drive of crushed stone at breakneck speed. Further conversation was impossible. Just outside the broken window Chilcot galloped alongside, his coattails flying. "Hold on, Gareth!" he shouted. "Almost there now!"

Gareth closed his eyes and held the baby, letting his head rock and sway on Juliet Paige's lap. He was still grinning; he couldn't help it. The girl probably thought him insane. But armed with what she'd just told him, he had no intention of succumbing to the blissful lure of unconsciousness—or whatever lay beyond it. There was no way in hell he was going to die. Oh, no. He wouldn't miss the impending events for the world....

Or the look on Lucien's face when he learned that the virtuous, never-do-anything-wrong Charles had sired a bastard babe.

Looking up, Gareth could just see the outline of Juliet's jaw, her firm, determined chin and the sweet curve of one cheek. He knew the moment she caught her first glimpse of the castle for her eyes grew huge, and she leaned close to the window for a better look,

35

giving him a better chance to furtively study her.
Ah, yes. She was a lovely creature, just as Charles
had described. Her skin was as white as snowdrops
and set off by dark, upswept hair. Her face was en-
chanting, with a delicate nose and fine, dark eyes set
beneath daintily arched brows. Physically, she was
diminutive and graceful—yet despite her small size,
there was something about her that conveyed courage, resilience, and fortitude. It was easy to see why
his brother had fallen for her. But where was the *joie
de vivre*, the innocent naiveté that Charles had so
praised? This woman seemed older than her years,
as though her spirit had been crushed beneath the
weight of sorrow and hardship.

By God, if he lived, he'd remedy *that*. She was far
too young—and pretty—to embrace age before its
time!

He closed his eyes, content to let his head sway in
her lap, content to feel her tightening up the curve
of her arm so that he wasn't jostled so. To think that
she, Charles's betrothed, was here in England. And
to think that this infant whose tiny body was so near
to his, whose heart beat so close to his own, was his
brother's little girl. . . .

"Whoa!" Perry was pulling the team up. "Whoa
there!"

Juliet placed Charlotte beside her and put her
arms around Lord Gareth so that he and Charlotte
wouldn't spill from the seat with the sudden, jolting
halt. The coach hadn't even come to a stop before
his friends were wrenching the door open. Gusts of
rain and wind swept in and Juliet, hastily picking
up Charlotte, felt him tense as they leaped inside,
sliding their hands beneath his body and trying not
to jostle him too much as they lifted him from her
blood-soaked skirts.

"Here, I've got his shoulders."

"I've got his legs."

"Easy with him, now! Gareth? Gareth, we're going to have to move you. Bear up there, man!"

They carried him out. Immediately, Charlotte started crying again. Her heart pounding, her hand patting the little baby's back, Juliet watched as Gareth's friends rushed him toward the great, medieval doors of Blackheath Castle. As they spirited him away, he lifted his hand to her. Whether the gesture was meant to convey a last good-bye, undying gratitude, or amusement at the sort of treatment everyone was falling over themselves to give him, she did not know.

Feeling a bit lost, she raised herself off the seat, shaking the wrinkles out of her blood-drenched skirts and wondering if she should follow the others inside or wait in the coach for someone to come for her and Charlotte.

But the decision was made for her. A man was there at the door, extending a hand inside to her. "Madam?"

Perry. He had remained behind, still the cool-headed gentleman in a storm of confusion.

Juliet smiled her thanks and, hastily bundling Charlotte up, allowed him to help them down from the coach. She stood for a moment on the drive, the rain on her face, the wind tugging at her hair and tangling her skirts around her legs. Then Perry offered his arm and escorted her toward the castle, not saying a word.

Blackheath was much grander than Charles had described it. Juliet stared at it, awestruck, as it rose up out of the darkness before her. High above her head, twin crenelated towers seemed to travel forever skyward into the night, older, it seemed, than time itself. She could just see the dim outline of a flagpole above one of them, its pennant snapping against the black and moody sky with each gust of wind. It was a magnificent palace of a place. A place that made Juliet feel daunted, lost, and very much like a creature out of its element.

Her courage nearly faltered at the thought of facing its duke. This grand castle with its own flag so far above, the village through which they'd just come, the countryside for miles upon miles around— it all belonged to one single man, who might or might not feel like being charitable. Back in Boston, the thought of going to Blackheath to seek his help had not fazed her. But now, in the face of such imposing, intimidating magnificence, it seemed presumptuous to throw herself and Charlotte on his mercy—even though he *would* have been family in happier circumstances, and Charles had bade her to do just that.

*Stop being so foolish.* She was here in England, with Charles's family, and she would not turn back now. But as the towering stone walls of the castle loomed closer and closer, Juliet almost wished she had never come here, never bought passage on the Loyalist-owned ship that had been part of the mass evacuation when the British had abandoned the town last month.

*Not that you were spoiled for choice,* she reminded herself. Her stepfather, Zachariah, had died of pneumonia in January, and she'd had nowhere else to go. As a suspected Loyalist, her life had been in danger in Boston. As an unwed mother whose baby's father was rumored to be a hated British officer, she'd been scorned, snubbed, ostracized, threatened. Like it or not, she'd done what she had to do. If not for Charles, then for his daughter.

*Be strong. He would have wanted you to be.*

They were at the foot of the stone steps now. At their top, the ancient oak door through which Lord Gareth had been carried stood open, spilling light out onto the lawn. The door appeared to be some two feet thick and was banded by heavy strips of iron, each one studded with heavy bolts. Perry, obviously a frequent and welcomed visitor here, hustled her up the steps, past two liveried footmen who stood to attention on either side of the door, and into a huge medieval hall, where Juliet stood gaping up at the carved, vaulted stone ceiling that rose some two stories above her head. The room was so big that the fine house in which she and Zachariah had lived back in Boston could easily have fit within it.

"Wait here," Perry ordered and hurried off, following the drops of blood that meandered across the polished marble floor. He tore open a set of doors at which the trail stopped and was gone.

And Juliet was alone.

"Gareth! 'Sdeath, man, don't die! Hugh rode for the doctor, he'll be here any moment. Hang on, just hang on!"

Gareth cursed the saints, the devil, and his well-meaning friends as they rushed him through Blackheath's stone passageways and corridors. Every jarring jolt, every skidding turn, brought him agony. He set his teeth and pressed a hand to his side. Through half-closed eyes he caught glimpses of sconces flickering orange against walls, of a chambermaid's startled face, of the row of portraits in the West Corridor, all of which blurred into a graying haze as he fought gamely to hold on to consciousness.

Pain jarred him back to reality when Chilcot stumbled, nearly breaking Gareth's spine in two.

"Damn you, Chilcot, if you're going to trip over the blasted rug, at least have the decency to let go of me!"

And then a door crashed open and he saw the plush rugs of his own room, the massive bed of dark, carved oak and the leaded windows that looked out over the downs. Servants ran to and fro,

scurrying to pull back the sheets, but Gareth knew
nothing but pain as Neil Chilcot and Tom Audlett
set him down on the bed.

Confused, excited voices penetrated the haze in
which he lay. Someone removed his shoes. His
breeches and what remained of his shirt were cut
away, and someone sponged his nettle-stung cheek
with blessedly cold water. Gareth lay unmoving.
And now Perry, good old Perry, was lifting his head,
supporting it so that Chilcot could dump more of
that wonderful Irish whiskey into him. It burned a
path down his throat and into his stomach, spreading numbing tentacles of warmth out through his
limbs, into his very fingertips and toes.

Gareth closed his eyes, his brain comfortably
fuzzy. "More," he whispered.

"Bloody hell, Gareth, stop grinning like a damned
fool," Chilcot was saying, putting the flask to his lips
once more. "This isn't funny!"

Gareth only made an obscene gesture with one
hand and drank.

Audlett commented, "Good thing that girl was
quick-witted enough to pack his side with this rag.
Hang on there, Gareth. Dr. Highworth's just arriving
now."

Gareth pushed away the flask before he reached
the point of no return. "See to her," he gasped, grip-
ping Chilcot's wrist. "Don't leave her out there to
face Lucien alone."

"But—"

"Go!"

And then they all heard it. The sound of footfalls
coming down the hall, echoing off the stone walls
and approaching with relentless, unhurried calm.
Chilcot froze. Audlett held his breath. And every
servant in the room went still as the footsteps
stopped just inside the room.

And continued forward.

*Lucien.*

Gareth didn't need to open his eyes to know his brother was there, gazing down at him with that black stare that was severe enough to freeze the devil in his lair of fire. And he didn't need to see Lucien's stark face to know what he would read there: blatant disapproval. Fury.

He felt Lucien's cool hand on his cheek. "Ah, Gareth," the duke said blandly, in a tone that didn't fool anyone in the room, "another scrape you've got yourself into, I see. What is it this time, eh? No, let me guess. You were posing as a target and taking bets that none of your friends could hit you. Or perhaps you got so foxed that you fell from Crusader and impaled yourself on a fence? Do tell, dear boy. I have all night."

"Go to hell, Luce."

"I'm sure I will, but I'll have an explanation from you first."

*Bastard.* Gareth refused to respond to the mocking taunts. Instead, he reached up, his fingers closing around Lucien's immaculate velvet sleeve. "Don't send her away, Luce. She's here. She needs us. . . . We owe it to Charles to take care of her and the baby."

Footsteps came running down the hall, into the room. "Over here, Dr. Highworth!" Chilcot cried, suddenly.

Lucien never moved. "Take care of *whom*, Gareth?" he inquired, with deadly menace.

Weakly, Gareth turned his head on the pillow and looked up at his brother through a swirling fog of pain and alcohol. "Juliet Paige," he whispered, meeting Lucien's cool, veiled gaze. "The woman Charles was to marry . . . She's here . . . downstairs . . . with his baby. Don't send her away, Lucien. I swear I'll kill you if you do."

"My dear boy," Lucien murmured, with a chilling little smile, "I would not dream of it."

But he had straightened up and was already moving toward the door.

Gareth raised himself on one elbow even as the doctor tried to hold him down. "Lucien . . . damn you, *don't!*"

The duke kept walking.

"*Lucien!*" With the last of his strength, Gareth lunged from the bed, but the effort—and the Irish whiskey—did him in at last. As his feet hit the rug, his legs gave out beneath him, and he crashed heavily to the floor in a dead faint.

Doctor, servants, and friends all rushed to his assistance.

The duke never looked back.

Juliet, still alone in the great hall, gazed about her in disbelief and wonder. She—raised in the woods of Maine, grown to maturity in Boston's comparative rusticity—had never seen, nor been able to imagine, anything quite like this room in her life. Stone staircases spiraled off to her right and left, presumably leading up to the massive turrets she'd seen from outside. An ancient tapestry depicting a hunting scene covered an entire wall. Huge mullioned windows rose from floor to ceiling, black against the night and reflecting the twinkling flames of a chandelier suspended above her head and containing what had to be at least a hundred candles. Such grandeur. Such *waste!* She made a half turn. Notches in the stone wall held suits of medieval armor, the slitted visors ominous, the space between each suit hung with heraldic shields, battle axes, and other primitive weapons of war.

To think that Charles had grown up here . . . had touched these same stones and strode beneath these very windows, had stood, perhaps hundreds of times, in this exact spot. . . .

A feeling of awe gripped her, building and building until all the trauma she had experienced these past twelve months—indeed, these past few hours—was swallowed up by the sudden, giddy relief that she and Charlotte were finally here, safe at last, in this home that had been Charles's. Here, in this strange castle, in this strange land, Juliet had found familiarity. A little bit of Charles. She could almost picture his spirit looking down on them from somewhere above, smiling and finally at peace, content that his new family would never again want for anything. The image alone pulled at her heartstrings, made her eyes shimmer with unshed tears. Not since his death had Charles felt so very close. . . .

Her lower lip was threatening to tremble again. Catching it between her teeth, Juliet peeled back Charlotte's blankets and lifted the baby high above her head so that she could see this magnificent home in which her father had been born, in which he had lived.

"Look, Charlotte!" Juliet took the baby's hand and pointed it at one of the suits of armor. "I'll bet your papa played with that thing when he was just a little boy!"

Charlotte, however, was more fascinated by the glittering chandelier above her head. Juliet, half laughing, half weeping, touched her nose to her daughter's and swung her high. Charlotte squealed with delight, kicking both legs now and punching at the air. *Oh, Charles . . . are you here? Are you here with me and your daughter?*

Caught up as she was in a giddy sense of closeness to her beloved, of relief at finally reaching her destination, Juliet didn't hear the distant footfalls. The steady, relentless beat of shoes against stone.

Suddenly a door opened and she froze, the laughter dying in her throat, the baby still high over her head.

Slowly, she lowered her daughter and held her protectively close to her breast.

Thirty feet away he stood, tall and elegant in a frock of black velvet, a ruby winking from the folds of his lacy cravat, his breeches molded to long, muscled thighs that tapered to silk-clad calves and shoes from which diamonds winked in each polished silver buckle. His eyes were dark and smoldering. His hair was as black as the night outside. His nose was narrow, his jaw set, his cheekbones planed, stark, severe. His was a hard face. An uncompromising face. He looked at Juliet with that ruthless black stare, looked at her muddy, blood-drenched skirts, and without batting an eye, gave a bow, coming up with an elegant sweep of his arm that made the lace at his wrist dance in the resultant breeze.

"I am Lucien, Duke of Blackheath. Gareth tells me you knew Charles." The obsidian gaze flickered briefly to the baby. *"Intimately."*

Juliet, taken aback, dipped in what curtsy she could manage with Charlotte in her arms. Then she raised her chin and, with more courage than she felt, met that chilling black gaze. "Yes. We were to have married."

He indicated the door through which he had come. "Then won't you join me in the library? I am sure we have much to discuss."

His voice was smooth, rich, cultured. The words gave away no emotion, no hint whatsoever of his temper, thoughts, or feelings. They were also, Juliet realized, not a question but an order.

Warning bells went off inside her head.

"Yes, of course," she murmured, and, painfully aware of her shocking, disheveled state, walked with as much dignity as she could muster toward the door.

And as she moved through the great corridors, liveried servants standing stiffly at attention with eyes staring straight ahead as though bloodstained young women were quite an ordinary sight at Blackheath Castle, a single, urgent phrase kept repeating itself over and over in her mind:

*Don't die, Lord Gareth. Please don't die. I think I'm going to need you.*

5

"**R**eally, Your Grace, I should like to change my clothes before we have this—this discussion."

He was striding several paces in front of her now, broad shouldered and tall, carrying himself like a general. Sconces lit the long, narrow corridors, and as he passed each one, they flickered and bowed as though in homage to him, their dim light gleaming in his hair.

"That will not be necessary," he said without so much as looking over his shoulder.

Juliet hurried to keep pace with him. "I am not presentable!"

"You are presentable enough for me. Come. I haven't all night."

"But—"

"There is an alcove just ahead, with a bowl and pitcher. Wash if you so desire, but be quick about it. This night shall be long enough without having to wait for you to indulge in the sort of silly nonsense in which females must engage before they dare show their faces to anyone beyond their pet lapdogs. I am not a patient man, Miss Paige."

He indicated the alcove, shielded by a rich drape of dark-red velvet, and, without slowing his stride, pushed open a set of heavy doors several paces beyond. "The library. I shall expect you within five minutes. Do not keep me waiting."

The heavy doors shut behind him.

*Dear God above.* What arrogance! What rudeness! If the Duke of Blackheath was your average English aristocrat, it was no wonder America had risen up against the motherland! Bristling, Juliet yanked aside the curtain, splashed some water in the bowl, and scrubbed poor Gareth's blood from her hands, her fingernails, the little creases in her knuckles while Charlotte watched her from a chair set in the corner.

And what of Gareth? The duke had not volunteered so much as a word about how *he* was faring!

Without further deliberation, she picked Charlotte up and, pulling down her bodice and chemise, put her to breast. The baby suckled greedily. Juliet cupped the downy gold head in her hand and eyed the curtain behind her. Lord only knew when she would have gotten the chance to feed her, given the duke's intolerance for the "silly nonsense" of females!

She emerged some ten minutes later. By then her anger had cooled, and apprehension was quickly filling its place. She forced her chin up, straightened her back, and, feigning a courage she didn't feel, pushed open the doors to the library.

There he was, leaning with casual insolence against a magnificent mantle of carved Italian marble, a glass of brandy dangling from his fingertips. He was a dark angel, some brooding god of judgment, and as he turned his black, smoldering gaze upon her, Juliet felt her courage falter.

"Sit down."

"I . . . don't wish to soil the furniture."

"The furniture is replaceable."

*Expensive, too,* Juliet thought. Arranged on a priceless Oriental rug were several chairs upholstered in rich plum velvet, a claw-footed sofa stuffed with horsehair and finished in an elegant brocade, a French loveseat on spindly legs, and, nearest the fire, a very large, very masculine chair of carved oak with a seat and back of leather.

*His* throne, obviously.

Juliet headed for it. Not because she wished to be difficult, not because she wished to challenge his rank, but because leather was easily cleaned, and her sense of Yankee frugality could not let her destroy one of the other expensive pieces by sitting on it with her bloodstained skirts. Replaceable or not, she was not one for waste.

"Do you mind?" she asked, with civil politeness.

He shrugged and waved his glass, never leaving his place at the mantle. "Suit yourself."

With Charlotte in her lap, Juliet sank into the deep, butter-soft leather, painfully conscious of her appearance. How carefully she had chosen her clothes that morning, hoping to make the right impression on this man whose help and charity she had crossed an ocean to seek. Now, her apple-green skirts, parted to reveal a petticoat lovingly embroidered with sweet little roses, were dark with blood. Chalky mud caked her boots, her stomacher was blood soaked, and blood smeared the front of the smart, pine-green jacket she had chosen to match the ivy that twined itself along the gown's hem. She looked a mess.

But the duke, true to his word, did not seem to care. He wasted no time in getting the discussion underway, sparing no thought for Juliet's feelings, her pride, or the fact that she was a guest in his house and deserved more kindness than he seemed capable of giving. She had no sooner sat down than he asked her, bluntly, how she'd met Charles. She told him the truth. His scowl, and the impatient look in his eyes as she related the tale, made her want to squirm with discomfort. This was not going well. Not going well at all.

"So. You first saw Charles whilst he was drilling his troops on Boston Common. Love at first sight, you say." He gave a bitter little laugh. "You'll understand if I find the notion rather difficult to swallow."

"Charles was a very handsome man."

"Charles was from one of England's oldest, most aristocratic families and would not have married beneath him. As a second son, he could not afford to. What is it about you, then, that commended you to him?"

"I find your question insulting, Your Grace," she said quietly.

"Nevertheless, I'll have an answer from you."

"I don't know what it was about me that he loved."

"You have a passably decent figure, a pretty face, and a fine dark eye. I suspect little else was needed to bring a man to his knees—and into your bed."

"You dishonor your brother with such talk, Your Grace. Charles was a fine man."

"Yes, well, far away from home and thrown into a nest of rebel vipers and their conniving females, the devil only knows what goes through a man's head. Any warm body will do, I expect."

"Charles and I loved each other. He wanted to marry me."

"Before or after he found out you were breeding?"

She blushed. "After."

"Did it never occur to you that he was merely being honorable and that his heart might have lain elsewhere?"

"Indeed, it did not."

"Did it ever occur to you that it might have been arranged at his birth that he marry a woman of his own station, whose money would have allowed him to live a lifestyle to which he was accustomed?"

"He made no mention of such a woman, Your Grace, and Charles was not one to worship the god of money."

"Did it ever occur to you that his family might not welcome an ill-bred provincial into their midst and would not approve of his union with you?"

She looked him straight in the eye and said quietly, "Yes."

"And yet you came here anyhow."

"I had no choice."

"You had no choice."

Juliet clenched her fist beneath a fold of Charlotte's blanket, trying to keep a check on her rising temper. Her face felt hot, and she knew her color betrayed her, but she vowed he would not get the better of her, no matter how hard he tried. If by forcing her to remain here in her disheveled clothes, attacking her with his insolent questions, and implying things that were not true he sought to put her off balance, he had another thing coming. She was made of stronger stuff than that.

Politely, she said, "I fear, Your Grace, that you suspect me of being some sort of fortune hunter. That I lured your brother to me so I could claw my way up the social ladder by use of his name and rank. But I'll have you know that that wasn't the case. Charles was one of the king's officers. I was a maiden of Boston, and maidens of Boston did not consort with the king's officers—no matter how well-born they might be—if they wished to maintain their standing in a community that had grown to despise the Regulars' very presence."

He merely sipped his brandy and watched her, giving no hint of what was going on behind those enigmatic black eyes.

"I was well respected by those who knew me," she continued, bravely. "I may not have your noble blood, nor possess your limitless wealth, but my stepfather was one of Boston's leading citizens and we lived well enough by pursuing hard work and good causes. I have nothing to blush for."

"Your stepfather was a Loyalist."

"My stepfather was a spy for the rebels."

"That is not what Charles told us."

"Appearances are deceiving. What is the use of being a spy if everyone knows who you are?"

"Indeed. And did you learn all you could from my brother only to pass the information on to your stepfather?"

"I did not."

"Rebel, Loyalist . . . and where do *your* sympathies lay, Miss Paige?"

She looked him straight in the eye. "With my daughter."

He arched a brow.

"I don't want to be here," she said, firmly. "I don't know a soul in England, my heart aches for home, and it is obvious that my presence at Blackheath is most unwelcome—as I feared it would be. I would like nothing more than to go back to America and pick up the remains of my life, but I made a promise to Charles, and I don't break promises."

"And what promise was that?"

"To seek you out in England if anything should happen to him."

"And just what did Charles think I could do for you?"

"He told me that you would take us in and make our baby your ward. He said that you would give her your name. I didn't want to come here, but things turned bad in Boston and I had little choice. My daughter's welfare comes first."

"Charles died a year ago. Correct me if I'm wrong," he murmured, with faint sarcasm, "but doesn't the crossing from America take but a month?"

"Yes, but—"

"Why, then, did it take *you* a year?"

"I had no wish to travel in my condition, Your Grace. I was very ill."

"And after the babe was born?"

"I would not have subjected her to the rigors of a sea voyage at such a tender age. Besides, my stepfather needed me to help run the store and tavern, so I felt beholden to stay."

"Yes, do describe just what it was you did there at this store and tavern, Miss Paige. I assume it was along the order of serving ale to lusty customers and playfully fending off unwelcome advances so you could save yourself for one of the king's officers?"

Blood rushed to her cheeks and her heart pounded with outrage. "Indeed not, Your Grace," she said levelly, refusing to be baited. "My stepfather valued me for my frugality and head for figures. He would not have put a tray in my hands and bid me to spend my time running from cellar to table. No, I kept the books for both store and tavern. I opened in the mornings and closed at night. I paid the help, purchased the merchandise for the store, haggled with tradesmen for fair prices, settled disputes between cook and chambermaid." She looked at him without shame. "I am not afraid of hard work, Your Grace."

"So I see." Something indiscernible flickered in his eyes. "And what does your esteemed stepfather think of your coming to England?"

"He died of pneumonia in January. I doubt he thinks at all."

"And what did he say about your little thing with Charles?"

"It was not a 'little thing,' Your Grace. We loved

each other deeply and were engaged to be married—"

"Answer the question, please."

"I beg your pardon, but must you be so rude?"

"Yes. Now answer the question."

She made a fist, savagely driving her fingernails into her palm in an effort to control her angry tongue. "Charles and I had to keep our feelings for each other clandestine, lest our safety be compromised. The British presence was detested in Boston."

"Yes, I know. You Americans certainly made that obvious."

"I am not *all Americans*," Juliet said firmly. "And I would give the world to have my Charles back. Please stop goading me!"

He raised his brows and stared at her down the length of his aristocratic nose. She, wet and uncomfortable in his brother's blood, stared bravely back. The fire snapped in the grate. Voices sounded from somewhere outside in the corridor. And then the duke allowed the faintest of smiles, as though rewarding her for her courage in standing up to him . . . or contemplating the pleasure he would receive in throwing her out on her ear.

Straightening, he moved to where a crystal decanter stood atop a desk of carved mahogany. He took his time refilling his glass, not saying a word as the spirits splashed into the vessel and burbled up toward the rim. His severe profile gave away nothing. And then he turned to face her, leaning against the edge of his desk with ankles crossed and eyes thoughtfully narrowed. He took a sip of his brandy, watching her. Just watching her. Judging her, assessing her, studying her like a scholar might examine a singularly interesting biological specimen. *Dear God, this is awful.*

She stood up. "May I please go now?"

"Go where?"

"Anywhere. Away. Back to America, if need be. It's obvious that Charles's faith and trust in his family's desire to care for his baby daughter were unfounded. Neither she nor I are wanted here."

"Don't be absurd."

She reached for Charlotte's blanket. "I am being practical."

"Practicality is not a quality I associate with most females of my acquaintance."

"With all due respect to the females of your acquaintance, Your Grace, I was born and raised in the wilderness of Maine. Those who were not practical, resourceful, and hardy did not survive."

"Maine? How is it, then, that you ended up in Boston?"

"My father died when I was sixteen, mauled by a black bear defending her cub. He had a cousin in Boston, who'd always fancied my mother from afar. After Papa died, he came for Mama and me, married her, and took us both back to Boston. Mama died in '74. You know about my stepfather." She picked up her cloak, preparing to leave this house and never look back. "Now, if you'll excuse me, Your Grace, I think I've answered enough of your questions and had best be gone. Good night to you."

He never moved as she breezed past his desk, Charlotte in her arms. "Don't you wish to know how Lord Gareth fares?" he asked mildly, in an abrupt change of subject.

"Begging your pardon, Your Grace, but you gave me no chance to ask."

"I should think he'd like to thank you for saving his life."

She paused halfway across the room, silently cursing him between her teeth. What tarnal game was he playing now? Without turning, she ground out, "He saved *my* life, not the other way around."

"Not according to Lord Brookhampton."

"I know no Lord Brookhampton."

"Perry," he amended with infuriating smoothness. "He told me everything."

"Look, I—"

At that moment, the door burst open without warning, sounding like a thunderclap in the vastness of the room.

"Go away, Andrew, Nerissa."

"We've just spoken to Gareth. He told us who she is. Who the baby is. He said—"

"*I said*, go away."

Juliet could only stare as the pair crossed the room. They were two more de Montforte siblings. They had to be. She saw Charles in the lines of their faces, in the arch of their brows and in the romantic shape of their long-lashed eyes. The mouths were the same. The planes of the cheeks were the same. The noses, the jaws, even the hair—wavy like Charles's had been but, in the case of Lord Andrew, a dark auburn—were the same. Ignoring the duke, Andrew came right up to Juliet, took her hand, and bent over it in a sweeping, courtly bow.

"You must be Juliet," he said warmly, looking up at her through thick brown lashes. He was young and handsome, with a look of sharp intelligence about him and eyes that, though smiling and lazy in the de Montforte way, didn't miss a trick. "I am Andrew, Charles's brother, and this is our sister, Nerissa. Welcome to England, and to Blackheath Castle."

But Nerissa was transfixed by the sight of Charlotte, sleeping in Juliet's arms. Her hands flew to her mouth, and sudden tears filled her pretty blue eyes. She took a hesitant step forward, biting her lip and raising her pleading gaze to Juliet's. "May I?" she whispered, stretching out her arms.

With a resigned smile, Juliet passed the infant to her aunt. So much for leaving—and escaping the odious presence of the duke. But her peevishness melted away as Nerissa, her head bent over the little bundle, carried the baby into the shadows. The girl's shoulders were shaking, and it was obvious she was weeping.

"That's *Lord* Andrew and *Lady* Nerissa," the duke corrected, irritably. "If you insist on introducing yourselves, at least do it properly."

Andrew waved a hand in dismissal and moved toward the decanter. "Oh hang it, Luce, she's from the colonies. She's not bothered by all that."

"I told you to leave us, Andrew. Do so immediately, before I get angry."

"That's *Lord* Andrew, if you don't mind."

The duke's glass slammed down on the table, his face no longer wearing its veneer of tolerance. A frigid chill settled over the room. Juliet held her breath, all too aware of the enmity between these two brothers—one so dark and formidable, the other fiery, brazen, and openly insolent. For one terrible moment she thought the two of them were going to come to blows; but no. The duke had his temper on a tight rein. He would not stoop to fisticuffs, not in front of a stranger and certainly not with his own brother.

She was correct. He inclined his head, conceding this small victory to Andrew if only to avoid what would otherwise be a scene. "Sit down, then," he said, darkly. "Both of you."

Nerissa, still holding Charlotte, complied, but Andrew obviously felt that this order had to be challenged, as well. Taking all the time in the world, he poured himself a drink, then tossed himself into one of the chairs, one long leg thrown over his knee and bobbing lazily. He raised his glass to Juliet and took a long sip as he studied her. "Ah, yes. You look just like Charles said you did. I can understand why he was so captivated by you, Miss Paige."

"Not just Charles," Nerissa chimed in. "Gareth's up there singing your praises as well, and he and his friends are all drinking bumpers to you. Gareth said you took control, calmed everyone down, and saved his life with your quick thinking. I think he's completely charmed!"

"I'm afraid Lord Gareth gives me far more credit than I deserve," Juliet said, head bent as she discreetly tried to cover her bloodied skirts with her arms. "He was the real hero of the hour, not me."

"On the contrary," said Andrew, waving his glass. "Gareth may be a rake, a wastrel and a scourer, but he doesn't make things up."

"Most assuredly not," his sister added.

Juliet glanced at the duke. The dark eyes were on her. Still watching her. Still studying her.

Worse, that faint little smile still played around his lips. It was unnerving.

"And how *is* Lord Gareth?" Juliet asked, directing her attention to this cheerful pair in an attempt to ignore that enigmatic stare.

"Oh, a bit faint from loss of blood and Irish whiskey, but otherwise quite well. But then, that's Gareth for you." Andrew downed the rest of his brandy with a practiced flick of his wrist. "The villagers call him 'the Wild One,' you know. Why, just last week he had the Den of Debauchery members make a pyramid of themselves down on the village green, took bets from all those who'd gathered to watch, and jumped Crusader over the lot of them. Won himself a fortune that day. The week before that—"

"That's enough, Andrew," the duke interrupted, straightening up.

"Come now, Luce, even *you* have to admit that his getting Mrs. Dorking's pig foxed was hilariously funny."

"It was not hilariously funny, it was uncommonly

stupid. Especially in light of all the damage the animal went on to cause."

Nerissa, examining each of Charlotte's tiny fingers, had her head bent and was trying not to laugh.

Andrew was undeterred. "Still, what he did tonight tops 'em all. Whoever would've thought Gareth would go and make a hero of himself, eh, Luce?"

"Indeed, whoever would have thought Gareth would go and make *anything* of himself," the duke murmured cryptically as he drained the rest of his glass. "And now, if you'll all excuse me, I must go into Ravenscombe to see to the unfortunate passengers of the coach, as well as the highwayman your brother *should have* taken care of but didn't. Pity. I expect there shall be a hanging. Are your traveling trunks still strapped to the coach, Miss Paige?

"Yes, but I think I should leave."

"And *I* think you are distressed and need to rest before making such a hasty decision," he countered, with infuriating benignity. "Surely, meeting Charles's younger brother so unexpectedly, and under such traumatic circumstances, has not helped matters any." He was smiling, but there was something she couldn't identify beneath that smile, and his dark eyes were watching her closely. *Too* closely. "Lord Gareth bears a certain resemblance to Charles, don't you think?"

"Your Grace, I don't want to argue with you, but I would be more comfortable staying someplace in the village—"

"*What?!*" cried Andrew and Nerissa in chorus.

"Are your trunks still outside on the coach, Miss Paige?" the duke persisted.

"Well, of course, but—"

"Are they emblazoned with your name or initials?"

"Yes, but—"

"Puddyford!"

The door opened obediently, and a liveried servant appeared, his face expressionless, his body erect and at attention.

"Puddyford, I have business to attend to in the village. Have Miss Paige's trunks brought inside and up to her room. Nerissa, you will see that our guest is made comfortable, and someone is sent to attend to her needs." He let his gaze sweep assessingly over Juliet. "You will be happy in the Blue Room, I think."

"Your *Grace*, I have no wish to impose upon your hospitality—"

"Nonsense, my dear girl. You have conducted yourself admirably, and your answers have satisfied me. Don't look so put out. Don't you realize I was only testing you with my studied rudeness?"

*Testing me for what?* she all but cried, not knowing whether to be outraged or humiliated. But she said nothing as he smiled, bowed, and without another word, was gone.

Andrew and Nerissa rushed to placate her as she remained staring at the door through which Lucien had passed. She could not know that he was a master manipulator. She could not know that he had plans for her. And she could not know that as the Duke of Blackheath strode out into the Grand Hall and called for his hat, his gloves, and his horse, Armageddon, his eyes were gleaming with cunning delight.

But then, no one knew but the servants, and they would never tell.

His Grace, after all, had his secrets.

# 6

Unpleasant dukes aside, there was something to be said for English hospitality, which started immediately.

Andrew, calling a servant aside and murmuring quiet instructions, made his exit. Beyond the open doors, footmen hurried past with Juliet's trunks. A matronly servant breezed in, took Charlotte, and whisked her away to wash and change her. Several fresh-faced, bright-eyed maids streamed into the library, lining themselves up for Lady Nerissa's inspection. The young noblewoman smiled and beckoned one of the girls forward. "This is Molly," she said, introducing Juliet and the girl. To the maid she said, "Please draw a bath and lay a fire for Miss Paige. She is to be our guest."

"Which room, milady?"

Nerissa turned and, thoughtfully tapping a fingernail against her teeth, looked at Juliet. "In Lord Charles's room, I think."

Juliet gasped. After the robbery, meeting Lord Gareth, and the rigorously exhausting interview through which she'd just been put, could she possibly endure sleeping in Charles's bed without falling apart completely? Nerissa gave her no time to think further upon the matter. Chattering happily, she bade Juliet to follow her from the library.

"Now, you must *not* allow Lucien to upset you," she said, lightly touching Juliet's sleeve as they walked side by side. "He can be a monster even at the best of times, but he's been particularly bad tempered ever since Lady Hartfield tried to blackmail him into marriage last month. Needless to say, my brother does not have the highest opinion of women at the moment! But never mind. Would you like to say good night to Gareth before you retire for the evening?"

Still trying to come to terms with the idea of sleeping in Charles's bed, Juliet was caught by surprise. "I, uh . . ."

Nerissa mistook the reason for her hesitation. "It would make him very happy, I think," she prodded softly.

"But is it proper?"

"Of course. I shall be with you."

She beckoned Juliet to follow her and, skirts whispering over ancient stone, led her up a flight of stairs so magnificent and wide that five people standing arm to arm could have climbed them with room to spare.

At their top was a long, paneled corridor with several doors leading off it. From behind one of them came a drunken verse of song and an answering roar of laughter.

Without hesitation, Nerissa pushed the door open and the guffaws immediately stopped.

"*Gentlemen?*" she said, stressing the word in a way that led one to think she didn't consider the inhabitants of the room to be such at all. "I have a visitor to see Gareth. Behave yourselves."

She opened the door wide for Juliet, motioning her forward.

Hesitantly, Juliet stepped over the threshold and paused just inside. The room was velveted in gloom and shadow. Ornately plastered ceilings rose some fifteen feet above her head. A few burned-down candles, their tongues of flame swaying in the drafts, struggled to give the huge chamber light. Juliet blinked, trying to adjust her eyes to the rich dimness.

And then she saw Gareth's friends, lying about the bedroom in various states of repose—Chilcot, perched on a window seat, his forefinger stuck in an empty bottle and swinging it back and forth; Perry, sprawled in a damask-backed chair with his waistcoat unbuttoned, his cravat askew, and a bleary smile on his handsome face. The names of the others had escaped her. There was the one with the big nose, his eyes bloodshot beneath the straggles of wavy brown hair that had escaped his queue; the one who was as wide and burly as a draft horse, flat on his back and snoring, his wig looking like a dead rat on the floor beside his head; a third, thin and cocky, hiccuping drunkenly and saluting Juliet with his bottle: "To the lady . . . *hic*! . . . o' the hour!"

And Lord Gareth de Montforte.

He lay propped against a mountain of brocaded pillows in a massive bed of carved oak, his hair tousled, a sheet drawn loosely over his bare torso, a sleepy little smile flirting with one corner of his mouth. His gaze lifted to Juliet, and for the second time that night, her hand went to her heart to still its sudden wild palpitations.

Beneath that sheet she knew he was naked.

It was suddenly too hot in the room. It was suddenly too hard to breathe. Juliet felt every part of her that made her a woman go up in flames, thrumming and tingling in wild response to the sight he made against the bedsheets and pillows. She would have turned and fled had Nerissa not been standing just behind her.

Candlelight made his skin glow like honey, bathing his upper body in warmest gold. It picked out the hollows created by bone, sinew, and beautifully honed muscle, flowed over the taut bulges of his upper arms and the base of his neck. Whorls of brown hair brushed his chest, but in the kiss of the bedside candle, each one glinted a mellow gold, as did the stubble just hazing his jaw. As he looked up at Juliet her knees went suddenly weak, for he had a certain, lethal charm that even Charles could not have matched. The thought—and her own physical reaction to the seductive picture he made against those sheets and pillows—made her feel oddly guilty, as though she was betraying the man she loved. She swallowed, hard.

"Come here," he said, softly.

The room went still, with only the candles throwing moving shadows and light up the walls, the carved moldings, and across the high ceiling.

Juliet moved forward, aware that every eye in the room was on her. Her heart pounded madly. Her palms went damp. As she neared the bed Lord Gareth reached out, took her hand, and kissed it.

"You're . . . an angel," he said thickly, his fingers warmly enclosing her own.

She smiled. "And you, Lord Gareth, are foxed."

"Shamefully so. But useful, under the circumstances."

"Are you in much pain?"

He grinned, still holding her hand. "To be honest, Miss Paige, I cannot feel a thing."

Behind her, Chilcot let out a bark of laughter, but Juliet, entranced, never heard it. As Gareth gazed up at her through the loose hair that fell endearingly over his brow and tangled in his lashes, she saw, at last, that his eyes were a pale, sleepy blue.

"I guess you were right," she said and, pulling her fingers from his grasp, reached over and brushed the strands of hair off his brow. Her hand was trembling. "You're not going to die after all."

"Wouldn't dream of it. I rather like being a hero,

you know. Think I'll stick around and rescue damsels in distress more often." He looked up at her, those beautiful blue eyes of his warm, earnest, and reaching areas of her heart that she'd forgotten had existed. "Don't let Lucien scare you off, will you?"

"I won't."

He nodded once, satisfied, and let his eyes drift shut. "Thank you for coming to see me, Miss Paige."

She swallowed, trying to find her voice. "And thank you, Lord Gareth, for what you did for me tonight." And then, on a sudden impulse, she bent down and, through the loose strands of his hair, dropped a kiss on his brow. "I owe you my life."

She was far from cold, but Juliet was hugging her arms to herself as she and Nerissa moved along the shadowy corridor, their passing the only sound in the now-quiet house. Her heart was still pounding, and she longed to rush outside and drink deeply of the cool night air. What was wrong with her? Why had she had such a reaction to Lord Gareth?

She hadn't experienced *those* sort of feelings since . . . well, since Charles.

She shuddered, throwing off her thoughts. Of course her heart was beating so hard because they were headed for Charles's room, an experience she was both dreading and eagerly anticipating. Of course the only reason she'd reacted so to Gareth was because he was Charles's brother, nothing more. It had nothing to do with Gareth. It had everything to do with Charles.

Didn't it?

"Are you well, Juliet?" Nerissa asked, beside her.

Juliet managed a feeble smile. "Yes, thank you—it's just been a rather trying day, that's all."

"Of course," the other woman said kindly, but her blue eyes were sharp, and Juliet had a feeling she had guessed more than she was letting on. What must Nerissa think of her, lighting up over one brother while supposedly still mourning the other?

They continued down the hall. On the walls, sconces glowed orange and cast flickering light over portraits and paintings, ancient statues and busts. Finally they reached a massive carved door. There Nerissa paused, her hand on the latch.

Juliet tensed, mentally bracing herself. She felt Nerissa's gaze upon her.

"Charles would have been proud of you," said the younger woman, quietly. "Coming all the way to England just to give your baby a name and a family. . . . Please don't worry about Lucien. If he shan't help you, one of us will." She pushed the door open slightly while Juliet hung back. "Martha?" Nerissa called softly, into the darkness within. "You can go off to bed now. And oh, good—you've brought the cradle up from the nursery."

Juliet, still standing outside, hugged herself and traced a design on the rug with her toe while Nerissa conversed with the maid.

The matronly woman who had made off with Charlotte emerged from the room, yawning. "Lord Andrew 'ad it done, milady. Said 'e didn't think mother and daughter'd want to be separated. Also said it was too short notice to find a wet nurse in the village, so the babe would 'ave to stay in 'ere with 'er mother instead of up in the nursery. The little mite's a-sleepin' now, but I 'spect she'll need a feedin' soon."

"My goodness! I am amazed that Andrew knows anything about such matters," Nerissa mused, raising her brows.

Juliet lifted her head. "Thank you for your help, Martha." She turned to Charles's sister. "And you, too, Lady Nerissa. You have all been so kind to us."

Martha beamed. "Think nothink of it, mum. We

ain't 'ad a babe in this 'ouse for far too long, if'n ye ask me."

"Indeed," Nerissa said wryly. "Off with you now, Martha. I am sure Miss Paige wishes to rest. We can both see Charlotte at breakfast."

"Yes, milady. Lookin' forward to it; I am!"

Martha bobbed in a curtsy and ambled off down the hall.

Nerissa watched her go. "I know you are unused to servants, but if you change your mind about letting Molly assist you tonight, there's a bellpull behind the bed." She put her hands on Juliet's arms, looking at her for a long moment before pulling her forward in a quick embrace. "I'm so glad you've come here. Good night, now, and I shall see you in the morning."

Juliet returned the other woman's smile. "Good night, Lady Nerissa."

Charles's sister moved off down the hall, her footfalls fading. Juliet stood watching her, hating to see her go. But she had to face the inevitable. Taking a deep breath, she slowly pushed open the door . . . and entered the room that had belonged to Charles.

All was still. Dark. A sleepy fire crackled in the hearth, and before it, in silhouette, stood a brass bath and a towel stand and the cradle that held Charlotte. Juliet took a step forward, softly closing the door behind her. A great curtained bed filled the shadows. Dim shapes marked out furniture. On a chest of drawers, a lone candle flickered in the drafts, a tiny finger of light against the darkness. Arms at her sides, her chest slowly rising and falling, Juliet stood very still in the silence, letting it engulf her.

*Charles.*

She had thought to feel him here, but the room was empty. There was only the little candle, herself, and her sleeping daughter. Nothing else. No overwhelming sense of his presence, no lingering hint of his scent, no rush of memories, nothing. It was just a room and nothing more.

She moved slowly around the huge, chilly chamber, her skirts whispering over the floor he had once walked, her fingers trailing atop the furniture that had once belonged to him. He was not here. He was as far away from her here, as he had been all these past lonely months in Boston.

*Oh, Charles . . . I have never felt so alone in all my life.*

The fire snapped. A little shower of embers trickled through the grate, a mournful sound in the darkness. She leaned against the bedpost and gazed dismally at their red glow, feeling somehow betrayed by his absence, feeling sad and confused and lonely and lost.

"Charles . . ."

But there was no answer.

The baby awoke, whimpering. Juliet went to the cradle, picked her up, and hugged her to her breast, rocking back and forth in quiet, dry-eyed agony. *Charlie-girl*, Lord Gareth had called the baby. What an endearment. Grief welled up in the back of her throat.

*He's dead, Juliet. Dead and gone. Doesn't this empty, lifeless room prove it?*

She held Charlotte close for a long time, gathering what comfort she could from her baby and trying, in vain, to cling to something she'd once had but would never have again. The wild and breathless euphoria of first love. A heart that had leaped with joy at just the thought of her handsome British officer. How young and naive she had been, assuming that with Charles she had found her "forever," that death would never touch someone as youthful, as virile, as he had been. And how far away those memories, that giddy, soaring, girlish excitement, now felt.

And yet something inside her had stirred tonight

when she'd seen his brother—beautifully masculine, powerfully muscled—lying in his bed, his nakedness covered only by a loose sheet. Something she hadn't felt in a long, long time.

Desire.

She shook her head. No wonder she didn't feel Charles here. How could she, with the image of that splendid younger brother emblazoned so vividly across her brain?

"Ouch!" Charlotte had grasped a lock of Juliet's hair, yanking it hard from its pins and reminding Juliet that she had someone else to think of besides herself. Gently, she pried the lock from the baby's fist and pulled up a chair, where she sat nursing her daughter and staring into the red embers of the dying fire. She thought of Charles. She thought of her reaction to Gareth. She thought how horrible she was for even having such a reaction.

And eventually, she became so tired, she didn't think at all.

The water was cool by the time she had finished tending to Charlotte, shed her soiled clothes, and crawled, shivering, into the bath. It had grown much colder still when she finally emerged. She toweled herself dry, put on her nightgown and crawled beneath the cool, crisp sheets, her cheek sinking into the feathery softness of the pillow that had once held *his* dear head.

His pillow, his room, his bed.

And he had probably been the last one to sleep in it.

She pulled the other pillow close and curled her body around it, hugging it and staring at the shadows flickering against the far wall. Then she closed her eyes . . . and dreamed of Charles.

She saw him again, the fine British officer on his mighty charger, surveying his troops with a coolly assessing eye as they filed smartly past. She lived again that moment when he'd first caught her watching from the window and had touched his cocked hat in acknowledgement. And she was there once more, on that day he'd finally stridden into the shop . . . spoken to her . . . met her behind the wood-shed two weeks later, where they'd shared that first magical kiss, and she had nearly swooned within the hard circle of his arms. *Oh, Charles.* She sighed softly and turned over, sinking back down into the depths of sleep.

The dream faded out.

*Charles?*

*Oh, my dearest love, come back!*

But Charles was no longer there. Someone else was coming toward her now . . . someone riding out of a rainy English night, lifting a pistol, tumbling through fierce, stinging nettles to shield the child in his arms even as the ball tore into his side.

She ran to him, and when she lifted his head from the nettles, the sleepy, down-slanted eyes that gazed up at her were not Charles's, but Gareth's.

## 7

**G**areth awoke, briefly, sometime just before dawn. Faint light was just starting to creep through the parted drapes, and from somewhere outside the first blackbird was calling. He shivered, pulling the covers up over his shoulders. The room was cold and empty, the hearth a pile of dead ashes, his friends long gone. Lucien must have kicked them out sometime during the night, he thought, not sure whether to be grateful or annoyed. As he lay there wondering if it was worth moving to retrieve and use the chamber pot, the words of the doctor played through his head like a litany.

*You were lucky, damned lucky, my lord . . . Another half-inch and you would've lost your rib; a little more than that your lung, and very likely your life.*

It was a sobering thought.

They'd told him the ball had peeled a strip of flesh off a lower rib, plowing a furrow in the bone and leaving a loose flap of skin that had bled profusely. As wounds went, it was far less serious than it had initially looked. But plague take his rib, Gareth had thought then—and thought now as he groaned and finally reached for the chamber pot, it was his head—the entire left side of his face—that was killing him.

He'd do well to stay out of the nettles in the future.

And, he allowed ruefully, Irish whiskey.

Still, he knew that if he had the chance to live the robbery all over again, he wouldn't set a foot differently. Despite his hangover, his raw cheek, and the throbbing of his nicked rib, he felt quite good about himself just now. Quite good, indeed. He slid back beneath the covers, smiling like a fool. It was rather nice, being the hero of the hour . . . and there were no words to describe how he'd felt when Miss Juliet Paige had come in to say good night to him and bent down to touch her cool, sweet lips to his brow. He sighed and lay back in bed with a happy grin. Such attentions made him feel quite special, indeed. And, appreciated.

He wasn't used to anyone appreciating him.

He closed his eyes. The blackbird was still singing, and as he began to drift away, he allowed himself to imagine that Juliet Paige was gazing reverently down at him, standing watch over him as though he were some mighty fallen warrior-hero and she, heaven's dearest angel.

When Lucien came quietly in to check on him an hour later, Gareth was fast asleep . . . and still smiling.

The mighty hero slept straight through breakfast. By then, the flowers, tributes, notes and poems of praise had already begun to arrive as news of the robbery, and Gareth's part in thwarting it, spread through Ravenscombe and into the surrounding countryside.

The Wild One had always been popular with the ladies, but never so much as he was this fine, late-April morning. His actions of the previous night—and the fact that he'd suffered a "grievous, life-threatening wound"—seemed to have driven every female in Berkshire into a frenzy. A group of blushing, giggling maids from the village brought him a bouquet of bright purple lilacs. A half-dozen red roses arrived from Lady Jayne Snow, only to be outdone by a full dozen from her sister Lady Anne. A box of sweet, juicy oranges were sent by Miss Amy Woodside, letters and notes poured in by the dozens, and a poem of ardent admiration came from the gushing pen of Miss Sally Chilcot, who was as brainless and silly as her fool of a brother, Neil.

Or so proclaimed an increasingly annoyed Lucien, as a footman entered the dining hall where they were all having breakfast, with the missive on a silver platter.

"For *heaven's* sake," he muttered, plucking the perfumed vellum and all but slamming it down into the growing pile before Gareth's empty chair.

He picked up his coffee and went back to reading *The Gentleman's Magazine.*

"Oh, do open it, Luce," drawled Andrew, buttering a piece of bread and craning his neck to read the flowery writing that covered the folded vellum. "Let's see . . . Ah! *A Poem: To the Brave and Dashing Lord Gareth de Montforte.*" He made a noise of amused contempt. "Whatever she wrote ought to be priceless as far as breakfast-time amusement goes."

"Whatever she wrote is for Gareth's eyes only," snapped Nerissa, who was bouncing Charlotte on her lap. "You're just miffed that Gareth is getting so much attention, and you're not."

"On the contrary, my dear sister. I have better things to do than fend off the attentions of pestilent females."

"Perhaps that's because there *are* no pestilent females giving you attention to fend off," Nerissa shot back.

"*Children,*" muttered the duke, without looking up from his paper.

Feeling uncomfortable and more than a little out of place, Juliet silently stirred sugar into her tea. She was still smarting over the way the duke had treated her during the previous night's interview, and even now she didn't know whether he intended to take her in and make Charlotte his ward—or not. He hadn't said a word about the subject, and until Nerissa had brought her down here to breakfast, Juliet had not seen him so that she could ask. She wanted to speak to him alone. Here at the table, with two bickering siblings listening in, did not seem the appropriate time or place in which to do so.

Perhaps she could request a moment of his time after breakfast. . . .

"Don't look so troubled, Miss Paige," Andrew said amiably, mistaking the reason for Juliet's preoccupied frown. "My sister and I fight like cats and dogs. 'Tis quite normal in this household, I'm afraid. In time you'll get used to us."

Juliet glanced at the duke, wondering whether or not he intended to give her that time, but he made no comment, only continued reading.

"And Andrew *would* have pestilent females chasing after him if only he'd get his nose out of those science books and venture out into the real world once in a while," his sister added. "Tell her about the invention you're working on, Andrew."

"It's nothing."

Juliet noted the sudden tinge of color along Andrew's cheekbones. "Invention?"

He shrugged and bent his head, making a big project out of buttering another piece of bread. "I'm trying to build a flying machine."

"A flying machine!" Juliet nearly dropped the cup of tea she was just bringing to her lips.

"Yes." He didn't look up, but kept smearing butter on his bread, the color spreading out along his cheekbones. "I know it sounds daft, but if birds can fly, and kites, and even leaves on the wind, I don't see any reason why it can't be done."

"Impossible," the duke muttered, still reading.

"I don't think so," said Andrew.

The duke turned a page. "If God wanted us to fly, He would've given us wings."

"Yes, and if He'd wanted us to ply the seas, He would've given us fins," countered Nerissa, as Andrew, red-faced, set down his knife. "But He didn't, so we had to invent ships. Why should flying be any different? I think Andrew's idea is worthy and fine."

"And I think it's damned ridiculous," the duke snapped, not bothering to look up. "Of all the men who've gone through Oxford in the last twenty years, Andrew was probably one of only a handful who didn't waste his time drinking, whoring, and carousing, but actually got down to the business of serious study. And for what? A flying machine. What a waste of a fine education. What a waste of a damned fine *brain*."

Andrew flushed hotly, his eyes sparking with sudden anger.

"Lucien, that was cruel and unfair!" cried Nerissa.

"It is the truth."

"If people like Andrew didn't invent things that others thought impossible, nothing new would ever be made!"

"Flying machines *are* impossible. He'll never do it."

Andrew slammed his chair back and stormed from the room, nearly knocking over a footman who was just entering. The servant never batted an eye as Nerissa also jumped up and went hurrying past him after her angry brother. The duke, meanwhile, calmly went on reading his paper as though the exchange had never happened. He didn't even acknowledge the footman—bearing yet another note on the silver plate he held in one gloved hand—

when the servant lowered it before his face.

"For Lord Gareth, Your Grace."

Wordlessly, the duke took the note and tossed it into the growing pile as the footman glided soundlessly from the room.

Then he looked up and saw Juliet still sitting there, her face tight with disapproval. "Ah"—he gave a rueful, bland little smile—"I see that you, too, think I'm cruel and heartless. But Andrew cannot focus his mind, and attentions, on a single project. He has an annoying and unproductive habit of hitting upon an idea, then failing to follow it through." He took a sip of his coffee and smiled benignly at Juliet. "If I do not mock and challenge him, he will never design his flying machine."

"You're a very manipulative man, Your Grace. Do you always employ such methods to get others to behave as you would wish?"

Again, that derisive little smile. "Only when it is necessary, Miss Paige. Now, be a good girl and take those letters up to Gareth, would you? I find that the scent of them is giving me a headache."

Juliet managed to find her way through the maze of rooms and corridors to the great staircase that led upstairs. She paused at the summit. Halfway down the hall, the door to Gareth's room was standing slightly ajar. Her hand gripped the carved banister and, with some surprise, she realized her heart was beating twice as fast as it should be. Now, why on earth was she nervous about entering that room? There were other things that deserved her concern far more than a common female reaction to the uncommonly handsome Lord Gareth de Montforte.

Such as whatever the Duke of Blackheath was planning.

It bothered her that he'd sent her on this errand when it would have been more appropriate—not to mention, proper—to have one of the servants do it. It bothered her because she suspected he was up to something, and she didn't know what it could be. She had seen firsthand how Blackheath pulled strings and people unwittingly danced. She had seen how he'd manipulated Andrew by purposely mocking and angering him; he had done much the same with her during last night's interview. In fact, he had even admitted as much—though what his motives were now, or even then, Juliet did not know and was not sure she cared to know. After all, she had nothing that His Grace could possibly be interested in, nothing he could possibly want of her. . . .

She continued down the corridor, pausing at Gareth's partly open door and listening for sounds within. All was quiet. Slowly, shyly, Juliet pushed the door open, breathing a sigh of relief when it made no noise on its well-oiled hinges. Oh, she was nervous, all right; the letters in her hand had absorbed its dampness, molded themselves to the curve of her palm. Slipping quietly over the threshold, she paused just inside.

The room was preternaturally still. She took a deep breath, casting about for a place to leave the letters while trying not to look at the bed. A pillow was on the floor; yet another; in fact, a whole jagged trail of them, hurled off the bed by a sleeper who was either restless or in a considerable amount of pain. Juliet's gaze followed this trail, across the floor and straight to the foot of the bed. She saw the tasseled ropes of deep crimson holding back the curtains of shimmering gold silk that dressed the bed; she saw the carved headboard framed between them; and she saw a man's form, partially covered by a loose sheet. Rising above this form was the bare skin of one handsomely rounded shoulder and a tousled head of hair upon the pillow.

Juliet's cheeks went feverishly warm. She jerked

her gaze away, feeling she was intruding upon something personal. Something private. A man's bedroom, for goodness sake! She would just drop the letters on the highboy between the windows and beat a hasty exit.

She was partway across the room before she realized Gareth would have to get out of bed to retrieve the letters, and injured as he was, he was likely to be very sore.

Oh, she could just strangle the Duke of Blackheath for putting her in this position!

There was nothing for it, then. She would have to put the letters on the table beside his bed and hope he didn't wake.

She steeled herself. Then, shielding her eyes as though from the sun, head down and watching the progress of her shoes—anything to keep from looking at that bed as she approached and at Gareth, who was probably still naked, who might even be half-exposed by the looseness of the sheet, for all she knew—she moved swiftly across the rug, her heart beating triple-time.

The edge of the bed came into view. She tried to keep her gaze downcast, but like Pandora with her box, it lifted, nervously strayed, crept up to stare at that which she had no business observing. She saw the curve of that bare, muscled shoulder, close enough to touch; the clean white bandage around an equally bare torso; and there, beneath the soft, draped sheet, the outline of hips, legs, ankles, feet. . . . *Oh, my!* And then he sighed and turned over, and Juliet froze, praying that he wouldn't wake and find her here, wide-eyed and uninvited, a silent voyeur staring at him as though she had never seen anyone asleep before.

And stare she did. He lay not quite on his side, not quite on his back, but halfway between the two, beautifully chiseled lips slightly parted, one arm bent at the elbow and thrown over his head, the palm of his hand showing beneath loosely curled fingers. He had a broad, sculpted chest. Powerful arms. She watched the sheet rising and falling in time with his breathing, noting the way the light and shadows came in from the windows and dappled his relaxed face, the strong column of his neck where it flowed into wide, capable shoulders, the loosely draped hips, thighs, and legs. *Oh, dear,* she thought, laying a hand to her burning cheek. *Oh dear, oh dear, oh dear . . .*

Juliet swallowed—hard. Then she tiptoed up to the bed and placed the stack of letters on the small marble-topped table. Her anxiety and attempt to be quick were her undoing. Her sleeve caught the edge of the stack as she withdrew, and the letters made a whispery little sound as they tumbled to the floor.

The man in the bed opened his eyes.

Juliet gasped.

And Lord Gareth merely grinned, instantly seeing her plight and giving her time to compose herself by emitting a very exaggerated, vocal yawn. "Mmmmm," he murmured, his eyes sleepy, heavy lidded, hopelessly seductive. "You are still here. Good."

"G-good?" She backed up and looked away, painfully embarrassed, her face so hot that she feared it might melt.

"Yes, good. You see, I had some strange dreams last night." He knuckled his eyes and then, letting his arm fall back, rested his loose fist across the pillow beside his ear. "I dreamed that my brother had fathered a darling little girl and lived on through her. I dreamed that a beautiful woman was in my room watching over me whilst I slept. And I dreamed that Lucien did not send her away." He smiled up at her, his eyes warm upon her face. "I see that perhaps I have not been dreaming."

"I, uh—" Juliet suddenly couldn't find her tongue, or the means to make it work. "I—I was just leaving."

"Leaving? Come now, I just woke up. If you go so soon, I may be offended." Sitting up, he flexed his arms, scrunched up his face, and emitted a yawn of such pure, robust pleasure that it sounded almost leonine; then he struck out sideways in a leisurely stretch, his fist hitting a pillow and sending it tumbling off the bed to join the others on the floor. "So"—he lay back and crossed his arms behind his head, treating Juliet to a view of hairy male underarms and strikingly defined muscle—"how are you getting on with Lucien, anyhow?"

Juliet's face flamed at the unconsciously seductive sight he made. She looked away. "Well, all right, I guess. But he is rather—"

"Difficult?"

She smiled and gave a little shrug, not wanting to say anything bad about his brother.

"Domineering?"

Her smile became a downright grin.

"Rude, oppressive, bad tempered, and unpleasant?"

She saw the twinkle in his eyes. "Well, I didn't want to say it myself."

"Why not? It is, after all, the truth." He immediately sobered, his expression becoming more focused, sharper. "What did he say about Charlotte? He *is* going to make her his ward, isn't he?"

"I don't know. He's given me no indication what his plans are."

Gareth swore beneath his breath.

"He didn't say a word all through breakfast, except to antagonize Lord Andrew—and ask that I bring these letters up to you. I tried to be quiet so as not to wake you, but . . ." She gave a little shake of her head. "Oh, I am so embarrassed!"

"Why?"

"I don't usually make it a habit of prowling around a man's bedroom, especially when he's in it, asleep!"

"Well, I do not mind." Arms still crossed behind his head, he gave her a look of twinkling amusement. "That is, if you don't."

"I think I had better leave."

"Oh, please don't, Miss Paige. I am enjoying your company."

"This is unseemly!"

"Says who? I'm bored. Restless. And I have no one else to talk to."

"You shouldn't be talking to me. Not when you're lying there naked beneath those sheets, and . . ."

His brows rose. "How do you know I am naked, Miss Paige?"

"I didn't look, if that is what you're implying!"

"Oh. But you did"—his lips were twitching—"in my dream, that is."

*"Lord Gareth!"*

He laughed, his eyes warm, teasing, and as blue as the sky outside. Confused and flustered by the warm interest she saw there, Juliet looked away, awash in a wave of prickly, pleasurable heat. She could feel his gaze upon her. Could feel her own response to it, to him. And then, despite herself, she began to smile. She liked Gareth. He liked her. And truth be told, his playful yet ardent attention felt rather nice.

"So, what do *you* do?" she asked, trying to change the subject to something . . . safe.

"Do?"

"Yes. I mean, Charles was an army officer, Andrew aspires to be an inventor, Lucien is a duke—what about you?"

"Oh. Uh, me."

"You."

He looked temporarily lost. She could not know what he was thinking: *I am a hopeless wastrel. The black sheep. The family embarrassment. What do I do? Nothing.*

"I . . . have fun," he said, and then looked innocently up at her through his lashes, bestowing upon her such a charmingly dimpled grin that she could only laugh.

"That's *all* you do?"

"For now. Though I must confess, I expect life will be rather boring whilst I am stranded here convalescing. Therefore, you simply must come and visit me every day, Miss Paige—I could *never* be bored if I have you here to amuse me."

She laughed, picked up the pile of letters, and rapped them lightly on his shamelessly naked chest. "Here. If you're so bored, I expect these will make your convalescence all the more bearable."

"But I am not in the mood for reading, Miss Paige. Besides, I'd wager they all say much the same thing. Read one, you've read them all."

"And have you read one?"

"Actually, I have not. I can do many things in my sleep, but reading is not one of them."

He gazed up at her, arms still crossed behind his head, a playful little smile on his face.

She took a deep breath and looked away—and all she saw were flowers. On the chest of drawers, on the windowsill, on the writing desk. Looking at them—and the pile of letters whose scent remained on her palm—Juliet felt a restless, twisting pang of something she would've identified as jealousy had there been any reason to feel such a thing. But of course she wasn't jealous. She barely knew Lord Gareth. Just because she'd had a claim on his brother didn't give her one on him.

"Pretty flowers," she said, inanely. She wiped her palm on her skirts, unconsciously trying to rid it of another woman's scent. "You seem to be quite popular with the ladies, Lord Gareth."

"You think so?"

"Don't you?"

He gave a little shrug, a modest acknowledgement that yes, he supposed he was, but did not at the moment find it particularly important. Or, relevant.

She asked, "Was your brother popular with the ladies, too?"

"Who? Charles?"

"Why, yes."

His gaze warmed yet further as it played over her face. "It would appear he was quite popular with at least *one* lady."

Her cheeks went pink and she looked down, hiding a little smile. "Besides me."

"Oh, Charles had his admirers. But he was an ambitious man, given to his studies and later his military career, and didn't have time to chase skirts. Or so he said. The truth was, our parents—and Lucien—had his life perfectly arranged, and Charles was not the sort to rebel simply for the sake of rebelling."

"I see. . . . The duke did imply that Charles was promised to someone else."

"He was promised to someone else before he was even born. That certainly did not mean he had any feelings for the girl."

"And what about you? As the new heir-presumptive, are *you* promised to another?"

He grinned. "My dear Miss Paige. I *am* the sort to rebel, simply for the sake of rebeling. When and if I ever marry, it will be to someone of my own choosing, not Lucien's."

"Yes . . . somehow, I cannot see you following a course laid out for you by him or anyone else."

"Ha! But that doesn't mean he doesn't try to force one upon me." He was still gazing fondly up at her; but as he studied her face, his grin faded somewhat, only to be replaced by an expression of sympathy and understanding. "You still miss him, don't you?"

Her smile dwindled, too. She stared wistfully out the window and across the green, green downs. "I think I'll always miss him, Lord Gareth." She was still for a moment, her gaze cresting the brow of the downs to the milky-blue horizon, as though she could see all the way back to Boston and that terrible day last April. "I can still remember it so well, that last night I saw him alive. I'd just told him I was going to have his child. Oh, you should've seen his face . . . so full of joy, then sober duty as he got down on one knee before me and asked me to marry him. And that is my last memory of him: Charles on his knee, his head bent, the candlelight flickering in that bright, gold hair of his."

"As last memories go, that is not such a bad one, Miss Paige."

"Yes—I know. Sometimes I'm thankful for the fact that I never did see his body, for that very same reason. It's much nicer to remember a person alive, don't you think? Still, in some ways, it makes it harder . . . there was no closure, you know. I never had the chance to weep over him, never had the chance to tell him good-bye. And that's the part that still hurts. It's horrible to lose someone you love; it's even more horrible when that person is snatched from you with no warning whatsoever, and you never get the chance to say good-bye."

"Yes . . . I know exactly what you mean." He was silent for a moment, sad, and she knew he was re-living his own memories, quietly relating to her words in a way that no one on the other side of the Atlantic had ever been able, or inclined, to do.

It made her feel suddenly close to him. Kindred.

"You still miss him, too."

"All the time."

"Your sister put me in his old room last night. I

know this is going to sound silly, but I'd thought—
hoped—I'd feel him there somehow."

"And did you?"

She hugged herself and, gazing somewhat wistfully at the floor, shook her head. "No."

He was quiet for a moment. Then: "I don't know
if it's of any comfort, but I've never felt him in there,
either."

"You, too, have gone in there, hoping to feel his
presence?"

He gave a gentle smile. "Many times."

A still moment hung between them as she fussed
with the lace at her sleeve. She could feel his gaze
upon her. "Are my feelings for Charles so very obvious, Lord Gareth?"

He smiled, kindly. "Yes—but they are not offen-
sive. In fact, I must confess that I am happy for my
brother, having loved someone who, even a year after his death, remains so loyal to him." His eyes
grew a little sad. "Happy for Charles, perhaps—but
not for the woman he left behind. You must get on
with your life, Miss Paige. He would have wanted
you to, you know."

"Yes . . . I know. I was doing fine until I met you,"
she admitted. "Seeing you, your close resemblance
to him, brought everything back."

"Ah, but physical appearance is the only resemblance Charles and I shared," he said, with another
of those warm, dimpled grins that made her insides
do somersaults. "Get to know me well enough, Miss
Paige, and you'll see that I am a very different man,
indeed."

He pulled the sheet up to better preserve his modesty—or perhaps hers—and, leaning sideways, tried
to reach the glass and bottle of spirits that stood beside the letters on the marble-topped table. As he did
so, he winced, his hand still four or five inches from
the glass, and settled slowly back against the pil-

lows, empty-handed, his face suddenly quite pale.

"Please, let me help you!" Juliet gasped, rushing forward.

"I am fine, just a bit of pain in my side, that is all." He grinned up at her as she hovered above him. "I daresay the Irish whiskey has worn off. Everything is beginning to hurt."

She picked up one of the pillows that lay on the floor. Then another. "You passed a bad night, didn't you?"

"I have had worse. And woken in a great deal more pain than I am feeling now. Miss Paige—I am sorry to impose, but will you pour me a measure of that whiskey, there? I must stretch to reach it, and . . ."

"Yes, yes, of course," she said, impatient with herself for not anticipating this simple need and seeing to it before he could try to do so himself. She grabbed both the bottle and glass, filling the latter to the brim as though to make up for her failings and handing it to him. Their fingers accidentally touched. He smiled at this simple contact and Juliet shivered, involuntarily, her fingers tingling as she watched him down the strong spirits with one practiced flick of his wrist.

Finishing, he handed the glass back to her, his skin a little flushed. "Ah. That is better. Thank you."

She refilled it for him. "Would you like me to fluff up your pillows, as well?"

"Oh, I daresay I would like that very much indeed."

They shared a shy smile. Then Juliet gathered the rest of the pillows up from the rug and dumped them near Gareth's left arm. He was keen to help her, leaning forward so that she could pile two or three pillows up behind him. As she plumped and fluffed them, she could not help but look at that stunningly beautiful masculine back so close to her

hand, tautly curved, sculpted with muscle, and
blessed with breadth across the shoulders. She
snatched her hand away as he began to lean back,
both tempted by, and wary of touching, that bare,
warm skin for fear of the purely carnal reaction she
knew it would ignite in her.

He lay back, sighing with pleasure as he sank
deeply into the pillows. From beneath half-closed
lids he watched her refilling his glass yet again. As
she handed it to him, he looked up at her, his eyes
warm with gratitude—and something else. Juliet
blushed. Without the life-and-death urgency of last
night, without talk of Charles to get the focus off
themselves, there was an awkward uncertainty between them, the sort felt by two people who are attracted to each other but don't know each other well
enough to admit it, or feel comfortable in displaying
it.

Or at least, that was the way *she* felt.

She wasn't so sure about Gareth, who seemed
completely at ease around her, with or without the
assistance of so much whiskey.

"I, uh . . . think I'd better go," Juliet said.

"A pity, that." He lifted the glass to his lips, his
eyes watching her from above its rim. "I cannot talk
you into staying, then?"

"No. But I'll come back later if you like. Maybe I
can bring your supper up to you or something. . . ."

"Would you? I would like that. In fact, I would
like that very much indeed. Otherwise boredom will
force me to read those silly letters, and I confess,
Miss Paige, that I would much rather spend the time
with you." He grinned. "And Charlotte, if you will
bring her."

"I will bring her."

"Good. I am looking forward to getting to know
both my niece *and* her lovely mama. When you return, I want to hear all about America, your sea

crossing, everything. And I want a full report on how—Oh, dear—'' He suddenly started and blinked several times in rapid succession, as though the whiskey had just caught him very much by surprise (which in itself was no surprise, Juliet thought, given the amount he had downed and the speed with which he had consumed it). He shook his head, slowly, and tipped it back against the pillows with an apologetic little smile. "That is to say, I want a full report on how Lucien is treating you."

"You shall have it then, Lord Gareth." She plucked the empty glass from his hand and placed it back on the table. "But for now, I think you had better rest."

"Yes . . . I fear I have no choice about *that*, given the way those spirits have just hit me! I am sorry, Miss Paige; I have no wish to be rude, it usually takes much more than three glasses to get me to this state . . . but oh, isn't it strange, how the loss of a little blood seems to carry a man's vitality off with it, as well. . . ."

"I wouldn't know." She smiled and moved forward to gently pull the sheet up over his chest. He looked up at her through his lashes and gave her a slow, sleepy smile, content to let her fuss over him, grateful for the attention, a man completely at ease in the company of a woman.

"Thank you," he murmured, smiling as he let his eyes drift shut. "I think I shall enjoy . . . my dreams."

She blushed wildly at the unspoken implication of what they might contain; then she touched his arm and crept silently away.

"One last thing, Miss Paige."

She turned and gazed fondly at him, at his eyes, drooping now, that he was trying so hard to keep open. "Yes?"

"This is a . . . rather oppressive house. I know better than anyone what Lucien is like, and I know how homesick you must be, far away from everyone and everything you know and love. But you just remember this. . . . Any time you start feeling out of place here or unwanted or just need to get away from it all, you know where to find me."

His words hit something deep inside of her, making her realize she'd found her first real friend in this strange and lonely place. A lump rose in her throat. "Thank you, Lord Gareth."

"Mmm. . . . the pleasure is mine, madam."

Gareth slept well past supper, not only because his body needed the healing rest, but because large quantities of Irish whiskey were enough to lay even the most debauched of English gentlemen low.

When he opened his eyes late that evening, the shadows were gathering, the room was still, and a figure sat in silhouette by the dying light of the far window.

"Ah. So the gallant hero awakes."

Gareth swore and rubbed his eyes. "Lucien."

"Feeling better, I hope?"

"I feel fine." He yawned, stretched with lazy, all-the-time-in-the-world abandon, and suddenly snapped to attention as he remembered. "Where is she?"

Lucien swept his arm to indicate the many bouquets that seemed to grow from every flat surface in the room. "Where is whom?"

"Don't play games with me, you know damned well whom I'm talking about."

"Ah, you must mean Miss Paige. Why, she's downstairs in the Gold Parlor with Nerissa and Andrew, playing with Charlotte. Tsk, tsk, Gareth. Did you think I had sent her away?"

"And why wouldn't I think it? You will."

A smooth, benign grin. "Perhaps."

"Oh, and what is your twisted, self-serving game

this time, eh?" Gareth muttered, sitting up and pressing the heel of his hand to his pounding head. "To see how quickly you can intimidate her into leaving? Frighten her into turning tail and fleeing back to Boston? Or perhaps it's something worse."

The duke raised his brows, all feigned innocence and surprise. "Why, Gareth. You disappoint me with your distrust and lack of faith in me. I am not such a monster as all that. In fact, I even brought you tea."

"You play with people's minds, Lucien. I'll not have you doing so with hers."

"My dear boy, I plan nothing of the sort." He flicked a bit of dust off his sleeve of black velvet. "Besides, the girl is not so easily frightened. You know that yourself."

"You can't send her away."

"I will if I have to."

"I won't allow it."

"You'll have no choice. I am not blind, Gareth. I see how quickly your tongue defends her, and I suspect you half fancy her already—as you do anything with two legs and a skirt. Now, don't get me wrong. I quite like the chit. Miss Paige is a fine woman, blessed with both beauty and courage, but she is a base-born rustic, and you are the heir presumptive to a dukedom—much as I rue that unhappy fact every day of my waking life." He gave a dramatic, exaggerated sigh. "Oh, how I wish Andrew was in line to inherit, instead of you. . . ."

"Don't lecture me, Lucien. I'm not in the mood to hear it."

"Of course you're not. You never are, are you? But here's something for you to think about whilst you're lying in bed, playing up your little scratch and enjoying the undeserved fruits of hero worship." He ignored Gareth's curses. "Whether or not

I send Miss Paige away, my dear boy, depends on you."

"What the hell are you talking about?"

Lucien's voice lost its mocking tone and hardened. "You know how I felt about Charles's wish to marry someone so far beneath him, and you can guess how I feel about any possible romantic attraction you might have for the girl, as well. I will allow her and the babe to remain at Blackheath. But should I see you staring after her when she leaves a room, or nipping at her heels like a lovesick puppy, I will send her away." Again, that infuriatingly benign smile. "For your own good, of course."

"Damn you, Lucien, you've no business telling me what I can or cannot do, I'm three and twenty, not fifteen!"

"Which brings me to the second half of my conditions."

"As if this isn't enough!"

"It isn't." The duke rose to his feet, cool, composed, infuriatingly unruffled. Gareth saw that he was holding a vase of flowers, which he had apparently brought upstairs with him. "As you've just said yourself, my dear boy, you are three and twenty now. Not fifteen. It's time your behavior reflected the age of your body, not your brain."

Gareth swore once more. Not this discussion *again*.

"I will see behavior from you befitting an educated young nobleman in line for a dukedom," Lucien continued, smoothly. "No more stupid stunts, immature pranks, drunken loutishness, or other nonsense. Put one foot wrong, Gareth, and I warn you: The girl goes. Do you understand me?"

Lucien's black gaze bored through the darkness into Gareth's.

"Go to hell," Gareth muttered sullenly, looking away.

"Good. I see that you do understand. Good night, then. And here"—he plunked down the vase he still held in one hand—"have some flowers."

# 8

As the week unfurled, Juliet found herself growing lonelier and lonelier at the castle. The meals she took with the family were always silent and tense; Andrew was usually in his laboratory "experimenting"; Nerissa rose late and made frequent social calls on the neighboring gentry; and the Duke of Blackheath, never pleasant, often aloof, and always more than capable of making Juliet feel as though she was a burden on his time and attention, continued to evade her question about making Charlotte his ward—*I have not made up my mind yet, Miss Paige, do not continue to harass me about it*. It was little wonder, then, that Juliet found herself spending more and more time at Gareth's bedside, laughing at the amusing things he would say, blushing at his flirtatious remarks, sitting in a chair while watching him play with Charlotte. Her new friend was a warm blanket in a glacier of cold English formality, a welcome relief from the oppressive austerity of the duke—which seemed to permeate the very walls of the castle itself.

Despite the signs indicating otherwise, she told herself that she was not attracted to him. Gareth— lighthearted, carefree, and not always grounded in maturity—was not, after all, her type. *Charles* had been her type. It was not practical, nor wise, to let herself think of Gareth in any terms other than what he was.

A friend.

Juliet, of course, was not the only one to benefit from this growing friendship; Gareth, too, found his convalescence much easier to bear with a beautiful young woman tending to him, bringing him his meals, his niece, and—if truth be told—a good excuse to needle Lucien. He knew his brother was aware of Juliet's visits and was not altogether pleased about them. Still, Lucien said nothing about the subject, though Gareth presumed the servants reported every visit Juliet Paige made to his room back to his omniscient brother.

A week and a half after the robbery, Gareth—restless from being stuck indoors, his muscles cramped from too much bedrest, his stitches newly removed— decided he'd had enough. He was going for a walk. He was certain he possessed the strength to undertake such a venture by himself; however, his "lingering weakness" was a perfect excuse to ask Juliet to accompany him, just in case he suddenly grew light-headed and needed her assistance. When she brought their lunches up to him that afternoon, they ate together—and then he asked her to walk with him to the top of Sparsholt Down.

He thought she would protest; instead, she surprised him by saying the fresh air would probably do him good. And so it was that an hour later the two of them, Charlotte safe in the care of Lady Nerissa, set off across the front lawn, heads together and laughing.

As they passed the library, the drapes at the window moved slightly—but neither noticed. The Duke of Blackheath watched them go, his expression unreadable. He was, of course, very much aware of Juliet's frequent sojourns to his brother's room. He was also very much aware of the attraction between the two, a fact that did not annoy him half as much as he wanted Gareth to believe; in fact, it was quite the opposite.

Quite the opposite indeed.

The faintest of smiles crossed his face, and he let the drape fall shut.

Gareth was purposely defying him.

Things were going precisely according to plan.

And when, a few hours later, he saw them racing a spring thunderstorm home, the two of them laughing like children—he was smiling even more.

By week's end, however, Gareth needed more than bucolic walks around the Lambourn Downs. He missed his friends. He missed doing things with those friends. By the time Saturday night came around—and with it, Perry and the other Den of Debauchery members—the Wild One was ripe for trouble.

"You're looking fit as a fox," Perry drawled, flicking open his snuff box and taking a pinch. "Never thought you'd want to go out and raise hell again so soon."

"I am hardly an old woman," Gareth returned, standing in front of the looking glass and carefully tying his cravat. He wore a tailored coat of plum silk, cream breeches, and a waistcoat embroidered with gold thread. His hair was tied back and lightly powdered, his sword already at his hip. Unlike his friends, Gareth had spent most of the last two weeks cooped up and bored, and he was not about to pass another day, let alone this night, in similar fashion. "Besides," he added derisively, "it was little more than a flesh wound—a *scratch*, as Lucien called it. Now." His gaze met theirs in the mirror. "Where to tonight?"

"Whist at Cokeham's?" suggested Sir Hugh Rochester hopefully.

"Boring," said Gareth.

Neil Chilcot pulled out a half-shilling and began flipping it in the air. "I hear Broughton's having a cockfight in his barn. . . ."

"I hate cockfights," Gareth declared.

"Lord Pemberley's mistress is rumored to be doing her famous 'forbidden fruit' act tonight. I say we attend that," murmured Tom Audlett, grinning and elbowing Hugh.

"No, no, none of that," Gareth muttered impatiently, still standing before the looking glass and pulling at the frothy lace until it lay just so against his shirt and waistcoat. He turned, perfectly handsome, perfectly tailored, and perfectly innocent.

Looks were deceiving. There was nothing innocent about Lord Gareth de Montforte at all.

"I am bored with endless rounds of drinking, whoring, and gaming," he announced. "There must be something else, something more exciting we can get up to without taking ourselves all the way off to London. . . ."

"Speaking of excitement, how's that fine bit of muslin who saved your life, eh, Gareth?"

"Yes, have you made a *suitable impression* upon her yet?"

Gareth grinned. "I am working on it."

"Ha! I can imagine what your despot of a brother thinks about *that!*"

"Who gives a damn what he thinks? Lucien may be Blackheath's master, but he sure as hell isn't mine. Now come, let's go. The evening waits, and I simply cannot abide being in this place another minute."

It didn't take long for the notorious Den of Debauchery—which had managed, through every fault of its own, to become the bane of the Lambourn Downs—to get up to its usual devilment.

The den members had gone to the cockfight after all, then to Pemberley's, and finally, after three bottles of Chilcot's Irish whiskey, to the Speckled Hen opposite the village green, which was where the trouble began. Jon Cokeham had started a fight with one of the locals. Tom Audlett had refused to pay for an ale whose taste he found inferior. And the rest of them had chatted up and then fondled Tess and Lorna, the two serving wenches. The girls were all too willing to drape themselves across the laps of these well-bred, badly behaved lads in favor of doing the work for which they were paid; it was Fred Crawley, the landlord, who finally got fed up.

He threw out the lot of them, including the two women.

"Bloody 'ell, Gareth . . . what're we going to do now, eh?"

They stood in the road outside, grumbling and cursing, all so foxed that not a soul amongst them could walk a straight line. The two barmaids, giggling and flirting, were partaking quite freely of Chilcot's Irish whiskey. One of them, already tipsy, sidled up to Gareth and put her hand on his bottom; the other ingratiated herself beneath his arm, slid her hand beneath his waistcoat, and began rubbing his chest.

"Yes, Lord Gareth—what *are* we going to do, hmmmm?"

He grinned down at them. Two weeks ago he would've taken the invitation and run with it; after all, spending an erotic night with two women at once was every man's dream—and one he had frequently lived out in reality. Tonight, however, he just wanted to go home.

To Juliet Paige.

"I don't know," he said, slightly baffled by this rather strange reaction in himself.

Cokeham declared, "*I* have an idea how we can

get back at that cheeky bastard for throwing us out. We can alter the scenery from his dining room window. You know, shock his guests so they go somewhere else."

"Oh?"

Cokeham took a long swig of the whiskey; then he pointed the bottle toward the village green and leaned toward the girl beneath Gareth's arm. "Tess? Got any idea where we can get some of that purple paint Crawley used on his front door?"

King Henry VIII on a rearing charger had been the focal point of the green—and the pride of the village—since Gareth's great-great-grandfather, the first duke, had had the statue erected some time back in the previous century. Towering above Ravenscombe's oft-used crossroads through which traffic to and from Newbury, Swindon, Wantage, and Lambourn all passed, it was a fine work, commanding the eye as well as the attention. The magnificent stone horse, rearing back on its hind legs with its front hooves slashing the air, was noble and fiery; the monarch who rode it, fiercely imperious. But tonight, poor old Henry had to have been as miserable as any of his unfortunate wives ever were, for a group of his most high-born subjects was clustered around the statue's base, and they were up to no good.

No good at all.

That is, all but one of them stood around the statue. Ten feet above their heads, their leader—who had agreed to do the deed only because everyone had bet money that he wouldn't dare (an incentive to get Gareth to do just about anything)—was hanging from a rope slung around the steed's neck, his feet braced against the statue's pedestal, his hand thrust up beneath the stallion's hind legs.

"Having a good feel up there, Gareth? Sure are taking a damned long time about it!"

"Can't blame him. 'Tisn't every day that a man gets to grope a stone horse!"

"Wish I was hung half so well!"

"You mean you aren't, Chilcot?"

"Lord Gareth is!" cried Tess. "Why, 'e's built foiner than any stallion *Oi've* ever seen, stone or not!"

Drunken laughter rang out, both male and female, and yet another bottle of Irish whiskey made its way among the shadowy figures who stood, or rather swayed, beneath poor Henry on his about-to-be-disgraced charger.

"Hey Gareth! Didn't know yer pref'rences ran to—*hic!*—bestiality! What else haven't you tol' us about yershelf, eh?"

"Shut up down there, you bacon brains," Gareth said. "D'you want to wake up the whole damned village?" But he was as foxed as the rest of them, and no one took him seriously.

"*Hic!*—c'mon, Gareth, it can't take you more than five minutes to—*hic!*—paint its bollocks blue!"

"This is not blue, it's purple. Royal purple. As befits its royal rider."

Chilcot gave a credible imitation of a neighing stallion. Cokeham snorted, horselike, and clutched his stomach as he tried to contain his laughter. But the Irish whiskey was too much for him, and, losing his balance, he fell face first into the damp grass, still guffawing and holding his side. "Oh! Oh, I fear I shall cast up my accounts if this keeps up . . . oh, dear God. . . ."

Without missing a beat, Gareth dipped his brush in the paint and flicked it over the bewigged and powdered heads of his friends below.

Howls pierced the night as he calmly went back to his task.

"A plague on you, Gareth!—*hic*—you've jesht ruined my best wig!"

"To hell with your damned wig, Hugh, look what he just did to my coat!"

Chilcot gave another equine whicker, tucked his chin, and with his beautifully turned out leg began pawing the ground.

"Shhhh-h-h-h-h-h-h!"

"Oh . . . oh, I do feel sick. . . ."

"Keep it up, you pillocks, and I shall dump the entire bucket on your heads," Gareth called down from above. Wrapping his hand around the rope, he pulled himself up a little higher to relieve the tension on his left arm and began smearing paint on the horse's other testicle. "One done, one to go, just call me . . . Gainsborough."

A mouthful of whiskey shot out of Hugh's mouth and he collapsed in a fit of laughter. Perry made choking noises, and guffaws echoed all around.

"Reynolds, Romney, Ho-garth—God help me, I'm going to barf," cried Cokeham, still rolling on the ground and laughing. "Oh, that's horrid, Gareth, positively horrid!"

Gareth grinned, quite amused with himself. "I'm no poet and well I know it. More paint, my dear fellows. And mind you don't trip and spill it. We're starting to run low."

He tossed the empty bucket down, not particularly caring where it landed. It hit the statue's base, making a dreadful, clanging racket that could probably have been heard all the way to the Seven Barrows. Hugh dumped in more paint. Chilcot, still pawing the ground, picked up the bucket handle with his teeth and, whickering, cantered once around the statue, the bucket swinging precariously and splashing paint all down the front of his elegant lace cravat and expensive waistcoat. Snorting and neighing, he pranced to a stop just beneath Gareth where, with the help of his cohorts, he managed to hook the bucket on the end of a long pole and push it up toward their leader.

It swayed back and forth near Gareth's ear, threatening to tip its contents over the primped and powdered heads below. He snared it and loaded the brush up with more paint so he could apply a second coat to his masterpiece. "I can't see a damned thing up here," he said, pushing the brush up into the darkened cavern between the steed's hind legs and hoping he'd found the right spot. "How the devil am I supposed to paint its balls if I can't even see them? Fine mess we'll be in if I paint its stomach instead!"

"Fine mess we'll be in if your brother finds out who did this."

"Bloody 'ell, Gareth, hurry up!"

Snickers, more laughter. The long-suffering king, silhouetted against the silvery night sky, stared off across the high brows of the downs as though seeking the help of a sympathetic god. Divine intervention would not be forthcoming but ducal intervention very well might, and every one of the Den members knew it.

Gareth's brother had a habit of turning up when he was least expected.

Or wanted.

"Finished!" Gareth announced. "I'm coming down now."

"Did you get its prick, as well?"

"Oh, sod you, Perry!"

Tess called up, loudly, "Paintin' its bollocks without doin' its prick ain't good enough, Lord Gareth!"

The bucket weaved close, swinging against the night sky. "Ouch!" Gareth cried as it smacked his ear, nearly knocking him from his perch. Angrily, he flicked more paint down on the hapless heads below. "Damn you, Hugh, watch it, would you?"

More laughter. Gareth, starting to get annoyed and wishing he really *had* gone home, leaned back against the rope, trying to find his footing. He was getting too old for this nonsense. This wasn't even *fun*.

Moments later he was finished, tossing the paintbrush blindly over his shoulder, not caring where it landed.

*Thump.*

"Son of a bitch!"

"That's it. I'm coming down as soon as I get the rope."

He stood up on the narrow ledge, one hand braced on the king's thigh for balance as he tried to reach the noose, snugged tight just behind the horse's left ear. Pain, faraway and detached, came from his rib, still a little raw. He ignored it.

"I can't reach it. Somebody pass me up a stick or something, and I'll try to slip it under the noose and off the head."

"Could always burn it off," Perry mused.

"Or make a halter out of it," added Audlett.

"How 'bout if you—"

"Just get me a damned stick!" Gareth snapped, growing impatient with both his friends *and* the situation.

Cokeham roused himself and, on hands and knees, fell to rooting around in the grass, snuffling and making pig-like noises. "Oink, oink!"

Audlett belched.

Sir Hugh Rochester, baronet, expelled a loud puff of gas that came from regions much lower.

And the two women began singing drunkenly.

*Oh, God help me. I think I need a new set of friends.* Fed up with the lot of them, Gareth hoisted himself up so that he was sitting astride the horse just in front of the king. He drew his feet up beneath him and, holding onto the rope for balance, got to his feet, stretching his body full length along the crest of the horse's neck as he reached for the noose.

He couldn't . . . quite . . . reach it.

*Damn.* He pulled himself forward another inch, his rib screaming in protest even through the haze of whiskey-induced numbness. Buttons popped off his coat. His shirt tore. Kicking for a foothold on either side of the horse's neck, he found only empty space. He made a desperate grab for the noose. Missed. Far below him, the others began calling bets.

"Two guineas he won't do it in the next thirty seconds!"

"I'll up you to five pounds—"

"Oink, oink, *ereeeeeeeeach!*"

And then Gareth felt himself beginning to slide backward.

Cursing, he dug both knees against the cold stone neck—and kept sliding. Scrambling madly, he made another grab for the rope and had just snared it when Chilcot cried, "Bloody 'ell, Gareth, someone's coming up the road! Crawley must've called in the constable or something!"

"*Damnation!*"

It all happened at once. Cokeham abandoned both the ground and his pig impersonations and fled, howling, into the night. Chilcot grabbed the bucket of paint, tossed it into a ditch, and took flight himself, running like a hare over the downs. Perry dashed toward a nearby tithe barn, the two tipsy women collapsed, giggling, against the base of the statue, and Hugh and Audlett scattered, one for the village, the other stumbling after Cokeham and yelling for all he was worth. One by one, his friends all deserted him—leaving Gareth stretched full length atop the horse's stone neck with the rope in one hand and his feet sliding mercilessly down toward Henry's loins.

And then he heard it. Hoofbeats, coming toward

him from off in the darkness. Unhurried, steady, like the grim reaper coming from Hades knowing it had all the time in the world.

Gareth let his cheek drop against the statue's cold neck and swore, knowing who it was even before the rider, astride a savage beast whose hide was as black as the sky above, materialized from out of the night.

The horseman halted just below the statue and did not even bother to look up.

"Party's over. You may come down now, Gareth." It was his brother. The Duke of Blackheath.

Morning. Or rather, early afternoon.

Gareth awoke to the sound of a cuckoo outside his window.

He dragged open his eyes and saw his bed curtains revolving in a slow circle around him. Comfortably enmeshed in the stuporous daze that always followed a night of heavy drinking, he watched their heavy folds, their crimson tassels, until the slow, lazy spinning began to overwhelm him and his stomach churned with sudden nausea. He groaned, his head pounding with each beat of his pulse, his mouth dry, stale, and sour. All to be expected after a night out with the Den of Debauchery, of course. But this morning, more than just his head hurt. In fact, every muscle in his body ached. He cursed and pulled the coverlet up over his eyes, trying to shut out the daylight, trying to remember what he had done last night.

*Cuck-oo. Cuck-oo. Cuck-oo.*

He put his fingers to his temples, straining his mind to remember.

*Purple bollocks.*

Ah, yes, he remembered now. Or partly, at least. Something about a statue and painting its balls purple.

And Lucien, spoiling everything.

Gareth pulled the counterpane from his eyes and gingerly sat up in bed. Faint light glowed through a crack in the bed hangings and he squinted against it, unwilling—unable—to face even this meager taste of morning. The devil, he felt awful. Groaning, he brushed from the pillow a small twig that had fallen out of his hair sometime during the night. Ah, yes. Now he remembered why his muscles ached. When Lucien had arrived, Gareth had tumbled off the statue, a victim of that damned Irish whiskey Chilcot had brought. Priceless stuff, that. He didn't even remember hitting the ground. And he certainly didn't remember the ride back to the Castle, though Lucien must have slung him across Armageddon's back and carted him all the way home.

He knuckled his eyes and ran a hand over his hair. Part of it was still caught in its queue, part of it was pasted to his neck by mud, and the rest hung in limp, heavy swatches over his eyes. As he loosened a patch of dried mud just behind his ear, a sprinkling of chalky white dirt sifted down onto the bed linens. Even the gentle tug of his fingers against his scalp hurt, magnifying his hangover.

"Oh . . . *hell*," he said, giving the bell pull a single yank. Then he held his head in his hands and groaned, in very real pain, as the bath was brought in and filled. Ellison, his valet, stood waiting to assist him.

"If I may help, my lord?"

Gareth stared down at himself. He was still dressed in last night's finery—or what was left of it. His fine lawn shirt was stiff with dried mud and missing several buttons. His breeches were minus one knee buckle, and a large rip showed the skin beneath. His coat, which his tailor had delivered only last week, was hopelessly crushed, probably ruined. 'Sdeath, he was even still wearing his shoes.

Good old Lucien. Tossing him into bed without even removing his shoes, let alone his clothes.

Anger beat behind his eyes. He swung his feet from the bed and was promptly sick, managing to grab the chamber pot just in time.

The damned bird was still going at it outside. *Cuck-oo. Cuck-oo. Cuck-oo*, with only a second's pause between each call.

"Ohh-h-h-h . . . shut up!" Gareth stumbled to his feet, digging his fists into his eye sockets as Ellison helped him out of his ruined clothes. "Just shut up!"

But it was not the cuckoo, a quarter mile away and singing from some tree on the downs, that was setting his teeth on edge. It was Lucien. Lucien, who always interfered. Lucien, who didn't know how to have fun, didn't want to have fun, and forbade others to have fun. Lucien—the all-powerful, all-controlling, Duke of Blackheath. Gareth stepped into the tub and sank into the hot water. How much better it would have been if Charles had been the first-born, he thought sullenly. He would have made a far more pleasant duke, just as Lucien, with his autocratic ways, would've made the better soldier.

Charles, at least, had been capable of having fun.

And Lucien would never have gotten himself killed.

Sadness knifed through Gareth's normally light heart as he bent his head and let Ellison soap and rinse his hair. His brother had been only a year older than himself, his friend, his confidante, his ally—and the standard by which Gareth had always been judged. He'd been the one with whom to climb trees and race horses, to follow to Eton, to Oxford, and back again to Blackheath Castle. Like himself, Charles had grown restless. He'd been home from University for only two months before buying himself a commission in the army and leaving the castle forever.

Best not to think about Charles. All the missing him in the world wouldn't bring him back.

And then Gareth remembered Miss Juliet Paige.

The beautiful woman who had won Charles's heart. Who had won Charles's request for her hand. Who, as Gareth sat here stewing in the aftereffects of his own debauchery, mothered Charles's own child.

*Put one foot wrong, Gareth, and I warn you: The girl goes.*

Cold dread washed over him. *Lucien.*

He swore and lunged from the bath.

**P**ausing just long enough to grab some money, Gareth charged down the stairs, his hair wet, his fresh shirt clinging to his still-damp body, his unbuttoned waistcoat flapping open beneath his frock of pale-blue superfine.

He met Andrew on the way up.

"Gareth! Thank *God* you're up and about. I was just coming to get you—"

"What is it?"

"Lucien, the bastard! He's sent her away!"

"'Dammit, Andrew, why the hell didn't you come get me earlier?!"

Andrew vaulted down the stairs after him. "I just learned of it this second! Nerissa went to Miss Paige's room and found her gone, and one of the servants told her Lucien sent her packing back to Boston on the morning stage! You've got to find her, Gareth, before it's too late!"

*I'll kill him,* Gareth vowed to himself, striding angrily through the Gold Parlour, the Red Drawing Room, the Tapestry Room and toward the Great Hall. "Where is he?"

"Outside, on the west lawn."

The report of a pistol cracked the midmorning quiet. Then another. Andrew didn't need to say anything more, for there was only one thing that Lucien ever used the west lawn for.

Dueling practice.

Another pistol shot banged out in the distance.

Gareth saw a footman standing rigidly near the door, pretending not to notice the drama unfolding beneath his nose. "Gallagher? Send word to the stables. I need Crusader saddled immediately."

"Yes, my lord."

"And send a message to Lord Brookhampton, telling him to summon the Den and have them waiting for me on the green in twenty minutes. *Move*, man!"

Another footman came running with Gareth's tricorn and surtout. Ellison was there with his sword. Gareth buckled it on and, his top boots ringing against the stone flooring of the Great Hall, strode out the door. Down the drive. Over the bridge that spanned the moat, through the gatehouse, and across the west lawn. There, a solitary figure in black stood with his back toward him, a pistol in his hand. A whipcord was hooked to the duke's breeches at one end and attached to a pistol wired into the hand of a wooden dummy at the other; as Lucien stepped back, the whipcord triggered the dummy's pistol to fire at him. It was the supreme test of one's ability to stand firm and unmoving while a pistol was fired at you, and it was an exercise that the Duke of Blackheath, one of the deadliest duelists in the land, practiced at least once a week.

*One of these days you're going to kill yourself,* Gareth thought furiously, *and it won't be soon enough for me.*

He marched across the velvety smooth carpet of lawn. Lucien had reloaded the dummy's pistol. He took aim at the dummy and stepped back at the same time he fired, and a ball whizzed past his shoulder, past Gareth's neck and tore a chunk of bark from one of the copper beeches that lined the moat.

Gareth strode straight up to Lucien, seized his shoulder and spun him roughly around on his heel. The pistol went flying from the dummy's wooden hand.

"I *beg* your pardon," Lucien said, raising his brows at Gareth's open display of hostility.

"Where is she?"

The duke turned back to his target and calmly reloaded his pistol. "Probably halfway to Newbury by now, I should think," he said, mildly. "Do go away, dear boy. This is no sport for children like yourself, and I wouldn't want you to get hurt."

The condescending remark cut deep. Gareth marched around to face his brother. They were of equal height, equal build, and almost of equal weight, and his blue eyes blazed into Lucien's black ones as he seized the duke's perfect white cravat and yanked him close.

Lucien's eyes went cold with fury, and he reached up and caught Gareth's wrist in an iron grip of his own. All civility vanished. "Don't push me," the duke warned, menacingly. "I've had all I can take of your childish pranks and degenerate friends."

"You dare call me a child?"

"Yes, and I will continue to do so as long as you continue to act like one. You are lazy, feckless, dissolute, useless. You are an embarrassment to this family—and especially to me. When you grow up and learn the meaning of responsibility, Gareth, perhaps I shall treat you with the respect I did your brother."

"How dare you talk to me of *responsibility* when you banish an innocent young woman to fend for herself, and she with a six-month-old baby who happens to be your niece! You're a cold-hearted, callous, unfeeling bastard!"

The duke pushed him away, lifting his chin as he repaired the damage to his cravat. "She was handsomely paid. She has more than enough money to get back to those godforsaken colonies from which she came, more than enough to see herself and her bastard babe in comfort for the rest of her life. She is no concern of yours."

*Bastard babe.* Gareth pulled back and sent his fist crashing into Lucien's jaw with a force that nearly took his brother's head off. The duke staggered backward, his hand going to his bloodied mouth, but he did not fall. Lucien never fell. And in that moment Gareth had never hated him more.

"I'm going to find her," Gareth vowed, as Lucien, coldly watching him, took out a handkerchief and dabbed at his mouth. "And when I do, I'm going to marry her, take care of her and that baby as Charles should have done—as it's our duty to do. *Then* I dare you to call me a child and her little baby a bastard!"

He spun on his heel and marched back across the lawn.

"Gareth!"

He kept walking.

*"Gareth!"*

He swung up on Crusader and thundered away.

Fred Crawley, landlord of the Speckled Hen Inn, was just lugging a cask of ale up from his cellar when the Wild One and his Den of Debauchery came charging up on their fancy horses.

"Aye, I saw 'er," he grunted, in reply to their frantic queries. "Bought a ticket for London, she did. Ye missed 'er by no more'n two, maybe three hours." He looked up at the group of rakehells, letting his disgust for them show on his face. Crawley was not inclined to exhibit his usual good humor to the scapegraces. He could see the statue's glaring purple bollocks from where he stood, and he wasn't altogether thrilled with the view his paying guests had from the dining room window—though admittedly, were he two or three decades younger, he might've found the incident as hilarious as did most of his neighbors.

"Come on, Gareth, we're wasting time!" cried Neil Chilcot, already turning his horse. "The more we delay, the harder it'll be to find her!"

"Wait, Chilcot." The Wild One put out a hand in restraint. "Was she upset?" he asked, his face shadowed by his tricorn and his blue eyes troubled.

"The devil if I know. But yer friend's roight. If ye want to catch 'er, ye'd best be off. I ain't got time to sit 'ere 'avin' a chin wag with ye, I got work to do."

"Such insolence!" exclaimed Lord Brookhampton, raising his pale brows. "Really, Crawley, have you no respect for your betters?"

Crawley put the cask down. "Respect? Harrumph! Maybe when me *betters* start doin' good deeds around this 'ere village, instead of treatin' life like a lark, raisin' 'ell, and goin' around vandalizin' our statues, then, aye, maybe I'll respect 'em."

"Gareth's *done* a good deed! He saved that coach from the highwaymen!" Chilcot cried defensively.

"An accident o' fate. Probably so far in 'is cups 'e didn't even know what 'e was doin'."

"I'm not listening to this." Muttering an obscenity, Chilcot turned his horse and galloped away. Perry, Lord Brookhampton, shot Crawley a quelling look and sent his horse charging after him. Tom Audlett, Jon Cokeham, and Sir Hugh Rochester all followed, guffawing and mimicking Crawley's humble, country accent. Only the Wild One remained behind, his horse blowing and foaming and fretting to be off with the others.

Lord Gareth studied the old innkeeper for a long moment, frowning.

"Er, Crawley . . . about that statue—I am sorry. Maybe I'll repaint it for you when I return." He flipped the innkeeper a coin in appreciation for the information about the woman. Then he touched his heels to his hunter's sides and sent the animal thundering off after his friends.

Crawley watched him go. Then, shaking his head, he hefted the cask of ale and carried it inside.

The Beloved One going off to America and getting himself killed.

The Defiant One trying to invent a flying machine.

And now the Wild One, vandalizing statues and ruining innocent young women.

The duke might be the devil's kin, but Crawley didn't envy His Grace the Wicked One one bit.

# 10

**S**he had caught the stage in Ravenscombe.

They made good time. The road, rutted and puddled, had taken them through spectacular chalk downs and pastures fenced by hedgerows, through humble villages and market towns and along the banks of a peaceful river that one of the other passengers said was the Thames. But heavy clouds foretold an early nightfall, and by the time they reached Hounslow, it had begun to rain.

Juliet watched the passing scenery with a sort of dismal fortitude. The weather reflected her spirits, though her future did not seem as bright as the green fields outside the window, the purple aubrietia that spilled over garden walls, the gay red and yellow tulips, the thousands of tiny daisies and dandelions that carpeted the grassy pastures. England's spring was well underway, but back in Boston, the flowers would only be just starting to bloom, as though unsure whether to emerge after a long and brutal winter.

*Boston.*

A town turned upside down, torn apart by war and strife. She gazed out the window, dry-eyed and unblinking. Not the best environment for a young, unwed mother to bring up a baby and certainly not a safe place to be right now. Especially when people thought you were a Loyalist.

And your baby's father was rumored to be one of the enemy.

She let her body rock with the motion of the coach. Best to stay in England, conserve the money the duke had given her, and find work in London as a wet nurse or something.

Rabbits sat up and watched from the verge as the coach hurtled past. Sheep grazed in distant pastures whose horizons vanished into gray mist and low, rushing clouds. A pheasant, calling in alarm, glided over a field of new, minty-green wheat. With a pang, Juliet thought of Andrew and his flying machine, of Nerissa defending him, of Gareth with his seductive, romantic eyes.

And of the duke.

From the moment Juliet had awoken that morning she knew that something bad must have happened the night before. She had heard the giggles of the chambermaids as they hurried past in the corridor outside. She had felt the tension in the air as she made her way down to breakfast. And she had seen it in His Grace's face when she quietly took her seat at the table.

He had not said a word to anyone as he sipped his black coffee and read his paper. His mood was such that even Nerissa and Andrew, exchanging swift, puzzled glances, had been uncharacteristically silent. Only the brief drumming of the duke's beringed fingers on the tabletop had betrayed some inner agitation that he had not allowed his face to show. He had waited only long enough for Nerissa and Andrew to make their excuses; then he'd stood up, his gaze falling on Juliet. "Come with me to the library," was all he'd said, and she had known then that the news was going to be bad.

She had seen the veiled shadows around his eyes,

the weariness in his bleak and forbidding face as he leaned against the mantle and raked a hand through his hair. She had quietly taken a seat in response to his invitation—and then sat there feeling everything crash inside her as he had calmly explained that it was not possible for him to make Charlotte his ward.

He offered no explanations for his decision, nothing. Just said he could not do it.

And Juliet had stared at him numbly, as stunned and empty as a ship suddenly becalmed, holed, beginning to sink. *This is it, then. Pretty much what I had expected, I guess. Farewell, hopes. Farewell, Charles, and your wish for your daughter's future. Farewell, de Montfortes, because I cannot stay here now. . . .*

"You are welcome to remain at Blackheath for as long as you desire, of course," the duke had murmured in that disaffected, benign way of his that said he really didn't care one way or another what she did. But Juliet couldn't remain. Not now. She had too much pride to throw herself on the charity of a man who did not want her little girl. She could not live in a house with him knowing how he felt, could not raise her daughter there so she would grow up knowing she was not wanted by the man who fed and clothed her. Never. Far better to take her little baby far away, where her mother's love would enfold her and protect her from such people as her unfeeling uncle. . . .

She had quickly packed her things. The duke had been waiting for her in the Great Hall, standing alone near the suits of medieval armor. The silence of the ages had echoed around him.

"I will tell my siblings of your decision after you have gone," he'd said simply. "Better not to make a scene, I think."

"But I should like to say good-bye—"

"It is for the best."

His face had been as much an enigma as the man

himself. Wordlessly, he had escorted her out to his own private carriage waiting out in the drive to take her into Ravenscombe. There he had courteously handed her up into the vehicle, passed Charlotte to her, and stood there studying her for a long moment while the footmen lashed her trunk to the top and a groom stood at attention by the horses' heads.

And then he had pulled a fat pouch from his pocket and pressed it into her hand.

"Take this. It will keep you and your daughter safe, even if I cannot."

Money. A *lot* of money. Her pride had told her to hand it back. Her practical nature, that he had so praised, bade her to accept and be grateful for it.

She had taken it. Thanked him for it. And seen the brief gleam of . . . something in his enigmatic black gaze before the door was shut, His Grace bowing deeply, and the coach rolled down Blackheath's long drive of crushed stone, taking her away forever.

She had not looked back.

Now, as the stagecoach thundered down the road, the gray Thames occasionally peeping from behind the newly clothed stands of English oak, hawthorn, sycamore and chestnut, Juliet told herself she had no reason to grieve. After all, she hadn't really expected that one so high and mighty as the Duke of Blackheath would ever deign to acknowledge his own bastard child, let alone his brother's. She had known all along that he wouldn't help her, hadn't she?

*But what about Lord Gareth? Why did he fail us, as well? I thought he was my friend.*

She blinked back stinging tears of betrayal.

When the stage stopped at a coaching inn in Hounslow, she took a room for the night, deciding to continue on to London in the morning. Carrying Charlotte and her smallest trunk, she stood at the counter and waited for the innkeeper to fetch a room key. The door stood open behind her. Rain fell steadily, plopping into puddles and making her feel all the more homesick and alone. Mixed scents of damp vegetation, horse manure, and hyacinth came in on the breeze, mingling with the stale aroma of beer and smoke that seemed to be the trademark of every English drinking establishment she had yet been in. They all seemed to leach that same distinctive smell, a scent that the rain seemed to bring out of the old stone walls all the more.

She carried Charlotte up to their room, fighting despair and vowing to make the best of things. Beyond her window and the slate roof that shone with rain, she could see the trees waving in the breeze, dark against a dark sky. English rain, English cobbles, English trees, English wind. How out of place she felt. How far away from home. Oh, what she wouldn't give to have Charles here by her side. . . .

Or even Gareth, for that matter.

A pang went through her. Best not to think of the de Montfortes. Best to look forward, not backward. She washed the baby's napkins and hung them up to dry beside the fire, trying to take her mind off things and telling herself she wasn't as lonely as she suddenly felt. She put the duke's pouch of money beneath the pillow, fed Charlotte, then picked at the supper the landlord kindly sent up to her. But she kept seeing Gareth's charming smile, those romantic blue eyes. Kept seeing him lying in his bed, playing with Charlotte, laughing down at her as they raced home the day of that spring thunderstorm. She pretended that he meant nothing to her, absolutely nothing. She pretended that it really didn't hurt at all that he had not come out to stop her from leaving—as she had thought that he would. And outside the rain still fell, that tarnal, infernal rain, streaming down the window's cracked glass and trickling down the slates, pulling at the awful lonesomeness until it became unbearable.

She felt suddenly alone in a world that was much, much bigger than herself.

A half hour later, her dark hair hung in a plait down her back, her petticoats, gown, and cloak were draped over a chair, and she, clad only in her chemise, was sliding beneath the cold bedsheets, Charlotte beside her.

Outside, the rain fell softly, and somewhere in the distance sheep bleated, a lonely sound in the vast English night. She felt every one of the three thousand miles that separated her from Boston, from home. Her eyes misted with sudden tears.

*I failed you, Charles. I failed you, and your brothers failed us. I'm sorry. God help me, I'm sorry.... I tried my best.*

The back of her throat ached. Her nose burned. Beyond the window, the rain came down and down and down.

*I will not cry.*

Tears wouldn't win her a duke's sympathy. Tears wouldn't gain her a home, a family, or a future for her baby. Tears wouldn't change her situation one bit. She tightened her jaw and determined to cry no more, to get on with her life and make the best of things. As her mama used to say, the only thing tears ever brought a person were wrinkles before their time. She would not give in to them.

But a single one slipped down her cheek and melted into the pillow.

Then another.

Suddenly there was movement on the pillow beside her—Charlotte, reaching for her in the darkness, her little hand grasping. Swallowing hard, Juliet pushed her forefinger into the baby's palm, feeling the tiny fingers close around hers with surprising strength.

She choked back the sobs, reached deep inside herself and found strength. They were in this together, the two of them. She had failed Charles, but she would not fail her baby.

On that thought, Juliet closed her eyes, and by the time the clock struck ten in the hall outside, she was fast asleep.

"Stop here—I want to check every major coaching inn from Ravenscombe to London!"

The Den of Debauchery members pulled up their steaming horses outside yet another inn. Before Crusader could even come to a stop, Gareth was out of the saddle, leaping puddles and charging through the front door.

He was back a moment later, frantic with disappointment and rising anxiety as he jumped back aboard the tired horse.

"Not there," he cried, yanking his hat down against the rain and setting his heels to the animal's sides. "Carry on!"

At about the same time that Juliet Paige was settling down to sleep, and a soaked and streaming Lord Gareth de Montforte was charging out of the Hare and Horses, the Duke of Blackheath was calmly finishing his evening meal.

He was not alone. His closest friend, who had dropped by for an impromptu visit several hours after Gareth had stormed off and set the house in an uproar, sat across the table from him. Sir Roger Foxcote, Esquire, had first met the duke in '74, just after the barrister had been knighted for his brilliant defense of a prominent Whig MP accused of murdering his wife. Lady Chessington had been found in the bedroom of their London town house with a knife through her heart, and, as everyone knew she and her husband were estranged, a hangman's noose had seemed quite imminent for poor old Sir Alan. No barrister in the land would defend him.

He was a good friend of the king, and if Chessington went to the gallows, so would any royal favors for the man who failed to save him. But Foxcote, twenty-five years old at the time and eager to prove himself, had accepted the case. On the stand, he had dramatically exposed Lady Chessington's lover as the murderer, and the news had swept the country. When the tumult had died down, the grateful king, beside himself with elation, had wasted no time in bestowing upon his "Clever Fox" a knighthood for his efforts.

The nickname had stuck. And so had the reputation.

Fox, the second son of an aristocratic Oxfordshire family, was not a diffident man. Nor was he particularly restrained, either in his opinions or his dress. He was a handsome man, something of a dandy. But those who knew him, or knew of him, were not deceived by appearances. Fox and his friend the Duke of Blackheath were two of the most dangerous men in England.

Tonight he and Blackheath lingered over their port in the duke's immense dining room while his private quartet struck up an after-dinner violin concerto. It was a glorious room, with ornate plaster columns, Italian art, and scenes of Bacchus and the gods painted on the high, friezed ceiling. Fox liked this room well, but not because of its rich ambience; he was in love with one of the portraits just over the doorway and enjoyed looking at the beauty's mischievous eyes as he ate. It didn't matter that Lady Margaret Seaford had lived and died nearly two centuries past. Fox still liked to look at her.

And he was looking now as the footmen cleared away the remains of their meal. Pity that only he and Lucien had been there to dine on the roast pheasant stuffed with currants and apricots and finished in red wine. It had been exquisite. Divine. But Gareth was gone, and Andrew and Nerissa, who weren't speaking to His Grace, had taken their meals in their rooms.

Nothing out of the ordinary at Blackheath Castle.

"I say, Lucien, this whole situation is *most* complicated," Fox mused, selecting a wedge of Stilton from the cheese plate the footman offered and studying it absently before popping it into his mouth. "You allowed the girl to stay just long enough to ensure that Gareth would become enchanted with her—then, when he annoyed you, as he inevitably would, you sent her away. How very cruel, my friend! To use the poor girl to punish your brother! But no. That is not like you to be so heartless. Thus, I can only conclude that you are up to something, though what it could be, I have yet to fathom." He shot Lucien a sideways glance. "Are you certain she's the one Charles was so mad about?"

Lucien was sitting back, smiling and idly watching the musicians. "Dead certain."

"And the child?"

"The spitting image of her papa."

"And yet you sent them away." Fox shook his head. "What *were* you thinking of?"

The duke turned his head, raising his brows in feigned surprise. "My dear Roger. You know me better than that. Do you think I would actually banish them?"

"'Tis what your sister told me when I arrived."

"Ah, but 'tis what I want my sister to *believe*," he countered, smoothly. "*And* my two brothers—especially, Gareth." He sipped his port, then swirled the liquid in the glass, studying it reflectively. "Besides, Roger, if you must know, I did not send the girl away—I merely made her feel so awkward that she had no desire to remain."

Fox smiled pleasantly. "Is there a difference?"

"But of course. She made the decision to leave,

which means she maintains both her pride and a small modicum of respect, if not liking for me—which I may find useful at a future date. Gareth thinks I sent her away, which means he is perfectly furious with me. The result? She leaves, and he chases after her, which is exactly what I wanted him to do." He chuckled. "Oh, to be a fly on the wall when he finds her and the two of them discover my hand in all this. . . ."

"Lucien, your eyes are gleaming with that cunning amusement that tells me you're up to something especially Machiavellian."

"Really? Then I fear I must work harder at concealing the obvious."

Fox gave him a shrewd look. "This is most confusing, as I'm sure you intend it to be. You know the child is Charles's and yet you will not acknowledge her—and this after Charles expressly asked you to make her your ward?"

"Really, Roger. There is no need to make the child my ward when Gareth, in all likelihood, will adopt her as his daughter."

The barrister narrowed his eyes. "You have some superior, ulterior motive that evades us mere mortals."

"But of course," Lucien murmured yet again, lifting his glass and idly sipping its dark liquid.

"And perhaps you can explain it to *this* mere mortal?"

"My dear Fox. It is quite simple, really. Drastic problems call for drastic solutions. By sending the girl away, I have set in motion my plan for Gareth's salvation. If things go as I plan, he will stay so furious with me that he will not only charge headlong to her rescue—but headlong into marriage with her."

"Bloody hell! Lucien, the girl's completely ill-suited for him!"

"On the contrary. I have observed them together, Fox. They complement each other perfectly. As for the girl, what she lacks in wealth and social standing she more than makes up for in courage, resolve, common sense, and maturity. Gareth, whether he knows it or not, needs someone just like her. It is my hope that she will—shall I say—reform him."

Fox shook his head and bit into a fine piece of Cheshire. "You're taking a risk in assuming Gareth will even find her."

"Oh, he'll find her. I have no doubt about that." Lucien gestured for a footman, who promptly stepped forward and refilled his glass. "He's already half in love with her as it is. Gareth is nothing if not persistent."

"Yes, and he is also given to rashness, poor judgment, and an unhealthy appetite for dissolute living."

"Yes. And that, my dear Fox, is exactly what I believe the girl will cure him of." The duke sipped his port and smiled, completely in control of the situation. "You see, I knew perfectly well that Gareth, having got a taste of heroics with the stagecoach, would be keen to play the gallant rescuer once again. By provoking both the girl—and him—I have created the perfect opportunity for him to do so. The fact that he is furious with me will ensure that he does not come crawling back to me when things begin to grow difficult for him." The duke leaned back, swirled his port again, and let a pensive little smile move over his face as he gazed into the depths of the glass. "And grow difficult, they shall."

"Oh?" Fox raised an inquiring brow.

"Gareth charged out of here with nothing but the clothes on his back. He has nothing with which to support himself and Miss Paige except for what he's wearing—and, regrettably, riding. He has some money, yes, and there is that which I gave the girl, but I can assure you he'll be through *that* before the week is out. But he will not come crawling back to me. Not this time."

Fox lifted a brow.

"It is time my brother learns to grow up," Blackheath mused, still gazing thoughtfully into his port. "A damsel in distress, a baby to look after, and limited funds with which to support his new family. Ah, yes. I daresay, nothing can bring on maturity like a bit of responsibility, eh, Roger?"

"What about the girl? The child? What if Gareth gets in over his head and someone's life becomes imperiled? For God's sake, that baby's only six months old!"

"My dear Roger. Do you think I would allow anything of the sort to happen? Tsk, tsk. Thanks to my trusty informer, I am well aware of my brother's destination and what he will soon get up to. Nothing will happen to his little family. I am, as you know, completely in control of the situation."

"As always."

Lucien inclined his head, smiling. "As always."

"I've got to hand it to you." Fox grinned, then saluted his wily friend with his glass. "You, Lucien, are a master manipulator. And too damned clever by half."

"And you, my dear Fox, have bread crumbs in your cravat. Whatever will the world think?"

# 11

"**S**hhhhhh!"

*Bang!*

"Damn it, Chilcot, I said toss the pebble, not break the damned window! Here, I'll do it."

They had found her—after checking every coaching inn on the London road in a desperate race to catch her before she reached the capital and was lost to them forever. The proprietor of this inn just outside Hounslow had confirmed their frantic queries. Yes, a pretty young woman with dark hair had taken a room for the night. Yes, she spoke with a strange accent. And yes, she had a baby with her.

"Put 'er upstairs, Oi did," the garrulous landlord had said. "She wants an early start, so I gave 'er the east bedroom. Catches the mornin' sun, it does."

But Gareth had no intention of waiting until morning to see Juliet. Now, standing in the muddy road beside the inn, he unearthed a piece of flint with his toe, picked it up, and flung it at the black square of the east-facing upstairs window.

Nothing.

"Throw it harder," urged Perry, standing a few feet away with his arms folded and the reins of both Crusader and his own mare in his hands.

"Any harder and I'll break the damned thing."

"Maybe you don't have the right window."

**125**

"Maybe you ought to just do it the easy way and ask the bloody innkeeper to rouse her."

"Yes, that would save time and trouble, Gareth. Why don't you do that?"

Gareth leveled a hard stare at them all. His temper was short tonight. "Right. And just what do you think that's going to do to her reputation if I go knocking on the door at three o' bloody clock in the morning asking after her, eh?"

Chilcot shrugged. "As for her reputation, she's already ruined it herself, getting a bastard babe off your brother and all—"

Without warning, Gareth's fist slammed into Chilcot's cheekbone and sent him sprawling in the mud. "'Sdeath, Gareth, you didn't have to take it so personally!" Chilcot cried, scowling and rubbing the side of his face.

"She's family. Any slur upon her name and I *will* take it personally. Understand?"

"Sorry," Chilcot muttered, sulking as he gingerly touched his cheek. "But you didn't have to thump me so damned hard."

"Another remark like the last one and I'll thump you even harder. Now, stop whining before you wake everyone in town and word gets back to my damned brother."

With his toe, Gareth dug up another piece of flint. He picked it up and threw it at the window.

Nothing.

At least the rain had stopped. Above, the wind made the trees rustle and hiss.

"Now what?" Perry asked, tapping his chin with his riding crop. "I daresay your damsel in distress is a heavy sleeper, Gareth."

Gareth stood back, hands on his hips, thinking. And then, as he stared up at the chestnut tree overhead—and its proximity to the window—he suddenly grinned.

"I've got an idea," he declared. "The tree."

"Surely you don't mean to climb it?"

"Well what else would I do with it?" Gareth shrugged out of his surtout, then removed his sword, gloves and tricorn. He handed them all to Cokeham. "Hold these. I'm going up."

"Don't fall and break your fool neck," Perry warned, lazily.

Gareth merely answered him with a cavalier smile. He rubbed his hands together, reached for a heavy, low-hanging bough, and effortlessly pulled himself up, hooking one leg over the thick branch until he straddled it. Pain flared along his side, but he ignored it. Moments later he was inching his way out along the thick, wet branch toward the black panes of glass.

The branch began to dip.

"*Damnation!*"

"What's the matter?"

"The branch. It won't hold my weight."

Indeed, the branch was slowly beginning to droop toward the ground, carrying Gareth with it. He clung like a monkey, cursing as it dipped lower and lower.

Below, the Den members started sniggering.

And then, an arm's length from the window, the branch stopped its descent.

Gareth looked down at his friends. "Hand me my riding crop so I can tap on the pane."

Sir Hugh moved forward and, stretching, offered the short whip to his friend.

"No good. I can't reach it. Cokeham, you're the smallest of the lot. Climb up on Audlett's shoulders and hand me the damn thing, would you?"

"How the devil am I supposed to do that?"

"I don't know; you figure it out."

"Crusader's a good seventeen hands; why don't I just stand up his back, instead?"

"Because he won't like it, that's why. Get onto Tom's shoulders, have him hold your feet, and stand up. I need the crop. *Now.*"

The branch was wet and perilously shaky. Gareth inched forward, snagging his cravat on an offshoot. Cursing, he yanked it free. Beneath him, his friends hoisted Jon Cokeham up onto Tom Audlett's shoulders. Tom, who weighed in at nearly sixteen stone, never even staggered under Cokeham's slight weight.

Gareth watched impatiently as the others crowded round Tom. On wobbly legs, Cokeham went from a crouching to a standing position. His narrow face was very pale in the darkness, and, anchoring himself with a hand on Tom's head, he reached up to pass the crop to Gareth.

Gareth's fingers had just closed around it when Cokeham lost his balance and began waving his arms wildly as he fought to regain it. "Help!"

"Hold him!"

*"Shit!"*

*"Aaaaaaahhhhhhh!"*

Arms flailing, shrieking loud enough to wake everyone in Hounslow, Cokeham tumbled backward, only to be caught by Hugh and Chilcot who both went down, laughing, beneath him.

"Hell and the devil, shut up down there!" Gareth barked, losing patience with all of them.

"Can't—Hugh's got his knee in my balls!"

More laughter.

Just then the window opened with a protesting squeal of water-swollen wood.

"Lord *Gareth?*"

He froze.

It was she, staring out at him with an expression of astounded disbelief on her lovely face. Gareth was caught totally unprepared. He knew he must look like an arse because he certainly felt like one. But the comic ridiculousness of the situation suddenly hit him, and his lips began twitching uncontrollably. He gazed up at her with perfect innocence. "Hello, Juliet."

A chorus of out-of-tune voices came up from below. "Romeo, O Romeo, wherefore art thou, Romeo?"

Gareth flung his crop down at their heads. Cokeham let out a yelp, then fell to laughing.

The girl's smooth, high brow pleated in a frown as she took in the scene. Perry down there with the horses. The other Den of Debauchery members all gathered below, beaming stupidly up at her. And Gareth, grinning, sprawled full-length along a tree branch just outside her window.

"Balcony scene, indeed," she murmured in her soft, colonial twang. She pulled a blanket around herself to conceal her throat and shoulders, which, Gareth noted, were as smooth and white as the chemise she had worn to bed. "Just what on earth are you doing, Lord Gareth?"

The way she said it made his cheeks warm with embarrassment. So he was a pillock. Who cared? Instead, he gave her his most devastating grin and said with cheerful earnestness, "Why, I have come to rescue you, of course."

"*Rescue* me?"

"Surely you didn't think I'd allow Lucien to banish you into obscurity, now, did you?"

"Well, I—The duke didn't ban—" She gave a disbelieving little laugh and leaned out the window, grasping the blanket tightly at her breasts. Her hair, caught in a long, dark braid, swung tantalizingly out over her bosom. "Really, Lord Gareth. This is ... highly irregular!"

"Yes, but it was too late to ask the innkeeper to disturb you, and as it took me all day to catch up to you, I was feeling rather impatient. I do hope you'll forgive me for resorting to such desperate measures. May I please come in and talk?"

"Of course not! I—I cannot have a man in my bed-room!"

"Why not, my sweet?" He pushed aside a small, leafy twig in order to see her better and grinned cajolingly up at her. "I had you in mine."

She shook her head, torn between what she wanted to do—and what she ought to do. "Really, Lord Gareth . . . your brother will never approve of this. You should go home. After all, you're the son of a duke and I'm just a—"

"—beautiful young woman with nowhere else to go. A beautiful young woman who should be a part of my family. Now, do collect Charlotte and your things, Miss Paige—I fear we must make haste, if we are to marry before Lucien catches up to us."

"*Marry?!*" she cried, forgetting to whisper.

He gazed at her in blank, perfect innocence. "Well, yes, of course," he said, wounded by her sharp tone. He clung to the branch as it dropped another few inches. "Surely you don't think I'd be hanging out of a tree for anything less, do you?"

"But—"

"Come now." He smiled disarmingly. "Surely, you must see there is really no other option for you. And I won't have my niece growing up without a father. What kind of a man do you think I am? Now, gather up Charlotte and get your things, my dear Miss Paige, and come outside. I am growing most uncomfortable."

Juliet pulled back from the window, rubbing her temples in confusion and disbelief. This was too much. Yes, she had felt let down that Lord Gareth didn't try to stop her from leaving the castle, had secretly hoped he'd chase after her, but this—this was insane.

Or was it? He was offering them his name and

protection. He wanted to take care of them, to do right by his dead brother and the woman who would have, should have, been his brother's wife. Noble gestures, yes, but . . . Juliet bit her lip, her stomach knotting with confusion and, yes, fear. *But I don't love him! I desire him, yes, but what if that's only because he's Charles's brother? What if I only feel that desire because he's as close as I can get to Charles, the next best thing? I should want this man for being the man he is, not for resembling, or being related to, the man I wish I could have!*

Confusion and fear mounted. Outside, the branch rustled as Lord Gareth shifted his weight on it. Desperation tore through her. God help her, what should she do? She wanted, needed, a man like Charles, and here was this brother of his—crazy, reckless, proposing to her from a tree branch!

Oh, he was offering the perfect solution, but wasn't it wrong to marry him when she still loved Charles? And wouldn't she be failing to honor that love if she accepted this offer from a man she *knew* wasn't right for her?

*Yes, but I do have a lot of fun with him.*

And there was Charlotte to think of.

Charlotte, who needed a father.

Juliet swallowed, hard. *That's it, then. I will marry him, but only for my baby's sake.*

She dressed and packed. Five minutes later, her braid pinned up beneath a plain white mobcap and Charlotte in her arms, Juliet crept from the room, quietly shutting the door behind her so as not to disturb any of the other guests.

The future was uncertain, but one thing was not:

Lord Gareth de Montforte had not disappointed her after all.

# 12

**D**eciding to get married was easy. Deciding *where* to get married posed considerably more trouble, for England's laws decreed that three weeks must pass while the banns were posted—and with Lucien no doubt in hot pursuit behind them, time was not a luxury. Scotland was exempt from the law, but as they stood debating it outside the inn, Gareth vehemently declared he wasn't dragging his betrothed and a baby all the way up to Gretna Green. Everyone argued. Everyone offered suggestions. Finally, Cokeham piped up. He had a cousin in Spitalfields, in London, who would probably marry them, provided he could get approval from his archbishop.

"Right, let's go then," Gareth declared, striding toward Crusader and glad to settle the matter at last. His bride-to-be was standing a short distance away, quiet—*too* quiet. It wasn't hard to see that she was having second thoughts about the idea, and the longer they delayed, the more uncertain she would get.

He had not misread her. Indeed, the more they had argued, the more Juliet's apprehensions grew. Gareth wanted to get her to the altar, but he had not stopped to think *how* he would get her to the altar. Such lack of preparation worried her. Would he be any better prepared to take on a wife and child?

*What are you getting yourself into?*

The Den members were mounting their horses, Chilcot passing her trunk to Tom Audlett who held it before him on his pommel, Perry buttoning up his coat, Lord Gareth leading his horse forward. As he approached he gave her his slow, heart-melting de Montforte smile, but this time it only left her cold and wanting and all the more nervous than she already was.

He touched her cheek. "What is wrong, Miss Paige?"

"Nothing," she lied, unwilling to hurt him. "It's been a long day, that's all."

"And I have only myself to blame for that. I was out rather late last night, and I'm afraid I slept in this morning—otherwise I would have caught up to you much sooner."

"A bit cup-shot, were you, Gareth?"

"Go hang yourself, Chilcot."

" 'Cup-shot'?" Juliet asked, raising a brow.

"The aftereffects of Irish whiskey on the morning after," Perry supplied, acidly. "I daresay I felt them myself."

"We *all* did," Audlett muttered, steadying Juliet's trunk.

"In any case," Gareth continued, "I could have murdered Lucien when I found out what happened. You know that my brother and I do not get on, Miss Paige. Never have, never will. I am only sorry that our differences have now affected you as well."

"Oh—I didn't realize that they had," Juliet said, puzzled. What on earth was he talking about?

"Well, he sent you away, didn't he?"

"Actually, no—I left of my own free will."

*"What?!"*

"Yes—he told me he wouldn't make Charlotte his ward but that I was welcome to stay at Blackheath

Castle for as long as I liked. He didn't send me away at all; I left."

Gareth swore beneath his breath. "He let *me* think he'd sent you away!"

"Why would he do that?"

"Yes, why would he, Gareth?" chorused the others, equally confused.

But Gareth's face was growing dark with fury and embarrassment.

Perry gave a little cough, amused. "I suspect it is because His Grace has something up his sleeve," he mused, "though the devil only knows what it might be *this* time."

"The devil, indeed," Gareth snapped, kicking viciously at a loose stone. "I'll kill that manipulative bas—" He caught himself, slammed a fist against a nearby tree, and walked a short distance away, cursing under his breath and trying to get his temper under control.

Juliet came up behind him and touched his arm. "I'm sorry, Lord Gareth. I know you blame your brother, but if it hadn't been for me, you and your friends wouldn't be standing out here in the middle of the night, far away from your homes and your beds."

"Beds?" Chilcot snickered, exchanging glances with Sir Hugh. "I can assure you, madam, that if any of us were in bed at this hour, it certainly wouldn't be our own—"

"Be quiet, Chilcot," Gareth said sharply. He stalked back to his horse, yanking the stirrup irons down with loud cracks that showed his increasing annoyance. "This is my future wife you're talking to, not some harlot. Show her some respect."

Chilcot lowered his gaze, but not before Juliet saw the sidelong glance he threw Audlett, the sly look Audlett gave Cokeham, the quick visual exchange between Perry and Sir Hugh. She knew Gareth's friends were discreetly studying her, measuring her worth against that of their leader. And why shouldn't they? She was just a colonial bumpkin who spoke differently, dressed differently, and thought differently than they did. No doubt they found her lacking.

"Forgive me, Miss Paige," Chilcot said, with exaggerated remorse. "I am indeed a bacon-brained idiot sometimes."

"You're a bacon-brained idiot *all* the time," Gareth muttered. He wiped the saddle dry with his coat sleeve, gave the big horse a pat on the shoulder, and then, before Juliet knew what he was about, he spanned her waist with his hands and lifted both her and Charlotte up onto the horse in one easy motion.

A moment later her was mounted behind her, his chest against her back, his arms framing her body as he gathered up the reins.

"You still going to go through with it, then?" Perry asked nonchalantly.

Gareth shot his friend a hard look. "Of course I am. If that cunning rascal thinks to play his little games with *me*, he's got another thing coming. It's time the mighty Duke of Blackheath got his comeuppance." He gave a smile of pure malice. "Lucien forbade me to have anything to do with Miss Paige. Therefore, I can think of nothing that will infuriate him more than if I marry her. Now, come on, let's go. Time's wasting."

Sometime during the next hour Juliet dozed off, lulled to sleep by the enveloping warmth of Gareth's arms, the gentle gait of the horse beneath her, and exhaustion. When she blearily opened her eyes, the clouds were moving off to the southwest, and dawn rimmed the horizon in distant bands of pink and gold. Her head was resting against a hard, masculine arm. With a start she jerked up, blushing and uncomfortable at such intimacy. Her sudden movement startled Charlotte, who began to whimper for her breakfast.

"Good morning," came Gareth's cheerful voice from above. "I trust you slept, even if just a little?"

Juliet, blinking, looked about her. Buildings, still dark in the predawn light, had taken the place of enclosed fields and roadside hedgerows. Coal smoke lay heavily on the air. "Probably more than you, my lord. Are we in London?"

"Yes, though we'll have to cross the bulk of it to get to Spitalfields."

Charlotte's cries strengthened, becoming lusty wails.

"What's the matter with her?" he asked, worriedly.

"She's hungry."

He stiffened. "Oh."

Perry, riding just ahead, turned and lifted an amused brow. Sir Hugh grinned.

Charlotte's wails grew piercing.

Gareth cleared his throat. "I, uh . . . suppose you'd better attend to things, then. We can stop here, and maybe you can take her off behind a tree or something. . . ."

Sir Hugh was downright snickering now.

"I think I can manage right here, Lord Gareth," said Juliet.

"*Here?*"

"Why, yes." She pulled the loose folds of her cloak up and around Charlotte, tugged down her bodice, and, behind the discreet veil, put the baby to her breast. Immediately, Charlotte quieted. No one could see, but nevertheless the Den of Debauchery members urged their horses into a trot and all but fled ahead.

"I . . . er . . . don't know about this," Gareth mumbled, deeply embarrassed.

"You'll have to get used to it if you wish to be a father, my lord."

"Yes, but . . . I mean—that is . . ."

"She can't just sit down to a pork pie and a mug of ale," Juliet chided gently. She twisted around to look up at him. His handsome face was as pink as the dawn, and it went downright crimson as Charlotte began making very loud sucking noises.

"God help me," Lord Gareth muttered, looking away.

*God help me, too,* Juliet thought, amused, for against her bottom she could feel him getting hard, stimulated, no doubt, by the mental pictures that Charlotte's loud suckling evoked. Her lips twitched helplessly at his unfortunate predicament—until *that* part of *him* twitched, and a swift blast of answering desire roared through her own blood.

Her own face flamed red, and she stiffened, shocked and alarmed. Suddenly it wasn't so amusing anymore.

*And what will you do tonight, Juliet, when you have to share a bed with him? Hmmmmm?*

Oh, God. She could not allow herself to think about *that*—not now, not yet!

Tension crackled between them. Unspoken words. They were both exceedingly aware of his excited state, he too polite and she feeling too awkward to call attention to it. But it was there, growing harder, growing larger, and as the baby suckled her nipple and that huge swelling pushed against her backside, Juliet found herself tingling, fidgeting, growing hot and damp. Her heartbeat thumped in her ears. Her breathing grew strained and ragged. Then, mercifully, Charlotte finished, and Lord Gareth was urging the big hunter into a trot, eager to rejoin the safety of his friends.

Perry turned as they approached. He, like the others, was grinning wickedly. "Fatherhood will agree with you, old boy," he drawled, ducking as Gareth's hand lashed out and knocked his hat awry.

"Yes, you were made for it, Gareth. The picture of domesticity, you are!"

"Shut up."

More guffaws, all around. But they were all exhausted from so many hours on the road, and eventually everyone—and every*thing*—calmed down, the Den members slumping in their saddles as the horses carried them ever closer to their destination. Shod hooves clattered against the cobbles, echoing against the still-dark houses that pressed close on either side of the road. The light grew stronger, the streets wider, grimy, soot-stained buildings of brick and stone beginning to rise around them. Beyond their rooftops, dawn's high, feathery clouds were mauve against the brilliant orange sunrise. And down every silent, narrow side street were long rows of houses, all boasting doors and windows alike in every way, and chimney pots that stood like blunt teeth against the pinking sky.

Juliet gazed about in wonder. So this was London. The great city whose government ruled—and had ruined—her distant homeland. It was from here that the Townshend, Stamp, and Intolerable Acts had come, inciting and fanning the seeds of rebellion that had torn Boston apart. Hard to believe that she, little Juliet Paige from Maine, was actually here in this immense, sprawling city from whence came the laws that had culminated in bloodshed three thousand miles away. . . .

Belatedly, she realized that Gareth was pointing out landmarks, naming each street. They were on Piccadilly . . . turning right onto St. James Street . . . right along Pall Mall, passing St. James's Square, and there, off over his shoulder, he was drawing her attention to a park, where the quacking of ducks on a glittering canal broke the early-morning stillness.

"Let's hope Cokeham's cousin is an early riser,"
muttered Perry, yawning as he brought his mount
up alongside Crusader. "God knows I'm not."

Indeed, his eyes were heavy with lack of sleep,
and just ahead, Hugh's head kept drooping, only to
snap up again as the baronet jerked himself awake.

"What time *is* it?" Gareth asked.

"Not quite four." Perry stifled another yawn with
one elegant hand. "Tell me, Miss Paige, what do you
think of our illustrious London?"

"It certainly rises early," she noted, looking about,
"as does your English sun." The sky was fiery beyond the rows of buildings, the sunlight just starting
to glow pink and gold on their grimy windows, but
even at this early hour the place breathed life. A
lamplighter was up on his ladder, yawning as he
trimmed and ordered a streetlight and, upon noting
their fine horses and expensive clothes, nodding def-
erentially to the Den of Debauchery members as they
passed. And there, a woman was standing just outside her open door, flicking water from her mop, a
pair of wooden pattens protecting her shoes from
the wet pavement she had just cleaned. A watchman
ambled past, lamp, watch, and rattle in hand, whistling as he turned down a side street. They rode up
the Strand, Fleet Street, and toward the imposing
dome of St. Paul's, a sight so beautiful in the early
pink-and-gold light that Juliet twisted around to
stare up at it in wonder long after they'd passed it.
Cheapside, now, and the heart of London; the Royal
Exchange, Leadenhall Street, and East India House,
all of which Gareth and Perry took turns pointing
out to a wide-eyed and wondrous Juliet. She saw
prostitutes lying drunk in gutters and doorways,
rag-tag gangs of child pickpockets, a few fancy carriages on their way home from somewhere. Down
side streets as narrow as a needle she saw glimpses
of the silvery River Thames, where the masts of

great sea-going ships caught the first light of dawn. Milkmaids, fishmongers, and bakers began crying their wares. The sky grew brighter. The smells of the great city were many and varied, and over that of fish and slops and horse dung hung the pungent scent of coal smoke.

They turned away from the river, heading northeast up Whitechapel until Cokeham, leading the way, turned left onto Brick Lane. The beery scent of a brewery hung heavily in the air here, and Juliet could see that this area was not as affluent as some of the ones through which they had come. As she wondered about the long skylights built into the roofs of the humble dwellings here, Gareth explained that Spitalfields was a velvet and silk weaving center, and the design and placement of the skylights made best use of the daylight that managed to get through the coal smoke, thus aiding the weavers at their looms.

Juliet shuddered. *Charlotte and I could have ended up here,* she thought, greatly humbled. *If Lord Gareth hadn't come along to rescue us, if we'd continued on our way to London uninterrupted, we might well have found ourselves in one of these sad little houses after my money ran out. Thank you, God, for sending Lord Gareth to us. I don't know if I'm doing the right thing by marrying him, but, oh, please let me at least be grateful to him for saving us from such a fate as this. . . .*

And then Cokeham pulled up his horse before a neat brick house and a stone church with a tall, graceful spire. Juliet felt her forced gratitude fading as stark reality took over—and the first wave of dread clawed at the shore of her resolve.

She was getting married. Here. Now.

*To a man who was as far from her ideal as London was from Boston.*

"Here we are," Cokeham announced cheerfully. "Let's go, you two!"

The others were already dismounting, joking with one another, making the sort of loud comments that equated marriage to prison, marriage to death, marriage to being devoured by lions or suffocated by petticoats. The sort of comments that *men* always made, Juliet thought distractedly.

Gareth leaned close to her ear. "Nervous, Miss Paige?" he teased.

She willed her pounding heart to be calm, fought the feeling of foreboding that was squeezing her chest, wished she had a weapon with which to brain Chilcot, who was hopping around on one foot, miming shackles and giggling like the idiot he was. "In truth, my lord, yes. But I'm sure we'll both be happier after the deed is done."

"You sound as though the idea does not appeal to you."

She watched Cokeham open the iron gate and swagger up to the minister's house, banging the knocker sharply and turning to laugh at Chilcot's foolishness. "I'm sorry. It's just that . . ."

*That you're nothing like Charles, and* he's *the sort of man I should be marrying, not you.*

"That what, Miss Paige? Do you find me wanting in some way, shape, or form?"

"No, Lord Gareth. It's nothing. Just bridal jitters, that's all."

And then the door was swinging wide, and Cokeham was hurriedly beckoning them all in.

# 13

Carrying a candle and still in his night shirt and cap, the Reverend Harold Paine swept into the room in a high dudgeon. A special license?! An immediate marriage?! Could this not wait until a decent hour? Could they not wait for the banns to be posted? He went on sputtering until Gareth calmly reached into his pocket and pulled out some money. The vicar stared, then went still. His eyes grew round, his lips parted in a perfect O, and he hurriedly sent the poor, yawning housekeeper off to bring his guests tea, bread, and butter.

"Sit down, sit down!" he cried, suddenly all smiles.

Gareth seated Juliet, then took a chair beside her. By the light of a candle, and with the Den of Debauchery members hovering over their shoulders, he began counting out money. It took a third of what he had to convince the clergyman to perform the ceremony—and another quarter of what was left to bring the man back on course when he balked upon learning that the bridegroom's brother was none other than the mighty Duke of Blackheath—who, Paine protested nervously, was sure to oppose this "hasty and clandestine union to a 'colonial nobody.' " But Gareth, not so unlike his older brother, was in total command of the situation.

"Then I suppose I must go elsewhere, my dear fellow," he said with cheerful nonchalance. "There are plenty of vicars in and around London who will marry us if you will not."

Paine hesitated, torn between greed and fear of the notoriously dangerous Duke of Blackheath. Gareth shrugged and began to take the money back. His bluff worked. Moments later a messenger was dispatched. By the time the sun was high and the traffic heavy in the street outside, the servant had returned with a special license from the archbishop.

Immediately, they all filed into the church.

It was cold and still inside. The scent of old, musty tapestries, of damp stone and candles long since burned, filled the huge nave. The vastness of the chamber echoed their every footstep, their every cough, their every nervous whisper. As the others moved down the flagstoned aisle toward the chancel, Gareth paused to take off his surtout, gently placing it around Juliet's shoulders. Hugging the baby to her, she flashed him a smile of gratitude and looked away, but not before he saw the anguish in her eyes, the tightness around her mouth and the tiny lines that pleated her forehead. He raised his eyebrows, surprised.

"Such a woeful face!" he teased, adjusting the overcoat. "Cheer up, lest they all think you do not want me!"

"It's not that, Lord Gareth."

"Then what is it?"

"It doesn't matter. Come, let's just get on with it."

*Let's just get on with it.* Her air of resigned defeat alarmed and hurt him. What was wrong? Did she find him wanting? Was she angry with him, thinking he was marrying her only to get back at Lucien? Or was she—*please God, no*—comparing him to Charles and finding him lacking?

After all, that's what everyone else had always done.

As he offered his elbow, she stayed him with gentle pressure on his arm. "But then again, maybe the reverend's right, Lord Gareth," she said slowly, for his ears alone. "I'm just a colonial nobody, and you can do much better than me."

"I'm not even going to honor that remark with an answer," he said with false brightness. *Bloody hell.* Is *it Charles?* "And furthermore, I think it's time we dispense with the 'Lord Gareth' and "Miss Paige' bit, don't you? After all, we shall soon be married."

"Marriage is not a union in which to enter lightly—"

"I can assure you, my sweet, we are not entering it lightly. You need a husband. Charlotte needs a father. And I"—he grinned and dramatically clapped a hand to his chest before executing a little bow—"am in a position to help you both. One cannot get any more serious than that, eh?"

"This isn't funny, Lord Gareth."

"It's not so very terrible, either."

"I don't think this is quite what Charles had in mind when he bade me to come to England—"

"Look Juliet, Charles is *dead*. Whatever he had in mind no longer matters. You and I are alive, and we must seek the best solution to your—and Charlotte's—predicament." He lifted her chin with his finger and smiled down into her troubled eyes. "Now, let's see some joy on that pretty face of yours. I don't want my friends to think you're miserable about marrying me."

Juliet swallowed. A few locks of tawny hair had escaped his queue and now framed his face. He looked divinely handsome, his chin set off by the flawless knot of lace at his throat, and that slow, teasing smile of his more warming than an August sun. Oh, no, Juliet thought, she could never be miserable about marrying him. It wasn't that at all.

And it wasn't that they barely knew, let alone loved, each other. It wasn't that she had no idea what sort of a husband or father he would make, or that she didn't even know where they'd sleep tonight, or that he had carelessly frittered away so much money—money that could have been spent on food and shelter and other necessities that were far more important than a bribe for a marriage license.

She looked desperately toward the altar where the others already waited, looked even more desperately toward the door, while inside of her everything began screaming in protest, the warning voices—*this is wrong, wrong, wrong!*—growing louder and louder until she wanted to clap her hands to her ears to block them all out.

God help her, it was because of—

"Ready now, Juliet?"

She closed her eyes as a deep shudder went through her. Dampness broke out all down her spine, and a sudden, sick feeling lodged in the pit of her stomach. "Yes, Lord Ga—"

"Ah!" He raised his forefinger and both brows.

Her shoulders slumped. "I mean, Gareth."

"That's better. *Now* you're ready, I think." Again that light, teasing grin that brought out his dimple and made his lazy blue eyes sparkle like the sea. "Shall we?"

He walked her up the aisle between the pews, his stride easy, confident, and assured. Their shoes echoed over tombstones laid flat in the floor, and flagstones worn smooth by the passage of many feet. Charlotte clung tightly to Juliet, staring about her with wide, curious eyes.

Juliet's heartbeat grew louder. Faster. She felt sick.

"If you'll both just stand up here, please," Paine instructed, directing them to a spot just before the altar. "Bride to the left of the groom, please. Who shall give her away?"

"No one," Juliet said.

Paine frowned. "Right, then. Whom do you want as witnesses?"

Gareth crooked a finger at his best friend, standing nearby and watching with cool gray eyes. "Perry? And you, too, Cokeham. After all, coming here was your idea."

Cokeham grinned and, puffing his chest out with importance, swaggered forward.

Paine wasted no time. He turned and lit several candles. They flared to life, solemn points of flickering light that did little to penetrate the church's heavy gloom. Someone coughed. Charlotte let out a complaining whimper, and Juliet, nervously hugging the baby to her, shuddered beneath the warmth of her bridegroom's expensive, silk-lined surtout.

She stole a nervous glance at him, standing there with his weight and hand on one hip, the hand rumpling up one tail of his frock as he traded a joke or two with Perry and laughed with as much abandon as if he were at a county fair instead of his own wedding. He was perfectly at ease, shamelessly handsome. Any other woman would have been happy to be standing in her place.

"Be a good fellow, Perry old man, and be my looking glass!" he quipped, as he tried to arrange the frills of his cravat around the sapphire brooch pinned in its center. "Do I look as well as I should?"

"You look a sight, Gareth," called Audlett, smirking.

"A sight, indeed," added a grinning Chilcot.

Perry, the only one of the lot whose eyes reflected the misgivings that Juliet herself felt, merely gave a thin smile and flicked his fingers over Gareth's cravat. "You could do with a shave," he murmured, dryly.

"No time for that," Paine interrupted, directing Perry to stand on Gareth's right. "Someone please take the infant so we can get on with this."

Wordlessly, Juliet turned to Sir Hugh, whose smiling face went suddenly blank with horror. He froze as the baby was placed in his arms, not daring to even breathe.

"Right." Paine stood before them. "Are we ready, then?"

Juliet shrugged out of Gareth's coat and placed it on the pew behind her. The chill hit her immediately. She took her place beside her bridegroom, tall and smiling. He was romantic, handsome, splendid, a man that any breathing female would be happy to take as her husband. . . .

*Anyone but me.* Guilt crashed over her, and tears rose in her eyes.

Paine, the *Book of Common Prayer* in his hands, adjusted his spectacles and cleared his throat. Gareth was positively glowing with excitement, beaming up at the vicar as though this was the moment he'd waited for all of his life.

"Dearly beloved. We are gathered together here in the sight of God, and in the face of this congregation, to join together this man and this woman in holy matrimony, which is an honorable estate, instituted of God in the time of man's innocency . . . and therefore is not by any to be enterprised, nor taken in hand, unadvisedly, lightly, or wantonly. . . ."

*Unadvisedly . . . lightly.* Juliet gulped and squeezed her eyes shut as the timeless words washed over her.

"It was ordained for the procreation of children . . . it was ordained for a remedy against sin, and to avoid fornication . . . it was ordained for the mutual society, help, and comfort that the one ought to have of the other, both in prosperity and adversity. . . . Therefore if any man can show any just cause why they may not lawfully be joined together, let him now speak or else hereafter forever hold his peace."

Nobody moved.

The church rose still and silent all around them while outside, carriages passed on the cobbled street.

Paine glanced once, twice at the door, as though expecting the Duke of Blackheath to come storming in to put a stop to the absurdity.

He didn't, of course. And Juliet stood on feet she could no longer feel, listening to words she could no longer hear, existing in a body that was no longer her own. She was merely an observer watching a terrible drama unfold. She felt no joy in what she was doing. And—oh, God help her—here came the tears, collecting in the back of her aching throat, in her burning sinuses and way up in her nose. . . .

"Wilt thou have this woman to thy wedded wife, to live together after God's ordinance in the holy estate of matrimony? Wilt thou love her, comfort her, humor, and keep her in sickness and in health; and forsaking all others, keep thee only unto her, so long as ye both shall live?"

"I will," the man beside her proclaimed loudly.

And then the vicar turned his attention to *her*, frowning above his spectacles as he saw her face, as gray as the tombstones in the floor behind her.

"Wilt though have this man to thy wedded husband. . . . Wilt thou obey him and serve him, love, honor, and keep him in sickness and in health . . . so long as ye both shall live?"

She bit her lip to stall the tears, blinked back the stinging, salty mist, and through it saw that Gareth's grin had frozen in place, his eyes darkening with sudden alarm as he stared down at her.

She looked down at her feet. "I will," she whispered.

She glanced up at him then and saw that she had wounded him, that he did not understand. His fair de Montforte brows were drawn tight in confusion as the minister placed his right hand over hers, the excitement fading from his eyes as he felt the ice-cold clamminess of her skin and the tremors that shook her hand.

"Repeat after me," Paine instructed. "I, Gareth, take thee Juliet to my wedded wife, to have and to hold from this day forward, for better, for worse, for richer, for poorer, in sickness and in health, to love and to cherish, till death do us part, according to God's holy ordinance; and thereto I plight thee my troth."

She heard him repeat the words, but something was missing now, and she felt sick with shame as she realized she'd killed the thing in his heart that had been singing, the music that had now fallen silent and still. Paine repositioned their hands, and she dully repeated the words in like manner.

"The ring, please."

She watched as Gareth bent his head and worked the heavy gold signet from his finger. She already knew what it would look like, that heavy chunk of gold emblazoned with the de Montforte arms and engraved with the family motto: *Valour, Virtue, and Victory*. She knew exactly what it would look like because she already wore the exact . . . same . . . ring—

*God help her, she'd forgotten to remove it, just before the ceremony!*

Too late. Gareth took her hand—and went dead still as he realized somebody else's ring was already there where his was supposed to go. Somebody else's that looked exactly like his, right down to the shape, the motto, the de Montforte crest that stared back at him with mocking cruelty.

Charles's.

The others saw it, too; she heard Perry's quick inhalation of breath, Chilcot's surprised curse, and the low murmur that coursed through the rest of the little group. Gareth looked up, his face stricken, unsure of what to do; but there was nothing he *could* do that wouldn't embarrass her, and so he slid his own ring partway down her finger and began to say the words that would unite them forever:

"With this ring I thee wed, with my body I thee worship, and with all my worldly goods I thee endow: in the name of the Father and of the Son and of the Holy Ghost. Amen."

A horrible silence hung over everything. Juliet wanted to die. She suspected her bridegroom wanted to, as well. Instead, with a little desperate smile, he leaned down and murmured, "For me to put this in place, you must first take the other off, my dear."

She blinked back the sudden tears, and with a jerky nod she offered her hand because she knew she could never find the heart to take Charles's ring off herself. As Gareth's fingers closed over hers, she lifted her gaze to look at him—*I'm sorry; so, so sorry*—knowing there were no words that could ever make up for what she had just done to him. But his eyes were downcast, his expression strained, and in that moment, Juliet knew he had finally grasped the truth of the situation.

That she was still in love with Charles.

Wordlessly, he pulled his dead brother's ring from her finger. His hand tightened around it, and for one long, awful moment Juliet thought he was going to hurl the thing across the room to send it *clink, clink, clinking* beyond the far pews. But no. Instead, he bent his head and in a gesture so humble, so selflessly noble that it brought a single tear pooling in her eye, he quietly slid Charles's ring onto her *right* forefinger—and put his own on her left ring finger, where it belonged.

The tear slid down Juliet's cheek.

Her husband looked at her then, cupped a hand

to her face to shield that single tear from the others, and in his eyes she read his heart: *I know I'm not Charles, but I'll do the best I can, Juliet. I promise.*

She squeezed his hand in acknowledgement, totally undone by his intuition, his selflessness, his generosity: *And I, too, will do the best that I can. After all, we're in this together now.*

She barely heard Paine directing them both to kneel, felt only the strength of her new husband's hand beneath hers as those final, binding words poured over their bowed heads.

"Those whom God hath joined together let no man put asunder . . . For as much as Gareth and Juliet have consented together in holy wedlock . . . and have given and pledged their troth either to other, . . . I pronounce that they be man and wife together, in the name of the Father and of the Son and of the Holy Ghost. Amen."

Gareth lowered his head to hers, thumbed away that single tear, and kissed her gently on the lips.

It was done.

# 14

~~~◦◦~~~

Chilcot gave a sudden whoop, and everyone rushed forward to congratulate them, as though overexuberance could somehow erase the awkwardness and embarrassment of that terrible moment with the ring. Thank God for Charlotte, who was a distraction in herself. Still in Hugh's arms, she let out a loud, piercing wail that shattered the din, screwing up her face and beating her fists in the air. Hugh paled. He turned desperately to Juliet, who knuckled the tears from her eyes and hurried forward to rescue the two of them from each other.

"I don't know much about babies," Hugh stammered, red-faced, as he gratefully thrust the infant into her mother's arms. "I hope I didn't upset her. . . ."

"With a face like yours, who could blame her?" Chilcot called, laughing.

"Aye, talk about making the ladies weep!"

The Den members guffawed, and poor Hugh flushed scarlet.

"You did just fine, Sir Hugh," Juliet murmured, holding the squalling baby against her. "She just needs changing, that's all."

"Er, yes . . ." He made a face. "I know."

Everyone laughed. So did Gareth, pumping the

vicar's hand while his friends congratulated him and clapped him heartily on the back. But his easy manner was nothing but a mask. Beneath their veil of golden-brown lashes, the eyes with which he perused his bride were as sharp as a falcon's.

No, not his bride.

*Charles's* bride.

Pain wrung his heart. So, then, it was to be the same in death as it had always been in life. He concealed the bitter ache, pretending to laugh at something Chilcot was going on about. It was inevitable that during all those years they were growing up, people had compared him and Charles with each other. After all, they'd both been so close in age, so similar in looks and build. But in the eyes of those adults around them—adults who behaved as though neither child had ears nor feelings—Charles had been the golden boy—the Beloved One. Gareth's carefree, devil-may-care nature had never stood a chance against Charles's serious-minded ambition, his dogged pursuit of perfection at whatever he did. It was Charles who had the keener wit, the better brain, the more serious mind. It was Charles who'd make a magnificent MP or glittering ambassador in some faraway post, Charles who was a credit to his family, Charles, Charles, Charles—while he, Gareth . . . well, God and the devil only knew what would become of poor Gareth.

Charles had never been one to gloat or rub it in. Indeed, he'd resented the inevitable comparisons far more than Gareth, who laughingly pretended to accept them and then did his best to live down to what people expected of him. And why not? He had nothing to prove, no expectations to aspire to. Besides, he hadn't envied Charles. Not really. While Charles had been groomed to succeed to the dukedom should Lucien die without issue, he, Gareth, had been having the time of his life—running wild over

Berkshire, over Eton, and most recently, over Oxford. Never in his twenty-three years, had he allowed himself to feel any envy or resentment toward his perfect, incomparable older brother.

Until now—when he found himself wanting the one thing Charles had owned that he himself did not have: the love of Juliet Paige.

He looked at her now, standing off by herself with her head bent over Charlotte as she tried to soothe her. The child was screaming loudly enough to make the dead throw off their tombstones and rise up in protest, but her mother remained calm, holding the little girl against her bosom and patting her back. Gareth watched them, feeling excluded.

Charles's bride.

Charles's daughter.

*Christ.*

He knew he was staring at them with the desperation of one confined to hell and looking wistfully toward heaven. He thought of his wife's face when he'd taken Charles's ring off and put it on her other finger, the guilty gratitude in her eyes at this noble act of generosity that had cost him so little but had obviously meant so much to her. What could he do to deserve such a look of unabashed worship again? *Why, she was looking at me as she must have looked at Charles.*

She still loved his brother. *Everyone* had loved his brother. He could only wonder what it might take to make her love *him.*

*But it's not me she wants. It's him. 'Sdeath. I could never compete with Charles when he was alive. How can I compete with him now?*

Lucien's cold judgment of the previous morning rang in his head: *You are lazy, feckless, dissolute, useless.*

He took a deep breath, and stared up through the great stained glass windows.

*You are an embarrassment to this family—and especially to me.*

He was second best. Second choice.

Perry was suddenly there, clapping him on the back and shaking his hand. "Congratulations, old boy!" he said loudly, before curving his arm around Gareth's shoulders and drawing him aside. He jerked his head to indicate Juliet, still standing by herself. "She all right?"

Gareth instantly recovered himself, his smile too quick, too wide, and far too bright as he tried to convince Perry that all was as it should be. "Don't be silly, of course she's all right. Bridal jitters, 'tis all. Nothing to look so damned worried about. Ours is not the first marriage of convenience, nor will it be the last. We'll work things out." He grinned and punched Perry lightly in the shoulder. "Hell, maybe I'll even come to love the girl in time."

Perry only eyed him narrowly. Plucking his surtout from the pew, Gareth left him to reclaim his bride before his friend could delve deeper.

*Hell, maybe I'll even come to love the girl in time.*
Indeed.
*The thing is, will she come to love me?*


They signed the register, thanked the vicar, and as a group emerged from the church, talking, laughing and blinking in the mid-morning sunlight. It was a beautiful day, with fluffy clouds of dove gray and mauve scudding briskly across a hard, cobalt-blue sky. The breeze drove bits of loose straw and debris across the cobbles, and horses, carriages, and pedestrians hurried past in both directions. They stood there on the pavement, buffeted by the mild wind, as Chilcot and Audlett went to get the horses.

Nobody mentioned that horrible moment when Gareth had tried to slip his ring on Juliet's finger, though Juliet knew it was on all of their minds.

"You made a right beautiful bride, if I do say so myself, Lady Gareth!"

She smiled, gamely. *Lady Gareth.* How strange it sounded. "Thank you, Sir Hugh. Though I'm sure the gloominess of that church hid all my flaws."

"What?" piped up Chilcot. "Listen to her! Flaws!" He yanked out a quizzing glass, pretending to scrutinize her from top to toe until she smiled and turned pink with embarrassment. "I see no flaws. Do you see any flaws, Perry?"

"Not a one."

"Really," Juliet said, embarrassed.

"Leave her alone," grumbled her husband, shading his eyes from the sun. "You're overwhelming her, all of you."

He moved close to her, his arm slipping possessively around her waist. Instinctively, Juliet moved closer to him, but there was a polite formality to his gesture, nothing more, and she knew then that things could never be the same as they'd been in these last two weeks at Blackheath—when he had been her easy-going, carefree friend.

To top everything off, Charlotte was still crying. Loudly.

"Here, I'll take her," her husband said. He scooped the baby from Juliet's arms and cradled her to his chest. Immediately the whimpering stopped. Charlotte stared at him in wide-eyed fascination.

Juliet watched a passing carriage, too ashamed of herself, and her conflicting feelings, to meet Gareth's blue, blue eyes. "She's wet," she warned.

"Ah, well, we've got more important things to worry about than that, don't we, Charlotte?" he said lightly, adjusting the baby's frilly bonnet around her tiny face. Juliet caught the double meaning and the tension in his words, knowing well what he meant. She threw him a quick guilty glance, but Gareth didn't see it. He was too busy ignoring her, playing with the baby, swinging her high over his head and laughing as she broke out in a smile as bright as the sunshine blazing down on them. Juliet looked on a little wistfully. What she wouldn't give to be so happy, so carefree; what she wouldn't give to be able to take back that terrible moment in the church when he had discovered Charles's ring still on her finger. Why hadn't she removed it once and for all this morning?

She had hurt him—deeply. And she felt sick about it.

"Like that, do you?"

Charlotte chortled in glee.

"Here, let's do it again," he said cheerfully, and out of the corner of her eye, Juliet saw that Perry was watching him with those cool gray eyes of his that didn't miss a trick. Perry knew that all was not right here, and Juliet suspected he knew Gareth's sudden silliness with the baby was just a cover for the pain he had to be feeling. And now her husband was swinging Charlotte up and over his head once more, making foolish faces and even more foolish noises at her until he had her shrieking in delight.

"Watch this—*wheeeeeee!*"

Perry, observing, just shook his head.

"If anyone knows how to act like a juvenile, it's you, Gareth."

"Yes, and the day one forgets how to be young is the day one gets old. Let's do it again, Charlie-girl. Ready, now? Here . . . we . . . go!"

Again he swung the infant—high, high, higher. Once more, Charlotte shrieked with glee, and even Juliet felt a reluctant smile creep over her face. Forced or not, her husband's good humor was infectious. The Den members were also grinning, elbowing each other and eyeing him as though he had lost his mind along with his bachelorhood.

"I don't believe I'm seeing this," murmured Chilcot.

"Yes, what *would* they say down at White's, Gareth?"

Perry was shaking his head. "Well, all *I* can say is that I'm exceedingly grateful I don't know anyone on this side of town," he drawled. "I daresay you are making a complete arse of yourself, Gareth."

"Yes, and enjoying it immensely. I tell you, dear fellow, someday you, too, shall make an arse of yourself over a little one, if not a woman, and then we shall all have the last laugh!"

A chorus of guffaws went through the group, and Perry, scowling, waved them off to indicate his contempt for such a preposterous idea. Juliet, however, stood quietly, watching the carefree man she had just married, who was laughing and swinging her daughter up to the sky, and wishing he was someone else. Wishing he could act more . . . mature.

Like Charles.

Sudden, wretched guilt clenched her gut, and she drove her fingernails into her palms, welcoming the pain. Whether she wanted him or not, Lord Gareth de Montforte deserved better than this. He deserved better than *her*. He had given them his name and sacrificed his own future just so she'd have a husband and Charlotte, a father. It wasn't his fault that he was not Charles. Maybe he wasn't happy about having to marry her, either. Maybe he, too, was in love with someone else. Had she ever stopped to think of *that*?

God help them. What would become of them tonight, when they had to share the marital bed for the first time?

Her maudlin thoughts were interrupted by the sound of hoofbeats coming up the street. Tom Audlett and Neil Chilcot, leading the horses, were just returning from the mews. As they approached, Gareth's hunter pricked up his ears, his dark, liquid eyes wide as he saw his master playing with the baby. He gave an inquisitive whinny.

Chilcot came to a stop, pulling the curious horse back with him. "Right. Now what?"

"Time to go, I think," Gareth said breezily. "But first, let's see if Charlotte's inherited the de Montforte horsiness."

"The what?" asked Chilcot.

"You know. Horsiness. I want to see what Crusader thinks of her." Still carrying Charlotte, he walked to his horse and held the baby up to the animal's soft, velvety nose. The big hunter arched his neck and blew softly, his ears and eyes on the baby. Charlotte shrieked at each tickling breath, kicking her feet in excitement. Grinning, Gareth lifted the child high and placed her in the saddle, where she sat smiling down at them like a tiny princess, safe within the cradle of her uncle's grip.

"No!" Juliet cried, alarmed. She ran forward.

"Don't worry, I've got her," her husband said easily, his big hands firmly around Charlotte's waist.

"Take her down now! She's too little!"

"She's a de Montforte, Juliet. All de Montfortes are horsemad; it's in the blood."

But Juliet pushed him aside and pulled the baby down even as everyone stared at her in dismay. Immediately, Charlotte screwed up her face and started crying.

Not just crying.

Screaming—fit to blow the glass out of the surrounding buildings.

Cokeham winced. "Well, I'm off to bed," he all but shouted as Juliet tried frantically to calm the howling baby. "I'll catch up to you all later!"

Audlett was moving toward his own horse, his face wearing a look of pain as Charlotte's screams grew louder. "Yes, me, too. Damned long night it was, I'm afraid! Catches up to a fellow, it does. . . ."

"I'd best be off, too, then," Chilcot said, throwing Gareth a look of false sympathy as he all but ran to his horse and hurled himself up into the saddle. "Good day, Lord and Lady Gareth!"

"Wait!" Gareth called as Charlotte's screams began turning the heads of those passing on the street.

But his three friends were already making a hasty exit, urging their mounts into a brisk trot, then a canter. Even Hugh made his excuses and left, until only Perry, politely pretending not to hear Charlotte's shrill screams, remained with them.

"What a fine lot of friends!" Gareth exploded angrily. "Leaving just when you need them most!"

"Well it *is* your wedding night," Perry drawled. He pulled out his snuff box and took a casual pinch, acting for all the world as though he didn't hear Charlotte's frantic wailing five feet from his right ear. "Surely you don't think they're going to hang around and share a bedroom with you, now, do you?"

"Very funny. I suppose you're going to desert me, as well."

"On the contrary, my dear fellow." Perry tossed the reins over his horse's head. "You have a wife and baby to carry up there with you. If I desert you now, then who, I ask, shall take her trunk?"

"Much obliged," Gareth muttered. But Juliet, patting Charlotte's back and trying desperately to calm her, noticed that her bridegroom was looking increasingly uncomfortable. He shifted his weight, ran a nervous hand through his hair, cleared his throat.

"What is it?" Perry asked, preparing to mount his horse.

Gareth fidgeted some more. He grinned, but Juliet saw a trapped look in his eyes that belied his easy manner. "Oh, well, it's nothing, really. Does your mother still loathe the sight of me, Perry?"

"Must you even *ask?*" Perry narrowed his eyes. "Why, Gareth?"

Charlotte was still screaming. In vain, Juliet tried to hush her, offering a rattle to play with. Charlotte merely screamed louder and batted it away.

"Oh, well, I'm just wondering if we could stay at your town house." At Perry's hesitation, he quickly added, "Just for tonight, of course. Wouldn't want to upset your mother any more than I already have, what with her thinking me such a bad influence on you and all. . . ."

Perry was clearly at a loss, and Juliet, watching this tense exchange and desperately trying to calm her shrieking daughter, felt her spirits sink like a leaf downed by a storm. It was glaringly obvious that Gareth's plan to "rescue" them stopped here at the steps of this church. She could tell by the confusion on his face, the sudden, fleeting panic in his eyes, that he had no idea what to do next, where to go—nothing.

God help them.

"What's wrong with de Montforte House?" Perry asked, raising his voice to be heard over Charlotte's ear-splitting wails. "Doesn't the duke keep his London residence staffed when he's not in town?"

"Of course he does. But we're *not* staying there, Perry."

"Why not? It's your home."

"No it isn't, it's *Lucien's* home, and I'll be damned if I'll take myself or my family to live under any of his roofs ever again."

"Oh, for *God's* sake."

Charlotte's screams grew deafening. Tears streamed from her eyes, and her face was tomato-red from the force of her tantrum. Juliet glanced desperately at her husband, knowing that he alone could probably calm her, but he was angry now, no longer the carefree man he had been a few moments past. Perry tried to reason with him. Gareth's blue eyes blazed with fury. "Don't try to argue me into it, Perry. I said no, and by God I mean it."

"Don't be ridiculous."

"And don't *you* be so damned insensitive! You think I'd take advantage of my brother's so-called hospitality after he not only refused to make his own niece his ward, but allowed a young woman and a baby to leave Blackheath with no escort, no protection, nothing? By God, I'm ashamed to admit I even share the same damned blood as that monster! Forget it, Perry! Forget I even bloody asked!"

"You know what they say, Gareth. Pride goeth before a fall."

"Oh, just sod off, will you? 'Sdeath, you're no better than the rest of them. Come on, Juliet. You can ride Crusader, and I'll carry your trunk."

"Gareth—" Perry said, reaching for his friend, but Gareth threw him off.

Charlotte was still screaming, beating the air with her fists, kicking out and howling at the top of her lungs. Carriages were slowing, people leaning out of their windows and shouting for peace and quiet. Juliet glanced from the baby to the two angry men and knew she had to do something.

She touched her husband's arm. "Really, Gareth, His Grace was not unkind to me. He gave me a huge amount of money—"

"I don't care what he gave you, you traveled three thousand miles to get here, and what does he damn well do? Pays you off like some—some *creditor* or something! You, who ought to be treated as a member of our family, not a piece of unwanted baggage! I cannot forgive him, Juliet. Do not ask it of me!"

"I'm not asking it of you, but surely you can swallow your pride just for one night, if only for the sake of your niece."

He stared at her, furious.

"Er . . . daughter," she corrected, lamely.

Through his teeth he gritted, "We are *not* staying at de Montforte House or Blackheath Castle or any of Lucien's other estates, and I'll hear no more about it!" He made a fist and pressed it to his forehead, trying to keep his temper under control even as Perry made a noise of impatient disgust and Charlotte's endless screaming threatened to drown out all thought, all sanity.

Perry chose the wrong moment to be sarcastic. "Well done, my friend. You have just succeeded in showing your unsuspecting bride that there is indeed another side to you. Were you beginning to think your new lord was all syrupy sweetness, Lady Gareth?"

Gareth's patience broke, and with a snarl, he went for his sword. Juliet grabbed his arm just in time.

"Stop it, the both of you! Really, Lord Brookhampton—must you antagonize him so?"

Perry merely raised his brows. "Me?"

"Yes, you! The two of you are acting like a pair of brawling schoolboys!" She pushed Gareth's hand away from its sword hilt and faced him with flashing eyes. "Charlotte and I have had enough. Either take us to de Montforte House or wash your hands of us, but I'm not going to stand here watching you two bicker while she screams London down around our ears!"

Gareth stared at her in shock.

And Perry, raising his brows at this sudden display of fire, merely reached into his coat and pulled out his purse.

He tossed it casually to Gareth. "Here," he said. "There's enough in there to buy yourselves room and board somewhere for a week, by which time maybe you'll have come to your senses. Consider it my wedding present." He mounted his horse and touched his hat to Juliet. "Good day, Lady Gareth."

He gave Gareth a look of mocking contempt. "I wish the two of you many hours of marital bliss."

And then, to Juliet's dismay, he turned and trotted off, leaving her standing on the pavement with a screaming baby and a husband who—it was growing alarmingly clear—was ill-equipped to take care of either of them.

# 15

Gareth stared after Perry in dismay. The baby was still screaming. His new wife was standing on the pavement trying to calm the infant, her mouth tight, her eyes flashing with the first anger Gareth had yet to see in them. His friends had all deserted him, he had cut himself off from Lucien's help—

And he hadn't a clue what to do next.

He stood there helpless, Crusader's reins knotted in his fist and that saddle looking terribly inviting as he resisted, with everything he had, the urge to go galloping off after Perry and the rest of the Den, and leave this problem far behind him.

This problem that he had rashly inherited.

An instant wife and daughter.

*Whatever were you thinking of, man?!*

The devil only knew, because *he* sure as hell didn't. And he had no idea what on earth to do with either of them. He was deep in the suds now, and there was no one to get him out but himself.

*Bollocks.*

He looked at his wife. She had turned her back on him and moved a few steps away, perhaps embarrassed that she'd lost her temper, perhaps just giving his a chance to cool. She was bent over the baby, who was finally—thank God—beginning to quiet, her piercing screams fading to choking, hiccupping sobs. Gareth raked a hand through his hair, trying to think, trying to steady himself. Then, leading Crusader, he came up behind her.

"Juliet?"

She didn't turn, and Gareth was suddenly filled with shame. Shame at the way he'd behaved in front of her. Shame that he was so unprepared to deal with this situation. And shame that he had regretted, even for a moment, that he'd married her and now had full responsibility for both her and Charlotte.

*Responsibility.*

'Sdeath, it was the worst word in the entire English language.

"Juliet." She still did not turn around. Her head was bent, and he could just see the pale curve of her nape beneath the upsweep of dark hair. Gareth swallowed—hard. Then, bowing his head, he said awkwardly, "My apologies. Perry's right, you know. I've got a temper, and sometimes it gets away from me."

She turned then and gave him a level, unforgiving stare. "I don't mind your temper, Gareth. What I *do* mind is the fact that we don't seem to have a place to stay tonight. I suspect we don't have a place to stay tomorrow night, either, let alone next week, next month, or next year."

He shrugged. "We can go to a hotel or something."

"Yes, and how long will our money last if we live like *that*?"

He flushed and looked away.

"Didn't you even *think* about any of this before you asked to marry me and took on the responsibility of caring for us?"

"Juliet, please."

She looked suddenly weary. And disgusted. "No, I didn't think so."

And now she was moving away again, as though

she couldn't bear to be near him, much less look at him.

"Juliet!"

He swore and hurried after her, Crusader trotting behind him. This scrape was getting worse by the moment.

"Juliet, please—"

"I wish to be alone for a few minutes, Gareth. I need to think."

"Everything will turn out just fine, I'm sure of it!"

"I'm glad that one of us is."

He picked up his pace. "Look, I know you're angry with me, but I am rather new at this husband stuff. I'll get better at it. Just takes a bit of practice, you know? Why, even Charles would surely have made a few mistakes along the way—"

She kept walking. "I doubt it."

"I beg your pardon?"

"I said, *I doubt it.*"

He halted in his tracks, Crusader's broad head crashing into his shoulder blades as he watched her walk away. The words had cut deeply, and he could think of nothing to say in his defense. The truth was, of course, that the incomparable Charles probably *wouldn't* have made any mistakes.

She took a few more steps before she, too, paused. Her shoulders slumped, and she gave a heavy, tired sigh. She stood there for a moment, her back to him as though she was fighting some inner battle, and then, slowly, she turned and faced him, her face haunted by sadness.

"That was unfair. I'm sorry."

He looked away, his jaw hard. "There's no need to apologize."

"No, really. You and Charles are—were—two different people, and I should never have compared you to him."

"Whyever not?" He tried to laugh it off, but his

anger showed in his voice, and the words were out before he could stop them. "Everyone else always did."

Immediately, her eyes darkened with sympathy, with understanding, with pity. She took a step forward.

Gareth raised his hand, stopping her. "I told you when we first met that if there's anything I'm good at, it's making a mess of things. And I've made a fine mess of this, haven't I?"

Her heart in her eyes, she took another step forward, slowly reaching out to lay her hand on his sleeve.

"*You* didn't make this mess, Gareth."

"No. Charles did, didn't he? My brother the saint, who never put a foot wrong, never gave anyone cause to blush for him, never made a mistake, never earned himself a caning, a whipping, a bad reputation. By God! Who would've thought."

She merely stood there, her hand burning a hole through his sleeve. He glanced sullenly at her, expecting—maybe even wanting—her to react, to snap back at him, so they could have it out right then and there and start their marriage with the air cleared between them.

But she did not.

"Aren't you even going to defend him?" he asked hotly. "Start proclaiming his virtue, his perfection, his god-awful sinless glory?"

She flinched, sadness filling her eyes. "No." Then, softly, she added, "Besides, he wasn't perfect."

"Wasn't he?"

"Of course not. As my grandmother always said, there was only one perfect person to ever walk this earth, and God took him back."

Gareth stared at a railing on the other side of the street, his eyes hard. He felt her let go of his sleeve and slowly pull away. They stood there awkwardly, neither saying a word.

A moment passed.

Another.

Carriages went by in the street.

"Well . . ." she said at last.

He gave a humorless little laugh. "Well what?"

"I guess we'd better find a place to stay for the night."

"I suppose."

They said nothing, each wanting to mend the rift between them, neither one knowing quite how. Juliet bit her lip, frustrated by her thoughtless words of comparison, by her inability to mend the hurt she had caused. Then she looked down at Charlotte, who had blown herself out and now whimpered in heartbroken misery in her arms.

She handed the baby—a peace offering—to her husband.

Charlotte immediately hushed and looked up at him through her tears, her blue eyes wide and imploring as she reached up to touch his chin.

And Juliet knew the exact moment when Gareth's kind, bruised heart melted into a puddle at his feet.

"Ah, hell," he murmured, and as the baby smiled up at him, he reached down and thumbed the dampness from her cheeks, a reluctant smile already tugging at one corner of his mouth. Looking at this tender scene, Juliet was undone. How large and powerful his hand looked against Charlotte's tiny face. How little she looked in the cradle of his strong, capable arm.

*And what a wonderful father he already is, despite his shortcomings.*

Juliet's own gaze softened—and in that moment her husband glanced at her and caught her odd expression. He went still, and something deep and unspoken passed between them.

"Well, I guess we'd better go," he finally said, tucking Charlotte's blanket around her shoulders. "It'll be tea time soon at this rate."

"Am I forgiven, then?"

"Forgiven?" He grinned, slowly, like the sun breaking through a bank of clouds. Out came the dimple. Out came the sparkle in his blue, blue eyes. When he smiled like that, it was impossible to be angry at him for anything.

Anything at all.

He took her hand and raised it to his lips before tucking it into the crook of his elbow. "Only, my dear, if you can forgive me for not being Charles."

"Oh, Gareth," she said, shaking her head and sidling close to him. "Let's just go and make the best of it, shall we?"

With that, they moved off down the street.

And neither noticed the tall figure that kept to the shadows just behind them.

The entry was duly recorded in White's Betting Book: *The Earl of Brookhampton wagers Mr. Tom Audlett fifty guineas that Lord Gareth de Montforte will return to Blackheath Castle within a fortnight.*

"What's going to happen to us, now that he's abandoned us for a woman?"

"We'll just have to make her an honorary Den member."

"Oh, yes, right. I can just see her getting drunk with us and vandalizing statues. I can tell you right now, *this* marriage isn't going to last."

"I sure hope it doesn't; I mean, what the devil are we going to do without Gareth?"

"I give him a week," Cokeham said, approaching the green baize table where his friends were just sitting down to a game of faro. He flipped his coattails back and took a seat near Perry, his eyes gleaming. "In fact, Perry, I'll up your bet to seventy guineas!"

"Done."

"A week?" Audlett stood up, his chair crashing backward. "The devil take it, I'll go you a hundred that he goes running back to Blackheath in three *days*!"

"One hundred and twenty!"

"One hundred and fifty!"

A servant arrived with a fresh bottle of wine, his expression perfectly blank at the frenzied betting going on around him while he topped up each man's glass. As he glided innocuously away to another table, Hugh leaned across the table and said heatedly, "You ought to be ashamed of yourself, Perry."

"Whatever for?"

"Leaving poor Gareth there to fend for himself, and with a woman and babe besides!"

"My bleeding heart."

"What a heartless bastard you are!"

"Why thank you, Hugh. I shall take that as the highest of compliments." Perry flicked open his snuff box and took a pinch. "I didn't see the rest of you sticking by his side."

"No, we went off so he could have a proper wedding night."

"Ha!" Cokeham said, "he'll get no proper wedding night with *her*. I couldn't believe what she did to him in that church, leaving her ring on like that! The bloody cheek of her!"

"Really, Jonathan, I hardly think it was intentional," Perry drawled. "And I'll tell you another thing. Despite appearances, Gareth's bride has more spunk than any of us gave her credit for. She's quite striking when she's angry."

"How do *you* know?"

"You forget—*I* stuck around after you all fled." Mirth danced in Perry's gray eyes. "Gareth's lovely little wife is no dull stick at all."

"Well, thank God for that!"

"Aye, after the last twenty-four hours, I just couldn't see what Charles saw in the wench that the rest of us have not."

"Happiness, probably," Perry remarked acidly.

"Happiness?! Let's hope she doesn't drag Gareth down in the dumps with her!"

Cokeham leaned forward. "Care to know what *I* think?"

"Not particularly."

"*I* think Gareth married too far beneath himself. He should've married money. Lots of it. How else is he going to survive in this world?"

Audlett nodded sagely. "Yes, he could've had his pick of the heiresses—Lady Eastleigh, Miss Beatrice Smith-Morgan . . . even Louisa Bellington, who's got to be the richest baggage in England, was panting after him like a bitch in heat. She would've married him in an instant if he'd only asked her—"

"Yes . . . funny, isn't it?" Perry murmured with a dramatic sigh. "To hell with money or a title, all it takes is charm and a handsome face and the best doors in England open to you."

"Not to mention the prettiest thighs," Cokeham muttered, a little enviously.

Perry shot him a sideways glance. "I take it none have been open to *you* lately, old boy?"

Cokeham spluttered and cursed. "Plague take you, Perry!"

Perry merely grinned and sipped his wine.

"I say, has anyone seen Chilcot?"

"Not since we parted outside the church," Audlett muttered. He raised his voice to imitate Chilcot's high-pitched nasal whine. "Said he was exhausted and had to get his beauty sleep."

Laughter erupted around the table.

"Exhausted? As though the rest of us aren't!"

"To hell with Chilcot," Hugh mused, his face tight with concern as he idly traced the edge of one of the painted cards that decorated the table's green baize. "What I worry about is how Gareth's going to take care of them. A young wife, that little baby, no money coming in and no place to go . . ."

Immediately, the mood sobered, for their friend was in trouble, and all of them knew it.

"The duke's got enough blunt to buy up half of England," Audlett proclaimed. "Gareth's got nothing to worry about."

"Except that Gareth's got too much pride to go running back to his big brother, especially after the row he had with him yesterday," Hugh countered worriedly. "He'll have to get money from some other source."

"How?" Cokeham asked.

"He's got credit."

"And us."

Perry, staring into his wine glass, shook his head. "Gareth's credit is about as bad as his ability to pay his debts. The duke shut him off, you know. Stopped paying his bills."

"Bloody hell!"

"Well, then, *we* can help him. We're his friends!"

"Right," Perry said, sarcastically. "Most of us are no better off than he."

"God's blood, Perry, what do you think he'll do, then?"

Perry's lips curved in a faint smile. "Perhaps he'll have to—God forbid—*work* for a living?"

"Gareth? *Work?* Preposterous!"

"How else are they going to eat? It's either that or beg, borrow, and steal," Perry mused. "And, frankly, I think our friend has too much honor to resort to the latter. Now—shall we get on with our game? I dare say I am feeling lucky this evening."

# 16

As luck would have it, Gareth's dilemma about where to take his new family for the night was solved for him just after an early lunch.

They had gone into a bakery, where they'd indulged in raspberry tarts glazed with sugar, and were taking a meandering route back across London when they ran into Lavinia Bottomley sweeping along in her fancy carriage. She stopped, of course—Lord Gareth was a client she wouldn't have minded servicing herself—and, upon hearing that the Wild One had just gotten married and that he and his family were in need of a place to stay for the night, she immediately offered them a room at her place.

"At no cost to you, of course," she said kindly, eyeing Juliet and the baby with sympathetic eyes. "In fact, you can have the Crimson Suite on the second floor; it's the best room, you know, and no one will disturb you."

"Good God, Vin, I cannot bring my family there!" Gareth cried, mortified.

"Don't be a prude, Gareth. Why, you can even consider this to be my wedding present."

"Absolutely not, this is unthinkable—"

"No, Gareth, wait...." Juliet, either ignorant or uncaring of what Lavinia's erotic perfume and low-cut bodice implied, put her hand up to silence his

174

protests. She turned to the older woman. "You're very kind. We have no place else to go tonight, and we would be happy to accept your offer."

Gareth nearly choked. "Juliet, we cannot—that is to say . . ."

"I'll not mince words here," Lavinia said, smiling. "What his lordship is trying to tell you is that I am an abbess. That is, I run a brothel."

"Oh!" said Juliet, darkening to crimson and looking quite embarrassed.

"However, it is a very *nice* brothel," Lavinia added. "Exclusive. I only allow clients who have wealth, wit, and breeding." She winked. "Keeps out the riffraff, you know."

"I, uh . . . I see," Juliet said faintly. She mustered a wan little smile. "Please forgive my hesitation, Mrs. Bottomley; staying in a brothel is not something I have ever done before, and I feel a bit . . . well, awkward about this. However, we *are* in need of a place to stay tonight, and you are being most generous—"

"There's no need to apologize, my dear, I understand perfectly," Lavinia said, patting Juliet's arm. "But a room is a room, yes? I'll make sure it's made comfortable for you and that no one disturbs you; why, I think I can even find a cradle for the baby. How does that sound? And if we leave now, whilst it's still fairly early, no one will even know you're there."

Juliet nodded once, her mind made up. "Very well, then. We'll take it."

"Now, wait just one moment," Gareth protested, growing angry. "I will not have my wife and daughter spending the night in a bawdy house!"

Juliet took him aside, leaning close to him and tilting her face up to whisper in his ear. "Gareth, I don't like this any more than you do, but it's only for one night, and it *will* save us some money."

"We have plenty of money, we don't need to be frugal!"

"That is the most absurd statement I've yet to hear you utter."

He set his jaw.

She continued, "You gave most of your money to the vicar, and what Perry and the duke gave us, though substantial, won't last forever. We cannot *afford* to be choosy, Gareth. Now, please—put aside your pride for a moment and be practical, would you?"

"It has nothing to do with pride. I want to bring you to a hotel," he said sullenly. "A *nice* hotel. It's our wedding night, Juliet; you deserve no less."

"A wedding night is a night just like any other," she said pragmatically, her unthinking words inadvertently cutting him to the bone. She saw the sudden hurt in his eyes and laid her hand on his wrist. "We don't have money to waste, Gareth."

He stared at her, crushed by how lightly she seemed to regard the symbolic parts of marriage that *he* considered special—that she, had she loved him, would consider special, too. Was that how she rated their marriage, as well? Dispensable? Not worth some extra effort? He wondered, rather bitterly, if her marriage to Charles would have meant so little that she would have dishonored it by spending their wedding night in a brothel, as she was happy to do with theirs.

Somehow he doubted it.

"Very well, madam," he said, retreating into formal aloofness to disguise his hurt. "Have it your way, then."

Gareth didn't want anyone to see his wife in the presence of London's fanciest whore, so he asked Lavinia to go on ahead of them, telling her they'd take their time in arriving. And take their time they did. Gareth took his time bringing his family back across town. He took his time finding mews in which to stable Crusader, rubbing the big animal down, feeding, watering, and making a fuss over him—anything to prolong the inevitable. Finally, when he could delay no longer, he chose narrow sidestreets so that no one would see them heading toward the brothel.

Juliet, walking beside him, was very quiet. He sensed her despair, her knowledge that she'd done something wrong coupled with an inability to put her finger on just what that something was. She probably thought he was upset because of pride; after all, no self-respecting nobleman would ever bring his lady to a brothel, let alone on their wedding night. But it was more than that. Much more. *If she had married Charles, she never would have dishonored their marriage by spending their wedding night in a brothel. She would have wanted everything to be as perfect as he was.*

She finally spoke. "Gareth?"

"What?"

"I don't know quite what it is I've done, but I do wish you'd tell me what is the matter."

"It shall pass."

"Are you angry because I didn't want us spending money unnecessarily?"

He winced. *Unnecessarily.* "No."

"Then is it because I took charge, and having a woman take charge does not sit well with your male pride?"

"No."

"Then what have I done?"

He shook his head. He didn't want to talk about it. What was he supposed to do, tell her he was angry with her because once again the inevitable comparison to Charles had been made—albeit in a roundabout way—and he had again been rated second best? No. That sounded self-pitying.

"It's nothing, Juliet. I'll get over it."

She looked at him for a long moment, shrugged, and fell back into quiet once more.

The brothel was in sight now, standing unobtrusively on the corner. Gareth avoided the main entrance and discreetly took his family around to the back one, horrified that someone of consequence might see them, horrified that his wife's name and reputation would be in shreds before he even had the chance to properly introduce her to society.

*By God, what a bloody, thundering mess!*

He stood on the steps and rapped the knocker sharply. Moments later the door opened, emitting a cloud of smoky incense, a glimpse of the foyer's high ceiling, painted with its colorful orgy of naked, cavorting figures, and Mario, staring down at them from his height of six and a half feet. He was exquisite in a powdered wig and suit of gold satin, but such elegance did nothing to disguise the brute strength of a man hired only to toss anyone who didn't quite fulfill madam's standards of birth, breeding, and cleanliness out on their ear. He took one look at Gareth in his slightly rumpled suit and a face that begged for a razor, at the petite young woman standing behind him with a fussing babe in her arms, and his heavy black brows shot straight up to his hairline.

*"My lord!"* he gasped; then, with a clearing of his throat and a sudden yank at the knot of his cravat, in a more dignified, subdued voice: "My lord."

Gareth was unflappable. "Lavinia said we could stay here for the night, Mario."

"Yes—yes, of course. Come right this way, please."

"The Crimson Suite," Gareth said, greatly humiliated. "We are *not* to be disturbed."

"You will not be, my lord."

"No interruptions. I mean it."

"No interruptions, my lord."

Bowing, Mario ushered them inside. From somewhere inside the building, Gareth heard the tinkle of feminine laughter. He glanced at his wife. Her face was very pale but resolved. Determined. Strong. Behind them, Mario shut the door.

Once inside the warm, familiar surroundings, however, Gareth's anger faded to dismay, then awkwardness, and finally a stifling-hot embarrassment. Above their heads was Lavinia's famous painted ceiling, highly colorful, detailed, and lushly erotic, depicting an orgy of some eight or nine cavorting, sultry, full-breasted women. They were all stark naked. Some were sucking on cherries and grapes, several were drinking from gold chalices, one was smearing wine over the nipples of another while a man crouched open mouthed beneath, catching the droplets on his tongue as they ran off her creamy, wine-blushed breasts. He had a huge erection. Beneath him, another woman lay on her back, her hand, and tongue, hard at work on him.

Juliet was staring up at the painting.

Juliet was not saying a word.

And Juliet was turning pink. Scarlet. Marble white.

Gareth wanted to die. He looked at the dark, panelled walls. At the ornate, gilt-framed mirror. He felt the plush burgundy rug beneath his boots, soft enough to pillow a bare foot, a bare bottom, a bare anything else, while the sound of husky feminine laughter, male guffaws and tiny shrieks came from a distant room. The walls, hung with suggestively lewd paintings that complimented the masterpiece on the ceiling, began to close in. The erotic mix of scents—expensive perfumes, incense, the subtler, more discreet aroma of sex—began to make him faintly nauseous, and memories entered his brain that he suddenly blushed to remember. Oh, hell. Oh bloody, thundering *hell!* And beside him, his gentle, virtuous wife was drawing Charlotte protectively against her bosom, her face carved in stone, her gaze fixed straight ahead as several of Lavinia's choicest girls came gliding out from around corners and behind closed doors, watching them in curiosity and high amusement.

And then madam herself, resplendent in diamonds, shimmering mauve satin, and a bodice cut so low that her rouged nipples were in danger of popping fully free, came sweeping out of her salon in a cloud of heavy perfume. In her wake trailed her two famous redheads, Melissa and Melita.

Gareth knew them both well.

*Too* well.

Heat burned through his blood as their sultry gazes caressed his body, and he remembered certain unique pleasures each was capable of bringing. One with her mouth, the other with her toes.

God help him.

"Ah, you've made it," the abbess purred, all smiles, all charming hospitality. She touched Gareth's arm, then turned her smile on Juliet. "Come, now; follow me. I'll have Melita bring up supper, as well as soap, a razor, and some clean sheets to tear up for baby napkins. You'll be quite comfortable, I can assure you."

"And a cradle?" Juliet asked.

"I do believe it's already there."

Juliet nodded. "I guess that's all we need, then." She glanced uncertainly at her husband. "Right, Gareth?"

"Right," he muttered and, taking her arm, wordlessly led her upstairs.

\*    \*    \*

London was growing dark.

To the west, fiery bands of salmon and gold streaked the fading sky, silhouetting hundreds of chimney pots and glinting like fire against window-panes caked with grime. In the streets and outside the fine houses, oil lamps were lit, and traffic was heavy as people hurried to get home. It was not safe for decent folk to be out after dark, for with darkness came the city's desperate and hardened criminals like a wave of scavenging rats: hundreds of thieves, housebreakers, purse snatchers, grave robbers, pros-titutes, beggars, and other riffraff best left unen-countered.

The alleys were already dark, already dangerous, and it was up the narrow passageway between Mrs. Bottomley's and a neighboring pawn shop that a shadowy figure moved, as silent and sinister as a phantom.

He reached into his pocket, his eyes gleaming as he fingered the money with which he'd bribe Mario. If the money didn't work, the sword at his thigh would. Mario did not frighten him. London after dark did not frighten him. Nothing frightened him as much as the man who had paid him to follow Lord Gareth, and he had no wish to rouse that de-vil's ire.

He gave the door three sharp raps with his knuck-les. He flashed the money, asked his questions, and got the answers he sought.

Yes, they were here. All three of them.

Satisfied, the figure melted back out into the dark-ness, the oil lamp in its decorative iron bracket above the brothel's front door trying, unsuccessfully, to find his face and form. He stood for a moment, the cobbles hard beneath his fine shoes, well pleased with himself. And then he tilted his head back to regard the high, second-floor window, where a slit of light showed between heavy drapes.

Lord Gareth and his little family would not be going anywhere tonight.

A thin smile stole across his face, and he turned and melted back into the shadows from which he had come.

# 17

Juliet, standing at the washstand and scrubbing the dust from her face, was so tired that she wanted to collapse. As she picked up a towel and patted her cheeks dry, she silently watched her husband removing his sword and placing it atop the mantle. Behind him, the rich crimson velvet with which the walls were hung made a perfect backdrop for his natural, aristocratic elegance.

He was not himself. His shoulders were set, his expression as severe as she'd ever seen the duke's. He was not only unhappy, he was downright furious—though for the life of her, she couldn't figure out why. Obviously, his being an aristocrat meant he did not understand, had never needed to understand, did not want to understand, the meaning of frugality. Perhaps he resented having it forced upon him. Perhaps he resented the fact that if he hadn't had her and Charlotte to look after, he would still have the rich lifestyle to which he was accustomed. Or perhaps he had lied to her and really *did* resent the fact that she'd been the one to take charge and accept the abbess's offer, after all.

But she'd had no choice but to take charge. Earlier, while standing outside the church, Juliet had realized with a sinking sense of resignation that responsibility for not only herself and Charlotte but also her aristocratic husband was going to fall on *her* shoulders. Now, however, that realization was teamed with fatigue and, in conjunction with the way her husband was acting, making her feel annoyed. Burdened. Angry.

The warnings had all been there, and she had ignored them. There were his family's cryptic comments, for a start. From Andrew—*Gareth may be a rake, a wastrel, and a scourer. . . . The villagers call him 'the Wild One'*—and from the duke—*Indeed, whoever would have thought Gareth would go and make anything of himself.* An impulsive marriage proposition, an attitude toward money she found both frightening and immature, and, of course, this morning's spending spree at the vicar's, when he'd thrown away so much her head had spun. Juliet put her fingertips to her suddenly throbbing forehead. It was obvious that *she'd* have to be the one to control the money— and where it was spent. *She* was going to have to be the one to make major decisions, locate a place for them to live, and, in all likelihood, find work so that they could survive. She could not see Lord Gareth de Montforte, with his elegant hands and even more elegant blood, lowering himself to something so base as *work.* Charming and pampered he might be, but he was as naive and directionless as a five-year-old.

*Stupid woman,* she rebuked herself. She had allowed her desperate situation, his handsome face— and the fact that he was Charles's brother—to annihilate her good sense. Had she been thinking correctly, she would never have married a man who proposed marriage from a tree branch. Had she been thinking correctly, she wouldn't have let his charm override her judgment. It was her own damned fault.

Disgusted with herself, she yanked the pins from Charlotte's napkin and tossed them into a nearby bowl. *You have no one to blame for this but yourself. He cannot help the way he's made, the fact he's nothing like Charles. You married him, and now you'll just have to make the best of things.*

Make the best of things.

She had weathered many storms in her life; she would weather this one, too. If she had to go out and work as a seamstress in one of those squalid places in Spitalfields, then so be it. If she had to be a wet nurse for some rich woman's babe, then so be that, too. She had a good brain and two capable hands, and she would do what she had to do for their survival.

She picked up Charlotte, who was fussing and kicking, and set her down on the bed. Out of the corner of her eye she saw Gareth hefting her trunk onto a chair. He popped the lid and rummaged about, pulling out a square of clean linen. Then he looked up and met her gaze.

He smiled, tentatively, trying to ease the tension between them.

Juliet ignored him and returned her attention to Charlotte. She removed the infant's wet, dirty napkin and tossed it into the chamberpot for washing later. Though soiled, the baby was still forgiving, managing to bestow a smile as sweet as heaven's sunshine upon her mother. Juliet felt a sudden stab of guilt. Of shame. Not only had she betrayed Charles by marrying this less-than-capable brother of his, but her poor little baby, as well. *Her poor little baby who should've been changed hours ago.*

Angry tears stung her eyes. Tension built and boiled inside her. Her cheeks grew hot with suppressed anger, her movements became jerky and abrupt. She shoved an errant strand of hair out of her face, stormed to the washstand—

And collided with her husband.

He had been coming toward her with a piece of wet linen and a bowl half filled with water. As he and Juliet bounced off each other, some of the water spilled onto the carpet, the rest down the front of his waistcoat. Ignoring it, Gareth held out the damp rag like a truce offering. "Here."

"What's that for?"

"She needs washing, doesn't she?"

"What do you know about babies?"

"Come now, Juliet. I am not entirely lacking in common sense."

"I wonder," she muttered, spitefully.

He summoned a polite though confused smile—and that only stoked Juliet's temper all the more. She did not want him to be such a gentleman, damn it! She wanted a good, out-and-out row with him. She wanted to tell him just what she thought of him, of his reckless spending, of his carefree attitude toward serious matters. Oh, why hadn't she married someone like Charles—someone capable, competent, and mature?

"What is wrong, Juliet?"

"Everything!" she fumed. She plunged the linen in the bowl of water and began swabbing Charlotte's bottom. "I think Perry was right. We should go straight back to your brother, the duke."

"You should not listen to Perry."

"Why not? He's got more sense than you and the rest of your friends combined. We haven't even been married a day, and already it's obvious that you're hopelessly out of your element. You have no idea what to do with a wife and daughter. You have no idea where to go, how to support us—nothing. Yet you had to come charging after us, the noble rescuer who just *had* to save the day. I'll bet you didn't give any thought at all to what to do with us afterward, did you? Oh! Do you always act before thinking? *Do you?*"

He looked at her for a moment, brows raised, stunned by the force of her attack. Then he said dryly, "My dear, if you'll recall, that particular character defect saved your life the other night. Not to mention the lives of the other people on that stagecoach."

"So it did, but it's not going to feed us or find us a place to live!" She lifted Charlotte's bottom, pinned a clean napkin around the baby's hips, and soaped and rinsed her hands. "I still cannot believe how much money you tossed away on a marriage license, no, a *bribe*, this morning, nor how annoyed you still seem to be that we didn't waste God knows how much on a hotel tonight. You seem to have no concept of money's value, and at the rate you're going, we're going to have to throw ourselves on the mercy of the local parish or go begging in the street just to put food in our bellies!"

"Don't be ridiculous. That would never happen."

"Why wouldn't it?"

"Juliet, my brother is the Duke of Blackheath. My family is one of the oldest and richest in all of England. We are not going to starve, I can assure you."

"What do you plan to do, then, *work* for a living? Get those pampered, lily-white hands of yours dirty and calloused?"

"Juliet, please. You try my temper."

"Well, what use is a rich and powerful brother if you won't go to him for help? This is not a game! This is a serious matter! I'm a young mother with a baby to consider, and I must know how you plan to support us!"

"I don't *know* yet. But I shall think of something." He turned away. "Have a little faith in me, for heaven's sake."

"I'm *trying* to, but . . . it's just that . . . oh, this has turned out to be the worst day of my entire life, and I don't see it getting any better." Tears gathered in her eyes and she shoved the heel of her hand against her temple, her bottom lip quivering.

He was there, immediately. "Ah, Juliet . . ."

"Leave me alone."

"I cannot stand to see you suffering so."

"Then go away. Please."

He shrugged out of his frock, tossed it over the chair back, and tried to gather her close. "Is it so bad?"

"Yes."

"Worse than the day you left Boston to come here?"

She waved him off, turning away to hide her sudden, angry tears.

"Worse than the day you got held up by the highwaymen?"

She took a steadying breath and bit savagely down into her tremulous bottom lip.

"Worse," he murmured gently, "than the day Charles died?"

She choked back a sob and pushed her fist against her mouth, trying to shove the tears back, to keep the great, gulping sobs at bay. "Nothing could be worse than when Charles died," she whispered, meeting his sympathetic blue gaze. She turned her back on him and walked a little distance away. *"Nothing."*

He came silently up behind her, too near, too close, and she felt the tender brush of his hand against her cheek as he caught the stray tendril of hair and tucked it back behind her ear. "Then I guess this isn't quite the worst day of your life, is it?" he asked, softly.

Tremors rippled through her body. Her nose burned and her throat ached and she balled her fists at her sides, but she would not cry in front of him. And she would not lean back against that strong, solid chest and let him shoulder her burden of pain, fear, and worry. At the thought, a bitter laugh nearly escaped her lips. He, who was incapable of figuring out where to bring them, what to do with them, how to support them! She jerked away, putting a safe distance between them once again and, sweeping up the baby, pressed her close to her chest. "You've made your point, Gareth," she said sharply. "Now, please leave me alone."

He looked suddenly weary. "And you, madam, have made yours. In future, I shall be more careful about where I spend our money."

His tone was one of polite and formal stiffness. Her cheek resting against Charlotte's downy head, she watched him move across the room to light another candle against the gathering gloom. They stood there in silence, she holding the baby, he staring at the candle. From downstairs came the distant sound of laughter.

Finally, her shoulders slumped. "I'm sorry, Gareth."

He shrugged, but didn't turn around. "Yes. I am, too. You deserve better than this. Both of you do."

"I suppose we'll just have to make the best of it."

He nodded, his gaze still on the candle as its light danced and flickered across his face, the wall behind him.

"I didn't mean to be cruel," she explained, her words sounding lame even to her own ears. She came tentatively up behind him, rested a hand on his arm. "It's just that I'm tired and—well, scared. You, on the other hand, don't seem worried in the least, and your total indifference about our predicament rather got to me, that's all." She gave an apologetic little smile. "I guess I just want you to be as worried about things as I am."

He turned then, taking her hand within his. "Ah, Juliet. Of course I'm worried," he admitted. "But I'm not going to dwell on it. I mean, how will it help us if I worry? It won't find us a place to stay tomorrow, put food in our bellies, or keep us free from want."

"No, I suppose it won't."

They were silent for a moment, heads bent, bodies close, hearts reaching to comfort and console one another. Her hand was still within his, and as his thumb tentatively stroked her knuckles, warm shivers hurried through her.

Shivers she was determined to ignore.

His mouth curved in the beginning of a sudden smile. "Know something, Juliet?"

"What?"

"I *was* terribly angry with you, but now that I think about it, it's all rather funny."

*"Funny?"*

"Yes; I mean, here we are, married and having our first row about money. My brother probably has half of England out looking for us. I'll wager he's gone to de Montforte House, Burleigh Place, and all of the Den members's homes in search of us, and where are we? Holed up in the most exclusive bawdy house in London!" His eyes crinkled with sudden amusement. "Oh, what an adventure we're having!"

She shook her head, pitying him for not seeing the seriousness of a situation she saw as grave. "I still don't think it's funny, Gareth."

"Don't you?"

"No."

"Well"—he folded his arms, jauntily, defiantly—"I do."

The teasing light was back in his eyes, his chin dimpling beneath its haze of golden-brown stubble, and despite herself, Juliet couldn't help her own reluctant little smile.

Just as she couldn't help the way she was noticing certain things about *him* . . . how his sleeveless waistcoat, fitting so snugly over the linen shirt just beneath, emphasized the span of his shoulders, the breadth of his chest, the lean tautness of his fighting-trim waist. How the snowy lace that spilled from his throat and over his wrists emphasized his chin and the natural grace of his big hands. How his buff breeches seemed to be painted on to his hips and long, muscular thighs; how very tall he was, and how powerful he looked. Sudden heat washed through her. He had a splendid form. He had a splendid face. He was splendid, period, a de Montforte through and through—and Juliet's sudden shock about the direction of her thoughts far surpassed her fears about how this charming wastrel was going to support them.

*I am not supposed to feel this way. This is Charles's brother—not Charles!*

Her husband misinterpreted the reason for her silence.

"Well then, Juliet, since *you* can't find anything funny about our predicament, let's see what Charlotte can do," he announced with a flippant, offhand charm. And then, before she could protest, he plucked the baby from her arms, laid her on the bed, and tickled her until she batted at his hands and began shrieking with delight. "See? Charlotte thinks it's funny, don't you, Charlie-girl?"

The baby, who obviously adored him, gurgled and squealed, and Juliet found herself staring at the tender picture the two of them made; he, so tall and strong and masculine, her daughter, so tiny and helpless. She swallowed, hard. There was something deep and moving in this powerful image of Lord Gareth de Montforte as a father—a role that seemed to come as easily to him as flight to a bird.

Her heart beat faster as she finally acknowledged what she'd been afraid to admit all along.

She desired him.

Desired him so badly it scared her.

He glanced over at her, grinning. She shook her head and folded her arms, feigning annoyance but unable to prevent the growing amusement from sparking her eyes. Then he bent over Charlotte, his nose nearly touching hers, a few locks of hair tumbling over his brow and brushing the baby's forehead. He put his fingers into the corners of his mouth and pulled his cheeks wide, all the while making an absurd gurgling noise and glancing playfully at Juliet out of the corner of his eye to ensure that she was watching, too. He looked completely ridiculous. Worse, he *knew* he looked completely ridiculous and reveled in it. Unbidden, a burst of laughter escaped Juliet, mingling with Charlotte's happy shrieks. Letting go of his cheeks, Gareth laughed right along with them, a big, happy sound that brightened the room as the candles never could have done. It was warm laughter, family laughter, the kind of laughter that Juliet had never expected to share in ever again.

Something lurched painfully in her heart. *I never had this much fun with Charles. He could never have found anything funny about spending the night in a brothel, would not have been able to find anything to salvage in this situation. He, far too serious by half, would have remained quietly furious with me.*

But not Gareth.

"See, Juliet? Your daughter thinks it's funny. Now, Charlotte, if we can only get your mama to laugh, too. I mean really *laugh*. She's so pretty when she smiles, don't you think?"

Juliet blushed. "Oh, do stop trying to flatter me, Gareth."

"Flattering you? I'm merely telling the truth."

"And stop grinning at me like that."

"Why?"

"Because"—she hugged herself and looked away— "it's making me all the more annoyed with you."

"You're not annoyed with me, Juliet." He climbed onto the bed, tugged off his boots, and, still in his stockings, lay back against the pillows, his long legs bent at the knee. Throwing one knee over the other, he placed Charlotte on his chest and grinned lazily up at Juliet. "At least, not anymore."

Her heart did a funny little flip, and desire swam through her blood. She could feel a hot, familiar dampness between her thighs. A sharp, tingling ache in her breasts. Dear God, he was shamelessly tempting. And the picture he made, lying back against the pillows like that, with his arms behind his head and that seductive gleam in his blue eyes as though inviting her to join him—

God help her.

"I'll make you happy, Juliet," he announced, still lounging on the bed with one leg propped over his bent knee, his stockinged foot bouncing playfully up and down. His eyes were warm and laughing. "Providing you can be patient and understanding with me whilst I fumble my way from wild young bachelor to tame and loving husband." He grinned. "I'm impossibly hopeless, you know."

"Yes. I know."

"Lucien says I need to grow up."

"You sound proud of the fact."

"Proud? No. Lucien, you see, never got the chance to be a child, and sometimes I think he almost envies me my total lack of inhibition. Poor devil. He was only a lad when he inherited the dukedom, you know. It wasn't easy for him."

"No—it never is, losing a parent." She knew well how *that* loss felt.

"Ah, but we did not lose just one parent, you see. My mother had a terrible time giving birth to Nerissa. My father couldn't bear to hear her screams of pain, so he tried secluding himself in one of the towers during her ordeal. Still, it was no use. He finally went rushing to her aid—only to fall headlong down the stairs." His foot stopped swinging for a moment, and his gaze was distant and sad. "It was Lucien who found him."

"Oh, Gareth..." Her eyes darkened with sympathy. "Charles never told me."

"No, he wouldn't have. Charles was very private about family, you know. But Luce, poor chap, he never got over it—nor over Mama's death from childbed fever several days later. Some men would drink themselves to death. Not Lucien. He buries his grief and horror at what he saw beneath a heightened sense of responsibility, not only for the dukedom but also for us. He takes that responsibility seriously. *Too* seriously, I'm afraid. Living under his roof has been about as happy as living at Newgate, I should think." He gave a rueful smile. "Why do you think Charles went into the army when he did? What do you think caused the rift between Luce and the rest of us? He never learned how to have fun. Never had the chance to pull a prank, play a joke, run wild, live it up as all young blades should have the chance to do. Everything is all seriousness to Lucien, but I could never live like that. Life is just too short."

She moved closer, perching herself on the very edge of the bed. "And so you amuse yourself by getting people's pigs drunk, instead."

"You heard about that, then?"

"I did. At the breakfast table one morning."

His eyes crinkled at the corners. "Well, I only do those sort of things when I'm foxed. I won't even begin to tell you what I've done whilst sober."

"I don't think I want to know."

"I confess, I don't think I *want* you to know!"

She laughed, and so did he, and for a brief, buoyant moment the troubles of their world went away, and there was only the three of them, alone in this room, safe from worry and want. But then Gareth's expression sobered. There was a message in what he'd just told her, and suddenly he was no longer teasing.

"Don't end up like Lucien," he said softly, reaching up to touch her cheek, that stubborn wisp of hair. "Don't throw away your youth, your spirit, and your love on something that is lost, Juliet. Something that can never be."

She looked down, the poignant—and unexpected—wisdom of his words filling her with pain. He was talking about Charles, of course. He, who'd said nothing about that terrible moment in the church this morning; he, who'd forgiven her for the cruel comparisons she had made between him and his brother; he, who'd never commented on the miniature she wore prominently displayed around her neck. He had noticed them all, these little shrines to another man, but he had never said a word, had never expressed resentment or anger or jealousy that he was not, and might not ever be, the prince of her heart. A lump rose in Juliet's throat. Not only was her husband noble and generous, he was far more perceptive—and wise—than she had given him credit for.

Picking at a thread in the counterpane, she said, "I cannot help it, Gareth. I still feel . . . loyal to him, even though he's dead, even though I'm now married to you. I know it's silly, but . . . well, I guess I just have too many memories."

"Memories are all well and good, but they will not warm your bed at night."

"He died in the prime of his life—"

"His life was completed, Juliet. And knowing my brother as I did, he would not have wanted you to pine so over him but to make the most of yours."

She stared morosely at the floor. He was right, of course, but that didn't make things any easier. Cuddling Charlotte, Juliet lay her cheek against the baby's soft curls and blinked back the sudden tears his words had brought on. She could feel her husband's gaze upon her—kind, gentle, understanding, patient.

"Are you angry with me?" she asked miserably.

He smiled, his eyes warm and forgiving. "Not anymore." And then: "Are you angry with me?"

"No." She shook her head and wiped away a tear that had rolled free of her right eye. Sniffled. Wiped away another. "I'm . . . I'm so sorry about this morning . . . in church, with the rings—"

"It is forgotten."

"No, I feel horrible about it. There you were with all your friends looking on, and I embarrassed you, hurt you—"

He shook his head patiently and gave a little smile. "Come here, Juliet."

"Oh, no, I can't, I—I'm not ready for—that is, I—"

"Shhh. I know you're not ready. I just want you to sit up here with me. That's all. You've been through enough all by yourself without going through this alone, as well."

He sat up in bed, making a space for her beside him.

She hesitated for a moment before joining him. She could feel the warmth of his big body beside her, its quiet, resting power. Immediately, her heart began pounding, skipping beats, sending blood racing to her cheeks and tingling out into her fingers and toes. She was helpless against his seductive attraction. Helpless against her feelings for him, which she could no longer pretend to ignore. Those heavy-lidded blue eyes, those long, sweeping lashes, that insouciant, irresistible smile—

She might have kissed him. For a moment their gazes met—his, warm and charming; hers, confused and scared—but then he grinned, draped an arm around her shoulders to pull her close, and the moment was lost. She lay stiffly against the hollow of his shoulder, heart pounding, reluctant to put the weight of her head against him and hardly daring to breathe—but very aware of the hard body beneath his soft shirt, the faint hint of his own unique, masculine scent.

True to his word, he did nothing but hold her as he prompted her to talk about her fears, her dreams, and, yes, even Charles. And sometime during that long hour that he held her, Gareth de Montforte ceased being the man she'd married and became her best friend.

# 18

**S**upper arrived. As Gareth set up their meal on an elegant French table, Juliet retreated behind the screen in the room's corner and fed Charlotte. When she emerged, putting the sleepy baby in the cradle, the aroma of hot food assailed her senses. Her stomach rumbled with need. How many hours had it been since they'd eaten a decent meal?

Gareth was standing attentively by her chair, waiting to seat her. Smiling, Juliet sat down, her gaze following her handsome husband as he walked back around the table and took his own chair across from her. Ever the perfect gentleman, he lifted the lids from the covered dishes and tureens, allowing Juliet to inspect each one before serving up her portions himself.

It was a veritable feast. Beneath the glow of the small candelabra there was hare simmered in port wine and stuffed with herbs and cinnamon. Veal pie with plums and sugar. A fluffy white cake filled with butter, sugar, and raspberry jam, an assortment of truffles and sugared pastries, and spicy, moist gingerbread, still hot from the oven. Bottles of sweet, fruity wine, biscuits, and a selection of cheeses—Stilton, Cheshire, and cheddar—completed the meal. As they ate, washing the food down with the wine served in sparkling crystal glasses, they continued the conversation they'd started on the bed. The more they talked, the more they relaxed. And the more Gareth drank, the more amusing he became.

Two glasses of wine and he was making her giggle with his word caricatures of Lord North and the other ministers whose doings had helped plunge America into revolution; three and he was telling her about the wicked scandals, affairs, and personal quirks of politicians whose names she had never heard, and aristocrats she hoped never to meet, until their own troubles seemed far away and she was laughing right along with him.

"No, I'm not joking!" he protested, laughing and waving a bit of cheese as he related a tale about Perry's mother. "The busks in her corset really did snap after she gorged herself at her daughter's wedding feast, and everyone at the table heard them go!"

"Oh, Gareth—you cannot be serious!"

"Oh, but I am. You see, I charmed her maid into bringing me the corset beforehand."

Juliet clapped a hand to her mouth to hold back her sudden laughter. "You mean you . . . sabotaged it?!"

"But of course. It was great fun, I can assure you. You should've heard the things go. *Crack!* Good thing she was swathed in so much fabric, or the damned things might've flown right out of her garments like arrows and hit someone in the eye."

"Oh, Gareth, that is quite impossible!" she gasped, holding her side with the force of her mirth.

"Ha! But I got you laughing!" He took a swallow of wine. "Another time, Perry's mother had a ball, and the Den members and I sneaked in beforehand, scooped out the inside of the cake, and stuck a dead salmon inside. Perry had caught it three days before, and it was the height of summer, so you can imagine how the thing stank. You should've seen everyone's faces when they started slicing the cake and the fumes burst forth; it was so bad that Hugh's mother passed out and fell face first right into the icing!''

Juliet was laughing so hard, the tears were rolling down her cheeks. "I think I understand why Perry's mother won't let you stay at her house!"

"Perry's mother? Ha! *None* of my friends' mothers will so much as allow me beyond their gates, never mind over their thresholds! Bunch of sour old gits; you'd think they could forgive me for things that happened four, five years ago." He grinned, all deceptive innocence. "Why, I'd never do such things now!"

She laughed. "Unless you're foxed."

"Unless I'm foxed."

"Perhaps you should stop drinking, then."

"And perhaps *you* should start eating, my dear wife. I've seen sparrows with bigger appetites. Here, try some of this Cheshire. It is splendid."

With his fingers, he plucked a small bit of cheese from the dish and, leaning across the table, held the morsel to her lips. Juliet hesitated—the gesture seemed uncomfortably intimate—but the wine had relaxed her, taking the edge off her inevitable wedding-night jitters, and she suddenly felt ridiculous for being so skittish. Especially when she looked into those romantic blue eyes across from her and saw shadows of Charles in that familiar de Montforte face, in that lazy de Montforte smile. Currents fluttered out along her nerve endings. Warmth settled in the pit of her belly. Slowly, she opened her mouth and accepted the cheese, trembling at the warm brush of his fingers against her lips.

She chewed and swallowed, her gaze still trapped by his, until she finally blushed and looked away, her face rosy and hot, her hands gripped tightly beneath the tablecloth. When she finally dared to look back up at him, he was gazing at her with an amused little half smile.

"Well, what do you think of it?" he asked, topping up her wine glass.

"Delicious." Every nerve in her body was thrumming in response to the intimate gesture they'd just shared, her lips tingling where his fingers had brushed them. "But I think I prefer the Cheddar."

"Oh. I haven't tried that one yet."

"You haven't?"

"No." His eyes were teasing, challenging, inviting her to summon her courage and—

*Good God, he wants me to feed him!*

Prickling heat danced through her. He was still watching her, little sparkles of laughter dancing in his eyes, his mouth twitching at the corners.

"You want me to force you to try some, then," she declared, her bold tone belying her shaky courage.

"My dear Juliet, I shall never force you to do anything that you do not wish to do."

She looked across the table at him. He gazed back, calm, relaxed, amused. Dear God, but he looked handsome in the candlelight. Handsome under *any* light. And now his grin was spreading, as though he was ready to burst out laughing at her predicament. What a rogue he was! And what a skittish ninny *she* was. She, who'd once faced Indians and bears in the wilds of Maine; she, who'd been caught up in revolution in Boston; she, who'd stood up to murderous highwaymen—she, who was letting this teasing English aristocrat, who was, after all, her *husband*, turn her courage upside down! Determined to prove to herself as well as to him that she was no coward, she reached down and selected a wedge of pale yellow Cheddar. Carefully leaning across the table so the candle would not singe her sleeve, she met that challenging stare with an equally challeng-

ing one of her own and placed the morsel of cheese
against her husband's lips.

His sensuous, lazily smiling lips.

His gaze locked on hers, but he did not open his
mouth. He merely gave her a warm, assessing look
that melted every bone in her body.

And then his lips parted, and his tongue came out
to lazily circle the edge of the cheese.

Raw desire shot through Juliet's blood, centered
between her legs. Her hand shook. Her heart
pounded. His lips, soft and warm, feathered against
her fingers as he slowly took the cheese, his gaze
still holding hers. He finally began to chew, and Juliet—trembling—started to pull away, but his hand
came up and closed warmly around her own, trap-
ping her fingers within his strong, hard grasp. He
brought her hand to his lips, and, watching her from
above her knuckles, slowly licked each fingertip
clean.

Juliet gasped and yanked her hand back. "I—
think I've had enough food for tonight," she said
shakily, pushing her chair back.

Laughing, he leaned an elbow against the table,
propped his dimpled chin in his palm, and calmly
swallowed the cheese. *"Coward."*

"I am not! It's just that . . . well, this is—"

"Wicked?"

"Well, yes!"

"Unseemly?"

"It's—"

*"Juliet."*

She froze. Everything inside of her was hot and
shaking, her throat as dry as cinders. Her bones
were suddenly so weak she didn't know if she could
stand up, anyhow. She clenched her hands to still
her wildly pounding heart and forced herself to
meet his amused gaze. "Y-yes?"

"You, my dear, do not know how to have fun."

"I do, too!"

"You do not. You are as bad as Lucien. And do you know something? I think it's time someone showed you how to have fun. Namely, *me*. You can worry all you like about our situation tomorrow, but tonight . . . tonight I'm going to make you laugh so hard that you'll forget all about how afraid of me you are."

"I am not afraid of you!"

"You are."

And with that, he pushed his chair back, stalked around the table, and in a single easy movement, swept her right out of her chair and into his arms.

"Gareth! Put me down!"

He only laughed, easily carrying her toward the bed.

"Gareth, I am a grown woman!"

"You are a grown woman who behaves in a manner far too old for her years," he countered, still striding toward the bed. "As the wife of a Den member, that just will not do."

"Gareth, I don't want—I mean, I'm not ready for *that*!"

"*That*? Who said anything about *that*?" He tossed her lightly onto the bed. "Oh, no, my dear Juliet. I'm not going to do *that*. . . ."

She tried to scoot away. "Then what *are* you going to do?"

"Why, I'm going to wipe that sadness out of your eyes if only for tonight. I'm going to make you forget your troubles, forget your fears, forget everything but me. And you know how I'm going to do that, O dearest wife?" He grabbed a fistful of her petticoats as she tried to escape. "I'm going to tickle you until you giggle . . . until you laugh . . . until you're hooting so loudly that all of London hears you!"

He fell upon the bed like a swooping hawk, and

Juliet let out a helpless shriek as his fingers found her ribs and began tickling her madly.

"Stop! You'll make me sick!"

"What's this? Your husband makes you *sick?*"

"No, it's just that—*aaaoooooo!*"

He tickled her harder. She flailed and giggled and cried out, embarrassed about each loud shriek but helpless to prevent them. He was laughing as hard as she. Catching one thrashing leg, he unlaced her boot and deftly removed it. She yelped as his fingers found the sensitive instep, and she kicked out reflexively. He neatly ducked just in time to avoid having his nose broken, catching her by the ankle and tickling her toes, her soles, her arch through her stockings.

"Stop, Gareth!" She was laughing so hard, tears were streaming from her eyes. *"Stop it, damn it!"*

Thank goodness Charlotte, worn out by her earlier tantrum, was such a sound sleeper!

The tickling continued. Juliet kicked and fought, her violent struggles tossing the heavy, ruffled petticoats and skirts of her lovely blue gown halfway up her thigh to reveal a long, slender calf sheathed in silk. She saw his gaze taking it all in, even as he made a grab for her other foot.

"No! Gareth, I shall lose my supper if you keep this up, I swear it I will—*oooahhhhh!*"

He seized her other ankle, yanked off the remaining boot, and began torturing that foot as well, until Juliet was writhing and shrieking on the bed in a fit of laughter. The tears streamed down her cheeks, and her stomach ached with the force of her mirth. And when, at last, he let up and she lay exhausted across the bed in a twisted tangle of skirts, petticoats, and chemise, her chest heaving and her hair in a hopeless tumbled-down flood of silk beneath her head, she looked up to see him grinning down at her, his own hair hanging over his brow in tousled disarray. He had one knee on the bed beside her—and one hand resting on her rib cage, just beneath her right breast.

Their gazes met. The room went hot and still. Then out came his dimpled grin—wicked, playful, seductive—and up moved his hand, now cupping her breast, his thumb roving slowly over the cloth-clad nipple in a silent question.

Juliet tensed. Gareth paused. And neither moved a muscle as they stared at each other like two fencing opponents waiting for the other to make the first move, their eyes conveying a silent invitation, a desire, that neither dared to voice.

Finally, he said, "Does this tickle?"

She swallowed, hard. "No. It does not."

"Hmmmmm . . ." He cocked his head as though in rapt observation, watching as his thumb began tracing a little circle around her nipple where the perimeter of her areola would be. "Does *this* tickle?"

She felt her heart starting to pound, her blood growing hot as her body fired in response to his playful seduction, and in a hoarse little whisper she managed, "Not yet."

His hand moved higher, his thumb anchoring itself against her nipple while his fingers crept up, hooking themselves over the top of her bodice, lingering there for a moment. His knuckles were warm against the soft swell of her breast, and everything inside her went still as he began to pull both bodice and chemise down, exposing her breast to his gaze inch by slow, torturous inch. The room grew hot, the only movement that of the flickering candlelight against the distant wall. Juliet, beginning to find the mere act of breathing difficult, stared up into her husband's face, her skin breaking out in damp heat as his hand moved lower and lower.

"And does *this* tickle, Juliet?"

Slowly, shyly, Juliet raised her hand to touch his

cheek. Her fingertips drifted down the side of his face . . . curved around his jaw . . . feathered to his lips. "No. I think—that you're going to have to try a little harder if you want it to tickle."

His eyes darkened, almost to azure. And it was then that she realized that he, too, was breathing hard, his body quivering with barely leashed desire.

He took hold of both chemise and bodice . . . pulled them all the way down past the erect, swollen nipple . . . and freed her breast to his gaze. Juliet swallowed hard, watching the appreciation and desire lowering his lashes over suddenly hungry eyes, banishing his earlier playfulness and replacing it with raw, naked desire. He cupped his big hand beneath her breast, feeling its heft, its shape, its satiny texture, its warmth. And then, with a groan, he moved fully up onto the bed, making the mattress sink beside her as it took his weight. Her heart pounded in expectation. She felt the singeing heat of his body, so much bigger, longer, stronger, than her own, as he moved up beside her, one hand still shaping her breast, his hair falling around his face, tumbling over his broad, noble brow. His knee was against her ribs. His thumb was stroking her swollen nipple. And then he moved over her, sliding his big warm hands up to cradle her flushed cheeks, his fingers plunging into her hair. He gazed down at her, his eyes just inches from her own. Unbidden, Juliet's tongue came out to moisten her suddenly dry lips.

"I think I . . . like being tickled," she whispered.

He smiled. His lashes lowered even more and his breath—so sweet, so warm, so fruity with wine— was suddenly upon her face as he slowly bent his head to hers. Her eyes slipped shut . . . and then there was nothing but that first, feathery touch of his lips against hers, of two hearts coming together for the first time. Juliet sighed, her arm curving around his back, her fingers exploring the hard muscles beneath his waistcoat and shirt before threading their way up his nape, up the back of his skull, tunneling through tawny hair that was heavy, silky, and lustrous. Desire washed through her, and, melting against him, she lost herself in the kiss.

After a time, he broke the contact and gazed down at her, breathing hard, his brow nearly touching hers.

"I can stop this if you wish, Juliet," he said hoarsely. "I told you I shall not force you; I swear to God I shall not—"

But she shook her head, not wanting to disturb this temporary escape from her sorrows, this floating, wine-lulled dreaminess of the moment. She drew his head back down to hers, and their lips met once again—hers, soft and moist and pliant against his harder, increasingly demanding ones. The point of his tongue traced the shape of her lips, then teased them apart to delve into her mouth and begin an erotic dance with her own. With a soft moan she pulled him closer, her other hand flat against his waistcoat, finding the buttons, slipping them through their holes until the garment fell open, one silken edge just brushing her exposed breast. She plunged her fingers into the folds of his shirt, thrilling to the feel of hard muscle and sinew just behind the fabric and a heart that beat as fast and frantically as her own.

"Oh, Juliet . . . by God, you taste so good . . . you are so very, very beautiful . . . you don't know how much I've wished for, waited for, this very moment. . . ."

His mouth slanted across hers, his kiss more forceful now, his tongue driving deeper and his breath hot against her cheek. Her fingers caught in his hair, raking through the heavy mass of it to loosen the ribbon that held his queue until the silken, golden-brown waves lay in loose disarray across his shoulders. Fleetingly, unbidden, her mind took her to another place, another time, when she had lain beneath another man not so very different in shape and appearance from this one—but she felt no shame in what she was doing, no regret, and certainly no disloyalty, and the image faded, banished by the new memory she was creating with this man who was her husband. She felt his fingers brushing her breasts, one still clad in fabric, the other bare to his touch; she felt his palm curving around each swelling crest, grazing each tautly swollen nipple until she was arching up against him, moaning softly and pushing herself into his willing hand. Bursts of pleasure radiated from every place he touched, and her mind was a spinning, whirling place of delight.

She explored him, as well. Her hand roved over the rocky ridge of his shoulders, down the valley of his spine, up over the taut curve of his bottom to one solidly muscled thigh. His breathing quickened, growing hoarse and ragged at her touch. He tore his lips from her mouth and buried his face in the hot curve of her neck, kissing the sweet, creamy flesh even while his hand kneaded and squeezed that bare, thrusting breast. Engulfed in rising flames, she moaned and flung her head back, feeling his breath hot against her collarbone, his kisses simmering down the side of her neck, the base of her throat, the crest of her breast—there to be replaced by the slick and raspy warmth of his tongue. While he kissed the soft flesh, nibbled the sugary-white skin, his fingers stoked and fired the nipple just beneath, and Juliet felt her senses careening toward a violent explosion.

"Oh—oh, Gareth. . . ." She made a sound that was half moan, half sob.

He laughed against her breast. "Ah, Juliet . . . I

have sorely underestimated you! You do know how to have fun, after all."

He heard her beginning to whimper with pleasure, making keening noises in her throat as he traced the perimeter of her areola with his tongue, and his hand began to move over the flat expanse of her stomach out over the prominent bones of her pelvis evident beneath the shimmering blue satin— down, down, down, toward her thighs. How sweet it was to hear his name on her lips, to know her wonderful, wanton response to his touch! He buried his face in her breast, his body quivering and his cock aching with a need so fierce, he could barely think.

He felt her fingers threading into his hair and clasping his head to her breast, urging him to continue, silently conveying her need. Her other breast was already half exposed; freeing it, he kissed its milky-white curve, nipped and licked and gently nibbled it until she was thrashing and making little inarticulate sounds of desperation beneath him. She was driving him mad. Wild. Insane. His hand moved back down her thigh, and the long, strong legs wrapped in delicious silk beneath their frothy tangle of skirts and petticoat. She moaned and shuddered violently, and his own hand was shaking as he pulled the heavy skirts up to the level of her knee, his fingers drifting over that smoothly stockinged leg, up the trembling inside of her calf, her pale white thigh, moving closer and closer toward the blushing center of her passion. . . .

She was slick and hot and wet, as he'd known she would be. Still suckling her breast, he parted the rosy petals and rubbed his thumb over her swollen bud, pushing down on it, kneading it, flicking it back and forth until her head thrashed on the bed and her heels drove into the mattress and frenzied little moans burst from her lips.

"Oh, Gareth!" she panted. "Gareth . . . please . . . oh, sweet Lord above . . . oh—"

He twirled his finger around her for a moment longer until she was nearly over the edge. Then, drawing back, he grasped the heavy, frilly layers of skirts and petticoats in his fist, pulled them up and over her stomach, and let out a sigh of appreciation at sight of the long, sinfully luscious legs laid bare to his gaze. At the pale, lean thighs, the silken mound of dark hair, the lush, sweet pink center of her. He could not help himself. His thumb and fingers stroking her once more, he leaned down, wanting only to taste her, to lick her, to tongue her until she blew apart . . . wanting only to plunge his throbbing rod all the way to the hilt inside that deliciously swollen pink cradle.

He bent his head, parted her with his thumbs, and touched the tip of his tongue to the quivering bud . . . and as he kissed and slowly licked her with long, torturous tongue strokes in that most intimate of places, and she began to sob, to spasm, and to mindlessly keen, his hot and lazy gaze lifted, drifting over her stomach, her rising and falling breasts and toward the door, where the subtlest of movements had caught his eye.

It was nothing more than the light glowing from behind the door's small, petal-shaped keyhole . . . being cut off . . . being suddenly restored.

A fiery red haze blinded him. Fury seethed in his temples, made every inch of him begin to shake, but he found enough control to cover her with his body as her climax came, clamping his mouth over hers and kissing her to muffle her impassioned cries. Then, pulling her skirts back down over her lovely long legs and swearing violently under his breath, he rose from the bed, grabbed his sword, and stalked toward the door, his waistcoat flapping open and his face thunderous.

"Gareth?" she breathed from somewhere behind him.

But Gareth saw only the doorlatch.

*I'll kill them.*

# 19

**H**e tore open the door with such force that one of the hinges gave.

And there they were. Several men out on the landing, none of them known to him, all of them taking turns peeping through the little keyhole in hopes of seeing some flesh. Juliet's flesh.

*His wife's flesh.*

Gareth went berserk.

*"You insufferable bastards!"* he shouted and, blinded by rage, threw down his sword and went for the one who happened to be nearest.

A saner man than Gareth would never have tackled Joe Lumford, a behemoth who had roughly four stone and some six or seven inches in height on him. A saner man than Gareth would never have attacked someone who was built like a Clydesdale stallion. A saner man than Gareth would not have chosen the undisputed king of the London boxing scene with whom to pick a fight.

But in that moment, Lord Gareth de Montforte was not sane.

His fist crashed into Lumford's jaw, and with a grunt of surprise the giant fell backward, arms flailing, his great body taking down several others who crumpled beneath him like weeds beneath a falling tree. There was not much room at the top of the landing, and someone, caught off balance, tumbled down the carpeted stairs, screaming in fear and pain all the way down. Gareth never saw him, never heard him. He had leaped upon his opponent and saw only the battered, ugly face beneath him, the broken nose and the mouth missing half its teeth, a mouth that was now twisted in a snarl of rage and emitting a deafening stream of gutter curses as Gareth's fists pummeled it with the fury of a man wronged. His knuckles split as they connected with the behemoth's jaw, a tooth, the hard edge of his cheekbone. And then, bellowing in outrage, the giant twisted, rose, and hurled Gareth violently off of him and into the plastered wall behind him with force enough to nearly break his shoulders and crack his skull. A picture crashed down, just missing Gareth, but he, maddened, was already up, throwing himself back in for more, his fists flying like cannon shot. He struck, blocked a blow with his arm, and struck again, hard and fast. Blood sprayed from the giant's lip, and he roared like a great wounded beast, his eyes murderous. Downstairs, people were shouting, yelling, and a mass of them came charging up the stairs, Lavinia Bottomley huffing and puffing in the vanguard like a flagship going into battle.

"Stop it, both of you! I'll not have this in my house! I will not!"

Gareth neatly blocked his opponent's fist, let fly with his right, and caught the other man just behind the ear. The giant staggered, swung, and landed a blow to his ribs that drove the air from Gareth's lungs and nearly made him vomit but never slowed him. Someone let out a piercing cheer from just behind his ear, and Gareth, insane with fury and still dazed from his impact with the wall, swung impulsively, his fist striking the fat onlooker a jaw-crunching blow that sent him reeling, senseless, back into the arms of the others. "Damn you for a pack of voyeurs!" he snarled as he lunged for the giant once more. "I'll teach you to go spying on a lady, so help me God!"

The giant came staggering back, the yells and shouts rising to a deafening crescendo all around. Fists collided with flesh. Blood flew, spattering the walls, the carpet. The behemoth was getting the worst of it. Gareth heard people shouting, felt hands clawing at his shoulders like so many spiderwebs as they tried to pull him off, but the interference only enraged him all the more as he and the giant fought for room in the small corridor. His face was damp, his hair in his eyes, his breath coming in fierce bursts. Someone, maybe Mario, made a grab for him, was deflected by one blow from Gareth's powerful fist, and did not come back. And now the giant was nearly finished. His fist struck out in a feeble, half-hearted arc; then his eyes rolled up in his head, and he pitched forward, and as he crashed heavily to the carpet, Gareth saw Juliet's pale face in the doorway just beyond.

She was looking at him in horrified shock.

Charlotte had woken and was screaming, fit to bring the ceiling down.

And a crowd of people were all staring, aghast, at Gareth, one or two of them even backing fearfully away.

"Great *God* above! He just knocked out *Joe Lumford!*"

A low, awed murmur. Charlotte's last little sobs. And then nothing but Lavinia Bottomley's piercing howls as she stormed over the fallen giant and came charging through the melee, coming straight up to where Gareth stood trying to catch his breath. "How could you!" she cried. "I took you in, gave you free room and board for the night, and you reciprocated by destroying my hallway, my stairs, my painting! Damn you, Lord Gareth, *damn you!*"

Gareth shook his still-dazed head and looked around. Slowly, sanity came back to him, and with a sickening sense of dread, he realized just what he'd done. Not that he regretted it; his wife's honor had demanded nothing less. But he'd probably managed to get them thrown out of the only place they had to stay for the night. Worst of all, he'd horribly embarrassed his wife.

Bloody hell. By tomorrow morning, this would be all over London.

*Oh, Juliet. I am sorry.*

He lowered his bleeding fists, then bent his forehead to them and leaned against the wall, his hair falling over his raw knuckles. From what seemed like a great distance away but was in fact only a foot or two, he could hear Lavinia hollering at him, could feel everyone staring at him like he was some terrible freak. God help him; honor dictated that dueling must only be conducted with other gentlemen; otherwise, he would've called out the lot of them and faced them outside with his sword.

After all, he was a much better swordsman than he was a pugilist.

A low murmur began among those gathered in the tiny hallway, on the stairs. Someone tried to seize his shoulder, and he angrily shook him off. Lavinia was still yelling about the damage done to her wall, her painting, her carpet. Gareth bent his head, driving his bloodied knuckles into his temple, his face twisted by self-disgust and loathing for what he had done to his wife.

And then he heard soft footfalls.

*Hers.*

And every person in the hallway went quiet.

She came forward, walking with a firmness of stride and purpose that would have done Boudicca proud. Her hair was down around her shoulders, and she wore a look of stoic resolve, of courage, of grace under the most terrible of pressures. She came up to him, pulled his gashed and bloodied hands down from his face and drew him, her warrior, against her slight form.

And then, holding him thus, she turned and faced them all, her eyes hard and angry.

Not a person moved.

"My husband, *was,* after all, told that we wouldn't be interrupted," she said to the glowering abbess. "Not only does he have a fiery temper but also a sense of honor that would put the most chivalrous of knights to shame. Your little peep show was enough to make that combination lethal. You only got what you deserved. Shame on you, all of you."

"He destroyed my door! My painting is ruined! I had it imported from France, do you know how much it cost me?! It's priceless! My carpet is ruined, my wall cracked, my reputation will never recover from this!"

Gareth straightened up, raking his hair back from his face, feeling a little sick to his stomach. "Look, Lavinia, I'll pay you for the picture," he muttered, wiping a trickle of blood from his mouth with the back of his hand. "Just tell me what it costs, and I'll pay you for it."

Lavinia Bottomley, however, was inconsolable. "*It's priceless!*" she shrieked, stamping her foot in rage. "Don't you understand? *Priceless!*"

"My husband *said* he would pay you," Juliet ground out, knowing there was a price for everything. Her slender arm was still around Gareth's waist, anchoring him, controlling him, when the great brute who lay unconscious on the carpet could not. "Send the bill to de Montforte House. I'm sure His Grace will see that you are reimbursed for all damages."

"Damn right he will! Now get out of here, you and that screaming brat, before I have you all thrown out on your ears! Mario! *Mario!*''

The Italian, confused and dismayed by this turn of events—not to mention wary of Gareth's deadly fists—took a doubtful step forward.

"No." Gareth put out a hand, staying him, not wanting to have to hurt him. "There is no need to exert yourself over me, my friend. There's been trouble enough here for one night." He pulled Juliet close, so fiercely proud of her for defending him, for standing by him, that he felt near to bursting. But when he turned to the abbess, his eyes narrowed, and anyone who knew the de Montfortes would have recognized the dangerous threat in that lazy blue gaze and shuddered with dread.

"We're leaving, Lavinia. And if word gets out that we were even here tonight, I'll make sure that none but the lowest scum in London ever again frequents this house. I'll make sure that no person in polite society will ever come near this place again, that you're closed down for lack of the right patronage. Do you understand, Lavinia? In short, *I will ruin you.*''

The abbess, one hand on her bosom, took a step backward, her face as white as paste.

Gareth let his icy gaze sweep over the lot of them. He pulled his wife close and escorted her back into their room, where they silently gathered their things and wrapped up Charlotte, still crying, against the chill of the night.

Then, silent and tight-lipped, they made their way down the stairs, Gareth's hand resting on his sword hilt in case anyone challenged them further.

Not a person spoke as they filed past.

And neither of them saw the sly, silent figure who slipped outside after them.

# 20

**T**he door shut behind them, and they were alone.

Cast out into the street, into the darkness, into the mercy of the night and all the dangers it held.

It was raining. Hard. Water poured out of the black sky in gusting torrents, one moment vertically, the next at a stinging angle, peppering the puddles, running in twisting, meandering rivulets down the uneven cobbles and into the gutters in hundreds of mad little races. Wind tore at their hair, whipped Juliet's skirts around her ankles like a loose sail, flung the odors of London into their wet faces: coal smoke and filth, the dirty river, wet stone, mud, dung, and despair.

Standing there with his small family, Gareth felt like the most hopeless failure in the world. Charles would never have done this to her. Charles would never have got them thrown out of warm, dry shelter. Oh, what must Juliet *think* of him? His fury that he'd let his temper destroy what had been a safe, comfortable night was nothing compared to his shame at letting them all down.

Beside him, his wife gave an involuntary shiver, drawing her cloak around herself in a pathetic effort to shield the infant in her arms from the rain. Gareth swore beneath his breath. It was chilly, as English evenings often are, and no night for a woman and baby to be outside. Hastily, he doffed his surtout and laid it over Juliet's cloak, wanting only to keep his two ladies as dry as he possibly could.

"No, Gareth, you'll get soaked," she protested, raising her voice to be heard over the angry drumming of the rain against the pavement, the street, the gutters. Her gaze was caught by his bleeding knuckles as he positioned the surtout over her shoulders and pulled her own hood up so her head would be shielded from the rain. The wind blew it straight back off again, releasing her cloud of dark hair and flinging it across her cheeks and eyes. She reached up, hooked a mass of it with her finger, and cleared it away. "I've already got a cloak, and if you give me your coat, you'll have nothing."

The way he felt, he *deserved* nothing. "Now, now. I've already played the fool, so now let me play the gallant rescuer," he said, securing and tying the hood of her cloak beneath her chin. He did up the top buttons of the surtout around the baby so that only her nose and the top of her head peeked out. "I won't have either of you catching a chill. Now, come. I don't trust that lot of scoundrely rascals in there, not in the least. It is unsafe to linger."

Juliet's trunk, hastily packed, stood on the steps where Mario had set it; Gareth picked it up, easily hoisted it to one shoulder, and, with Juliet beside him began to slosh through the puddles that stood like oil on the dark, grimy pavement, heading vaguely south. Rain slashed his face. Water streamed from his hair, and pain flared through his shoulders where he'd hit the wall. He felt a dull, pounding ache in his head, though whether that was because of that same impact or his own throbbing fury with himself—and those bastards back at Lavinia's—even he would've been hard pressed to know.

Neither spoke. They hurried through the streets,

heads down, walking quickly. Gareth hadn't the faintest idea where to take them. Back to the mews, he guessed, to collect Crusader, and then—then he'd have to figure something out. Soon. He couldn't have his wife and baby out on a night like this. Danger lurked in each alleyway they passed, in the darkened, miserable streets, in the shadowed doorways. And now the rain was coming down harder, drenching his face, his hair, the back of his neck beneath his cravat, soaking through his clothes and chilling his skin. It did nothing, however, to dampen his fury with Lavinia and her lot, and as Gareth stole a glance at his wife, hurrying along beside him with her head bent over Charlotte to protect her from the rain, he fought the impulse go to back to the brothel and take out his wrath on not just the one who'd happened to be nearest, but each and every one of the vulgar louts who'd been spying on them. If they'd received the privacy they were promised, none of this would've happened—and they'd be safe and warm instead of walking the dangerous London streets after midnight in the pouring rain.

He glanced sideways at Juliet, hurrying along beside him. She had barely spoken to him as they'd dressed and packed. He knew that she was not angry with him for fighting and getting them thrown out of Lavinia Bottomley's. No, it wasn't that. It was that she was dreadfully embarrassed about their session on the bed, and everything about her carriage—from the way she could not meet his eye to the way she seemed to huddle protectively within herself—told him so.

*Bloody hell.*

The mews were only a few minutes away. He would get Crusader and bring his family to a hotel, that's what he'd do. He'd spend the money and take them to the finest one in London to make up for what had happened back at the brothel. If frugal Juliet complained of the expense, so what. It was their wedding night. He cursed himself for not taking her to a decent establishment in the first place, as he'd wanted to do all along.

They had just turned the corner onto New Bond Street when Gareth realized they were not alone.

His hand went automatically to his sword.

Juliet faltered, shooting him a concerned glance. "Is something wrong?"

"Keep walking, Juliet."

"What is it?"

"I think someone's following us."

She was no silly, vaporous female who was likely to go into hysterics. She hugged Charlotte even tighter and did as she was told.

They moved through the rainy darkness of New Bond Street, walking quicker now, neither speaking, Gareth's surtout flapping around Juliet's slight body. Puddles splashed underfoot. The rain beat down, and the wind gusted through the streets as though alive. Gareth glanced over his shoulder, seeing something that might've been a shadow.

Something that was no shadow at all.

Hell and damnation. The mews were still a good distance ahead, and so was Berkley Street, Piccadilly, his club on St. James. Safety.

"Faster, Juliet."

She complied. The footsteps behind them kept pace. Sensing her mother's tension, Charlotte began to whimper from within the heavy folds of Gareth's surtout.

"Juliet?"

She glanced at him, her face a pale oval beneath the dark hood of her cloak. Another woman would have showed fear, but not her. In her face was only a mother's anger that someone was threatening her baby, her husband, all that she held dear.

He bent low toward her ear as they all but broke into a run. "Can you shoot a pistol?"

"Of course I can."

He kept his voice low. "Mine is in my belt. Push aside the tails of my frock coat and retrieve it—as unobtrusively as you can. If we are attacked, I want you to take it and run whilst I hold the blackguard off. Nothing matters except getting you and Charlotte to safety."

She shot him a fierce look. "You think I'd run off and leave you?"

"My dear, I can assure you, I am well able to take care of myself. *Now, take the pistol.*"

She did, hiding it within the voluminous folds of Gareth's surtout.

Their pursuer was closer now, splashing through the puddles behind them, his shoes hitting the pavement with increasing rapidity. Gareth turned right onto Bruton Street, pulling Juliet abruptly with him. Immediately, he set down the trunk and flattened himself against the wet stone of the corner building. As his unsuspecting pursuer also turned the corner, Gareth's hand lashed out, seizing the man by the throat and flinging him against the wall with such violent force that his breath came out in a startled *whoosh.*

Gareth drew his sword, the blade scraping from its scabbard with a raw, ugly sound that drained the blood from the other man's face.

"I do not *like* being followed," Gareth snarled, tightening his hold on the man's necktie and throat and bringing the point of his sword up against the bottom of his jaw. He gave the cravat a savage twist, until the man, bug-eyed and gasping, flung up his hands in surrender. "Are you alone or are there others?"

The man coughed, gesturing wildly that he needed air.

Gareth yanked him forward then shoved him roughly back against the wall, his sword still held at the ready. Out of the corner of his eye he could just see Juliet standing in the rain, the baby cradled in one arm, the pistol in her opposite hand.

The man put a hand to his throat, coughing. "I am alone, I swear it."

Gareth was not taking any chances. He stepped back, glanced quickly down New Bond Street, saw it was empty save for a few carriages moving off through the rain. And then he cuffed his wet hair from his eyes and, lowering his sword by a few inches, glared at his prisoner.

"I recognize you," he said coldly. "You were at Lavinia's, weren't you?"

"I was." The man was calmly adjusting his cravat, relaxing now that he realized Gareth was not about to kill him. "Though I'm surprised you noticed, Lord Gareth. You seemed quite involved with what you were doing." He smiled politely, disarmingly. "Never have I seen a man fight as well as you did! They'll be talking about it all over London tomorrow, I dare say."

"Don't flatter me. What do you want?"

"Why, merely to talk to you, my lord. But please, not in the rain. Can we go someplace drier, perhaps?"

"It depends on what it is you wish to talk to me about."

"An opportunity that might benefit us both. One that could be quite ... lucrative, if I do say so myself."

Gareth narrowed his eyes. The man was of middle age, a tall, gaunt-faced fellow with close-set eyes, a long, narrow face, and a carefully dressed wig whose rolls were already drooping in the rain. His clothes were fancy to the point of garishness, his shoes boasted fine buckles, and his sword—still in its sheath—had an elaborately worked hilt. He was obviously a man of some affluence. But breeding? Gareth's every instinct told him he was no gentleman, only one who pretended to the rank by an excess of trappings.

"If you had something to say to me, why didn't you say it back at Mrs. Bottomley's?" he demanded.

"Certainly it wasn't the time, nor the place. And by the time I had the chance to approach you, you were gone. Which is why I followed you. I *am* sorry."

"Very well, then, I'll hear you out." He motioned impatiently with his sword for the man to move. "Get in front of me where I can see you, and start walking."

The man shrugged. "Fair enough."

With a deferential smile that was almost mocking, he stepped away from the building and began moving down Bruton Street. Gareth kept his sword tip poised just inches from the man's back, Juliet following quietly beside him.

"Next street on the right, then left into the mews," Gareth snapped.

The man nodded and obeyed.

Moments later they were in the mews, surrounded by cold stone walls and the scent of hay and horses. The big animals moved about, munching their feed in the gloom while the rain beat down outside.

"Right," Gareth said, trying to study the man in the shadowy darkness. "State your name and your business. *Now.*"

The man bowed deeply, but there was something in his manner that set Gareth's teeth on edge. Something that marked him as an opportunist, a flatterer, a fellow who did not know his place and aspired to one to which he was not born and could never pretend to belong. "I am Jonathan Snelling, of Swanthorpe Manor in Abingdon, Berkshire." He watched

Gareth's face, his eyes sly behind his overly polite smile. "Perhaps you've heard of it, my lord?"

Gareth allowed no evidence of his sudden shock to pass over his face. *Swanthorpe Manor.* Of course he'd heard of it. In fact, if history had played itself out slightly differently than it had, he would know it quite well. The estate, once part of the vast ducal holdings owned by Lucien and occupying many acres of good, fertile ground along the River Thames, had been lost by his grandfather over a card table before Gareth was even born. It had been years since he'd heard its name, and the suspicion and distrust he already felt for this sneaking dog of a fellow increased tenfold.

"You know I know it," he growled. "It once belonged to my family, before my grandfather lost it gaming."

"Indeed. My uncle was the man playing cards with your grandfather that night. When he died, Swanthorpe passed to me."

Gareth eyed Snelling with fresh dislike. "So. How did you know who I am? I've never seen you before in my life."

The man shrugged. "Everyone who's anyone knows of the de Montfortes, my lord. You and your brothers—not to mention your friends—have cut quite a swath through London. Besides, if I had any doubts about your identity, I had only to ask Lavinia to confirm it. You can rest assured that is precisely what I did."

Gareth tightened his grip on the sword, his eyes narrowing. He did not trust this man, did not like him, did not want him anywhere *near* his wife and daughter.

"Go on."

Snelling chuckled, and Gareth realized that the man was studying him as keenly as he was studying Snelling. "Tell me, Lord Gareth . . . are you as good with fine steel as you are with your fists?"

Gareth raised a brow. "Are you challenging me?"

Snelling laughed. "Not at all, my lord. Trust me, I wouldn't care to be on the receiving end of either your fists or your sword. I was just thinking, that's all—thinking that I could provide a man like you with a venue to turn that speed and strength into sterling."

"I am afraid I don't understand."

"Two months ago, I saw you fight a duel with Lord Lindsay in Hyde Park. And rumor has it that you're a bit down on your luck right now."

"Is that so?" Gareth asked coldly, wondering which of his so-called *friends* had let slip *that* information.

"Come now, my lord! Everyone in London has ears, and a mutual acquaintance of ours—the Viscount Callowfield, that is—overheard your friends discussing your fate down at your club earlier this evening. I understand they even placed a few wagers in the betting book about you. Oh, no need to look so angry, my lord. Word does get around, you know!

"In any case, the man you knocked senseless tonight—the big fellow, not the other one who happened to step foolishly into the way—happens to work for me. I guess you could say I rather . . . well, own his contract. His services. Have you been to the fights lately, Lord Gareth? If so, you'll know him as Joe "The Slaughterer" Lumford, the undefeated king of the London boxing scene." Snelling chuckled. "Undefeated, that is, until you laid him out cold on Lavinia's carpet tonight. I say, what *ever* will poor Joe think when he comes to?"

Gareth said nothing, watching this man distrustfully.

Snelling folded his arms. "Anyhow, I was just thinking, that maybe you'd consider doing a few fights for me. You know, a few county fairs, local matches, that sort of thing. You'll draw big crowds. And you can make a *lot* of blunt off this, I'll tell you that right now. Just to make it all the more appealing, why, I'll make you an offer you can't refuse. We'll split the proceeds fifty-fifty, and I'll give you and your family free room and board at Swanthorpe. What do you say, young man? Sound like a good deal, eh?"

"You're out of your mind!" Juliet cried.

But Gareth had gone very still. He stared at Snelling, so shocked and insulted by this outrageous suggestion that for a moment words failed him. Finally he gave an incredulous little laugh. "You insult me, sir, by even suggesting such a thing. Gentlemen do *not* engage in swordplay for money, but only for the settling of affairs of honor!"

"Sixty-forty, then, and use of the Dower House at Swanthorpe."

"The devil take you, I will not stoop to such vulgarity!" Gareth cried angrily. "If I thought you were a gentleman and therefore worth challenging, I'd call you out myself for even suggesting such a thing to me!"

"I am a businessman, nothing more. But you take some time, my lord; have a think about it," Snelling said affably, clapping Gareth across the shoulders before reaching into his pocket and drawing something out. "Here"—he grinned wolfishly and held the object out—"take my card."

Gareth did not accept the card. He did not even look at it. Instead, he regarded Snelling as he might a particularly disagreeable piece of offal, then turned and sheathed his sword.

"If you are not away from here by the time I turn around, Snelling, I am going to make what I did to your fighter look gentle compared to what I shall do to you."

Snelling held up his hands in truce, then tossed the card into the straw at Gareth's feet.

"A good night to you, then," he said, pleasantly, and with a sly, private grin, turned and left, waving casually over his shoulder before disappearing into the rainy darkness.

"The nerve of that rogue!" Gareth cried. "What a bloody cheek! Does he think me some dancing bear at a traveling show, to be exhibited for money? What in God's name is this world coming to!"

But Juliet was handing him back his pistol. "Never mind him," she said, as practical as ever. But Gareth noticed that her face was very white, her mouth tense. "We have a bigger problem. A much bigger problem."

"Yes, we need to find a place to stay for the night."

"Worse." She held out his surtout. "The pouch containing the money the duke and Perry gave us? The one we tucked in this pocket?"

Gareth felt everything inside of him stop. He stared at her, knowing what she was going to say before the words even left her mouth.

"I think it must've fallen out while we were running from Snelling. God help us, Gareth, it's gone."

# 21

**W**hat do you mean, it's gone?"
        "I just looked through both pockets,
Gareth—it isn't here."

He swore softly and checked the pockets himself,
even turning them inside out. She was correct; the
pouch of money was lost. Grim-faced, he took her
arm and turned back in the direction from which
they had come. They backtracked through the rainy
streets, desperately searching the cobbles, the pave-
ments, the puddles. They looked down the alley-
ways; they even went all the way back to the brothel.

Nothing.

"That's it, then. It's gone. We're in a fine mess
now," Gareth muttered, ranning a hand through his
wet hair. "Damn it, Juliet, why didn't you mind the
thing more carefully?"

"I thought the pocket was buttoned!"

"It doesn't *have* a button!"

"Well, how did I know that? Besides, there's no
use getting angry with me, *you're* the one who put
it there!"

"And *you're* the one so worried about money—
you'd think that such a person would safeguard it a
little better when it's entrusted to them!"

They stood there in the pouring rain, getting more
and more wet, panicky and angry. Finally, Juliet

drew a heavy breath and said through her teeth, "That's it then, Gareth. We *have* to go to de Montforte House, whether you like it or not."

"No."

"For God's sake, would you please be reasonable? We have no money, no place to go, and we're standing here getting soaked; we don't have a choice!"

"No. *You* have a choice. *I* will not stay there."

"Fine, then—I've made my choice!"

"What?"

"I want you to take Charlotte and me there at once!"

He stared at her, his nostrils flaring with ire, his whole manner one of stiff affront. And then he took her arm and brought them back to the mews, where he saddled Crusader and led them all back out into the rain. It beat down, cold, driving, merciless. Charlotte, growing damp despite her protective covering, began to cry.

Tension mounted. Neither spoke. Tempers simmered, barely banked beneath set, angry faces.

"Are we almost there?"

"Another five minutes," Gareth replied tersely. God help him, he'd had enough—of responsibility, of problems, of having to think too much. In short, of everything that had happened since he'd spoken the words "I will." Is *this* what marriage was all about?

He took them straight to Lucien's town house, standing in all its imposing splendor behind a tall, wrought-iron fence. He shoved the gates open and marched Juliet up the steps, barely coming to a stop before pounding his fist on the door.

It was opened by Harris, the duke's impeccably dressed butler.

"My lord!"

"Harris, this is my wife and daughter. They will

be staying here until I can return for them. Good night."

"Gareth!" Juliet cried angrily. "You can't just leave us here!"

"You wanted to come here, and so I've brought you."

"You can't just go off like this!"

"Juliet, I am *not* going to stand here arguing with you!"

"But what about you?"

"What about me?"

"Where will *you* go, then?"

"Does it bloody matter?"

"Yes!"

"I don't know," he muttered. Retrieving his damp surtout from her, he turned away, storming back through the rain toward where Crusader waited just beyond the iron fence.

He never looked back.

*They were safe.*

It was all he could do not to send Crusader galloping off down the street in relief. The weight of the world had been lifted from his shoulders, and he had his life back, if only temporarily. No wife, no baby, no responsibility, *nothing*. It was wonderful! It was liberating! It was . . . strange. And with every stride that Crusader put behind them, Gareth grew more and more confused, not knowing whether to celebrate his newfound freedom—as was his first impulse—or drown the weird and underlying sense of loss that went with it in a bottle of whiskey. Normally, he would've rejoiced. But now . . . now, as his anger began to abate (maybe it really *was* his fault they'd lost the money; after all, he *had* been the one to put it in the pocket) and Crusader carried him farther and farther away from his wife and daughter, he wasn't so sure. He felt empty, confused, and almost a little lost without them.

What the devil was the matter with him?

He slowed the horse to a walk. The wind flung a sheet of rain into his face as he turned the corner and made his way through Hanover Square. He pulled his tricorn low, watching the water spout from its peaked front in a little stream that splashed the pommel of the saddle and raced down the dark, drenched leather. Steam, and the strong scent of horse, rose from Crusader's wet hide as the big hunter moved easily beneath him. What a god-awful, hellish night.

He went south, uncertain where to go, what to do. He was wet, miserable, and cold, and his momentary relief (he could not quite call it euphoria) at having no one to worry about save himself was already fading. He tried to resurrect it. No use. He considered going to his club on St. James but decided on second thought that that might not be such a good idea. Soaked, unshaven, and looking like the worst sort of riffraff, he was in no shape to rub elbows with the elegant gentlemen at White's. Besides, he had no money.

*No money.*

Fear whispered through him, and for the first time, the extreme gravity of the situation hit him.

*He had no money!*

What was he going to do?

He could ask his friends if they could lend him something, but that solution came with its own dead ends. For one thing, he had no idea where any of the Den members were. For another, most of them weren't in any better a financial state than he was, save Perry, who—unlike the others—had come into his inheritance and therefore had blunt to burn.

Perry. Yes, he'd seek him out. Good old Perry would help him.

He turned Crusader down St. James toward White's. The street was wet and shiny with rain, the windows of the various clubs glowing a warm and welcoming gold through the sheets of water pouring out of the black sky. He looked at them wistfully. How he longed to go inside his own, to shed his drenched clothes and spend the night drying out before the fire, but he wouldn't be caught dead inside, looking the way he did. It was embarrassing enough just to have to walk up the steps to inquire after his friend.

The answer, when it came, was grim. No, Lord Brookhampton was not there; he had left an hour before with a group of his friends. Gareth knew just what friends Perry must've left with. He swore and continued on, soaked and miserable and never needing those friends as much as he needed them now.

He went straight to Brookhampton House, where Perry's mother told him her son was abed, then slammed the door in his face. He went to his other friends' town houses, and was given a similar reception by their mothers, who had listened too much to Perry's, bore grudges against him, or just plain thought him a bad influence on their darling sons.

By one in the morning, he was shivering and hungry. By two, he was getting a sore throat. He continued on, numb with fatigue and growing despair. By three, exhaustion had caught up with him, and he began to wander aimlessly. He rode to Grosvenor Square, back to Hanover Square, up and down Pall Mall and Piccadilly endless times. No Cokeham, no Chilcot, no Audlett, nobody. Huddled against the cold rain, he turned Crusader north once more, the horse's hoofbeats echoing against the dark and silent buildings that lined Albemarle Street. A young urchin slid out of the shadows begging for a penny, and Gareth, feeling as miserable as the lad looked, reached into his pocket for a coin, forgetting that it was long since empty. The boy cursed him furiously, spit at Crusader's feet and fled back into the rainy night. Gareth was alone once more.

With no other recourse, he let the big hunter carry him back to the mews near Bruton Street. The building was damp and cold, but at least he was safe from the rain that sheeted down outside. Shivering, he pulled the wet saddle from Crusader's steaming back, rubbed him down with a few handfuls of straw, and, carrying the saddle, stumbled wearily to a corner, where he tossed the tack to the stone floor and stood contemplating it for a moment, so tired that he could not muster a single coherent thought from the jumble of meaninglessness they'd all become.

In a stupor of fatigue, he scraped and kicked a few bits of old straw together over the uneven floor. Then he lowered himself to the cold, damp stone, pulling his drenched surtout up over his shoulders and resting his head against the saddle. Beneath him, the stone reeked of horse manure and felt like a slab of ice. Trails of cold water still drizzled from his hair and down his neck. He had never been so uncomfortable in his life.

Exhaustion eventually won out. His eyes drifted shut, and Lord Gareth de Montforte fell into a deep and troubled sleep.

# 22

I t was a wet and wild night on the Lambourn Downs, too. The wind drove through the vale in which Ravenscombe nestled, tearing off a roof tile here, snapping branches from a copper beech there, whistling up and over the high downs and through the gatehouse of Blackheath, where it made the roses in the garden thrash and bob, moaned around the mighty castle, rattled the windows in their casements, pummeled the ancient stone with rain. But the castle stood firm and high and invincible. It had thwarted both man and the elements for five hundred years and would probably thwart them for five hundred more. Its great towers stood out against the black sky, its close-cropped lawns were an expanse of dark velvet. Only the library windows glowed with light, proclaiming the presence of one who had not yet gone to bed.

In a chair beside the cold hearth sat the duke, his face grim as, by the light of a single candle, he opened the missive that had just arrived from his man in London.

*My dear duke,*

*I hope it will set your mind at ease to know that his lordship your brother married Miss Juliet Paige*

235

*this morning under special license (and at great expense, if I may say so), and that all went as well as could be expected. This evening, Lord Gareth brought his family to Mrs. Bottomley's; careful inquiries have assured me that they have merely taken a room there for the night, nothing more, and so, satisfied of their safety, I have taken my leave of them and will reassume my clandestine vigil in the morning, at which time I shall report again.*

C.

Lucien leaned forward, set the note on a table, and kneaded his brow. So he'd married her. Good. But as he gazed out over the rainy, night-shrouded downs and thought of them all off in London, he could not take pleasure in his success. Leave it to Gareth to bring his family to a whorehouse, of all places. God only knew where he'd take them tomorrow. . . .

He rose to his feet, pacing slowly back and forth, hands clasped behind his back. Was he right to have placed any faith in his brother? Was he right to have any faith that the girl could turn him around, make something of him? And why had *she* consented to stay at a whorehouse? Lucien swore softly beneath his breath. If it weren't for Gareth's fierce pride— and Lucien's own dwindling hopes that, through adversity, Gareth would finally straighten himself out— he'd order Armageddon saddled, ride to London, and drag them all back here himself. Nerissa had begged him to do it. Andrew, who wasn't speaking to him, had threatened to go himself. And now to hear that Gareth hadn't taken his family to respectable lodgings but to a damned brothel . . .

He shook his head. No. He would not intervene, no matter how tempted he was, no matter what lows his brother had sunk to. He had to give Gareth this chance to prove himself.

Had to allow him this chance to grow up.

He picked up the candle, pocketed the missive, and moved silently from the room, the meager flame glowing against Blackheath's ancient stone walls as he moved through the silent, shadowy corridors. He began to climb the stairs. Sleep might evade him, as it often did on these nights when the wind moaned around the castle and he relived that terrible moment when he'd discovered his father dead on the tower stairs all those years ago, but at least he could find peace in one thing: Gareth might be up to his usual depravity some miles away in London, but through his informer, the Duke of Blackheath was watching over him most keenly, indeed.

He had already lost one brother.

By God, he would not lose another.

In a lavish bedroom at de Montforte House, a humble young woman from the colonies lay dreaming on soft, goosedown pillows. A thick, fluffy counterpane warmed her body, her skin was silky after a bath in lavender water, and the fire that crackled in the hearth filled the room with heat and light.

On a cold stone floor in a nearby mews, the heir presumptive to an English dukedom also slept, his pillow the hard leather of a saddle, his blanket the wet surtout that covered his shivering body. His skin was damp and raw, and the rain that beat down outside found its way in through the leaky roof, creeping beneath his sleeping body via grooves and channels in the filthy stone floor.

The nightman came in leading his tired horse, a lantern in his hand. He saw the nob lying apparently drunk on the floor, stepped over his huddled body with total indifference, and put his horse in its narrow stall. A few feet away, the drunk was mumbling something in his sleep, tossing fitfully.

But Lord Gareth de Montforte was not drunk. He was dreaming. . . .

*You are lazy, feckless, dissolute, useless. You are an embarrassment to this family—and especially to me. When you grow up and learn the meaning of responsibility, Gareth, perhaps I shall treat you with the respect I did your brother . . . the respect I did your brother . . . the respect I did your brother. . . .*

Gareth tried to storm away. But this time he could not just go riding off to escape Lucien's savage rebuke, could not just laugh in his face and go find some other trouble in which to involve himself, because this time it was a dream, and there was nowhere else to go. Instead, he tried to escape by clawing toward wakefulness, but the dream held him in its clutches as ruthlessly as an iron shackle around the leg of a prisoner, and there was no getting away.

And still, Lucien, gazing down his nose at him with the highest contempt, those damning words echoing over and over.

*Lazy, feckless, dissolute, useless.*

"Oh, just sod off, will you?" Gareth cried, lashing out at that austere, forbidding face. "Bugger off and leave me the hell alone!"

He turned over and saw Charles.

"Hello, Gareth."

He froze, staring in open-mouthed shock. Then his heart began to beat in sudden, fragile excitement. He blinked, disbelieving. "Charles?" he croaked.

Charles smiled. He was in his regimental uniform with its blue facings and shining gorget, his sword hanging at his side. For a long moment he looked at Gareth, his face tender with brotherly love; then he shook his head, gave a tolerant little smile, and, turning on his booted heel, began to walk away.

The command to follow was an unspoken one. Gareth picked himself up, shot Lucien a triumphant glance over his shoulder, and dashed off after Charles, hardly daring to breathe.

Incredibly, Lucien did not try to stop him.

His brother led him through the fields, never turning to see if Gareth followed, never pausing to wait, but continuing on his way as purposefully as if he were leading his company into battle. How long they walked Gareth did not know. Where they were going he could not even guess. But eventually Charles paused, and as Gareth came up beside him, he stood back and pointed to something just . . . becoming . . . discernible through a drifting envelope of gray mist. Gareth gasped. It was their mother, having tea in the garden with Perry's mother, her smile as gentle, loving, and heartwarming as he remembered. His heart leaped. Mama! he cried excitedly, but she went right on talking to the Witch, never hearing him, never even knowing he was there. And as the mists cleared even more, Gareth saw that a fine summer day surrounded them, with the pond sparkling like a blue mirror in the distance. Far off in the muck and bulrushes that ringed it, he could just see a bit of color: himself as a little boy, hiding in the weeds with Perry and giggling in preparation for their grand prank.

He glanced excitedly at Charles. His brother inclined his head, directing Gareth to turn his attention back to this long-ago scene that was unfolding before them. . . .

"Really, Mary," Lady Brookhampton was saying waspishly, "I don't see why you defend him so. I don't think his antics are charming at all! He's a mischievous brat, and he'll cause you nothing but heartbreak and embarrassment. Charles is the one who will be the heir if anything happens to Lucien, Charles is the one who deserves your time and efforts—not that horrid little hellspawn!"

Not that horrid little hellspawn.

Charles looked pained. He gazed quietly at Gareth, who faltered, undone by the blatant love in his brother's eyes.

He knew that Charles had hated the comparisons between the two of them as much as he did, if not more. He knew that Charles had always felt guilty about coming out on top, as though it was his fault that he and Gareth were made so differently. The sympathy in Charles's gaze was almost unbearable. Pretending to be cold, Gareth shifted his feet and shivered. And then Charles turned and began moving once more, leaving the two women in their cozy summer scene far behind. Like an obedient dog, Gareth followed.

"Where are we going?" Gareth called after him. "Are you a ghost or a memory? Where are we? Charles!"

The scarlet-clad figure neither turned nor answered, merely kept moving, the sunlight glinting off his accoutrements and catching the gold in his hair. And when he stopped again, it had grown dark, and the two of them stood before the statue in the village green.

Gareth knew immediately what he would see. Chilcot with the bucket of purple paint in his teeth, Cokeham rooting in the grass and making pig noises, and all of them foxed out of their heads on Irish whiskey. An involuntary burst of laughter escaped him, for it really was quite funny.

He glanced at Charles.

His brother wasn't laughing. He looked infinitely sad.

The guffaw died abruptly in Gareth's throat. He cleared his throat and looked away, suddenly ashamed of his behavior. While he had been running wild over Berkshire, his brother had been out fighting for his king. While he had been up to his usual drunken debauchery, his brother had been dying a lonely death in a land far from home. Suddenly, Gareth could not bear to meet Charles's gaze. Could barely force himself to raise his head and look again at what Charles had brought him to see. And when he did, he saw himself clinging to a rope slung from the statue's neck, a paintbrush in his hand and a foolish, drunken expression on his face that now made him cringe with embarrassment. He heard his silly words, saw his *friends acting like fools, felt Charles's infinite despair as he stood quietly beside him.*

*"Please, no more, Charles," he said, turning away from the scene of mayhem. "This is damned embarrassing."*

*Charles merely studied him for a moment, thoughtfully, then turned and began walking again.*

*And when he stopped once more, it was in the Spital-fields church where Gareth had married Juliet just that morning. The Den members were laughing and insulting each other, the vicar looked harassed, and everyone was behaving as though marriage was some grand joke. Everyone, that is, except Juliet. There she stood, alone, looking sad and mature beyond her years, pledging herself to a man who didn't know the meaning of the word "responsibility." There she stood, still and silent, facing the adversity that was marriage to Lord Gareth de Montforte with the same stoic resolve with which she must have faced everything else in her young life. She, who had crossed an ocean to secure a future for her baby; she, who was putting her entire faith, trust, and future in the hands of a fellow who was sadly undeserving of any of it.*

*Gareth swallowed, hard, and looked away. He did not deserve her. He was everything Lucien said he was, and* he did not deserve her.

*He put his hands over his eyes, overcome with shame and self-disgust.*

You are lazy, feckless, dissolute, useless. You are an embarrassment to this family, and especially to me.

*He bent his head to his balled fist, seeing all the stupid things he had recently done, seeing Juliet—his sad, woe-begone little Juliet—standing trustfully in that church once again. Oh, God. . . . He did not know how long he stood there, rocking silently back and forth in his self-imposed agony. But when he finally looked up, the scene was gone, and he and his brother were alone in the deep quiet of a Lambourn night, the stars pricking through the* black sky that arced up over the downs, the insects humming all around them.

Charles was staring out over the downs, his hawkish profile dim against the night sky. And then, for the first time since this strange journey had begun, he spoke.

"You have two choices," he said quietly. "You can either abandon your pride and go back to Lucien—or you can make something of yourself." He turned then, his clear, intelligent gaze holding Gareth's own. "Whatever you do, I trust you not to let her down."

They stood looking at each other for a long, silent moment, two brothers, two friends.

Then Charles turned and walked down the hill, leaving Gareth all alone. And this time he knew he could not follow.

He stared after that scarlet-clad figure, growing smaller and smaller, now fading into the darkness. Tears rolled down his cheeks. Pain gnawed at his heart. And now the wakefulness he'd tried so hard to reach was starting to drag him away.

"I'll prove myself!" Gareth shouted into the darkness that had swallowed up his brother. "I swear it, I will! I'll prove myself worthy of Juliet's loyalty, her trust, and her hopes for me! I'll be a good husband and a good provider! By God and heaven, I will, no matter what it takes!"

He opened his eyes. The dream was still very near, Charles's quiet words still ringing in his head. For a moment he lay there in the darkness, disoriented. Then he heard the rain drumming on the street outside. He felt the cold, hard stone beneath his back, smelled the pungent aroma of horses, and knew that he was still in the mews, where he'd been all along.

And Gareth suddenly knew what he must do.

A finger of light was just creeping toward him through the open doorway, stretching across the dirty hay scattered across the floor, the patches of bare stone, and bits of litter until it finally glowed against a crumpled white wad that lay several inches from Gareth's face.

His heart pounding, he reached out and picked it up.

It was the card that Snelling had offered him earlier.

# 23

"*I* think you should go straight back to the duke," the Dowager Countess of Brookhampton declared, setting down her teacup with an abrupt clatter. "Here it is, nearly two days since he deposited you here, and where is that reprobate you married? Probably lying drunk in a gaming hell somewhere— or in the arms of some woman of sin. You'll not see the likes of him for another fortnight, I tell you!"

Perry's mother had come round on the pretense of a social call, but Juliet knew that was just an excuse; like the dozen or so other nosy harridans who'd called at de Montforte House since word had got out that the Wild One had married, Lady Brookhampton and her daughter wanted to glean information for the gossip mill, see for themselves the woman Lord Gareth had wed, and take the opportunity to malign him to his new wife.

Lady Brookhampton was a particularly unpleasant creature, and her daughter, Lady Katharine Farnsley—a tall, icy blonde whose beauty made Juliet feel shadowed—was equally mean-spirited. As they all sat down to take tea, it became glaringly obvious that Perry's sister had set her own cap for Lord Gareth—and was deeply resentful that Juliet had got to him first.

"I suppose it's just as well that *you* married him,"

Lady Katharine mused, stirring sugar into her cup and eyeing Juliet's plain clothes—and baby on her knee—with raking contempt. "After all, Lord Gareth *did* ruin his share of young women, and he's not likely to change. Better you have to worry about him than me, is that not so, Mama?"

"Indeed, my dear. You can do much better than that libertine."

"I understand he's currently having an affair with Lord Pemberley's wife."

Juliet smiled tightly. "Not anymore he's not."

"Oh, I wouldn't be so sure about that . . . after all, he's not here with *you*, is he?"

Juliet bounced Charlotte on her knee and leaned sideways so the baby couldn't make a grab for her teacup as she picked it up. She was not naive; it was evident that these two troublemakers wanted nothing more than to sow dissent in the newly tilled garden of her marriage. Still, she could have done without their pessimism. She had seen neither Gareth nor his friends since that rainy night he'd brought her here, and she was worried enough about his safety without these two giving her something else to be concerned about. Surely the man who had made such tender love to her—she blushed even now, just thinking about it—on their wedding night would not be in the arms of another woman. Surely he had not abandoned the wife and daughter he'd gone through hell and high water to wed, in favor of someone else.

Had he?

Juliet said, "You misjudge my husband. He's a fine man."

"A *fine man*?! Ha, did you hear that, Katharine? Ha, ha, ha, she says he's a fine man!" Perry's mother raised her brows, much affronted, and turned her stare on Juliet. "Let me tell you, gel, I've known the

Wild One since he was a little boy, and he hasn't changed one bit!''

And with that, Lady Brookhampton related the tale of a summer afternoon nearly seventeen years before, when Lord Gareth had been a mischievous blue-eyed prankster who'd been anything but innocent. The duchess had come by for tea in the garden, bringing Charles and Gareth with her; Charles had sat cross-legged on a blanket beside them, studiously reading a book while Gareth and Perry had gone off to play.

"Oh, I can still see it all so well!" Lady Brookhampton said, holding her cup out so that Juliet could pour more tea. She went on to describe the scene: the duchess, pregnant with Nerissa, smiling and rubbing her swollen tummy, her nanny suddenly charging up the lawn, skirts high as a strumpet's and screaming that little Lord Gareth had tumbled into the pond and disappeared beneath the water. The alarm was raised. Mass confusion and chaos had ensued, with servants—even those who couldn't swim—leaping into the pond, dashing to get the small boat, racing this way and that. Even her husband, the Earl of Brookhampton, had come running, shedding his waistcoat and diving into the brackish water in search of the boy, and as he'd come up for air, Lord Gareth—with Perry following reverently behind—came strolling out from behind one of the ancient yew trees, soaking wet, and laughing at having tricked some fifty people into thinking he had drowned.

"He should've been *whipped*!" Lady Brookhampton declared vehemently. "But the duchess wouldn't hear of it; why, I doubt he got anything more than a gentle admonition not to do such a thing again. Had she punished him as she ought to have done, perhaps he would have turned out all right, but no, he was her favorite, you know, her wild child, and he could do nothing wrong. She didn't even punish him when he turned six and shocked everyone in Ravenscombe by offering threepence to any of the village girls who would let him look beneath their skirts!"

"What about Charles? Did she ever punish *him*?" Juliet asked with faint sarcasm.

"Of course not, Charles never did anything wrong. But Gareth—he was too charming, too full of naughty, sparkle-eyed innocence for anyone to take him seriously . . . or remain angry with him for too long. He'd do something awful, and his mother would just smile and say that the years would cure him of his uncontrollable ways. But they never did. If anything, he grew more daring, more outrageous the older he got—especially after the duchess died."

"Perhaps he did those 'awful' things for attention," Juliet said flatly, her teacup coming down a little too hard. "Especially as everyone seemed to pay more of it to his brother."

"That is because his brother deserved it!"

Charles, she was told, had remained studious, serious minded, and unfailingly polite, but Gareth had become the black sheep of the family, the bane of the Lambourn Downs—and, much to Lady Brookhampton's dismay, Perry's closest friend.

"Perry's a grown man now; of course, I cannot keep him away from your husband's corruptive influence. But I *can* ensure that everyone who's anyone knows how wicked he is—a crusade I started after I found he'd dragged my darling Perry into some den of corruption where wild orgies were held every Saturday evening, and duels over the loose women who inhabited the place erupted at least once a fortnight. And do you know how I know about those duels, gel? I know because Perry was involved in one last February, and I heard all about it over tea at Lady Waltham's the following afternoon. Enough was enough, I said. Right then and there, I vowed that the duchess's wild son would never again darken my door." She picked up her tea and eyed Juliet with something like malicious triumph. "Oh, don't look at me like that. I know he's handsome; I know he can charm the maidenhood right out of a virgin—and no doubt has. But if you married him thinking he'd make a decent husband, you're going to be sorry till the day you die. The only thing he'll make you is miserable, I tell you. Miserable!"

Katharine said, "Charles was the better of the two, don't you think, Mama?"

"Absolutely. He was a credit to his family, to his rank, and to his country. Went out of his way to help people, was always good and kind and giving—"

"Lord Gareth is just as kind and generous as Charles was," Juliet said tersely.

"How would you know? You never even met Charles, whereas my daughter here was promised to him since birth. *We* knew both brothers quite well. As for Lord Gareth, ha! *Everyone* knows he is nothing but a useless wastrel, a rake!"

"Actually, I did meet Charles," Juliet returned, concealing her shock at Lady Brookhampton's announcement and resisting the impulse to add, *And I knew him in a way you never did.* "And as for Lord Gareth, he is my husband, and I resent how everyone seems to feel a need to say something cruel about him or compare him to Charles. It's not fair, and it's not right—to *either* of them. They were two different people."

"Yes. Of course." Sipping her tea, Lady Brookhampton stared out the window at the pigeons walking on the roof of the opposite town house. "Chalk and cheese, they were. Sometimes I wonder why the good Lord took the one instead of the other."

"Lady Brookhampton!" Juliet cried, appalled. "What a wicked thing to say!"

"Is it? Well, I can't help it; that's the way I feel," she snapped. "It's all Gareth's fault that my poor, dear Perry is wrapped up in that dreadful Den of Debauchery business, Gareth's fault that Perry goes to drunken parties and orgies, Gareth's fault that Perry's involved in daring midnight steeplechases, sabotaged hunts, and the ruination of decent women—"

Juliet felt her temper rising.

"—and here I am, a God-fearing mother, trying my best to teach my son morals and good behavior, but despite all I've done, Gareth has ruined everything and turned Perry into the worst sort of rogue. If it weren't for him, my Perry would be home, looking after his mother and sister and being a dutiful son, not running wild through London, getting up to the worst sorts of mischief and socializing with all manner of unsavory characters. Oh, I can't help but think how my son would have turned out if he'd never met that . . . that scoundrel!"

Juliet bit back the retort that was itching to escape her lips. With this termagant for a mother, meeting "that scoundrel" was probably the best thing that could've happened to Perry. God knew how he might have turned out if he *hadn't!*

She leaned over Charlotte and reached for the sugar. "You speak as though your son had no choice in the matter. Are you saying that Perry, a grown man, doesn't have free will to do as he pleases?" she asked, feigning innocence.

"I'm saying that Gareth has blinded him to what is right and wrong. Gareth was a wicked child, and now he's a wicked man, and you might as well face the fact, gel, that he's never going to change."

"Lady Brookhampton," Juliet said firmly, "from the moment you arrived, you and your daughter have been saying terrible things about my husband. You'll forgive me, but I'm beginning to question your motives."

"Motives?" Lady Brookhampton, taken aback about being so directly confronted, gave a nervous little laugh. "Oh, we have no motives, do we, Katharine?"

"Indeed not, Mama. We just want his wife to be ... prepared."

"I don't need any *preparation*," Juliet said sharply.

"Oh, but you do. That rogue you married will break your heart, I can tell you that right now. Is that not so, Mama?"

"He will indeed, Katharine."

Juliet, fuming, had had enough. She slammed her teacup down so hard, it nearly cracked the saucer. "I don't know the man you're talking about, but the one *I* married risked his life to save me—and a coach full of other innocent people he didn't even know. He sacrificed his own future to do right by his dead brother, and he defended my honor when it would otherwise have been compromised. If you cannot find something nice to say about him, I think it's time you both leave."

"What cheek!" Lady Brookhampton declared, staring at Juliet in offended shock.

"Yes. We colonials speak our minds."

"Perhaps, then, I too should speak *my* mind," Katharine said, with a superior little smile as she nodded toward Charlotte. "Why, look at you, married less than a week and already toting his brat. I dare say, Lord Gareth works fast, does he not, Mama?"

"Juliet is not the first woman Lord Gareth has ruined. But she just said she doesn't want to hear anything *bad* about her husband, Katharine."

Juliet smiled sweetly. "Oh, but Lord Gareth wasn't the one who *ruined* me."

Both women looked at her.

"Charles was."

*"What?!"* The word flew out of Lady Brookhampton's mouth like shot from a musket; beside her, her daughter's jaw nearly fell off its hinges.

Juliet said, "You know, Charles? The one you all think was so perfect?" *Good Lord, would you listen to me, defending Gareth over Charles!* "He and I met in Boston in the winter of '74. We were engaged to be married, but he died in the fighting near Concord last year, and the legal union was never made. I came to England seeking the Duke of Blackheath's help, as Charles had bid me to do should anything happen to him." Juliet's steady, dark-green gaze never wavered as she faced down her husband's detractors. "Lord Gareth is an honorable and selfless man. He married me so that his brother's baby would bear the de Montforte name. I think that is most noble of him. Don't you?"

Lady Brookhampton's jaw was working up and down as she fought to find words. "Well, I . . . well, yes, I suppose it is."

Her daughter's face had gone a very unattractive red. "You mean to say you were engaged to . . . *to my Charles?!*"

"Was he *your* Charles?" Juliet smiled sweetly again and got to her feet. "I'm sorry. He didn't mention it. I thought he was mine. And now, if you'll excuse me, I have things to do. Good day."

The Duke of Blackheath, his two gundogs trotting at his side, his walking stick parting the brambles and nettles before him, was just heading home after a long walk over the downs when he heard hoofbeats pounding toward him from the direction of the castle. He raised his head and frowned, calling the dogs to heel. His rambles were part of his morning ritual, and everyone at Blackheath knew he was not to be disturbed except for one thing.

A message from London.

The rider came galloping up on his cob, bits of chalk flying from the steed's heavy hooves. It was one of the servants, flushed and breathless. He pulled the horse up sharply, dismounting before the animal had even come to a halt.

"Your Grace! A message for you—from London!"

The duke cradled his walking stick in the crook of his elbow—actually no ordinary walking stick, but a deadly rapier concealed inside that knobbly length of wood—and calmly took the note. He broke the seal and began to read:

*My dear Duke,*

*I regret to inform you that I have lost the trail of your brother Lord Gareth, who was, along with his wife and child, evicted from Mrs. Bottomley's late Monday night after a disturbance in which several of her clients were injured at his hand. I have already spoken to the other members of the Den, all of whom confess ignorance and worry as regards his whereabouts, and am shortly on my way to call on his new wife, who is staying at de Montforte House until such time as his lordship returns for her. The usual haunts have not yielded any sign of your brother, and at this late hour, I am beginning to fear the worst. I implore you to come to London with utmost expediency to assist me in my search.*

*C.*

Lucien's face went black with fury. "By God and the devil, what will it be next? Am I to hire an infernal nanny for him at the age of three and twenty?!"

"Your Grace?"

He crumpled the note in his fist, his eyes blazing

with such wrath that the servant took an involuntary step backward.

"Ride ahead, Wilson, and inform the stables that Armageddon is to be saddled at once. I leave for London immediately."

# 24

The de Montforte footman who answered the urgent knock at nine past the hour the following morning didn't recognize the man who stood just outside.

"I *am* sorry," the servant said, already closing the door on the tall fellow dressed in a humble suit of green broadcloth, "but her ladyship is not receiving callers."

"Oh, I think she'll receive me"—he smiled—"I am her husband."

The footman's mouth dropped open as he recognized the figure standing just outside. "Lord Gareth!" He choked out a sputtered apology. "Why, the whole household has been worried sick about you; they thought—"

"Yes, I can imagine what they thought," Gareth quipped, grinning ruefully. "But as you can see, I have not abandoned my wife and daughter after all. Please summon my wife, would you, Johnson?"

The footman bowed and hurried off. He had always liked Lord Gareth and didn't believe all the wicked tales making the rounds about him "abandoning his wife."

A moment later, Juliet herself was hurrying down the stairs in a flurry of skirts.

"Gareth?"

She came up short, pausing at the foot of the stairs, hesitant, uncertain, unsure. He stepped over the threshold, his hat in his hand, a little smile on his face that only hinted at how his heart had leaped at sight of her, and everything inside him had begun to sing. For two days he had anticipated this moment, alternately mad to see her again—and dreading the reception he was sure he would get. He had, after all, had a row with her, dumped her here, then disappeared for three days.

"Hello, Juliet," he said with boyish sheepishness.

She leaned against the balustrade and eyed him with a mixture of wariness and relief. "Hello, Gareth."

And then both chorused: "I'm sorry."

They rushed toward each other, she flinging herself into his arms and he lifting her high to swing her once, twice around, her skirts flying up over her legs, her shining face just inches from his own. He set her down and was kissing her before she even found her balance, his mouth hungrily meeting hers, seeking forgiveness, seeking faith that she still cared. She responded with all the passion with which she had missed him, worried about him, and—despite herself—wondered about him.

"Ah, dearest," he murmured, setting her back on her feet so that he could gaze down into her face, alight with joy and relief. In that moment he realized she'd been just as worried about *his* reception as he'd been about hers. "I am sorry for going off and leaving as I did; can you possibly forgive me for not sending word back to you?"

"Only if you can forgive *me* for losing the money."

"That was my fault, not yours."

"No it wasn't, it was mine—"

"Shhh." Smiling, he leaned down and stopped her protest with another kiss that left them both reeling.

She put her arms around him and hugged him.

"Oh, I am so glad you're back, Gareth. I was worried sick about you!"

"I don't feel as if I deserve your worry, Juliet." He swallowed, hard, all but undone by the magnitude of her forgiveness. "After all, Charles would never have—"

"Stop it. I don't want to speak of Charles. I'm positively sick of the way everyone keeps comparing you to him. I just want to stand here for a moment with *you*, the man I married."

Gareth's brows shot straight up. Shocked into speechlessness, awash in a sudden, all-enveloping pleasure at her words, he held her for a long, happy moment, pressing his cheek against her soft hair, loving the feel of her body against his, the delicate bones of her shoulders beneath his hands. *I just want to stand here for a moment with* you, *the man I married.* Could he read into those words what he wanted to read into them? Had she finally put his all-too-perfect brother aside, in favor of him?

If so, he was truly blessed, the happiest man in England. And as he stood there holding her, he got a tantalizing whiff of her soap, felt her breasts pushing against him, her hand roving down his back. Oh, he couldn't wait to continue what they'd started on their wedding night!

"So, aren't you even going to ask me where I've been?" he finally asked, holding her at arm's length and grinning down at her. He pulled down his lower eyelid to expose his eyeball and shoved his face playfully into hers until a burst of laughter escaped her. "Don't you want to look into my eyes and see how bloodshot they are from two nights of steady debauchery?"

"Oh, do stop teasing me so!" she cried, smacking him lightly. "I have more faith in you than that."

Her words warmed him in a way that strong spirits never could. "Do you? I must confess, it's a very humbling feeling, to find that someone in this world has faith in me after all."

"You've never given me any reason *not* to have faith in you. Though I should tell you that every harridan in London—culminating with Perry's mother and sister, both of whom I finally threw out—came here to speak ill of you." She grinned. "But I didn't believe them, of course."

"You threw them out? *Perry's mother and sister?!*"

"Well, yes. They were ripping you to shreds."

He threw back his head in laughter. "Oh, what a plucky woman you are, my brave little colonial!" He sobered then, suddenly worried. "I probably shouldn't ask what they said about me, though curiosity begs that I do."

"Oh, just that you've ruined every woman in England, and you're having an affair with Lord Pemberly's wife."

He guffawed. "Lord Pemberly's *wife*? His mistress, maybe, and *that* ended three months ago! What rubbish!"

"Yes, I rather suspected as much."

"Oh, Juliet. How can I ever thank you for believing in me?"

Her eyes warmed; she reached up and ran her soft, dainty hand over his jaw, then removed it and put it behind her back, gazing up at him with a coy shyness. Her cheeks flared pink, and he knew she was thinking about their aborted wedding-night lovemaking. "I can think of a way."

"Dear God, why didn't I come back two nights ago!"

"I don't know. But I *do* know that my trust in you must be rewarded," she said playfully. "I'm certain that you haven't spent the last few days with another woman, and I can tell just by looking at you that you haven't spent them carousing, either; your face is clean shaven, your eyes are too clear and bright, and you have this . . . this rather humble set of new clothes. What have you done, Gareth?"

He grasped her upper arms. "I had a dream, Juliet. Actually, it was more like a vision than a dream. I—" He abruptly decided not to tell her that Charles had been his mentor in the dream; she would make him tell her everything about Charles, neglecting the message of the dream in favor of Charles's presence in it. Jealousy rose within him at the very thought; he'd had a tantalizing taste of this woman's passion, rather liked the idea that she had actually worried about him these past two days, and was not inclined to share his wife—*his* wife—with his dear departed brother. "I dare say there was a message in the dream," he continued. "It scared me. In it, I saw what I've been, realized what I would become if I continued on the path I was on. I saw that I was well on my way to losing you and . . . well, I know we don't really know each other just yet, but I *am* growing rather fond of you, you know? So I sold my expensive clothes, sold my jewels, and"—a brief shadow of pain crossed his face—"I sold Crusader."

"Oh, Gareth, you didn't! I know how much he meant to you—"

He shrugged, as though selling off his beloved horse had been as easy as pawning his jewels. "You and Charlotte mean more. And we needed the money so we could have a place to live, food in our bellies."

Juliet frowned. She hated to destroy his newfound confidence, but she had the sneaking suspicion that he had not thought things through beforehand. "Er, Gareth . . . that was very noble of you, but what will we do when the money runs out?"

He shrugged, looked down, and kicked at the edge of the carpet, obviously embarrassed. "I . . . well, I've found work. I think we shall be all right. I mean, we won't live in the lap of luxury, but—"

"Work?"

"Yes. I know you're probably wondering where I've been the past few days. Well, I swallowed my pride and went to see that fellow Snelling up in Abingdon; you know, the one who followed us the other night and offered me a job. I wanted to talk to him and see just what it was he wanted me to do before bringing you and Charlotte all the way back to Berkshire."

"You mean you've been up in Abingdon the past two days, trying to work out a way to support us?"

"I have indeed." He grinned. "Proud of me?"

"Well, yes, but—just what is it he wants you to do?"

He shrugged. "Oh, nothing really . . . just a little fighting, that's all."

"Gareth, I don't like the sound of this."

"Everything will be just fine, Juliet. I can take care of myself."

"You were furious with him when he made that offer the other night. You were insulted and ready to kill him. And now you tell me that everything's just fine?"

He reached out and grasped her by the shoulders. "Juliet, we need the money."

"I thought gentlemen didn't engage in swordplay for money."

"They don't, but—Oh, never mind, it doesn't matter. Even gentlemen have to find ways to feed their families, don't they?"

"Gareth, I—"

He turned, picked up a bundle he'd left propped against the steps, and, grinning, held it out. It was a beautiful bunch of red roses, tied with an expensive silk ribbon. "Here, I got you a present. It's to celebrate."

"Gareth"—she shook her head and looked at him in mock exasperation—"if you're going to start being frugal, you can't be wasting money on buying me flowers. Money should be spent on necessities!"

He grinned. "Do you like them?"

"Of course I do, but that's not the point—"

"I said, do you like them?"

"Well, yes, but—"

"Then they are a necessity. Now, go fetch Charlotte and let's get out of London before the neighborhood awakes, shall we?" He gazed down at his humble clothes with a mixture of amusement and ruefulness. "I don't want to give those miserable old gits anything more to talk about than they already have."

"What do you mean, she left London?!"

The bellow came rolling through the foyer and into Lady Brookhampton's parlor like a thunderclap. Nervously, she set down her little telescope—with which she had been perusing de Montforte House across the street, from where the Duke of Blackheath had just stormed—and hurried out to the door where the chalky-faced footman was shrinking from the wrath of that very same duke. Lady Brookhampton paled. Never had she seen Blackheath so furious.

"Your Grace! What a pleasure it is to see—"

He tore off his hat and stalked inside, the walls themselves seeming to shrink in terror of his fury. "You know everything that goes on in this city; where is she? *And where's that confounded brother of mine?*"

There was no use pretending ignorance; the duke knew she had a telescope, knew she was a valuable font of information. Lady Brookhampton waved the footman off and bravely met Lucien de Montforte's black glare. "He abandoned her for three days, you know. Married her, lost all their money, then dumped her." She cupped a hand to the side of her mouth and whispered, "Is it true that the brat is Charles's?"

"Never mind that, where did they go?"

"Surely, Your Grace, your own staff would be better prepared to answer such a question than I—"

"*Where—did—they—go?*" he ground out, a blood vessel throbbing in his temple.

"Well! If you must know, I *did* just happen to see Lord Gareth arrive this morning, then come back out with that . . . that woman. But as to where they were headed, why, that is beyond me, Your Grace." She saw him growing angrier and angrier, and, in an attempt to pacify him, wrung her hands in a pretense of concern. "Oh, Lucien! You know as well as I that your brother will never be able to care for her and that babe! He'll have them sleeping in the street and starving for want of food! He'll have them begging like waifs! You have to find them!"

"Where is Perry?"

"I don't know, I never know where Perry is nowadays, thanks to—"

"And those useless friends of theirs?"

"I'm sorry, but I don't know that, either. . . ."

The duke swore angrily and strode back out the door, jamming his tricorn on his head as he went. His face was thunderous. His grip on his riding crop was savage. He swung up on that vicious black beast he called a horse and, without a backward look, went galloping off down the street.

Her knees shaking, Lady Brookhampton released her pent up breath, leaned back against the wall, and dabbed at her forehead. For the first time in seventeen years, she actually pitied the Wild One.

God only knew what the duke would do to his errant brother when he found him.

They caught the stage out of London. This time, there were no highwaymen to lend excitement and danger to their journey, no muddy roads to slow them, no rain pouring out of the sky to make the trip a miserable one for those riding on the roof. The team was eager to be off, and they were out of London and on their way in no time.

Sitting inside with Charlotte on her lap and her husband dozing in the seat just across from her, Juliet was lost in thought as she stared out at the shifting clouds and changing scenery. Uncertainty prickled up her spine. She may have trusted her husband's fidelity during his three-day absence, but she didn't have quite so much faith in this dubious scheme that filled him with such excitement. He was a nobleman, bred to a life of leisure and elegance. As a second son blessed with charm and charisma, she could see him as an MP, or even an ambassador to some foreign post; but she could not envision him lowering himself to something so vulgar as sword-fighting for show. What was he getting them into?

At least Abingdon, just south of the university city of Oxford, was not so far from the Duke of Blackheath that she could not send to His Grace for help, if they needed it.

Not that Gareth ever would. At her questioning, he'd confessed—somewhat reluctantly and in no great detail—where he'd spent the remainder of their wedding night. Just the thought of him sleeping in the cold, wet mews made her want to strangle him. His pride was going to be the downfall of them all if she didn't keep a check on it. It was what had kept him shivering in the mews when he could have joined her at de Montforte House. It was what prevented him from bringing them all back to Blackheath Castle and the duke's more-than-competent care. But he *had* decided to accept Snelling's offer, and, as an impoverished aristocrat, that had to be plenty galling in itself.

Why had he done so?

She gazed at his peaceful face, framed by hair that had come loose from his queue and now tumbled haphazardly over his brow. He had no trouble setting aside his pride to work for a man who ranked far below him in status and breeding—yet the world might end before he would seek Lucien's help. Was that pride, then, all tied up with his relationship with his autocratic older brother? The inevitable—and, damn it all, annoying—comparisons to Charles? Whatever it was, it was obvious he wanted to prove himself, if not to her, then to Lucien, and Juliet found herself desperately hoping that he would succeed.

They stopped to change horses at a coaching inn. Several passengers alighted from the roof, and three more got on. On the seat opposite, Lord Gareth stretched his long legs, yawned, and leaned the side of his head against the squab, giving her a sleepy, confident smile before drifting off once more. His knees were crammed against hers, and only the fact that there were other passengers inside the coach kept her from putting her hand on that hard thigh of his and leaning over to kiss his parted lips. How boyish and charming he looked, as though he didn't have a care in the world. She shook her head with a little smile. In all likelihood, he didn't.

Of all the nonsense Lady Brookhampton had gone on about, one thing was certain. He and Charles were chalk and cheese. She could not quite see Charles bringing them all on some half-baked adventure and then dozing off with total confidence that everything would turn out just fine. She could not quite see Charles drawing his rapier and displaying his fighting skills for money.

She could not quite see Charles, period.

Her brow furrowed in bewilderment. She had not looked upon Charles's face for over a twelve month, and it came as something of a shock to realize that his features had now grown fuzzy and distant in her memory. When she tried to envision Charles's serious mouth, all she saw was Gareth's slow, teasing grin. When she tried to recall the timbre of Charles's voice, all she heard was Gareth's careless laughter. When she tried to remember what it had been like to make love to Charles, all she could evoke was that steamy, intense night at Mrs. Bottomley's, when her virile husband had brought her to heights she hadn't known existed, heights that had robbed her of air and made her feel dizzy and faint and gloriously alive.

Inadvertently, her gaze went to those long-fingered, aristocratic hands lying loosely in his lap, and as she recalled what he had done with them—and with that mouth that looked so lazy and relaxed at the moment—she squirmed, her body aching with sudden longing. Her breasts tingled and her heart gave an erratic flutter. And then she remembered, almost guiltily, the man who lay dead and buried three thousand miles away. The man who had fathered her little daughter.

"Charles," she whisperered, trying to call his memory back. She quietly reached for the miniature that hung from around her neck, letting it rest upon her palm as she looked down at it. It had been painted in Boston two months before Charles's death, the artist's tiny, exquisite brush strokes perfectly capturing his likeness. She gazed at it for a long time. Gazed at the pale hair that he had powdered for the portrait, the firm, soldierly mouth, the ambition in those deceptively lazy blue eyes.

And felt only a strange nothingness.

Carefully, Juliet tucked the miniature back beneath her bodice so that it rested once more against her heart. Then, cuddling her daughter, she looked out the window, thinking about her growing feelings for Gareth—and her dwindling ones for Charles.

She never noticed that on the seat opposite her, Gareth was not dozing at all, but keenly watching her from beneath a fan of lowered lashes.

# 25

**S**wanthorpe Manor was the most beautiful house that Juliet had ever seen. Nestled on the fertile banks of the River Thames and surrounded by manicured lawns, meadows, and acres of young wheat, it was built of lovely pink brick, with quoined stone and spectacular views over the river and distant green hills to the south. As the carriage they'd hired at Abingdon's Lamb Inn brought them down a drive bordered by budding roses, carefully clipped yew hedge, and damson, peach and cherry trees in full blossom, Juliet could see the spire of St. Helen's, one of the town's two ancient churches, thrusting above the trees a mile away. A cuckoo called from a nearby sycamore, and beyond, sunlight dappled the water where swans, mallards, and coots paddled lazily in the current.

"What a lovely home," she murmured as the carriage came to a stop just outside the front steps.

Gareth smiled a bit ruefully. "Yes. Too bad my fool grandfather lost it over a game of cards." His gaze met hers, and in it she saw something like regret before he looked out the window once more. "They say I'm just like him, you know. Looking at what he had—and what he so carelessly threw away—I begin to understand what a life of debauchery can cost."

265

"Oh, Gareth . . . surely you're not as debauched as you think you are."

"Put it this way. Not as debauched as I would have become, had I not met you." He gave her a teasing wink. "And, of course, Charlotte."

"You mean to say we've had an influence on you already?"

"My dear lady, you had influence on me from the moment I saw you bravely facing that highwayman from behind the mouth of a pistol."

The door to the manor was opening, and in the shadows beyond it, Juliet could just see an elegant chandelier and a graceful wooden balustrade leading upstairs. Then a footman was opening the carriage's door, and Snelling himself was coming down the steps toward them, his smile as false and overly wide as it had been when Juliet had seen him last.

"Ah, Lord Gareth, Lady Gareth! You've had a pleasant journey, I trust? You'll be happy here, I know you will. We've prepared the dower house just for you. Come, come. I'm eager to show it to you!"

Gareth inclined his head in what might have been a nod and got out of the carriage. He stood just outside, the sun lighting up his hair as he, ever the perfect gentleman, assisted Juliet and Charlotte out. His intense dislike of Snelling was almost palpable. Juliet could only wonder how humiliating it must be for him, a duke's son, to be relegated to the dower house of this magnificent home that had once belonged to his family while its new owner, a self-made man of the lower orders, slept in the master's bedroom. As much as she'd loved Charles, she couldn't imagine him tolerating such a humiliating arrangement.

She certainly couldn't imagine Lucien or Andrew tolerating it, either.

A wave of respect and admiration for her husband

came flooding over her, overwhelming her with its intensity and bringing a sudden lump to her throat. And as they crossed the lawn—Snelling carrying on a one-sided conversation about the grounds, the estate, and the weather—Juliet tucked her hand in the crook of her husband's elbow and gazed up at him with warm, glowing eyes. Her heart thrilled to his nearness. It was a wonderful feeling, one that put a bounce in her step and a flush on her cheeks and made her feel like a young girl all over again.

*My goodness, what* am *I feeling?*

But she knew. For the first time since she'd met him, she was allowing herself to recognize and examine her desire for this man she had married, without letting guilt—or her so-called better judgment—move in to steal it away, and it felt good. Liberating. Wonderful.

"And this is the dower house," Snelling was saying, fitting a key in the lock and triumphantly pushing the door wide. "What do you think, my lord?"

Juliet flinched. Addressed as it was to a down-on-his heels aristocrat accustomed to living in one of the most magnificent homes in England, the question in itself was an insult—and something in Snelling's wide smile and watchful eyes told her he knew it, as well.

Was he deliberately provoking her husband?

But Gareth didn't move, didn't step over the threshold, didn't deliver a swift reply of cutting rudeness. He merely stood outside for a moment, his hands on his hips as he tilted his head back to look up at the house with lazy, unhurried detachment.

"It will do," he finally said. "You may leave us."

Snelling had been grinning; now his mouth opened and closed like a landed fish in response to this abrupt and autocratic dismissal in his own home. For a moment he sputtered helplessly, before retrieving his too-wide smile and gushing flattery and laying a hand across Gareth's shoulders in a false gesture of friendship—a gesture that caused Gareth's pale eyes to glitter with warning beneath their lazy sweep of lashes. "Of course, my lord, of course! You've had a long journey, you're tired, it is perfectly understandable that you both wish to rest. Good day, then, Lord Gareth, and I shall see you at seven o'clock tomorrow morning, in the barn just beyond the stables."

"You shall see me at nine o'clock," Gareth countered easily, still coolly assessing the house, "for I do not keep such early hours."

"Lord Gareth"—Snelling no longer looked amused—"you work for me now. You shall do as I say."

"I shall do as I please"—Gareth smiled benignly—"or you may find someone else to fight for you. Do you understand me, sir?"

"I—" Snelling's face went a dark, ugly red, and his mouth thinned as he bit back an irate retort. Then he managed to recover that nauseatingly false smile, though Juliet noted he had his fists clenched at his sides. "I understand perfectly," he said with sudden, fawning brightness. "Nine o'clock. Till then."

He bowed to Juliet, then strode off, anger radiating from him like stench from a skunk.

As soon as he was out of sight, Gareth threw back his head and let out an amused guffaw. "What a buffoon!"

"If you keep irritating him so, you'll be out of a job before you even start."

"If he keeps irritating *me*, he'll be out of a fighter before I even throw the first punch."

"*What?*"

"Nothing." He grinned and took her arm. "Just an expression, my sweet. Come, let us have a look round the grounds, shall we?"

She eyed him narrowly, but he merely gave her

his innocent dimpled smile and, plucking Charlotte
from her arms and ruffling her blond curls, led her
back down the steps.

Viewed from the grounds, the dower house mirrored the manor house, with the same pink brick,
graceful stone quoining, and lovely views over fields
of young wheat, barley and rye. A small plot for
gardening was to one side, and to the rear of the
house a border of brambles, bulrushes, and trees
choked with bright green ivy stood between the
lawn and the Mill Stream, which branched off from
the River Thames and paralleled it all the way into
the town proper. Sunlight filtered through the trees,
creating a sleepy, peaceful effect, and birdsong filled
the air.

It was too good to be true.

Juliet gazed at the moving shadows the trees
threw across the dower house's roof. "Gareth," she
said slowly, "as pretty as this place is, I have a bad
feeling about all this."

He swung Charlotte up in his arms and laughed.
"There you go, worrying again!"

"No, really, I don't trust—or like—that man."

"Well, neither do I, but so far he's done nothing
wrong except subtly needle me. He's offered me
work, Juliet. *Easy* work. What is the problem? If
we're not happy here, we shall simply leave." Grinning, he bent down and kissed her full on the lips,
laughing at her sudden flush. "Come, let's go inside."

But as they stepped over the threshold, disappointment greeted them. The place smelled of damp
stone and smoke from fires long since dead. The curtains needed washing, the floors wanted sweeping,
and the place had a general unkempt look about it.
Snelling had told them the dower house had been
made ready for them—but obviously it had not
been.

"Ah, well," Gareth said at last, shrugging and mustering a cavalier smile, "better than Mrs. Bottomley's, eh, Juliet?"

"It's not so bad," she returned, trying, like him, to pretend that the place was nicer than it really was. "A bit of cleaning, a spot of paint, some new rugs on these floors, and we'll have a nice, happy home."

"Yes . . . I'm certainly not afraid of a little hard work."

"Neither am I—however, I shamefully confess the very idea is alien to me. I'll give it a go, though. You just tell me what to do, Juliet, and I swear I'll do it."

They stood together, gazing at the few pieces of furniture that had been left in the house, the rising damp on the walls, the grimy windowpanes. At last, Juliet gave a heavy sigh. She was not very good at keeping up pretenses.

"I am sorry, Gareth. You shouldn't have to live like this."

"What are you talking about? This is a fine little house."

She shook her head. "It's not the house. It's Snelling. Swanthorpe. *You.* You're trying so hard to make this work, to care for Charlotte and me, but all I can think of is Blackheath Castle and what you had there; all I can think of is what you were born to, what you're accustomed to." She shook her head. "And here you are, reduced to living in the dower house of an estate that once belonged to your family. . . . I cannot imagine how humiliating it must be."

He was leaning down, examining the soot-stained fireplace, holding Charlotte protectively as he did so. "Not as humiliating as crawling back to Lucien with my tail between my legs—which, I am afraid, is the only alternative." He straightened up and looked directly at her, and in his eyes she saw a fierce determination to succeed, a vow to show the world that he was not the useless creature that everyone thought him to be. "I will do whatever I must to avoid *that*."

Her heart went out to him, standing there holding the baby. She pulled Charlotte from his arms and set her, still swaddled in her blanket, down in the nearest chair. Then, stepping close to her husband, she put her hand in his, looked up into his face, and said quietly, "I believe in you, Gareth."

He gave a pained smile and bent his head so that his forehead just rested against hers. "Believing in me could be dangerous."

"Believing in you is all that Charlotte and I have."

"And you and Charlotte are all that *I* have."

She smiled.

He grinned.

"I guess we're in this together, then," she said.

"Yes. And do you know something, Juliet? There is no one else I would rather have at my side."

They moved closer, their clothes just touching, their body heat mingling.

"You'll prove Lucien wrong, I know you will, Gareth. You'll prove *all* of them wrong."

"I do not know if I'm worthy of such blind faith."

"*I* think you are."

"Do you?" His brow was touching hers, and he was beaming now, obviously pleased and flattered.

"I do." She looked up at him through her lashes, enjoying this light, challenging banter even as a blush crept over her cheeks. "If I thought otherwise, I would have left you and gone back to America."

"Juliet!" He drew back, pretending to look genuinely horrified. "What if I fail you both?"

"Whether you fail or succeed doesn't matter. It's the effort that counts—and as long as you make it, I shall always stand by you." On impulse, she stood on her tiptoes and kissed his cheek. "Thank you, Gareth. Thank you for—well, for being a hero all over again."

The delight and gratitude on his face made her ashamed to think that there had ever been a time—albeit brief—when she had *not* believed in him. And then he took her hand and lifted it to his lips, gazing at her from over the top of her knuckles. "And thank *you*, Juliet. I must admit that I am not accustomed to having anyone place such confidence in me."

*And therein lies the root of your problem.*

His gaze was darkening now with something deep and gentle, and Juliet knew, as women throughout time have always known, that he was in love with her. The knowledge both thrilled and scared her. Thrilled her because her body had come alive at the brush of his lips across the back of her hand. Scared her because she knew that he, if anyone, could make her forget Charles, was already making her forget Charles . . . and for Charles's sake, as well as his daughter's, she did not want to forget Charles.

Passion and guilt warred.

And now his lips were grazing the crest of one knuckle while his eyes watched her from beneath their veil of lowered lashes. She felt each hot little puff of breath against her skin. Felt his mouth moving over the next knuckle and down into the hollow between her fingers. Faint tremors pulsed through her, but she did not pull away.

Could not pull away, for she was transfixed by the invitation in those lazy blue eyes.

Still watching her, he nuzzled aside the lace sleeve of her chemise where it fell across the back of her hand and brushed his lips over her inner wrist . . . the base of her thumb . . . the warm cup of her palm, where he planted a deep and penetrating kiss with the hard point of his tongue.

Juliet blushed. "Gareth!"

But he merely smiled, holding her gaze with his own as he made little circles in her palm with his tongue. Juliet's body caught fire. Squirming, she

clamped her legs together against the gush of desire
that suddenly flared between them.

"G-gareth, I think we'd better—"

"Go upstairs?" he prompted in an inviting drawl.
"What a fine idea. I think I would like to ravish
you."

"Oh!"

"Unless"—he reached out, brushing his fingers
over the suddenly frantic pulse at her throat, and
found the chain that held the miniature—"you find
yourself unwilling to betray the man you still love?"

The words were said without rancor, jealousy, or
anger. It was simply an honest question, with none
of the emotion she knew he must feel, attached.

And Juliet felt terrible. In that moment she realized he had not been sleeping in the coach when
she'd examined the miniature with such detached
and puzzled longing. He had seen her take it out,
caress it with her thumb, and talk softly to the man
whose image it held. Shame and mortification
blazed through her.

"You saw," she said, red-faced with guilt.

"I saw. But I do not condemn. I told you I would
give you all the time you need, Juliet. I shall never,
ever push you."

"I know you won't, but Gareth, although I like
you, am very, very fond of you, I . . . I may never be
able to love any man the way I loved Charles, and
that is unfair to you."

"Juliet." He smiled with gentle tolerance, his hand
caressing the side of her face. "My dearest Juliet. I
knew when I asked you to marry me that you still
loved him. I knew where your heart lay, where your
thoughts lingered. I have always known, and I do
not suffer any delusions that you may ever come to
think of me in the same way that you did Charles.
I accept that. Do you not see?"

"Oh, Gareth. . . ." She shook her head, guilt twisting her heart. "What about you? What about how *you* feel about me?"

"My dear," he said gently, "I should think that that is painfully obvious."

She gulped and looked away, unable to face the blatant love in his eyes. How guilty she felt at her inability to admit as much to him. And yet, how she wanted him, ached for him, lusted after him, like a budding rose straining toward a spring sun. How could she feel so torn?

And as she stood there in that small, spartan room with this man who had so selflessly married her despite the fact that she might never love him as strongly as she had his brother, her choices were suddenly clear: She could retreat back into penned sadness or make a thrilling leap out into the liberation she had tasted earlier—a liberation that could open the doors to a loving, shining future for both herself and Charlotte.

She seized what courage still fired her and made her decision.

"Make me feel, then, Gareth." She pressed close to him, her eyes almost pleading. "Open my heart again, so we can have something of a life together."

He lifted her hand to his mouth, pressing his lips against each knuckle, studying the myriad of pain and hope and confusion that moved across her face.

"Are you certain that is what you want, Juliet?"

"How can I know if it's what I want unless I muster the courage to find out? I hurt so badly inside, Gareth. I hurt because on the one hand I still feel loyal to Charles—but on the other, I find myself having . . . wifely thoughts about *you*. Not him, *you*." Her eyes pleaded for understanding and forgiveness. "Can you make me forget him, Gareth? *Can you?*"

"I honestly don't know." And then he smiled,

slowly. "But I can promise you this; I shall enjoy trying."

She nodded and shut her eyes, trembling with sudden anticipation. Measuring each long, loud breath that went into, and back out of, her lungs. And now, his tongue was probing each pad of flesh at the base of her fingers, his breath whispering over the back of her hand, and Juliet, her heart pounding furiously, was as stiff as a sapling after an ice storm.

"Juliet?"

"Yes?"

"I am trying," he murmured playfully.

She opened her eyes. He was silently laughing at her, his eyes twinkling. And in that moment, Juliet's trepidation faded because it was awfully hard to take yourself seriously when someone you trusted, someone you knew cared about you, probably even loved you, was teasing you so.

"Oh, Gareth!" she said with a little laugh.

"*Oh, Gareth!*" he mimicked, grinning. And then, gazing down at her, he raised her hand to his face and painted his cheek with her fingers. "Touch me, Juliet."

Shyly, she pulled free of his grasp and let her hand move over his face. His cheek was slightly rough beneath her fingers, his skin warm against her own. Everything inside her began to heat up, and she suddenly found it hard to breathe. She ran her hand down the side of his neck and then out over his shoulder, feeling the shape of his body beneath his clothes: the bulges of his upper arm and then the solid breadth of his chest, the bumps that were each rib, the flat, taut belly beneath the loose, white shirt. She shut her eyes, trembling, knowing that she had to be the initiator if only to prove to herself that she was not afraid of letting go of the past, if only to prove to herself that she was indeed capable of loving another man. Her hand dipped, lower. He tensed and caught his breath. Her fingers hesitated at the waistband of his breeches as she fought both flight and desire. And then, bashfully, Juliet touched him through the cloth.

He sucked in his breath and went rigid.

And Juliet bent her head against his chest and looked down at where her hand was.

"Is this . . . all right?" she asked. *What a foolish thing to say to one's husband.*

"I am enjoying it."

"A lot?"

"Mmmm . . . yes."

Her hand shaking, she ran her fingers over him once again. He was hard beneath her touch, and she could feel every throbbing inch of him through the flimsy barrier of his breeches. Heat suffused her blood, her face, broke out all over her skin. She had forgotten how very large a man actually was, and the knowledge both excited and emboldened her. She wanted more.

Much more.

She wanted him inside her. Not Charles, not a fantasy that Gareth was Charles, but Gareth himself.

*Her husband.*

As lightly as a butterfly, she ran her fingernails over the warm, cloth-covered bulge and looked up at him. He gave her a satisfied smile, inspiring her confidence. She bore down harder upon him. His breathing changed and his eyes drifted shut, almost on a grimace. He took a step backward, leaning against the wall behind him. "Oh . . . oh, Juliet."

Charlotte was still in the nearby chair.

"Put the baby over there on the sofa," he said in a strained voice as she continued to stroke him. "Put her where . . . she won't be able to see us."

"She's asleep, Gareth."

"Regardless . . . I don't want her to wake up and see . . . I—"

And now *she* was laughing at *him*, amused by his modesty. She left him only long enough to do as he asked, then returned, picking up where she'd left off.

"That's better," he breathed, his eyes half closed, his hand running up and down her arm, and the back of his head resting against the wall as she touched and explored and caressed him through his breeches. He had not so much as even kissed her, but already he was making her forget, simply by allowing himself to be seduced by her femininity— a femininity that held him hostage in her hand and brought a singing excitement to Juliet's slowly awakening heart. She had forgotten how wonderful it felt to seduce a man. She had forgotten this hot, blood-to-the-cheeks sensation of growing arousal. She felt strange and shaky and not herself, her skin afire where her clothes lay against it. A tendril of hair fell from its pins to cling damply to her neck. And now she could not help herself. Could not stop herself from running her hand all over and around him, cupping the twin sacs that lay between his legs, palming the swollen, straining bulge that pushed to break free of the breeches.

She sank to her knees and kissed him through the warm fabric.

"By God!" he gasped, nearly collapsing against the wall behind him. His hands were on her head, stroking her crown, pulling the other pins free until her silken tresses tumbled down her neck, her nape, her back. She rubbed her cheek against him. She shaped the hard contour of his thighs and buttocks with her hands and kissed and nibbled the length of him through his breeches, until he was groaning with pleasure. Then, her fingers shaking, Juliet began to work on the flap of his breeches, pushing the buttons through their holes one by one until the fabric fell loose and he sprang out against her cheek, huge and hot and engorged with desire. She took

him in her hands, rubbed the warm length of him
against first one cheek, then the other, and began
planting gentle kisses up and down his rigidity.

"Juliet . . . oh, *God!* . . . I . . . I am sorry . . . I don't
know if this is . . . is a good idea . . . I mean, I . . .
want to make it last."

She parted her lips and touched him lightly with
her tongue.

"*Oh!* Juliet, *please!*"

But as she took the swollen head into her mouth,
he gasped, braced himself against the wall and began making helpless sounds of defeat. His hand
clenched a thick swatch of her hair with a despair
that almost pained her as she licked and sucked and
pulled at him. He stood it for only so long, before
finally hooking his hand around her damp neck and
urging her back to her feet. She slid her hands up
beneath his long, loose shirt as she rose, thrilling to
the hard-muscled feel of his torso, the warmth of his
skin, the splendor of his physique. His mouth, fierce
with passion, crashed down on hers, his tongue
thrusting between her teeth. And now he was pushing her steadily backward, his breath pulsing against
her cheek as he kissed her, her fingers still stroking
the hard, hard muscles of his inner thighs, the rigid
tumescence between his legs.

"Juliet . . . by God, Juliet, you are driving me beyond wild. . . ."

Yes, she had done the right thing. She would
never regret this, not ever, not in a million years. Her
lips clung to his, her hips grinding helplessly against
his swollen shaft. Her hand, closed around him, was
crushed between their bodies as he curved an arm
around her waist and bent her nearly double over
it, still kissing her, still driving his tongue against
hers. He broke the kiss, breathing hard, and she
gasped as his lips grazed her exposed throat, his fingers smoothing the silken skin of her neck, her chest,

and finally dipping beneath the lace-edged neckline of her chemise.

"Oh, Gareth . . ."

His hand was big and hot and wonderful against her skin. He pulled down both chemise and bodice, cupping one plump breast in his hand and popping it free. His thumb flicked over the nipple, and then his mouth was grazing the soft white swell, nipping around her nipple, licking, kissing, and loving her.

Juliet gasped as she felt the first violent waves of climax building within her. She moaned and pushed herself against him, wantonly grinding her hips against his, even as her lips blindly sought his mouth, and her fingers slid up the back of his nape and into the soft waves of his hair.

"Oh, Juliet . . ." He was cupping her breast, feverishly kissing it. "You are so beautiful . . . so very, very beautiful."

She moaned, lost in the haze of mounting passion.

"Say my name, dearest," he whispered hoarsely, his mouth moving to the other breast even as he slid his hands beneath her skirts and began to pull them up, "say my name so that I can hear it on your lips and know that I am the one who fires you."

"Gareth!"

He laughed.

"Gareth, Gareth, *Gareth!*"

This last came out as something of a breathless cry, for his hands had framed her outer thighs, clasping and lifting her straight off the ground. Caught by surprise, her feet dangling, she grabbed at his shoulders to brace herself as he held her, poised, just above his stabbing hardness. His fingers kneaded her bottom, cool air swept up between her open legs to kiss her most intimate flesh. She looped her arms around his neck and kissed his brow, his temples, even the loose hair that clung to them. Kissed his lashes, the bridge of his nose, his slightly roughened cheeks, his hard, demanding mouth, even as she opened her legs as wide as she could, instinctively seeking him, desperately wanting him. And then there was only the hot, probing head of his manhood, poised at her entrance.

She tensed.

He went still, refusing, as was his word, to coerce her into doing anything she didn't wish to do.

And then Juliet, aching for him, wanting all of him inside her with an intensity that threatened to blow her apart, dropped her lips against the top of his head and squirmed toward him.

"Oh, Gareth—*please! . . .*"

It was all the encouragement he needed. Holding her effortlessly, he slowly lowered her onto himself, his engorged shaft completely filling her, spreading her, touching upon wet, intimate walls and moving deeper and deeper inside of her. He was huge. He was wonderful. Her head fell back in mindless ecstasy. A last pin tumbled from her hair and tinkled to the floor, the heavy mass rippling down her neck, down her back, swinging sensuously against his hands. Still clasping her at the hips, he lowered her until she fully sheathed him, her legs resting atop his hard thighs, her feet dangling; then, when she thought she might explode from the exquisite torture of it, he slowly lifted her up, sliding her up and off each long, delicious inch of himself.

"Oh, *Gareth!*"

Back down he slid her. Her head fell forward, her fingertips driving into the rock hardness of his shoulders as she fought to delay the brilliant shards of feeling that were already whirling her up and into their spinning vortex. Her breasts were level with his mouth now, and she cried out as he took first one, then the other, into that hot wetness, to be kissed and loved even as he began to slide her back up his rigid length once more.

Back down.

Back up.

Faster now, their breathing growing hoarse and ragged and strained, his breeches falling farther and farther down his legs, and her skirts and hair lashing her back, her rump, with each savage, mighty thrust.

"Oh, Gareth . . . *Gareth!*"

He whirled her around and they fell across a table behind them. Hard wood behind, hard body above, her hair hanging over the edge and her husband pounding into her. His mouth hot and hungry on hers, his hands everywhere, the table squeaking and shaking and bumping with every thrust. Juliet felt climax rushing toward her as each savage thrust sent her body inching down the table's smooth surface, cried out as her name burst from his lips and his seed burst from him, exploding into her and sending her spinning out over the edges of reality. She bucked and arched, climaxing not once but twice, three times, tears of joy and fulfillment running down her face as the fierce, rapturous waves rocked through her.

Presently, their breathing returned to normal. They realized they were lying on a bare table, he atop her with his weight on his arms, she with her legs spread open and her feet dangling over the sides—and, spontaneously, both of them began to laugh at the total ridiculousness of their positions.

For Juliet, everything inside of her still rang like air around a reverberating bell, free and joyful and alive. And everything inside of her knew that her carefree, loving, rakehell of a husband had finally banished the ghost that had claimed the last year of her life.

"Gareth?"

"Yes, dearest?"

"I think . . . that there may be hope for us after all."

# 26

From his brother's friends, the Duke of Blackheath learned that Gareth had not been seen
since parting company outside the church in which
he'd been married. From Lavinia Bottomley, he
learned that he owed several hundred pounds for
damages incurred to her establishment when Gareth
had felled London's reigning boxing champion. And
from the Plough Inn, which sold tickets to the stagecoach, he learned that a man answering Gareth's description, along with a woman and child, had
bought tickets and appeared to be heading vaguely
north.

So, then, Gareth had failed after all, and was slink-
ing home, just as Lucien had feared.

And, predicted.

His face bitter with disappointment, Lucien
turned Armageddon north, his faithful informer galloping beside him.

Juliet woke to the sound of Charlotte whimpering
for her breakfast. She opened her eyes, stretching lazily and blinking against the bright sunshine that
streamed through the windows. A chaffinch was
singing just outside, and a breeze pushed at the
dingy old curtains that had been left in the dower
house by the previous occupant. Yawning, she

reached for the man in whose arms she had just spent the night.

The bed was empty. She turned over.

"Gareth?"

No answer. She sat up.

"Gareth?" she called again.

Nothing but Charlotte's increasingly impatient whimpers.

Rubbing her eyes, she swung her legs from the bed. A small shelf clock was on the mantle, and she gasped as she saw the time. It was almost half past nine! She had never slept so late before!

But then, she thought, blushing, she had never spent the night in a man's arms before, either. Her time with Charles had been brief and intense, consisting of stolen moments behind her stepfather's woodshed or clandestine meetings with her dashing British officer dressed as a civilian farmer so as not to arouse suspicion. But she had never spent a night with him. Had never lain her head atop his chest and fallen asleep while he stroked her hair and told her stories about his childhood, never dreamed in the protective circle of his embrace, never laughed until the tears rolled helplessly down her cheeks— as she had done last night when Gareth had told her what he and the Den of Debauchery members had done to a certain statue back in Ravenscombe. . . .

She laughed just thinking about it. Purple parts, indeed!

She was still giggling as she crawled out of bed and stretched. It was then that she saw the note propped on the table beside the bed:

*Dearest Juliet,*

*I have gone off to begin my work for Snelling; I do not know what time I will be home, but it may be late. Please do not wait up for me if this should be the case.*

*With love and kisses,*

*Gareth*

*P.S. I miss you already. More love and kisses.*

Happiness flooded her heart and she cradled the note to her breast for a long moment, filled with a strange longing, an inner peace. *I miss you already.*

She touched the note to her lips. *I miss you, too.*

Charlotte's cries were getting louder, more demanding. Carefully setting the note back on the table, Juliet crossed to the wooden cradle that stood near the hearth and lifted her daughter out. Gareth, bless him, had gone into Abingdon the night before and found the cradle, trading it for a fencing lesson that he promised to give the baker's son later in the week.

"What's the matter there, little girl? Are you hungry?"

Hungry wasn't the word for it. Charlotte all but grabbed for Juliet's breast. As the baby suckled, the blood rushed to Juliet's cheeks. All she could think of was her husband's erotic kisses on this very same breast just last night. All she could think of was the searing joy she had found in his embrace. Oh, how she wished he was there, instead of off working for Snelling. It would have been nice to wake up in each other's arms on their first real morning together.

As she sat there nursing the baby, her gaze fell upon the bedside table. There, the miniature of Charles lay beneath her kerchief, the ribbon on which she'd restrung it peeping out and just catching the morning sunlight. Thoughtfully, Juliet reached out and picked it up. She felt no urge to put it on. Instead, she simply let the tiny painting lie in her palm as she stared into the face of the man who now seemed to belong to another lifetime.

"Charles ... How much younger I was when I knew you," she whispered to his painted likeness. She looked down at it, trying to find the right words. "I was an impressionable girl and you, a god on a mighty charger, resplendent in officer's dress, all glitter and gold. I was so enamored of you—but I know now that we would never have been happy together. We were too much alike—both too serious, too practical, too ... cautious, perhaps. You were right for me then, and I shall never, ever forget you—but it's your brother who's right for me now."

She swallowed, hard.

"I hope you don't mind what I have done," she added, as she gazed down into those blue, blue eyes. "But I know you wouldn't have wanted me to be unhappy."

There was no answer, of course. And she had not expected one. The answer, as she well knew, was in her heart.

A half hour later, Juliet was washed, dressed, and eager to explore her new home. Plenty of work needed to be done around their little house, but it would wait till the afternoon. This morning, maybe she'd walk into Abingdon and see what the town was like. Or stroll around Swanthorpe, bringing Charlotte down to the river to see the swans, mallards, and coots that paddled in the current. Better yet, maybe she would wander around until she found her husband, and surreptitiously watch him through increasingly appreciative eyes. The possibilities were endless.

With Charlotte in her arms, she headed downstairs, pausing at a window to look outside. It was a delightful spring day, with high, fluffy clouds drifting across a sky of hazy blue and a thousand daisies and dandelions scattered across the back lawn. As she came down the stairs and entered the sitting room, she was startled to see a rather thin young woman on her hands and knees before the hearth, shoveling old coals into a cast-iron bucket. The girl looked up as Juliet entered the room, lunged to her feet, and bobbed a quick curtsy.

"M'loidy!"

Juliet was taken aback. Not only was she surprised to find a stranger in her home, she was not, and would never be, used to being addressed as "my lady."

"I'm sorry—I don't think we've been introduced," she said, eyeing the girl in some confusion.

"Beggin' yer pardon, mum. Moi name's Becky. The master said Oi could come and be yer maid, 'e did. Hope ye don't mind. Oi've brought ye a breakfast straight from the manor 'ouse, Oi 'ave—cold gammon wi' some bread and butter and a pitcher of fresh milk, since Oi knew ye wouldn't 'ave anythin' in." The girl jerked her head, bird like, toward the table. "It's all roight there waitin' for ye, it is."

"That's very kind of you," Juliet said, her face flaming as she saw the table and thought of what she and Gareth had done on it not twenty-four hours past. Thank God Becky could not read her thoughts! She sat down and poured herself a mug of milk, her stomach rumbling at sight of the food. "Won't you join me?"

Becky eyed the tray with undisguised longing, then quickly shook her head.

"Oh, no, mum, Oi couldn't."

"Go on," Juliet said, clandestinely eying the girl's bony hands and too-thin frame. "Besides," she fibbed, "I can't eat it all."

With a nervous little shrug, Becky wiped her fingers on her skirts and selected a piece of ham. Juliet noted that she took the smallest one, as though she felt undeserving of any more than that. It took some urging to convince the girl to take a second slice, let alone a mug of milk, but by the time she did, Becky had relaxed, obviously thinking Juliet was someone she could trust.

"So tell me about Mr. Snelling," Juliet murmured, washing down her breakfast with sips of milk. "You said he sent you down?"

"That 'e did, mum. And 'tis glad of it Oi be, too. Oi worked up in the manor house, ye see, but the master, 'e said Oi was lazy and slothful, and 'e wanted to send me away. But Oi heard ye was comin' and knew ye'd 'ave yer 'ands full, what wi' a babe an' all, so Oi asked Snelling if Oi could stay on and work down 'ere for 'alf me pay. I didn't want to leave Swanthorpe, ye see." She blushed hotly and cupped her hand to the side of her mouth. "Oi've got me a feller 'ere."

Juliet grinned. "I guess that makes two of us!"

"Oh, blimey, Oi've seen *yer* man! Everyone at Swanthorpe's talking about 'im, they are, 'specially all the town girls who work 'ere. Ye'd best keep a close eye on 'im, lest one of 'em try to steal 'im away from ye!"

Juliet laughed. "Oh, Becky," she said, shaking her head. "I'm so glad you're here. I've been a little homesick, and . . . well, it's nice to have someone to talk to. I don't know anyone here, I'm afraid, and I feel like such an outsider, coming from partway across the world and all. . . ."

"Ah, ye'll soon foind that people is the same no matter where ye go," Becky returned with quiet country wisdom. "And Oi knows what it's loike to be alone and not knowin' no-one. Tell ye what. Snelling always schedules a big foight for Froiday noights, down at the County 'all in the Market Place. That's tonoight, it is. All the foine folks from Oxford'll come down for it, and it'll be as fun and loively as a country fair. We can get me sister Bonnie to look after yer babe; she's got three of 'er own. 'Ow 'bout you and Oi go down together and watch?"

"Well, I—"

"It'll be great fun. I hear Bull O'Rourke's foighting, and 'e always draws a big crowd, 'e does. Ever 'ear of Bull? Strapping Oirish farmer, 'e is—'ands the soize of buckets an' arms so big, they split 'is shirt when 'e moves. 'Twill be a good match, I think—Bull's never lost a foight yet. What do ye say, eh?"

"I'm not much for blood sports," Juliet said, hesitating.

"Oh, ye can just close yer eyes if ye don't want to watch. Any'ow, the crowd'll be so thick and rowdy, we probably won't be able to get near the ring, let alone see anythin'."

"Well . . ." Juliet could think of twenty other things she'd rather be doing tonight, but Gareth *had* said he might not be home until late. What else was there to do, really? Besides, it would do her good to get out of the house. "All right, you've talked me into it," she finally said. "What time should I be ready?"

He had not told her, of course.

Had not told her what he and the others who worked for Snelling would be doing for most of the morning in this barn floored with hay, its leather bags stuffed with sawdust swinging from ropes hung from the rafters. Had not told her because he'd known she'd be angry with him, and what with the way she'd been looking at him lately—her eyes soft and almost adoring—Gareth could not stand the thought of bringing on either her disapproval or ire.

Besides, she did not have to know. There was no *need* for her to know, really. It was simply a way to earn a living—more base than some, more noble than others—and wasn't an income all that mattered at this point?

Of course it was. For the first time in his life, he was actually earning money instead of having it handed to him for no other reason than the fact that his brother was one of the five wealthiest men in England. For the first time in his life—excepting his rescue of the stagecoach passengers and that of Juliet and Charlotte by way of a wedding ring—he actually felt good about himself. Proud of himself. He was not relying on someone else to support him. He was not searching for some new way to chase away the endless boredom of his life or making a spectacle of himself for the amusement of others or getting himself into trouble with the knowledge that Lucien would bail him out. With his own brain and hands, he was supporting his wife and his daughter—the two people he loved most in the world.

*The two people he loved most in the world.*

Ah, there was no question about *that*. He'd adored his little Charlie-girl from the moment he first met her and saw his brother's blue eyes peering up at him from beneath those thick de Montforte lashes. And as for Juliet, beautiful, dark-haired Juliet with the creamy-smooth skin and loving hands and long, luscious legs . . .

He grinned like a fool. He was the luckiest man in England, and, by God, he wasn't going to jeopardize things by telling her what Snelling had *really* hired him to do!

With a cheerful farewell to the others, he left the barn bare chested, his shirt slung over bulging shoulders that were still damp with sweat. His muscles tingled and sang after his vigorous exercise, and everything inside of him felt alive and eager and free. He knew he was walking with a bit of a swagger; he could not help it. He was on top of the world, and if he proved himself tonight, Snelling, the bastard, had promised to give him half of the proceeds the fight brought in.

*'Sdeath, I just hope Lucien doesn't get wind of this.*

That would be almost as bad as if Juliet found out. Eventually she would, of course—and possibly quite soon—but he would deal with that when it happened.

*Aren't you afraid of the sort of reputation your fighting will bring down on your family, yourself, and Juliet?*

No, no, and, of course, yes.

But he would deal with *that* later, too.

Through the trees, he could just see the pink brick of Swanthorpe Manor and, some distance beyond, the dower house itself. And there, off to his right, the cold waters of the Thames beckoned, swelling against its clay banks, glittering in the sunshine.

Gareth paused. The sun was warm on his bare shoulders; the river looked cool and smooth and inviting. And, 'sdeath, he couldn't go home looking—and smelling—as though he'd just spent a day laboring in the fields, now, could he?

She might know. She might *ask*. And he really didn't want to lie to her. He had misled her a little, yes—but he wouldn't actually lie to her.

Whistling happily, Gareth turned and strode back across the meadow, heading away from the houses and toward the riverbank. Around him, wild dog rose was still in bloom. Buttercups, dandelions, and daisies sprang up in the grasses through which he strode, and sunshine turned the ivy that hugged the trees to a brilliant, shining green. He felt happy to be alive. Happy with his lot in life. As he neared the Mill Stream that branched out from the river, the ground beneath his feet grew dark and richly fertile, and not for the first time that day—that hour, even—he envied Snelling his fine estate with a passion that bordered on lust.

God, how he wished it were his own.

But such empty dreams would get him nowhere. If he thought about how he much he loathed Snelling—and coveted what he had—it would only spoil his exceedingly good mood. Besides, he thought cockily, *he* had Juliet and Charlotte; they were more valuable to him than a hundred Swanthorpes.

He found the footpath and crossed the bridge that spanned the Mill Stream, pausing atop it for a moment to watch a swan and her downy cygnets in the waters below. Then he continued across the springy turf to the banks of the river itself.

As he'd expected, no one was around. Nothing but a robin in a nearby hawthorn and a few mallards eyeing him from halfway out in the river.

He tossed his shirt over a low-hanging branch, removed his boots and stepped out of his breeches. Flexing his muscles, he waded into the icy river, gasping at the bracing shock of it against his skin. His teeth chattered. His legs went numb. And then he dived beneath the surface, letting the water wash away all evidence of his morning toils.

Ah, yes. Life was indeed grand.

# 27

**B**ecky hadn't exaggerated about the far-reaching popularity of Snelling's fights, Juliet thought as they walked through the fields and into Abingdon early that evening. Foot, carriage, and horse traffic were all converging on the center of town from all directions. Drivers shouted at each other to make way. Dogs ran loose, barking, among hurrying pedestrians, through the legs of prancing horses, in and around carriage wheels. Vendors stood on the street corners selling ale, pastries, and other refreshments, and the very air held a festive ambience.

"What a crowd!" Juliet exclaimed, looking around her.

"Bull always draws 'em," Becky said, her voice echoing in a medieval archway as she led Juliet through a row of ancient buildings bordering the Mill Stream. "'E ain't never been beat, Bull 'asn't, and you won't foind a stronger bloke in Berkshire. Why, once Snelling 'itched 'im up to an ox and made each of 'em pull against the other—Bull's so strong the animal couldn't budge 'im!"

"Surely no human is *that* strong!"

"Most of us wonder if Bull even *is* 'uman!"

Juliet merely laughed and followed Becky out of the medieval buildings onto Thames Street, where the rushing waters of the mill all but drowned out the sounds of the festivities. Caught up in the excitement around her, she was feeling increasingly happy and free of the cares of her world. She had said her final good-bye to Charles, releasing him from her heart. And, aside from Gareth's sister, how long had it been since she'd spent time with a female friend? She didn't even want to think about the answer. Motherhood had been a full-time occupation, and grief for Charles had robbed her of any desire to do anything fun. But she was feeling more like her old self these days, thanks to Gareth.

Dear, dear Gareth.

Her gaze softened as she thought of him. She hadn't seen much of him that day, save for a brief few minutes when he'd dropped by the dower house late that afternoon. She and Becky had been on their hands and knees scrubbing the kitchen floor when he'd come in with an ear-to-ear grin, his skin glowing and his hair damp, unruly, and deliciously tousled. With him around, getting any work done had been impossible. He'd been munching an apple, prowling the kitchen like a restless cat, and driving Juliet insane with his playful feints to her face, to the wall, to the leg of a chair.

"Would you *stop?*" she'd finally cried, looking up at him and laughing as she'd swatted him away.

"Can't," he'd said and, winking at Becky, leaned down and kissed Juliet fully on the lips. He'd tasted of sweet apples and sunshine, and she'd felt a rush of desire for him that had made her wish Becky was anywhere but in their kitchen.

"What's got *you* in such a good mood?" she'd managed after he finally broke the kiss and straightened up, leaving her breathless and flushed, her hand to her suddenly pounding heart.

"Oh, nothing." Another playful feint to her shoulder. "Nothing at all, dearest!"

"The way you're acting, one might think *you* were going to the fight tonight."

His eyebrows had risen, and then he'd laughed, loudly. "Well, maybe I am," he'd said, cheerfully; then, saluting her with his apple, he'd swung back out the door.

Juliet had watched him as he crossed the lawn and headed toward the manor house, his stride cocky and giving him the appearance of owning the world. When she'd turned back to Becky, the other girl was simply sitting back on her heels and shaking her head in amusement. "Men! They just never grow up, do they?"

"Do you know, Becky . . . I hope that one never does. He can make me laugh when all I want to do is cry. He can make me see the good in a situation when all I see is the bad. He knows when life should be taken seriously—and when it shouldn't. He's delightful and funny and clever—and not afraid to make a total cake of himself." She had smiled and given a little sigh. "No, I never want him to grow up . . . not if it means seeing him change into something other than what he currently is."

Becky had sat back on her haunches, a sly look on her face as she regarded Juliet.

"What?"

"Yer love for 'im is so obvious. 'Tis sweet to see, it is!"

"Becky!"

The girl, still grinning, had shrugged. "Ye can't hide it, ye know. And Oi'll wager yer man—charmin', kind, an' 'andsome as 'e is—is a real easy one to love."

"Well yes, he is, but . . . it's just that—" Juliet had turned as pink as Swanthorpe's brick and looked away, suddenly flustered. "I guess it's just rather difficult to admit my feelings, even to myself."

But Becky had merely laughed knowingly. "'Well,

then, maybe ye'd *better* admit 'em, 'cause it's plain that yer man's roight in love with *you*, 'e is!"

"Becky, you're embarrassing me!" Juliet had said, and the girl had merely chuckled before they'd gone back to scrubbing the floor. Mercifully, Becky had said no more about the subject, but the conversation had weighed heavily on Juliet's mind the rest of the afternoon, just as it weighed on her now as the two of them made their way down Thames Street, Becky tossing a few crumbs of bread to the ducks that paddled in the Mill Stream's current.

*Yer love for 'im is so obvious.*

She considered their marriage. He was fun loving and larkish. She was serious and pragmatic. He was reckless and impulsive and loved to put on a show. She was cautious and reserved and did not welcome undue attention. He was an aristocrat who'd never done a day's work in his life. She was a provincial who balked at the very thought of idle hands. What on earth did they really have in common?

Nothing.

Everything.

After Charles had died, she had thought the sun would never shine on her life again. But it had. By bringing Gareth—a man who, she now realized, fit all her crooked edges like two pieces of wood joined together in perfect dovetail; a man who could make her laugh like Charles had never done, a man who might make her happier than Charles could ever have dreamed. Charles, with his dignified polish, would have been shocked if called upon to behave as Gareth was wont to do. Charles had been too serious, too full of inhibiting maturity—and the two of them probably would, in time, have become bored with each other.

She gazed over the bridge, over Abingdon's rooftops, and up at the high, orange-tinted clouds. One thing was sure about the Wild One: She would *never* become bored with him. Not today, not tomorrow, not in a million years.

*Purple parts!* she thought with a little laugh.

"What's so funny, eh?" Becky asked as they joined the traffic heading up Bridge Street. Around them buildings rose, the sun's last rays slanting off the tiled roof of a coaching inn on their right, shadowing the warm brick and stone structures on their left.

"Oh, nothing. . . . I was just thinking about something my husband did, that's all."

"Think of 'im a lot, don't ye?"

"Oh, go on with you!" Juliet said, laughing. Becky laughed, too, chattering on about her own man, Jack, and pointing out various townsfolk that she knew. The street climbed and curved, and there, dominating the Market Place, was the County Hall, a tall, open structure of golden stone, its stone flooring a few steps higher than street level and creating a sort of open-air theater for the crowds that surrounded it. Someone had erected a ring of rope in the center of this open arena where several people, including Snelling, were milling about.

"So, does Snelling make his living promoting fights?" Juliet asked.

"'E doesn't need foights to make a livin'. Swanthorpe brings in all the blunt 'e could ever know what to do with, it does. No, 'e does this because 'e loikes 'ob-nobbing with 'is betters. That's all it is. Foights attract important people—nobs, statesmen, that sort. Snellin', 'e ain't no better than the rest of us, but by rubbin' elbows with 'is betters, wearin' fancy clothes, and apin' manners 'e's got no business apin', it allows 'im to pretend to be somethink 'e's not."

"You don't like Snelling, then."

"Nobody 'ereabouts does. Wouldn't trust 'im as far as Oi could throw 'im, Oi wouldn't. Oh, look! There's Bull O'Rourke!" Becky stood on tiptoe and tried to point over a hundred heads. "Can ye see 'im, Juliet?"

Juliet craned her neck until she could just see the ring that had been set up for the fight. It wasn't hard to identify Bull O'Rourke. She had never seen an uglier man in her life. His nose was broken, his lips were huge, his brow looked like a ledge of granite, his hair was a shorn orange rug. But his shoulders were what commanded the eye, for they dominated his body as surely as his lips did his face.

"My goodness, I do pity the man who has to fight him," Juliet murmured, shuddering. "You weren't joking when you said he had hands the size of buckets!"

"Knows 'ow to use 'em, too," Becky said. "Bones crack loike plaster beneath Bull's fists, they do!"

"Indeed," added a well-dressed man in the crowd who'd been breathing down Juliet's neck in his eagerness to see the stage. "I was here last summer when he took on Savage Sean. You remember that match, eh Jem?"

"How could I forget?" answered a neighboring gentleman, crushed like a kipper between the first man and the surrounding crowd. "Called himself the Pride of Ireland, but Bull felled him like an ax to a tree. Blinded him in the third round, if I remember right."

"Second."

"Aye, you're correct, second. 'Twas the end of *that* match, I daresay."

"*And* of Savage Sean's fighting days!"

"Anyone know who'll be taking Bull's punishment tonight?"

"Don't know. Some newcomer, I hear. Supposed to be good."

"How good?"

"Snelling's put it about that he beat Joe Lumford."

"Psaw! Lumford's the London champion; he's

never been beat. Snelling's making up stories to make the betting hotter, that's all. This newcomer? Bull'll cut him to ribbons in less than five minutes."

"Ha, I'll up you a guinea that he'll do it in three!"

Guffaws broke out all around, and for some strange reason she couldn't fathom, Juliet felt suddenly uneasy.

Then Snelling was raising his hands and calling for quiet, strutting before the crowd with the easy confidence of a seasoned actor as Bull's second—for pugilism was not unlike dueling in that respect— joined the prize-fighter. Snelling handed the second a large flask, and, laughing, the man passed it on to Bull, who promptly tipped it to his lips and guzzled heartily before tossing the vessel out into the audience. There was a mad scramble as some fifty people tried to catch it, and several men went down, fists flying as they fought each other for the prize.

A small roar went up as Snelling, turning to the shadows, called for Bull's opponent to come out on the stage.

"And now, may I introduce to you, tonight's challenger . . . all the way from the Lambourn Downs, it's *the Wild One!*"

The blood drained from Juliet's face.

No. It couldn't be.

But it was—

*Gareth.*

For a moment she couldn't move, couldn't breathe, could only stand there trying to absorb what she was seeing as the crowds jostled her to and fro in their haste for a better look at O'Rourke's challenger. Shocked into numbness, she watched her husband walk once across the stage and then back again, grinning confidently, as though telling this scornful crowd he'd soon put to rest their jeers.

"Who the hell is he?" complained the gentleman just behind Juliet in obvious disappointment.

"Don't know, never heard of him. But I'll tell you this: Bull's going to put him to sleep by the end of the first round, I'll bet you a crown on it!"

"If he lasts that long!"

"Dear God," Juliet murmured, the nightmare becoming reality as the two pugilists began stripping off their shirts and sizing each other up from across the ring. She could not watch any more. Could not stand there and see Gareth hurt and humiliated and possibly—probably, by the look of Bull—killed. Was this his so-called job? *Was this how he planned to support them?*

Feeling sick, feeling betrayed, she spun on her heel and tried to shove her way back through the milling masses, earning curses, lecherous leers, and a few nasty pinches on her bottom in her haste to escape.

Becky was right behind her. "Juliet! Oi swear, Oi didn't know!"

"He deliberately misled me!"

"What are ye talking about?"

"He let me believe that Snelling had hired him to fight with swords, not his *fists!*"

Becky stared at her blankly.

"He's going to get himself killed! Oh, forgive me, Becky, I cannot stay and witness this, I just can't, it'll be the end of me!"

"Juliet! *Juliet!*"

And then Becky's voice was drowned beneath the sudden frenzied roar of the crowd as the first blows were exchanged. Blindly pushing people aside in her haste to get away, their cheers and yells ringing in her head, Juliet fought to reach open road and once there, ran for all she was worth.

She charged down Bridge Street, through the meadows and fields that bordered the river, and over the footbridge that spanned the Mill Stream. She raced past Swanthorpe Manor, tore across the lawns, and flew into the dower house. It was shadowy inside, empty and eerily quiet. She could hear the crazed roaring of the crowd a mile away, and, with a little sob, she collapsed into a corner, clapping her hands over her ears to block it out even as her eyes frantically sought out ink pot, pen and paper:

*Your Grace,*

*You must forgive my shaky hand, but as I pen these words, your brother, who has taken a position as a pugilist for Jonathan Snelling, is engaged in a boxing match which has drawn the better half of Berkshire and Oxfordshire. Please come quickly, Your Grace. We are at Swanthorpe Manor, which, as you know, is in Abingdon-on-Thames.*

*Godspeed,*

*Juliet de Montforte*

She ran back out the door and up the steps of the manor house, where she persuaded a footman, just coming off duty, to deliver the note. Ten minutes later, it was on its way south toward Ravenscombe—and the only man Juliet knew who could put a swift end to this nonsense in which Gareth had embroiled them.

# 28

Gareth's head was reeling as, supported by Snelling on one side and Woodford, his second, on the other, he stumbled home through the darkened fields.

He was not hurt. He was not even exhausted. He was drunk on victory—and nearly half a bottle of celebratory champagne. Indeed, aside from some bruising high on his left side, where O'Rourke had caught him a real thumper before he could block the blow, he was unmarked. Sore and a little tender in a few places, but unmarked. It was a blessing, really. Unless Juliet had heard about the fight from someone at Swanthorpe, she'd have no reason to suspect he had been up to anything out of the ordinary. . . .

"You'll be the new English champion if you continue on as you did tonight," Snelling gushed, laughing in Gareth's face. 'Sdeath, what he wouldn't give to send his fist crashing into *that* obnoxious visage; at least it would give him some real satisfaction, which he hadn't got from this evening's match, ending as it had before it even seemed to begin. "Nobody's ever taken O'Rourke down, *ever*—let alone as quickly as you did! Bloody hell, I thought that crowd was going to go crazy for wanting their money back."

"Aye, you were something," grunted Woodford,

a solid, bandy-legged farmer who also fought occasionally for Snelling. "Thirty-five seconds into the third round and *bang*, that was it for ol' Bull!"

Gareth frowned and shook his head, trying to clear it of champagne. Instead, the movement dizzied him and he stumbled, nearly bringing both other men down with him. "I don't understand what all the fuss is over your man Bull," he mused, recovering his balance. "I'd go to hit him, and he was so slow about blocking my blows, it was like fighting a man whose hand was tied behind his back."

"Oh, the big ones are like that," Snelling explained. "All that brawn and heavy muscle, you know—takes time to get it moving, eh, Woodford?"

"Oh, absolutely."

"Just didn't seem right," Gareth persisted. "'Sdeath, I almost felt bad every time I hit the fellow. . . ."

"Now, don't you start thinking that way, I'll not have you going all soft on me! You're going to be *great*, Gareth. You're going to be famous, I can tell you that right now—"

"Christ," Gareth swore, thinking of what Lucien's reaction would be when *he* heard about all this. . . .

"You're going to be drawing crowds all the way from London, I tell you!"

"Look, I don't *want* to be famous, I just want to make enough money to support my family, all right?"

"You keep fighting, my boy, and you'll make enough money to put diamonds around your wife's neck and a tiara atop her head!"

"Aye, he's not as big and beefy as some, but he sure can hit," Woodford babbled. "I'd like to see him against Lumford in a staged match."

"*I'd* like to see him against Nails Fleming!"

"No, we've got to pit him against the Butcher. Now, *that'll* be a good fight. . . ."

Their prattle dissolved into a confusing jumble of words around him that Gareth didn't even try to keep up with. He cursed himself for drinking so much champagne. He felt sick and unfocused and unsteady. Hard to believe there'd ever been a time he'd *enjoyed* this feeling. Something was not right about tonight, like an ugly stench seeping from a shallow grave, and he couldn't quite put his finger on it. Something that had to do with the glazed look in Bull's eyes, his sluggish punches and slow reaction time. . . . Gareth shook his head, cursing beneath his breath. It would be nice if his brain was on dry land, instead of floating in a sea of champagne bubbles.

He wanted, needed, to *think*.

"Look," he muttered, "you can plan all you want, Snelling, but you'll not get any more fights out of me until I see my share from tonight."

"Back at the house, my boy, back at the house! You just be patient, now—"

"Patience has nothing to do with it. And while we're on the subject, I want the cracked window in our bedroom replaced. There's a cold draft coming in, and we have a baby to think of."

Snelling clapped Gareth expansively across the back. "Now, listen here, my good fellow, I don't want you worrying yourself about windows; I want you to start training for next week's match against—"

Gareth lurched to a stop and swung around to face his employer. "I will tell you once, Snelling, and only once. *I want the window fixed.* By tomorrow afternoon. Is that understood?"

Snelling's smile froze; he removed his hand from Gareth's back, his eyes narrowing, his lips thinning, and an ugly look coming over his face. He opened his mouth to retort; then, thinking better of it, he relaxed, breaking out a huge, beaming grin that didn't fool Gareth in the least. Snelling didn't like him, but Gareth didn't give a damn; the feeling was mutual.

"For you, my lord, anything," Snelling said tightly. "You want the window fixed, I'll fix it. You want your earnings now, you'll have them. Just ready yourself for next week's match, that's all I ask."

And then the trio continued walking, all three men very silent now.

*Sod you, you bastard,* Gareth thought.

The lights of Swanthorpe Manor blazed through the trees up ahead. Just looking at the big house, Gareth felt the customary stab of longing. *That* was where his Juliet and little Charlotte deserved to be, not in a tiny dower house with shabby curtains, damp rising up the walls, and, yes, an awful cracked window that had made the room so cold the night before that they'd brought Charlotte into bed with them. And as Snelling led him inside, and Gareth stood in Snelling's richly appointed parlor in a strange reversal of roles while his employer counted out his earnings, the longing only intensified until it felt like something was gnawing at the chambers of his heart.

*I want this house. I want this estate. I want it so badly I can taste it.*

And why not? A de Montforte had built it. A de Montforte had always lived here, cared for it, loved it. Now it belonged to a man who was not, and would never be, its rightful owner, and the house seemed to strain toward Gareth like a faithful dog whose leash was suddenly held by a stranger.

*If it were mine, I would clear this room of all these foolish statues, paint the walls happy colors like sunny yellow and heather pink and sky blue, put a thick rug on the floor, and make it my Charlie-girl's. This could be her very own play area. This could be where she'd learn to take her first steps, tumble with the puppies I would get for her, have her first tea party. Oh, if only this house were ours. . . .*

"Here you are, Gareth," said Snelling, dropping a heavy leather pouch into his outstretched hand. "It's all there. Count it if you want."

Gareth didn't bother. If it wasn't all there, he knew where to find Snelling. He pocketed the pouch, and through the hazy blur of champagne that still fogged his head it occurred to him that Snelling was no longer preceding his name with his title. That bothered him. He wasn't a snob; he was simply not comfortable with Snelling's over-the-top attempt at easy friendship with him. It annoyed him, put his hackles up, set his teeth on edge. He considered making an issue over it but decided he'd irritated Snelling enough these last few minutes. Maybe it would be best to let it go.

For now.

Moments later he was walking unsteadily across the lawn, heading for the dower house. It was dark, save for a glow in a downstairs window.

*She's waiting up for me, bless her.*

He gulped several deep breaths of night air to clear his head, mounted the steps and pushed open the door.

"Juliet?"

It took him a moment to find her in the shadowy gloom. She was sitting in a chair by the cold hearth, still and silent. At the sound of his voice, she turned her head in a manner that suggested the effort had cost her all the energy she had.

"So, you survived after all," she said woodenly.

He flinched. "You . . . know about it, then."

"I was *there*."

*Oh, hell.* He gulped and grinned, trying to take the heat off himself. "I was pretty good, don't you think?"

"Good? I wouldn't know. I left as soon as I saw who it was that Bull O'Rourke was fighting."

"Why?"

"Why do you *think*? Because I didn't want to see you hurt, that's why."

"Now, Juliet. Do you have so little faith in me that you think I cannot hold my own in a simple boxing match?"

"A simple boxing match? Gareth, the man was built like a . . . like a medieval fortress!"

"So was that bloke at Mrs. Bottomley's, but you didn't seem to mind that."

"*Gareth.*" She turned her level stare upon him, and he saw the hurt in her eyes, the betrayal, the sorrow. "Your abilities are not the issue here—and you know it."

A bucket of ice water thrown over his head wouldn't have sobered him faster. A guilty heat spread over his cheeks, and he kicked at a knothole in the wooden floorboards, staring at his foot and trying to figure out what to say, what to do, how to make amends. When he looked up, she was still gazing at him. Waiting.

"I am sorry, Juliet."

She looked away, blinking, as though his quiet apology had brought tears to her eyes.

"I should have told you," he added lamely. "I was wrong."

"Yes, Gareth, you should have told me. Why didn't you?"

Sighing, he crossed the room and sank to his knees on the floor beside her chair. Her hand rested on the chair's arm, and he picked it up, kissed it, and laid it gently against his heart. "Because I knew you'd be worried. And . . . well, you have enough to worry about, dearest. That's why I didn't tell you."

"I thought you were going to teach fencing, do an

occasional swordplay exhibit at a country fair or something. . . ."

"That's what I thought, too. But when I came here last week to arrange things with Snelling, he asked me if I'd like to do some boxing instead, since I was so handy against Lumford back at the brothel." He shrugged. "I was desperate, Juliet. We were hard up, had no place to go, and it seemed like the only thing to do." He squeezed her unresponsive hand and pressed her palm to his cheek, his eyes imploring as he gazed up at her. "Please forgive me, Juliet. I only wanted to take care of you and Charlotte. That's all I want."

She shook her head, sadly, and smoothed the tumbled-down hair off his brow. "How are you going to care for us, Gareth, if you get hurt? Killed?"

"I could get hurt or killed falling off my horse."

"You no longer have a horse to fall off."

"Juliet, please. I need your support, your encouragement—not your condemnation. Don't you understand how important this is to me?" He held her knuckles against his mouth and gently kissed each finger. "For the first time in my life, I've actually *earned* money instead of having it handed to me. *I* earned it, Juliet—with my own two hands. Me: lazy, useless, good-for-nothing Gareth, actually earning money—"

"Stop it!" she cried angrily, her eyes suddenly glinting with unshed tears. "You're not useless, were never useless."

"Yes, I was, but I shan't be any longer." Still kneeling beside her, he eagerly fished in his pocket, found the money pouch, and placed it triumphantly in her palm. "Here, open it up. Have a look. Wait until you see how much Snelling paid me just for tonight's scuffle."

She shook her head and handed it back without even opening it. "Oh, Gareth . . ."

"Oh, Juliet," he mimicked, making a face at her.

She looked away, in no mood for his attempt at humor.

He bowed his head, feeling suddenly deflated and confused. Hurt.

The silence was nearly unbearable.

"You're not useless." she finally said, reaching down to tousle his hair. Then, with a forced little smile, she added, "But I still want to strangle you."

"I know."

"You ever keep anything from me again, Gareth, and I just might."

"I'll not keep anything from you ever again. I swear it."

Another long moment of silence passed, heavy and awkward.

Finally she spoke. "Are you hurt?" she asked in a small voice.

"No."

Her eyes told him she didn't believe him. "Good at ducking punches, then, I suppose . . . ?"

"My dear Juliet, any fellow who ducks or shifts to avoid an honest punch is cowardly and unmanly. I never *duck*."

"So what *do* you do then?"

"Why, block them with my arm." He made a fist and raised his arm to demonstrate. "Like this."

"I see." She paused. "Does . . . your arm hurt, then?"

He laughed, relief breaking over him at her unspoken—and, he thought ruefully, undeserved—forgiveness. "Oh, it hurts. But here"—he stretched his arm out toward her—"if you kiss it, I'm sure it will feel immediately better."

She gave a watery smile and touched her lips to his forearm. Then she turned slightly in her chair and, watching him in the meager light, laid the flat of her hand against his cheekbones, his jaw, his temples. He knew she was feeling for swelling, looking for injury, and he saw her shoulders settle with relief when her search turned up nothing out of the ordinary.

She was quiet for a moment. "Gareth . . . when I got home this evening, I was . . . very upset. I have something to confess to you, as well. Something I know you're not going to like."

"And what is that, my love?"

She faced him squarely. "I sent a message to Lucien."

He caught her hand, which rested against his temple. "You *what?*"

"I sent a message to Lucien, asking him to come here immediately."

For a moment he stared at her, unable to believe what he was hearing, what she had done.

"Juliet—how *could* you?"

"I'm sorry, Gareth. I was sick with worry about you, and I acted rashly. I regret it now."

He swore beneath his breath and lunged to his feet, driving his fist against his brow as he stalked across the room. "I suppose you thought Lucien could just ride in here, make everything better, and then take us home?"

She gave an embarrassed little shrug. "Something like that."

"I'm not going back. You go, take Charlotte if you wish, but, by God and the devil, *I* am not going!"

They faced each other from across the room, his eyes blazing with hurt, hers silently apologetic, neither moving. Then, with a sigh, she rose from the chair, her skirts rustling as she crossed the floor to where he stood, sidling close to him and laying her cheek against his heart. "Then I'm not going back either, Gareth." She put her arms around him and stared at the flickering candle. "If you want to stay here and prove something to yourself, to the world,

I'll stand by you. If you want to fight for Snelling, I'll bite my tongue and pick up the pieces when you get hurt. I don't like what you're doing, I'm going to worry myself sick over it—but if this is what you must do, I won't leave you."

He hesitated a moment. "Aren't you worried about what people will say?"

"The opinions of Perry's mother and others like her don't concern me. My only concern, Gareth, is my daughter." She held her hand against his chest. "Please don't get yourself killed."

"Or you'll never forgive me."

"Or I'll never forgive you."

His anger faded as quickly as it had come. He pulled her slight body against him and rested his cheek on the crown of her head, grateful for her reluctant support, yet already anticipating the repercussions of her actions. *Lucien.* Bloody hell. That was *all* he needed. But he really couldn't blame her for what she had done, couldn't be angry with her—especially after she'd not only forgiven him for misleading her about the fighting, but had just pledged to tough it out with him when she could so easily go back to Blackheath and Lucien's more-than-capable protection.

"Juliet?"

"Gareth?" she mimicked, in a hopeful little voice.

They stared at each other, their lips twitching.

"Ah, the devil," he muttered, laughing, and, bending his head, claimed the parted lips turned so eagerly up to his own.

# 29

**D**awn.

Juliet was snuggled cozily against her husband's chest, her head pillowed in the cup of his shoulder, his arm cradling her body close to his, when something penetrated her slumber and nudged her awake. Blearily, she opened her eyes. In the early-morning stillness she could hear a commotion off in the direction of the manor house.

She didn't need to be a fortune teller to know what it was all about.

*Lucien had arrived.*

She lifted her head. Gareth, on his back, was sound asleep and snoring lightly, his eyelids dancing slightly in a dream. He felt warm and sleepy and delicious, and Juliet hated to wake him.

But the commotion was coming closer. She could hear a servant's voice raised in protest, Snelling's wheedling attempts to placate—

And the duke.

"Stand in my path, Snelling, and I promise you my horse will take great pleasure in walking over you. Now, *bugger off*."

"Really, Your Grace, don't you think it's just a *little* bit early to go disturbing the lad, especially after he fought so well last night?"

"Your sniveling protests are beginning to irritate

311

me beyond the restraints of my patience. I shall see my brother, and I shall see him *now*."

"But Y-Your Grace, he's *working* for me. . . ."

"*Not any more, he's not!*"

They were just outside the dower house now. On the steps. In the next second, the Duke of Blackheath would be pounding the door down.

"Gareth!" Juliet shook his shoulder, the powerful muscles wonderfully sculpted by the soft, buttery light of morning. "Gareth, wake up—Lucien's here."

"Hmmm?" He opened his eyes, staring blankly at the ceiling for a moment. Then the pounding downstairs started, and he flung a hand across his brow, wincing with each loud bang. "Oh bloody hell, my aching head. . . ."

"Gareth, you've *got* to see him. He's going to break the door down if you don't."

But the duke was not so barbaric as all that. As Gareth crawled wearily from the bed, scowling and rubbing his bloodshot eyes, they both heard Lucien's terse orders.

"Bring me the key, Snelling."

"'Sdeath," Gareth swore and pulled on his breeches. He went to the window and flung it wide. "For God's sake, Lucien, do you know what time it is?" he shouted.

"Get down here *now*, Gareth!"

"Sod off—I'm going back to sleep."

And with that, Gareth yanked the window shut and sank down on the bed, elbows on his knees as he rubbed his aching temples.

Juliet sat beside him, curved an arm around his shoulders, and pulled him unresistingly close. She kissed his ear, the side of his head, the silky, sleep-mussed hair that hung over his brow. "Go; get it over with," she said quietly, sliding a hand across his chest and reveling in its breadth and strength as she rubbed it lightly. "You'll feel better afterward."

"Mmmmm . . ." He was kissing her back, now, his lips making trails of fire all down the side of her neck. "You think so, do you?"

"I do." She smiled and laid her cheek against his. "Besides, you know he's not going to go away. He's not going to leave you alone until he's satisfied that you're all right. So go down there, confront him, prove to him he has no reason to fear for you. He's your brother, Gareth. He's here because he loves you—not because he wants to make your life miserable."

"He's here because he's a right controlling bastard, Juliet. Nothing more."

"No, Gareth. *He's here because he's your brother and he loves you.*"

He sat there beside her for a long moment, a hundred emotions playing over his face. Then, with a heavy sigh, he slid his palms up over his cheeks, blinked, and got to his feet. His shirt was draped across the back of a chair. When he picked it up and began to put it on, the big purple bruise visible beneath his right arm caused Juliet to wince as though it were her own. But he paid it no heed. He merely tucked the shirt into his breeches, raked a hand through his hair, and leaned down to kiss her. "Keep my side warm, all right?"

"Of course," she said softly.

And then, still in his bare feet, he opened the bedroom door and walked out.

*He's here because he loves you.*

Her words rang in Gareth's head with every step he took down the stairs, across the foyer, and to the front door. He paused for a moment before it, taking a deep, bracing breath. And then he unlocked it and pulled it open.

There was Lucien.

His brother stood on the lawn holding Armageddon's reins, his back toward the door. Snelling and the servant were halfway back to the manor house, gone, no doubt, to fetch the key. And then Lucien turned, and for the briefest of moments, Gareth saw the tiny worry lines that bracketed the duke's eyes, the tension around his mouth—until his brother's face hardened and those black eyes began to glitter with fury.

*He's here because he loves you.*

"Ah, there you are, my dear boy—"

"Don't patronize me," Gareth snapped. "I know why you're here. I know what you want from me, what you want to say to me. Well, I'm not leaving, Lucien. I'm not leaving, and neither is Juliet, and if you want me to go back to the castle, you're going to have to drag me off by the ear."

Lucien's brows rose. "What is this?"

"You heard me. For the first time in my life I am actually supporting myself, instead of living off your charity and holdings, and it feels good. Damned good. I won't have you take that away from me, Lucien."

"My dear boy. There is no need to be so defensive. I have no intention of taking anything away from you . . . but really, there *are* other ways to make money besides fighting."

"I have to start somewhere, don't I?"

Lucien cast a quick glance at Snelling's retreating back and led Armageddon over to the stairs atop which Gareth so defiantly stood. He stared harshly up at his younger brother and in an angry whisper, snapped, "You are a fool, Gareth. Do you know what sort of man you're dealing with?"

"I have a damned good idea."

"You have a damned good idea," the duke muttered in disgust. "Now, you listen to me and listen well. Snelling is dangerous. He's an opportunist and a cheat who will go to any lengths to make money, and he doesn't give a damn whom he crushes along the way. Do you understand me, Gareth?''

Gareth made a noise of scoffing dismissal. ''My, my, for a man who associates with kings, princes, statesmen, and other assorted bluebloods, you certainly do know a lot about the lowly Jonathan Snelling,'' he mocked.

''I only know what Fox told me last night. And *he*, as a barrister, is certainly in a position to know.''

Gareth shifted uncomfortably and looked away.

''Three years ago, Snelling was accused of fixing horse races,'' the duke continued heatedly. ''The only thing that saved him was his acquaintance with an influential member of the Jockey Club whom, it is widely believed, Snelling bribed to keep quiet. The year before *that* he was caught cheating at cards at his club in London. Sir Maudsley, who lost four thousand pounds to him that night, saw him do it and called him out on the spot. But the duel was never fought. And do you know why it wasn't fought, Gareth? Because Snelling never showed up for his dawn appointment. He quit the country and went to the Continent, hiding out there until Maudsley conveniently died!''

''So he's a coward with a tainted past,'' Gareth said, shrugging. He folded his arms and, curling his toes around the edge of the top step, leaned negligently against the doorframe. ''Who cares? He's paying me good money.''

''I'll pay you five times what he's giving you if you'll just come home where you belong.''

Gareth gave a bitter laugh. ''Why should I do that? Why should I—after all your taunts about how worthless I am, how I'm a good-for-nothing wastrel, how you're sick to death of having to rescue me from one scrape or another—why should I come back with you, only to suffer more of the same abuse?''

"Because," Lucien said gruffly, "I think you are in danger here, that's why."

"You're treating me like a child again, Lucien. I dislike it."

"Yes, I suppose I am . . . but, God help me, you were a damn sight easier to handle when you were acting like one."

Gareth raised his brows and stared at his brother. Lucien unflinchingly held his gaze, then looked out over the river, his jaw hard. An awkward silence hung between them. Finally, Gareth sighed and sat down on the top step, raking both hands through his hair. "I daresay that's the closest thing to a compliment I've yet to hear from you."

"Yes, well, keep at it the way you're going, and you just might get an apology out of me, as well."

"That'll be the bloody day."

Lucien, still holding Armageddon's reins, mounted the steps. He, too, sat down, the tails of his black frock just inches from his younger brother. The two sat together in silence for a long moment.

"I treated you abominably," Lucien finally said.

"Yeah, you were a right bastard."

"So will you come back to Blackheath?"

Gareth shook his head. "I cannot."

"Care to tell me why?"

"I'm determined to make a new life for myself. I know Juliet summoned you, though she regrets the rashness of doing so; I know you came here thinking you had to rescue me from yet another scrape. But those days are behind me, Lucien. I have a wife and baby to look after now. They have faith in me, believe in me when no one else thinks I'm worth the polish on my boots. I won't let them down."

"I see," the duke murmured, slowly. And then: "Would you like any assistance? I can send a servant to help—"

"No. I want to do this by myself. *Have* to do this

by myself. I don't need my big brother to help me."

"You sound very determined."

"I am."

"Well, then." The duke rose to his feet, unsmiling. "I guess there is no need for me to remain here." He walked down the steps, turned, and stood there for a moment looking up at Gareth. An odd look touched his stark features. Not quite admiration, not quite pensiveness, not quite worry—but maybe a combination of all three. "Just promise me one thing."

Gareth raised a brow in question.

"That if you get in over your head, you'll contact me." His black eyes stared levelly into Gareth's, and Gareth realized that for the first time his brother was treating him as an equal. "Sometimes it takes more courage for a man to put aside his pride and admit he needs help than to try to manage on his own."

"I shall remember that."

"You do that," Lucien said. Then, without a backward glance, he swung up on Armageddon, touched his heels to the stallion's sides, and rode off.

# 30

**B**y the time Gareth showed up at the barn to begin his morning's training, his head had long since ceased to ache.

This morning his sparring partner was Dickie Noring, a likeable, up-and-coming young lad whom Snelling had recruited during a trip to Bristol. Dickie had worked in and around ships for most of his eighteen years and was more of a brawler than a boxer. But he was strong, keeping Gareth on his toes as the two circled each other and traded punches. Gareth was enjoying himself, taking pleasure in his own fitness and strength. But try as he might, he could not keep his mind on what he was doing. Lucien's dawn visit kept replaying itself through his mind:

*You're treating me like a child again, Lucien. I dislike it.*

*Yes, I suppose I am . . . but, God help me, you were a damn sight easier to handle when you were acting like one.*

"Guard your face better than that, Dickie!" Snelling called out as Gareth's fist glanced off the other man's cheekbone.

"I'm trying, Mr. Snelling, but 'e's too quick for me!"

"Then you'll have to be quicker, won't you?"

Dickie lashed out with renewed vigor. Gareth neatly blocked and deflected the blow, getting in a good punch to Dickie's jaw.

"Son of a bitch! Blimey, ye're damn good for a nob ... where'd ye learn to fight like that, anyhow?"

"I have brothers," Gareth answered, grinning as he blocked another hit. He didn't bother mentioning that the village lads with whom he'd grown up had also taught him all they knew, and that he and the Den members often practiced their pugilistic skills simply for fun and exercise, and that he'd been thrown out of inns and alehouses because of his penchant for using his fists—because in his mind he wasn't watching Dickie. He was seeing Lucien sitting there beside him on the steps, treating him with wary respect and talking to him as an adult. He was seeing Lucien swallowing his pride to offer a half-baked apology—and then that strange look on his face, almost of admiration, as he'd prepared to leave. What had it taken his brother to *ask*, instead of demand, that he return to Blackheath? How much had it cost him to back down—probably against his better judgment—and let Gareth make his own decisions, right or wrong?

*He's giving me the chance to prove myself. I will not let him down.*

"All right, that's it for today," Snelling declared. "For you, anyhow, Dickie. Gareth? You're going to be up against Nails Fleming on Friday night. It's a big match, and I'm putting lots of blunt into promoting it, so make sure you train especially hard this week. If you do well against Nails, then we're going to pit you against the Butcher."

"The *Butcher*?" Gareth asked, grinning. "Is that his ring name or his trade?"

"Both. And believe you me, the name's well earned. I've just bought his contract, so he'll be coming in next week to fight for me."

*"The Butcher's coming 'ere?!?"* asked Dickie, in something like awe.

"He is, indeed. He's the best Scotland has to offer. And the way our Gareth is looking, I predict he'll soon be the best *England* has to offer. Oh, what a fight that will be: Scotland versus England, the Butcher against the Wild One!"

"Hell, I'm game," Gareth crowed happily, feinting toward Dickie. "Bring the mon on!"

Everyone laughed at his clowning attempt at a Scottish accent.

"Don't look so damned eager," Snelling said. "You have to fight your way through Nails first."

Nails, who also worked for Snelling, was sitting nearby on a bale of hay, thoughtfully watching Gareth. Gareth had seen him in practice against others in Snelling's stable; he was quick and energetic and as lean as a spike of iron—hence his name. He had a shaggy cap of coffee-colored hair, a receding chin, several missing teeth, and fists that were disproportionately large for the rest of his body. He looked at Gareth and grinned.

"Why don't I fight him now?" Gareth asked, amiably slapping Dickie across the back as the two ended their practice session. He was pulsing with energy, more determined than ever to prove himself.

"I don't want you fighting him now; it'll spoil all the suspense of Friday's match," Snelling said.

"We'll just do a little sparring," Gareth countered dismissively. "What do you say, Nails? Care to give it a go?"

"Beats sittin' 'ere watchin' *you* 'ave all the fun!"

"All right, all right," Snelling muttered, waving Nails toward Gareth. "Get in there, then. But don't kill each other, that's all I ask. Save it for Friday night."

Grinning, Nails stripped off his shirt, put up his fists, and waded through the hay to meet Gareth. He got in the first hit, neatly getting under Gareth's guard and catching him a glancing blow off the chin. Gareth managed to block the next, but Nails was quicker than a mosquito. He was clever, seasoned, and strong, and Gareth, concentrating so hard on what he was doing that he promptly forgot all about Lucien, knew he was going to have his hands full on Friday night.

Thank God.

Another easy conquest like Bull O'Rourke and he would die of boredom.

The reminders were everywhere.

Juliet saw posters promoting the match on the corner of the High Street, along East St. Helen's, in the Market Place, and along the Vineyard. When she and Becky went into town to do their shopping, people stopped and pointed her out in the street as "the Wild One's wife." Even more distressing, the betting had already started—and Nails was the ten-to-one favorite.

Such odds didn't dim her husband's enthusiasm for the upcoming match in the least. If anything, he trained even harder, talking excitedly about the money Snelling was paying him, anticipating the following week's fight with some fearsome Scot named "the Butcher," reveling in his newfound sense of worth.

It was that which kept Juliet from admitting how much all this fighting, and talk of it, upset her. She bit her tongue when he spoke excitedly about his upcoming Friday night match with Nails. She turned away when he came home and threw playful feints at the wall, the mantle, the doorframe. And something in her heart lurched painfully when she entered the house one afternoon and found her husband lying on his stomach on the floor, both he and Charlotte giggling as the infant crawled all over his back—for all it would take was one blow, and her baby would grow up without the gentle man who was, in every way but one, her father.

He had turned into a diamond after all, her Wild One, and as she watched him cheerfully making a cake of himself over their daughter, she wondered how she could ever have preferred Charles.

The days fell away, and the match against Nails loomed ever closer.

On Friday night, Gareth easily defeated Nails Fleming in the second round. The crowd went wild. They carried their new hero all the way back to Swanthorpe, cheering him to the skies and hailing him as the next English champion. "Bring on the Butcher! Bring on the Butcher! We'll show Scotland you don't tangle with an Englishman!" was the cry that burst from hundreds of throats. They left him at the gates of Swanthorpe, and with no more damage than a cut high on his right cheek, Gareth strode into the dower house an hour after the fight had ended.

Juliet, waiting up for him and trying to read by the light of a single candle, nearly wept with relief when she heard the door open.

*Thank you, God. Thank you for keeping him safe.*

"Juliet? I didn't di-ee," he called out in a sing-song voice that made two syllables out of the last word and teased her for worrying about him so. Obviously, he knew what *she'd* been doing all night.

She put down her book and, candle in hand, hurried past Charlotte, sleeping in her cradle. Just outside the kitchen she paused to compose herself. She didn't want Gareth to know she'd shut all the windows so that she wouldn't hear the distant din surrounding the fight. She didn't want him to know that she hadn't been able to eat her supper, that she didn't remember a single word of the book she'd been trying to read, and that she had nearly paced a rut in the floor of the sitting room.

But her worries, she soon saw, had all been for naught. He was standing by the hearth, unhurt, and looking no more exhausted than if he'd taken a walk through the fields. She noted a small cut on his cheek, but nothing more. A wave of crippling relief washed through her, nearly buckling her knees as she ran into his arms.

"Gareth!"

"Hello, dearest." He caught her up and kissed her. "Mmmmm, you look good"—he cupped her breast in one hand, rubbed the nipple through the fabric, and slanted his mouth across hers once more—"and taste even better!"

She pushed away from him so that she could better regard him. "And *you* look ... virtually untouched. Are you sure you've even *been* in a fight?"

"Actually, no," he said, frowning, and it was then that she realized something was troubling him.

"Gareth, what is it?"

He sobered. "I am not sure, Juliet. But something's wrong. Something I just don't understand." He moved away and paced once before the fireplace, twice, then threw himself into a chair. "I sparred with Nails, my opponent, earlier this week. He kept me on my toes, he was so quick. But tonight ... tonight he fought as though he was half asleep. It was the strangest thing...."

"Was he ill?"

"No. I don't think so. He began the fight with all sorts of nervous energy. Caught me a good one right here," he said, tapping his cheek. "But late in the first round, he began ailing. It was most peculiar, Juliet. It was almost as though he was—I don't know, drugged or something."

"Perhaps he was drunk."

"No. He had a few good swigs of ale before the

fight, but not enough to get foxed. It wasn't that at all."

Juliet felt the first real tremors of uneasiness. Biting her lip, she walked over to his chair, sat on its arm, and waited for him to continue.

"He was just like Bull O'Rourke last week," her husband said, curving an arm around Juliet and drawing her close so that her head rested on his shoulder. "Rather sluggish, not very quick off the mark. Maybe the crowds didn't notice something was amiss, but I sure as Hades did. There was no sport in my defeating him tonight, none at all. When a man hits you, you don't just stand there and take it. . . ."

"So what did you do?"

"The only merciful thing I *could* do," he said bitterly. "I ended the fight. I swung, he just stared through me, and I refused to hit him again. Instead, I gave him a good push that sent him to his knees. The crowd jeered me, but the devil take them. I couldn't stand there and abuse him for round after round, Juliet. It just wasn't right."

His arm still curved around her, he leaned his head back against the chair and stared dismally up at the ceiling. "I don't know what to do. I've thought about telling Snelling, but I don't want to expose Nails if he and Bull have an opium habit or something. Maybe they need that sort of thing to brace up for a fight. 'Sdeath, I don't know . . . I just don't know."

Juliet moved off the chair, came around behind it, and began kneading his shoulders. They were stiff with unspent energy, the muscles knotted beneath her fingers. "Gareth . . . if those fighters need opium to give themselves courage before a match, their speed and reflexes would have been compromised long before now, in matches with other people—

which means they would never have become such renowned fighters."

"I know."

"And furthermore, if they'd been smoking opium, wouldn't they have *arrived* at the fight in that state, not become that way after it started?"

"Yes." With a heavy sigh, he bent forward so that his forehead rested in the heels of his hands, his fingers splaying up through his hair. "Those same questions have been running through my head all night. I just don't want to believe the alternative. It is too . . . too monstrous."

"Foul play?"

"Yes." She watched his knuckles clenching and unclenching where they poked up through his hair. "That's what it's beginning to look like, Juliet. Someone is drugging my opponents before the fights to ensure that I win."

"Dear God." Juliet drew a deep, shaky breath, then bit her lip to keep back the words that threatened to spill from her mouth: *Take us away from here, Gareth. Take us far away—from this awful fighting and whatever evil thing is going on here. Please . . . before it's too late. Take us away, and back to—*

Back to where? Blackheath Castle and the duke's all-encompassing protection? Even as she considered it, her heart rebelled. Gareth had worked hard to find a sense of responsibility, maturity, and self-worth. If he returned to Blackheath, all that he had so recently discovered in himself would probably go straight out the window.

"Juliet." He must have sensed the direction of her thoughts, for he rose from his chair and came around it to stand before her. He took her face in his hands—his powerful hands that were no longer white and pampered, his strong, capable hands that had sent men reeling into oblivion—and, gently cradling her jaw, lifted her face to his. "Juliet, my love, we will not be here forever. Please trust me on that."

"But Gareth, what if you're correct and there *is* foul play going on? Your life could be in danger."

"The fact that I already suspect as much will give me the upper hand." He ran his thumbs over her cheeks, then bent his head to kiss her brow. "All I have to do is continue to play along with the game, pretend I don't know something strange is going on—and with any luck, I'll catch whoever is behind this in the act and bring him to justice before someone gets hurt." He sighed and gazed deeply into her worried eyes. "I know you would have me take us far from here, Juliet, but I cannot run from this any more than I could have run from those highwaymen when I came upon them robbing the stagecoach that night. Please understand, my love. This is something I must do."

She shut her eyes and tried to take comfort in his strength, his faith in himself, the warmth of his arms as they enclosed her. She did not want him to play the hero again. She was afraid for him, afraid for all of them. But even as her heart quaked at the idea of the danger in which he was involving himself, she knew that she loved and respected him all the more for it. Another man would turn and run. But not her Wild One. *He* would not rest until justice prevailed.

*I love you, sweet Gareth. I love you so much it hurts.*

Sudden tears filled her eyes.

"Now, don't you worry," he told her, as he noted and mistook the reason for her tears. "Tomorrow I shall go talk to Nails—and Bull O'Rourke, as well. See what they have to say about all this. They're professional fighters, Juliet; I should not have won either match. But I promise you this. If something evil *is* going on, I'm not leaving until I get to the bottom of it."

She gazed up into his romantic eyes, his dear, dear face, for a long moment. How very noble he was.

How righteous and determined, for all his so-called wildness. And she knew, as she stood there in his arms, that the time had come for her to tell him that which she should have told him long before now.

"Gareth?"

"What is it, dearest?"

She took a deep breath and reached up to touch his cheek. "I . . . love you."

"Oh, Juliet . . ." He actually blushed, so pleased was he by her long-overdue admission. "You couldn't have chosen a nicer time to tell me."

"I should have told you ages ago, when I first knew. But I couldn't admit it then, not even to myself."

"And when *did* you first know?"

"When you took that bullet meant for the little boy. When you nearly died trying to save him—and all of us on that coach. I think I started to love you then. I think I've loved you ever since. I just . . . haven't told you."

"But—what about Charles?"

She gave him a patient little smile. "I'll be honest, Gareth. Once, I was like everyone else in that I was always comparing the two of you. But as I've grown to know you, those comparisons have happened less and less, and when they *do* happen . . . well, you always come out on top." She leaned up to kiss the smile breaking out on his face. "Lately, I've come to realize that Charles and I would never have been this happy together. We were too much alike. You, on the other hand . . . well, I've never had as much fun with anyone as I have with you."

"Oh, Juliet. I don't know what to say." He was grinning fiercely. "But I will tell you this. I've always been sure."

"Of what?"

"That I love you."

"Are you, now?" she asked, trying to muster a

grin even as a tear leaked from one eye. She knuckled it away. Sniffled. Heavens, she was beginning to
bawl like a baby.

"Yes. And you know something else, my dear,
darling little wife? I'm going to take you upstairs
and prove it."

Laughing, he swept her into his arms and carried
her up to their room—where he loved her so well,
and so thoroughly that he drove all thoughts of
fighting and foul play from her mind.

# 31

After making love to Juliet well into the wee hours, it was no wonder that Gareth's eyes felt like lead when he opened them the following morning. Even so, as he gazed lovingly at his sleeping wife, he wanted nothing more than to gather her up in his arms, bury his face in her silky, unbound hair, and cuddle away the morning. The afternoon. The whole day.

If only he could. But that was not possible, of course. He had to be at the barn at nine, and he wanted to get into town to begin asking questions before training started. Subtle questions, of course. He didn't want anyone to start wondering about *him*—and the reasons why he was suddenly asking those questions.

Carefully, so as not to disturb Juliet's slumbers, he lifted the blanket and crawled out of the bed. The floor was cold on his bare feet, and after gently replacing the blanket, he all but hopped over to the chair where he put his socks, shivering as he hastily drew them on. Despite his fatigue—and the concerns he'd shared with Juliet last night—he was in a good mood. And why not? Those three words she had spoken to him when he got home were still floating through his head like fair-weather clouds across a summer sky.

*I love you.*

He smiled and looked at her lying there under the blanket, her dark hair spread across the pillow like a Spanish fan. God, he loved her, too. He loved her lustrous hair and silky skin, her dark-green eyes and pert little nose, even that soft, twangy accent that left everyone who heard it scratching their heads, wondering where she was from. He loved her slim, strong body, the fullness of her breasts, and the way her waist flared into curving, womanly hips . . . hips that would, he hoped, bear many more children. She was a calming, practical influence on his reckless nature, the voice of reason where he was the soul of impulse. Oh, yes, he loved her. He loved her courage, her level-headedness, and her devotion. Most of all, he loved the fact that she now trusted him without question, supporting his decisions and standing by him when another woman might have demanded he bring her and the baby straight back to Blackheath and the all-powerful protection of its mighty duke.

But she had not demanded that he take them all far away from here, had not become hysterical, shrewish, or weepy with worry. She was, of course, nervous; he'd seen it in her eyes. But she, like Lucien, was placing her faith in him, and Gareth knew he would have to stand very tall indeed to measure up to what each of them hoped for, and expected, from him. Once he wouldn't have given a damn. Now he'd die before he'd let either one of them—or himself—down.

Outside, the blackbirds were calling, the first song to greet the dawn, and he could hear the distant quacking of ducks down on the river. He checked the clock on the mantle. It had just gone five. *'Sdeath.* Early, yes, but at least he had several hours before having to report for training . . . which left plenty of time to hunt down Nails and Bull O'Rourke.

He stopped beside the bed on his way out, where he bent down, cleared a strand of hair from Juliet's face, and kissed her gently on a cheek as soft and white as a magnolia petal. Charlie-girl was in her cradle, her body rising and falling beneath a light blanket; Gareth paused there, as well, kissing his little daughter. Then, very carefully so as not to wake either, he crept from the room.

Ten minutes later, he was munching on a piece of buttered bread and striding up the leaf-shaded path between the Mill Stream and the Abbey Meadow, heading toward town. The sun was shining, sparkling on the water and glowing green through the ivy that choked the trees that surrounded him, and if he didn't know anything else, he bloody well knew one thing:

It was going to be a beautiful day.

Dickie Noring hailed him just as he was passing beneath the Gateway of St. Nicholas Church.

"Lord Gareth! Lord Gareth! 'Ave ye 'eard the news? 'Tis a terrible thing, it is—'specially as 'e 'as family an' all!"

Gareth, suddenly alert, paused just beneath the Gateway's vaulted stone ceiling, his gaze moving from the County Hall across the street to the lad who, all out of breath, came running up before him. "What are you talking about, Dickie?"

"Nails died last night! 'E never woke up after 'e went down! Some are sayin' it was the strength of your hits that killed 'im, but the doctor thinks Nails 'it 'is 'ead when 'e fell. They're burying 'im tomorrow!"

For a moment, Gareth, blinking, could only stare at Dickie as his brain tried to absorb what he'd just been told.

"*What?!*"

"Aye, 'e died last night!"

Denial rose like a brick wall before him. Nails *dead?* 'Sdeath, he hadn't even hit him that hard!

"You all right, m'lord? Ye're looking a bit pale—"

"I am sorry, it's just that . . . this comes as rather a shock." He shook his head, trying to clear it. "Dear God." He pushed his fingers against his brow and leaned back against the church's cold, unforgiving stone, his thoughts racing and a prickling sense of unease icing its way up his spine. "Do you know where Nails lived, Dickie? I—I must go and pay my respects to his widow. . . ."

Moments later he was standing outside a small terraced house on East St. Helen's Street, his tricorn in his hands and his face grim. He saw the neat white curtains at the windows, the black crepe that someone had already hung above the doorway. Guilt twisted his guts. Confusion warred in his breast. And the same thought kept going through his mind, over and over again like a litany: *But I didn't hit him that hard. . . . I didn't hit him that hard. . . . I didn't hit him that hard. . . .*

What a lame excuse to offer Nails's grieving widow. He felt sick.

Taking a deep, shaky breath, he raised his hand toward the knocker. Despite the hour, he knew Nails's wife would be up; country folk rose early, and besides, he doubted anyone who had just lost a spouse would sleep much in that first night following such a loss. Still, he hesitated, wondering if he ought to just quietly turn away and leave this family to grieve. He was, after all, the last person they probably wanted to see just now.

*Coward.*

He tried the knocker and waited.

There was movement behind the door. He cleared his throat, wondering what to say to these people. The latch swung upward, and the door opened to reveal a gaunt woman with red-rimmed eyes. A handkerchief was wadded in her hand, and two toddlers huddled against her skirts. She gasped at the sight of Gareth, her eyes filling up all over again as she shoved the handkerchief against her nose.

Gareth's heart went out to her. "I am so sorry to hear about your husband," he said quietly. He clutched his hat, feeling awkward and terrible and sick at heart. "I . . . just wanted to stop and pay my respects. I shall leave you in peace."

He turned and began to walk away, but her voice stopped him.

"M'lord, please!"

He took a deep breath and turned back around, not knowing what to say, what to do.

She stood there in the doorway, looking small, lost, and forlorn. "Don't go," she whispered, her bottom lip quivering. "Oi know ye think ye killed me 'usband . . . but ye di'int."

"Thank you for that reassurance, Mrs. Fleming, but I hold myself responsible for what happened. Had I been Nails's second, I would have called off the fight. As his opponent, I only did what I could. . . ."

"M'lord, ye don't understand. Oi've watched ev'ry foight Nails ever did." Her eyes grew desperate behind her tears. "Oi was *there* last noight, and Oi saw what state me 'usband was in. Ye di'int 'it 'im that 'ard. And when 'e fell, 'e landed on 'is knees—'is 'ead never 'it the floor, no matter wot the doctor thinks."

Gareth stared at her and frowned.

"Don't ye see?" She gazed tearfully up at him, her eyes willing him to understand. "Me 'usband di'int die at yer 'and. *'E died because someone gave 'im laudanum just before the foight!*"

\* \* \*

At about the same time Mrs. Fleming was telling Gareth about the severely allergic reaction Nails had had to laudanum, Lucien's informer was standing at the window, reading the missive that had just arrived from the duke.

*My brother is at Swanthorpe Manor in Abingdon, Berkshire. I am not easy with the situation in which he has involved himself. Go there immediately and report back to me daily, and if there is trouble I wish to know about it at once. This time, do not lose him.*

*Blackheath*

The last four words were double underscored. This was serious, then. Very serious.

Chilcot folded the note, put it into his pocket, and called for his horse. He would go immediately to Abingdon, keeping a low profile until the rest of the Den members could join him there.

By the tone of Blackheath's note, there was no time to lose.

Snelling gave all of his fighters the day off out of respect to Nails. Most of them went to get drunk, but not Gareth.

He found Bull O'Rourke sitting in the Old Bell Inn, bent morosely over a pint of ale. Bull had, by all accounts, been drinking more or less steadily ever since his humiliating loss to the younger, less seasoned Gareth and was not much help when Gareth questioned him about events preceding their match. All he could tell him was that he remembered feeling "bloody strange" just after the first blows were exchanged, but he'd attributed it to the strength of Gareth's hits. Gareth pursed his lips and made a mental note of what he'd learned.

On Monday, after his morning's training, he paid a visit to the local chemist. His questions turned up nothing, but, then he didn't think his foe would be so stupid as to buy the drug in Abingdon. On Tuesday afternoon he borrowed a horse from Becky's brother Tom and went to Wallingford to see the chemist in that town. Nothing. On Wednesday he tried the one in Wantage. Nothing.

He was beginning to think he was pursuing a dead end when he finally found what he was looking for. It was late on Thursday afternoon when he walked into the small shop in Oxford and asked the apothecary the same questions he'd put to the others. Yes, a man with a narrow face and close-set eyes had recently bought a large amount of laudanum. No, he didn't know who the customer was.

But Gareth did.

And as he rode home that night, he recalled Lucien's words:

*Just promise me one thing. . . . That if you get in over your head, you'll contact me.*

His brother was right. Sometimes it did take more courage to put aside your pride and ask for help than try to do everything yourself.

Arriving home, he immediately wrote to Lucien.

# 32

**F**riday afternoon.

Six hours to go before the fight with Scotland's dreaded Butcher.

And no Lucien.

Gareth had spent the morning pacing the floor like a caged lion, jumping at every sound of voices outside, wondering if he was overreacting. After all, he had no hard proof, only suspicions, and it would be damned embarrassing if Lucien came charging in, only to find that Gareth had built a mountain out of a molehill. . . .

He stalked to the window and glanced nervously outside. Juliet was there in the vegetable garden, squatting down and planting seeds in the narrow furrow she had dug. He let out his breath with relief. He must've checked her ten times in the last five minutes at least. Must've checked Charlotte, who was crawling around on the floor playing with the rattle he had made for her out of a hollowed-out piece of wood filled with coins, ten times more than that.

He began to pace, and Charlotte looked up at him with her big blue eyes, watching him go back and forth, back and forth like an inmate at Bedlam.

Gareth paused. *What are you worrying so about?* those eyes, so like Charles's, seemed to say, and he suddenly relaxed, feeling like the biggest fool in the world. Two apparently drugged fighters and the word of a chemist and he was off like a ball from a cannon. Shaking his head at his own skittishness, he let out a sigh and dropped down beside his little girl. Immediately, she scrambled over to him as fast as her hands and knees could take her and climbed happily up into his lap. He picked her up. Her very presence was a balm to his nerves, a reassurance that purity and innocence still shone in a world that had, of late, seemed dominated by wickedness and evil.

But it soon became obvious that Charlotte wanted more than just a cuddle. Gareth had learned enough about her to recognize that particular pinched scowl as the one that preceded a bout of whimpering, which, in turn, preceded a lusty bout of crying.

"Hungry, Charlie-girl?"

Raising himself to his knees, he picked up the bowl he'd excitedly prepared a few minutes ago in preparation for this event and sat down, anticipation lighting up his face. Charlotte was beginning to eat solid food now, which delighted him beyond words because that meant he could have a hand in feeding her. Still, Juliet had looked dubious when she'd left him with the baby an hour before. *Mash up her food carefully*, she had instructed him, explaining the procedure with as much care as if she'd been advising an overeager two-year-old, going on and on while he'd stood there and nodded and nodded and nodded. *Make sure there are no lumps in it, and don't make her eat it all if she doesn't want it.*

He realized his first mistake as he dug the spoon into the bowl and eagerly began to feed the baby. "All right, so maybe you should have mashed up those peas or even the carrots, instead of these red beet roots left over from supper last night," he told himself aloud. Indeed, it soon became difficult to know who was faring worse in this new venture—

his daughter, who now had red pulp all over her mouth and down the front of the dress Juliet had just completed for her, or her papa, who had it all over his fingers and his lap. Ah, hell. They were both laughing and having fun.

They were half way through the bowl when a loud hammering at the door nearly caused Gareth to jump out of his skin. *Lucien.* Scooping up the baby and holding her easily in one arm, he went to open it—and found Perry and the rest of the Den of Debauchery standing just outside.

"Bloody hell!" Perry's jaw nearly hit the floor. "What on earth have you done to her?!"

Gareth looked at Charlotte and fully comprehended just what a mess the two of them had made. Huge red blotches stained the delicate skin of the baby's face. Her hands were bright red, her dress was ruined, and bits of crimson pulp clung to her chin. *Oh, hell,* he thought wildly, *Juliet's going to kill me!*

He grabbed up a napkin from the table and began scrubbing at Charlotte's face, to no avail. "Damnation!" he cried, much to Perry's amusement and the guffaws of the others.

"Playing papa to the hilt, are you, Gareth?"

"So much for *your* days of debauchery!"

"I say, next thing you know, he'll be changing napkins—ha, ha, ha!"

"Sod off," Gareth said, realizing how much he had *not* missed their immaturity. He was in no mood for their silly antics, their teasing, nor Chilcot, who had grabbed Charlotte's rattle and was shaking it in his face with relentless obnoxiousness. He seized Chilcot's wrist and all but ripped the rattle from his fingers. "What are you all doing here, anyhow?"

"Why, we've come to see you fight tonight."

"Yes, there are posters up all over Ravenscombe: 'Will the Scotsman Butcher the Wild One?' Oh, they're playing this up big, Gareth. You're a celebrity!"

Gareth swore under his breath. "Listen," he said, "I'm glad you're here because I believe something evil is going on, and I may need your help."

"What are you talking about?"

Hurriedly, he explained to them what he had learned and what he suspected.

"Yes, but Gareth, you can't *prove* any of this—"

"No, I can't. *Yet.* But I will. A man has died, and I shan't rest until I expose the snake who murdered him."


Eager to explore the town, the Den members did not stay long, but Gareth at least felt reassured that they were there in Abingdon. Chilcot was a fool, the others thought it was all a big adventure, and only Perry seemed to take him seriously. Good old Perry. He knew he could depend on his best friend.

But damn it, where was Lucien?

It was now just past four o'clock, and the fight was scheduled for six. Gareth had expected the duke to come charging in like death on the back of a black horse, but there'd been no note from him, no acknowledgement of the one he'd sent, and worse, no Lucien. Something was wrong. Dreadfully wrong.

He went to the window and stared out over the river, his hands in his pockets. In the distance, the pastoral hills off toward Culham, opaque with haze, rose blue-green against the sky.

*Come on, Lucien. Where the hell are you?*

A sharp knock sounded on the door downstairs. He heard Juliet—who, thank God, had decided the beetroot stains were not worth killing him over—crossing the floor to answer it. A moment later, he heard Becky's distressed voice.

"Gareth!" It was Juliet calling up to him, her voice urgent. "Come quickly!"

He spun on his heel and took the stairs three at a time. In the foyer stood Becky and her younger brother, Tom. Becky looked pale and shaken, her eyes red from crying.

"What's this, now?" he asked, gently putting an arm around the shoulders of each and ushering them into the sitting room. "Sit down and tell me what's wrong."

"Oh, Lord Gareth—Tom's got somethink awful to tell ye!"

And as Tom, rubbing the back of his head, began to speak, it soon became apparent why Lucien had not come. Tom had not even made it out of Abingdon with Gareth's urgent missive when something— or someone—spooked his horse. He remembered falling, then someone charging up on him in the darkness—and nothing more than that. Next thing he'd known, he opened his eyes to find himself lying in a back street of Oxford, bound, gagged and nursing a headache a hundred times worse than any hangover. It had taken him the better part of the day to free himself and find his way home.

"And what happened to the letter I gave you?" Gareth pressed.

"Gone, m'lord. Me mare was waitin' for me back 'ome, but the saddlebags, they was gone."

Gareth swore and, running a hand through his hair, met Juliet's eyes from across the room. She was as white as the starched mobcap that crowned her glossy curls, her expression stony.

She shook her head very slowly, from side to side. "Gareth, you cannot fight tonight. Someone now knows what *you* know, and your life could very well be in danger."

"But Juliet, I have to fight."

"No. You do *not* have to fight."

"There are people coming from all over England! There are thousands of pounds being bet on this! If

I don't fight, I shall never live this down, never be able to hold my head up again, because everyone will think I'm a coward—why, we'll have to leave the country, for God's sake!"

She raised her chin, hugged her arms to herself, and stared defiantly at him from across the room. "Gareth, I *beg* you not to do this fight."

"Juliet, I beg *you* to understand."

"There is nothing to understand. Your life is in danger. *I do not want you fighting tonight.*"

Gareth threw a quick glance over his shoulder at Becky and Tom, who read the unspoken message there and beat a hasty exit. And then, changing tactics, Gareth crossed the room to his wife. He slid his hands up her arms, trying to loosen them. She had no more give than a locked door.

"Dearest," he said, leaning down to kiss her brow, her temple, putting a finger beneath her jaw to raise her face to his. He lowered his mouth to hers and found it stiff and unyielding. Angry. "I promise you that nothing shall happen to me tonight."

She tightened her arms, refusing to let him seduce her into agreement. "And I promise you, Gareth, that if you go through with this fight, I'm leaving."

He pulled back, stunned. "What?"

"You heard me."

"I thought you were going to stick by me, support me. Damn it, Juliet, you've been saying all along that you have faith in me; here's your chance to prove it!"

"I'm not staying here to watch you die. I have a little girl to take care of. Go meet the Butcher tonight if you have to, Gareth, but I'll tell you right now that you'll be coming home to an empty house—that is, *if* you come home at all."

"Juliet!"

"Make your choice, Gareth. Your pride or your family." And with that, she turned on her heel and

left him standing there in the middle of the floor.
All alone.

*"What do you mean, you won't fight the Butcher to-night?"* Panicking, Snelling waved Lord Gareth into Swanthorpe's lavishly appointed parlor, impatiently gesturing for a servant to bring a decanter of wine and two glasses. "Everyone in town's talking about this fight! People are coming from three counties to see it! You can't back out on me now, it'll be a damned mob scene!"

The young fighter was adamant. "Forget it, Snelling. I am not doing it."

Snelling's heart was pounding, then racing, as he tried frantically to think of a way to salvage this emergency situation. *Calm down!* he told himself, wiping suddenly sweaty palms on his breeches. *Find out what the problem is and then do what you have to do to get him back on course.* "Now, you sit right there and tell me what's wrong," he soothed, using the parental tone that had often worked with other nervy young fighters. But he knew he'd taken the wrong approach the moment he saw the sudden coolness in Lord Gareth's pale eyes; the lad might be confused, possibly even scared, but he was certainly not a boy.

*Bloody hell, does he* know? *He can't know, only Woodford and I know, he's just got a case of nerves, that's all it is!*

He began sweating as he thought of how much money he'd wagered on the Scot and nearly keened with terror. *I'll lose everything I own if he doesn't meet the Butcher tonight!*

"I've had a bellyful, that's what's wrong," Lord Gareth said simply. "What more explanation do you need?"

That cool blue gaze bored into his.

Snelling began to fidget. The perspiration was already beading on his brow, and he was thankful when the servant arrived with the wine. His hand shaking, he poured two glasses, setting one in front of Lord Gareth—who, he noted, looked at it the way he might a poisonous adder and declined to touch it. Did he know? *Did he*!?

"Ah, so *that's* it, you've lost your courage, then!" Snelling said. He wiped his brow and managed to find his politician's smile somewhere down in the abyss into which it had fallen. "Happens to the best of them, you know. And you *are* the best, Gareth, probably the best in all England. Knew it the first time I saw you fight." He gulped his wine. "Now, I know you might be a little nervous but that's understandable, after all, the Butcher's got a reputation to strike fear into the heart of *anyone*; but damn, that shouldn't scare you, there's not a man in England who can hit like you. Why, look at the two worthies you've already defeated! Three, if you count Joe Lumford back in London! You're a natural, lad. A damned natural. You'll take the Butcher down by the third round. I'll lay money on it!"

Lord Gareth only stared at him for a moment, then looked away, his eyes bleak.

"I know, I know, it's because of what happened to Nails, isn't it? Now, Gareth, that was an accident. You can't be blaming yourself for what happened—"

"I don't." The pale-blue eyes looked at him directly, almost accusingly. "I just don't want to fight the Butcher tonight. In fact, I don't want to fight anyone. I am through, Snelling. I've lost my stomach for it."

"But—"

Lord Gareth stood up. "I am taking my family and going home."

A torrent of raw, uncontrollable rage blew through Snelling, nearly blinding him. His hands trembled with the effort it took to remain calm, and he knew, wildly, that if he'd had a gun, he would've pulled it out and shot this arrogant young rake dead in his tracks. But he had no gun. He had only the terrifying knowledge of how much money he'd put on the Butcher tonight—and how much he would lose if Lord Gareth did not fight. ·

"You can't leave me like this!" he all but shouted. "Damn you, de Montforte, *we had an agreement!*"

"And I have a wife and daughter. I don't want them ending up like Nails's family if something should happen to me. I don't want my wife mourning me, nor my little girl growing up without a papa." He picked up his hat and moved toward the door. "Goodbye, Snelling."

Snelling shot to his feet and raced around the table. "My, oh, my," he said, flinging all caution to the wind, "I never thought that you, of all people, would turn out to be such a lily-livered coward. *You,* a de Montforte!"

Lord Gareth paused, and Snelling was reminded of how very tall and formidable this young man actually was. How powerfully muscled he was beneath that loose shirt—and how very foolish he himself was for provoking him so. He caught his breath, fearing he was going to be the next person to feel Lord Gareth's fist—but, no, the Wild One had himself tightly under control, no longer the impulsive hotspur he'd been that night at Mrs. Bottomley's. "I would call you out for such a remark," the younger man said evenly, with a cool smile that only made the coming insult worse, "but I make it a practice to duel exclusively with gentlemen—not those who aspire to be. Good evening, Snelling."

"Wait!" Snelling tossed back his wine and leaped over the sofa, desperate to reach the door before Lord Gareth did. Gasping, he flattened his back against it and gazed up at his fighter with panicked eyes. Lord Gareth merely stared right through him and kept coming, and for a moment Snelling thought he was simply going to pick him up and throw him out of the way. "Listen," he said, grinning broadly and spreading his hands in supplication. He knew he was begging, but he was desperate, unable to help himself. "I've put a lot of money and time into promoting this match between you two. I've given you a home, a livelihood, and a name for yourself. And this is how you think to repay me?"

"I don't owe you a damned thing, Snelling. Now, stand aside."

"But—"

Lord Gareth simply reached around him, found the latch, and pushed the door open. Snelling stumbled, nearly fell. And now Lord Gareth was striding past him and down the hall, his footfalls echoing off the walls and high ceiling.

"Wait!" Snelling cried, knowing he would give ten years of his life to possess that elegant, bred-in-the-bone grace; another ten for that cool, aristocratic arrogance—

And everything he owned if only he could get the young rakehell to fight tonight.

"Lord Gareth!"

The tall figure was almost into the foyer now.

"*Lord Gareth!* What will it take for me to get you to do this fight? A thousand pounds? Two thousand? Name your price, Gareth, and if you win, you shall have it!"

His words reverberated through the hall.

The young man paused at the threshold of the open door, looking out onto a hundred acres of wheat, rye and barley, and some of the most fertile ground in Berkshire. Above his head was Swanthorpe's gorgeous leaded fanlight; beneath that, the de Montforte coat of arms, forever enshrined in the stone.

Lord Gareth's fair head tipped back as he, too, looked up and saw his family's arms above the door. He stood there for a moment, just gazing at that carving in the stone. And then, very slowly, he turned. His face was perfectly calm, his gaze almost triumphant.

"Very well then, Snelling," he said. "I want Swanthorpe Manor."

Snelling was in need of a stiff drink after Lord Gareth left. His heart was still pounding, though shaky relief was already beginning to spread through his veins. He poured himself a shot of brandy and sank back into the sofa. Thank God he'd found a way to get the lad to do the fight, after all. For a harrowing moment there he'd thought all was lost.

*Very well then, Snelling . . . I want Swanthorpe Manor.*

Snelling cursed out loud as he recalled Lord Gareth's words. That wasn't all the arrogant young nob had wanted. He wanted his friend Lord Brookhampton to be his second for the fight instead of Woodford. He wanted Snelling to give Nails's widow enough money to allow her to live comfortably for the remainder of her life. And, not content to trust Snelling's word, he wanted Brookhampton to witness the impromptu agreement the two of them made regarding the terms of the match.

"Otherwise, I'm not fighting."

*Bloody hell.* Snelling had just poured himself another shot when Sanderson, his butler, announced that he had a visitor.

"Woodford!" He smiled in relief. "Where the *hell* have you been?"

"It's de Montforte."

Snelling's smile vanished. "Shut the door."

Wordlessly, Woodford went back and pushed it closed. He glanced nervously around, then pulled up a chair opposite Snelling. "He's on to us."

"What are you talking about?"

For an answer, Woodford reached into his coat pocket and pulled out a sheet of folded vellum. "Creedon the gardener caught Tom Houghton trying to take this to the Duke of Blackheath late last night." He tossed the note onto the table before his employer. "The idiot just brought it to me now. I thought you'd better see it immediately."

Snelling hurriedly read, his face going purple with rage. "Damn that de Montforte for a clever, sneaking rogue!" he snarled, crumpling up the vellum that, had it actually reached the powerful Duke of Blackheath, would've had Snelling swinging from the nearest tree, so damning were the words. He shook the thing in Woodford's face. "He knows everything, damn his eyes!"

"Yes, I figured he was on to us when Osgood, the chemist, mentioned he'd been snooping around and asking rather strange questions, so I paid Creedon to keep an eye on him. When Creedon saw him ask Tom Houghton to carry this note for him, he knew something was up. He followed the lad, bashed him over the head, and took the saddlebags—which contained the letter."

"Why the hell did it take him so long to get the letter back to us?"

"There was also a flask of gin in the saddlebags."

"Bloody *hell*."

Woodford put both hands on the table, shot a nervous glance over his shoulder, and leaned close. "What are we going to do, Jon?"

Snelling held the damning letter over a candle, watching as it dissolved into a black, writhing curl. "Well, it's obvious, isn't it?" He flicked the ash from his fingers. "Lord Gareth knows too much. He must be dealt with—before he can tell Blackheath everything he knows. Christ, if that happens, I'm a dead man."

Woodford drew himself up. "Fine. I'll go take care of him now. Did you say he's gone into town to find Brookhampton? I'll just waylay him as he's coming back through the Meadow, stick a knife in his back, and toss him into the Thames—"

"No, no, that won't do at all. I've sunk enough money into de Montforte; I'm not going to waste it all by throwing him into the damned river." He rose and poured himself another drink, his jaw working furiously as he sloshed the liquid around his mouth and swallowed. He turned to Woodford, his eyes blazing. "No, Woodford, I've made a staggering amount of money off of him . . . but that will be *nothing* compared to what you and I are going to make off of him tonight."

"And how are we going to do that? He's on to us. He'll be expecting us to drug the Scot so that he'll win yet again, and then all he'll have to do is denounce us right there in front of everyone—"

"Don't be a pillock, Woodford. I am not going to drug the Scot. I didn't wager all my money on the Butcher just to see him lose."

Woodford raised a heavy brow.

"Lord Gareth is English," Snelling continued, "and I can tell you right now, every Englishman at that fight tonight is going to back him—no matter *how* big the Scot is, no matter how likely it is he'll make pulp of our young Wild One by the end of the first round. We're talking about national loyalty here."

Woodford, all ears, rubbed his jaw and listened.

"Everyone will be betting on Lord Gareth," Snelling said, his eyes gleaming. "But *my* money—every penny I own—is on the Scot. And do you know why? *Because Lord Gareth is going to lose tonight.*"

Woodford shook his head. "Really, Jon, if you think he's stupid enough to drink anything you offer him before the fight, you've got another thing com—"

"I don't need him to drink anything, Woodford. Have you actually *seen* the Scot fight?" He gave a little laugh. "There's no way in a million years Lord Gareth will ever beat him. He's good, but not *that* good." Snelling stood up, hatred and fury radiating from him like gas from a flame. "Oh no, Woodford, this time, his opponent will not be drugged. *This* time, our Wild One is going to get the stuffing knocked out of him."

Woodford raised a brow.

"You see, Woodford, it's not just my fortune that's at stake here, but also Swanthorpe. I had to offer it up just to get Lord Gareth to fight tonight. If he wins, it's his; so he *has* to lose, do you understand me?" Snelling's fist came down hard on the table. "*He has to lose!* And just to make sure that he never, *ever* opens his mouth and tells what he knows, I think we'd better offer the Butcher a hefty financial incentive for doing something a little special tonight. . . ."

"And that is?"

"Not just knocking Lord Gareth out—but *killing* him."

## 33

A bingdon hadn't seen such excitement since the previous autumn's Michaelmas fair. Crowds thronged the roads leading into the town. Fancy carriages bumped hubs with farmer's carts. People hung out the windows that overlooked the street, cheering Gareth as he and Perry, encircled by the Den of Debauchery members and flanked by Snelling, Woodford, and Angus "the Butcher" Campbell, made their way up Bridge Street. Patriotism was high. The red-and-white cross of St. George flew from windows, draped shop fronts, and was carried on great banners by crowds of shouting, reveling supporters who sent up a roaring *Huzzah!* as they caught sight of their champion. Gareth refused to think that he might not be worthy of their ardent loyalty. There was no room in his head right now for self-doubt—nor that heartbreaking scene not twenty minutes past, when, after getting ready for the match, he'd come downstairs to find Juliet silently packing her trunk, tears running down her set-in-stone face. . . .

It seemed unreal. It could not be happening to him. She could not be leaving him, not when everything had been so good between them, not when she'd just told him she loved him, not when he was risking everything he had—his health, his reputation, his life—to win Swanthorpe back for his family and provide a home for the two people he loved most in this world. *Damn it, I need you Juliet! Please— oh, God, please—come to your senses; please have faith in me; please, please, please be at the house when I get back.* And as the butterflies began to beat against his stomach, he realized he was not afraid of facing or losing to the Butcher.

He was afraid of losing his wife.

His dear wife, whom he loved more than life itself.

"By God, Gareth, all the flamboyant things you've done before are nothing compared to this!" Audlett shouted over the din, rousing Gareth from his thoughts. "Talk about daredevil stunts!"

"I'm not sure I can call it a stunt," Gareth called back, ducking as a bundle of red roses came arcing down on them from above. Looking up, he saw several pretty maids leaning from the windows of a coaching inn, waving frantically and blowing kisses to him. He bent down, picked up the roses before they could be trampled, and drew one out; then, with a grin he didn't feel, he tossed the bundle back up to the girls, eliciting a chorus of excited squealing.

Cokeham was yelling, trying to be heard over the crowd. "If Perry's going to be your second, then who's going to be your bottle holder, Gareth?"

Gareth threw a surreptitious glance at Snelling, walking several paces away. "It doesn't matter who holds my ale, as long as it's fiercely guarded. Who's got it, anyhow?"

Chilcot was there, close to Gareth's side. "I do!"

"Right. Don't you dare let that out of your sight, d'you understand?"

Chilcot gave his brainless grin and saluted. "Aye, cap'n!"

"'Sdeath," Gareth muttered beneath his breath,

wondering if perhaps he should have given that task
to Cokeham instead.

They fought their way up Bridge Street. Rose petals of every color—pink, red, white, and cream—
came drifting down from the windows above, and
Snelling's shouts of "Get back! Clear away there!"
were lost in the din. Just ahead and already decorated with banners, the County Hall, where the fight
would take place, rose high above a sea of what had
to be a thousand people, all shouting, cheering, and
milling about in anticipation; Stert, Bridge, and the
High Streets were clogged from pavement to pavement with incoming spectators, horses, barking
dogs, and vehicles of every description. Realization
of just what he was about to do suddenly hit Gareth,
bringing on the first involuntary prickling of nerves.

He thought of all the other times in his life he'd
been on show—from the time he'd pretended to
have drowned at Lady Brookhampton's to the time
he'd gathered just about everyone in Ravenscombe
to watch him jump Crusader over a human pyramid. He thought of all the reckless, exhibitionist
things he had ever done and told himself that this
wasn't going to be any different.

After all, since when had he—who would do anything for a laugh, for the sake of outrageousness, or
simply to make a spectacle of himself—been one to
experience stage fright?

*Since realizing that even if he won against the Butcher
tonight, he would still be going home to bitter defeat.*

"Hey, Gareth, cheer up there, man!" It was Chilcot, leaning close and frowning. "You're not nervous, now, are you?"

"Don't be a pillock," Gareth scoffed, waving him
off.

"I know you're worried that Snelling might try to
do something to Juliet, but Hugh's staying with her;
he'll keep her safe."

*"I know."* But he cannot keep her from leaving me.

Snelling, just ahead, had pushed through the throng and was climbing the County Hall's stairs. The magnificent stone building had a ground floor open on all four sides so that the upper stories appeared to be on stilts; on this ground floor, also of stone, the ring—fashioned of poles and ropes—had been erected. When the crowd saw Snelling, they sent up a thunderous cry of excitement, nearly drowning his full-bodied shout:

"And now, all the way from Edinburgh, Scotland, let me introduce Angus 'the Butcher' Campbell!"

The Scot shoved his way through the crowd and charged up into the ring, where Snelling and Woodford, who would act as his second, waited. The crowd roared in excitement, rabidly eager to see the match begin. As the din rose all around him, the Butcher, grinning confidently, shook his fist in the air, his great voice booming out over the Market Place:

"Sendin' yer Wild One off to dreamland is what I'll be doin', and when I'm done with him, I'll challenge any mon in this crowd to come up on stage and take me on!"

"Bloody hell," Cokeham breathed, his the only comment among Den members who had suddenly gone abnormally quiet. Gareth felt the first prickle of uneasiness creeping up his spine, for at six feet three inches, the Scot towered over everyone like a fortress over a battleground. Built as though Nature had tailor-made him especially for the ring, he had a bull neck, a massive chest, and overly long arms that ended in great scarred fists the size of a plow horse's hooves. This massive upper body tapered to a lean waist and strong, powerful thighs that were as stout as two oaks growing side by side.

"Holy shit," said Audlett, finding his voice.

Cokeham was still staring. "Er, Gareth, maybe this might not be such a good idea—"

"Shut up," Chilcot hissed from just behind them, making one of the first sensible comments of his life. "Gareth's going to drub the daylights out of him, aren't you, Gareth?"

"Either that or die trying," Gareth quipped, studying his opponent, and in the next minute Snelling was beckoning him into the ring and the crowds went wild, cheering so loudly that Snelling's introduction of him was lost in the clamor. A grim-faced Perry joined him as his second, and Chilcot took his place just outside the ring, the bottle containing Gareth's ale held protectively close against his chest.

"I've done some checking on this strutting Celt," Perry murmured, leaning close to Gareth. He watched Snelling's men chalking out a square in the middle of the floor, keeping within the ropes that marked out the ring itself. "He's a determined, rushing fighter and a tremendous hitter. He's as agile with his left as he is his right, and hits remarkably straight. Watch yourself, okay? He's going to try to put you out in the first round."

Gareth stretched his muscles and rolled his shoulders, concentrating on his eagerness to get the fight underway. "Stop worrying, Perry. I'll take care of him."

"I dare say you will. Just watch yourself, that's all I'm asking. I'll be right here if you need me."

"Right." Grinning, Gareth waved to the crowd, which obviously wanted to see their roaring cheers acknowledged. "Just one thing."

"What?"

"Don't stop the fight. No matter how badly I may get hurt, *don't stop the fight.*"

"Gareth, as your friend and your second I'm going to stop it if I see fit."

"Fine; then switch places with Chilcot, and I'll have *him* be my second instead."

Perry looked away, swearing helplessly under his breath.

"Thank you, old chap." Gareth clapped his friend across the back. "I knew you'd come through."

Across the ring, he watched the Scot flexing his muscles and eyeing him with undisguised malice as the rules were hurriedly explained: A man on his knees was reckoned to be down. . . . If a man was down, his principal had half a minute to bring him back to the side of the chalked square, opposite his opponent, lest he be deemed a beaten man. . . . No fighter was deemed beaten unless he failed to come back up to the line within thirty seconds. . . . A man was beaten if his own second declared it so. . . . Once the fighting began, no person was allowed on the stage except the principals and their seconds. . . . No person could hit his adversary when he was down or seize him by the ham, the breeches, or any part below the waist. . . .

*Let's just get this thing underway!* Gareth thought wildly, his heart beginning to pound in a potent mixture of anxiety, anticipation, and mad-dog eagerness.

And then the seconds were escorting their fighters up to the line. They were both stripping off their shirts when Gareth, his not even off yet, heard the sudden roar of the crowd a half-second before Campbell's body slammed into his with the force of a cannonball fired at close range. His neck snapped forward, the ropes collapsed behind him, and then there was nothing but empty space beneath him as he was hurled out of the ring and off the raised stone stage. He landed atop the heads and shoulders of several spectators and fell, twisting, to the street with a bone-jarring crash, there to lay in the dirt in humiliation while a circle of faces closed in on him from above, all shouting, screaming, and yelling at the top of their lungs for him to get up, get up, *get up!*

Enraged, Gareth was up like a game cock, taking the several steps leading to the stage in one bound, vaulting the reerected ropes, and going straight for the smirking Scot with fists flying.

The crowd went insane.

And Campbell was loving every minute of it. He was grinning as Gareth's fists, in lightning succession, connected with his jaw, his torso, his cheek, just standing back and taking it as if it amused him to allow his opponent to work himself up for the benefit of the roaring crowds. Only when Gareth's bare knuckles caught him square in the stomach, slightly doubling him over, did the Butcher's easy grin fade, and as Gareth came back with another punishing blow to his chin, he saw the mean glitter coming into Campbell's eyes and knew the time had come when the Scot would get down to business.

And get down to business he did. Gareth never saw the great fist coming. One moment he was striking hard with his right, and the next thing he knew, it felt as though someone had whacked the side of his face with the butt end of a musket; he was down on his hands and knees, numbly shaking his head and wondering what the devil had hit him while the referee was screaming above him:

"Five . . . six . . . seven . . ."

*"Get up!"* the crowd was roaring, then Perry was hauling him roughly to his feet, barely getting him into his corner and back into the ring before the thirty seconds were up. Furious now, Gareth charged the grinning Scot. *Calm down. Take your time; make each hit count; use skill and science here since he's got it all over you in brute strength!*

Bang, bang, bang—a hard chop to Campbell's jaw, his chin, his arm, and then that lethal fist streaking out, right for Gareth's face. Gareth's own arm flashed up, blocking it neatly, although the blow rocked him like an earthquake might a building as his entire body shook with its force. He hit out again, fell short of his mark, and now the Butcher, smiling, was lashing out with short, leashed feints and punches, one aimed at Gareth's eyes, another at his cheek, all the while backing him toward the ropes. Gareth blocked them all, his right arm as faithful a guard as it was a hitter, and then Campbell's knuckles collided with his gut and he doubled over, gasping, biting back the involuntary surge of vomit even as the crowd went wild around him. The Scot seized him by the hair, bent him beneath his massive shoulder and began pounding him, hard, raining blows against his head like a hail of bricks. Wildly, Gareth struggled to get free, hair tearing from his scalp as he twisted, kicked out, and hammered his elbow into Campbell's ribs, but the Scot held him tightly and was set to deliver a bruising punishment. Through his ringing ears, Gareth heard the crowd roaring like storm waves against a beach, screaming, shouting, hollering, but all he knew was each jarring thump against the side of his skull, the imprisoning grip of Campbell's arm, those iron-hard knuckles hitting him again and again and again. . . . Blood was running down his face now, and he felt his strength beginning to fail him even as courage roared in to take its place, felt awareness begin to leave him even as a single thought started running like a mantra through his dazed brain:

*Glad Juliet's not here to see this*—bang! went Campbell's fist—*Glad Juliet's not here to see this*—bang! *Glad Juliet's . . .*

And then Campbell released him and Gareth dropped, exhausted, to the stone floor, one hand flashing instinctively out to break his fall. Bruised and dazed, he swayed there on his hands and knees as Campbell strutted a victory dance around him, and the crowds's enthusiasm for their countryman turned to jeering, disappointed contempt.

"Get up, you pathetic excuse for an Englishman! Get up and show us a good fight, damn your eyes!"

"Get up, get up, get up!"

"Ten . . . eleven . . . twelve . . ."

"Gareth!" It was Perry, squatting down before him. "Gareth, he's killing you! Let me call off this lunacy—"

"The devil"—Gareth coughed, tasting blood—"the devil take you, Perry. Help me up or be forever damned. . . . Water . . . ale . . . where's . . . Chilcot? . . ."

Perry had him under the arms, hauling him up to his feet, staggering beneath his weight as Gareth slumped heavily against him.

"Fifteen . . . sixteen . . . seventeen . . ."

"Get a hold of yourself, damn you!" Perry hissed in his ear, and Gareth's eyes flew open as Perry's palm smacked him hard on one cheek, then the other. Reflexively, he almost hit him back with a closed fist before realizing, belatedly, that it was his friend who had struck him, not that bastard Campbell, and—

*Oh, God help me, why won't my legs work?*

"Twenty-one . . . twenty-two . . . twenty-three . . ."

An egg came streaking past his face and splattered against the wall.

"Get out there and fight, you miserable nob!"

The chalked line swayed and reeled beneath Gareth's blinking eyes, and then Perry planted a hand between his shoulders and shoved him mightily back in toward Campbell. Just outside the ring Gareth caught a glimpse of Snelling, standing with arms folded and a triumphant smile on his face.

That was all it took.

With a roar, he rushed at Campbell, feinting with

his left as he came in with his right. The Scot's tree trunk of an arm came up to block it, and Gareth, recovering, came in under it, landing a brutal blow to his opponent's ribs that split the skin of every one of his knuckles and rewarded him with the sound of a loud crack. *It's about time,* he thought, with sudden, frenzied glee, and then the two were fighting in earnest, striking, feinting, blocking the other's punches and slugging it out like there was no tomorrow. The crowd went insane, rushing up the steps, pressing against the ropes, yelling themselves hoarse. Snelling's assured grin froze, began to look strained as Gareth beat the Scot back against the ropes, hitting so hard and fast that Campbell could do nothing but block and guard. Perry, dutifully following Gareth around the ring, looked as smug as a cat who'd just caught a robin. And the Butcher was no longer smiling, devoting all his concentration to fending off Gareth's powerful punches as he looked for an opening to get in a few of his own. Both fighters were breathing hard now, sweating, their muscles pumped up and the veins standing out on their mighty arms.

"Come on, you ugly-faced, porridge-eating haggis head!" Gareth taunted, circling the Scot and teasing him with sharp jabs designed to make that mighty fist lash out again so he could plant another blow beneath it. "Come on, hit me, you yellow-livered—"

*Bang!* Out came that murderous fist. Gareth's right forearm flew up to guard his face, and Campbell's knuckles, with all seventeen stone of his weight behind them, hit it with the force of a boulder from a catapult, maiming muscle, cracking bone, and sending agony shrieking up the arm in a blinding torrent of pain. Gareth staggered backward, his arm rendered useless for hitting, for guarding, for feinting, even—leaving him only his head, left arm, and heart to defend him as the Scot came charging down on him like a bull at a matador.

*That's it. I'm done for now.*

The Butcher hit him hard. Impulsively, Gareth threw up his injured arm to guard the next blow, screaming hoarsely as Campbell's fist connected at the site of the break. Nausea flared in his stomach. Sweat ran down his face, and as he hit out frantically with his still very capable left, he happened to catch a glimpse of the swelling crowds just beyond Campbell's bulging shoulder.

There, sitting well above the world atop his mighty black beast, was a grim-faced, and monstrously angry, Lucien.

Beside him was Fox, mounted on what looked to be . . .

*Crusader?*

*Bang,* the Butcher's fist caught him square on the chin, and Gareth reeled backward, seeing stars. Bugger this. He was furious now. Furious with Lucien for taking his time in getting here, furious his brother was giving him that cold, I-told-you-you're-an-idiot stare from his lofty throne atop Armageddon, furious with Campbell, with Juliet, with the crowds, with everyone. Sod this for a lark, he wasn't going to stand here and take this sort of abuse, not with Snelling leaping up and down in excitement as Campbell hammered him like a woodpecker might a tree, not with his brother watching in disgust and disdain, and damn it all, not with Swanthorpe hanging in the balance. There was only one way to defeat this oatmeal-eating bully, and it had nothing to do with brawn, only brains.

*I may be down, but I'm sure as hell not out!*

His useless right arm cradled to his chest, Gareth lunged in with his left, aiming for Campbell's eye and instead connecting with the shelf of bone just above it. *If I can only blind him, with blood or a blow,*

*I may yet win this fight!* The flesh opened like meat beneath a cleaver, sending blood trickling down through Campbell's bushy eyebrow and into his lashes. The crowd went wild. Campbell, roaring, pawed at his eye and shook his head, and Gareth took advantage of his opponent's disorientation by charging back in with renewed confidence, his knuckles slamming into Campbell's nose, his eye, and again, that fearsome brow. Blood was running down the Scot's face now, the eye already beginning to close, and Gareth knew that if he could only close them both, the fight would be his. Buoyed by success, he struck with lethal speed, pounding the Scot's face and further opening the cut above his eye with each blow that connected, again and again and again until the big Celt had both arms up to shield his face—an action that brought on a thunderous roar of disapproval from a crowd that found such a cowardly defense worse than contemptuous.

Maneuvering his opponent, his one fist flying and his body sheened in sweat, Gareth looked out over the crowd and saw Lucien.

No longer furious, but smiling.

And now he was driving the Butcher straight back into the ropes while around him he heard Snelling cursing, the Den members yelling encouragement, the crowd cheering him on. He was going to win. He was going to defeat the Butcher fair and square and Swanthorpe was going to be his—

But Campbell rallied. With a mighty roar, he lowered his head and came straight for Gareth, seizing him round the waist, crushing his broken arm against his ribs as he lifted him high into the air, and hurling him with colossal force straight down at the stone floor. There was a loud crack as the back of Gareth's head hit the stage. Then Campbell landed heavily atop him, and Gareth knew no more.

\* \* \*

"Damnation!"

The shouts of the crowd ringing in his ears, the referee's toll of a count already beginning, Perry charged forward, both he and Woodford frantically trying to lift Campbell off of Gareth's still body.

"Four . . . five . . . six . . ."

"He's not getting up. Call off the fight," growled Woodford.

"Sod off!"

"Seven . . . eight . . . nine . . ."

Perry desperately tried to rouse his friend. He slapped his cheek and shook him and leaned down and shouted in his ear. Nothing.

"Eleven . . . twelve . . . thirteen . . ."

He couldn't hear with the rising roar around him, couldn't think with the panic that was making his heart race, didn't know whether to call off the fight or what. Again, he slapped Gareth's cheeks, but there was no response, not even a groan of pain, and beneath still, half-closed lashes, Perry could see the milky crescent of his friend's eyes, rolled back in his head and seeing nothing.

He looked up, saw the Den members gesturing and waving, and there, off above a sea of heads, the Duke of Blackheath coming forward, the crowd parting before Armageddon like waves before a ship.

"Seventeen . . . eighteen . . . nineteen . . ."

*"Damn you, Gareth, wake up!"*

The Butcher, bleeding heavily, was strutting around his fallen rival in amusement and high contempt, holding his arms over his head in a victory salute, shouting. The Den members were all yelling at the top of their lungs, the duke was still coming, and Perry, desperate, bent down, bodily picked up Gareth and threw him over his shoulder, and, staggering beneath his weight, rushed him back to their corner, rudely dumping him on the cold stone and ripping the bottle of ale from Chilcot's stunned hand. He poured it straight over Gareth's face—

"Twenty-two . . . twenty-three . . . twenty-four . . ."

—and was rewarded with a sudden flutter of his friend's lashes, a sharp, spastic jerk of his head, and a groan of pain. Dizzily, Gareth tried to raise himself, only to sway and fall back against Perry's arm with a sigh.

"Twenty-five . . . twenty-six . . . twenty-seven . . ."

Three seconds left. Cursing, Perry grabbed Gareth's injured arm and twisted it right back, and his friend lunged to his feet with an inhuman howl of pain, lashing out with a fist that nearly took off the top of Perry's blond head. But he was up, if dazedly awake, and Perry wasted no time rushing him back to the line and shoving him at the Butcher once more.

Gareth, reeling and all at sea, saw only a blurry vortex of faces spinning around him. He saw Campbell's bloody visage moving in and out of his vision, heard the crowd shouting at him to pull himself together, felt only pain . . . throbbing viciously in his arm, his bruised ribs, pulsing in the back of a skull that felt as if it had been mashed like a potato. And now Campbell was hitting him again, hard, but the pain seemed to come from far away, and Gareth had little interest in defending himself, only standing there, swaying on his feet, blinking dumbly with each blow. From some distant part of his brain that was still functioning, he found himself hoping that Juliet wasn't here to see this . . . that she would never hear about it . . . that the Butcher would just hurry up and put him to sleep because he could feel stone beneath his knees now, and Campbell was still hitting him, and Perry was yelling "Foul!" and Lucien—'Sdeath, was that Lucien?—was bellowing in a voice that could've shaken the very heavens:

*"Perry! Stop the goddamned fight! Stop it this instant*

*or by God, I'll haul you straight to the gallows for manslaughter!"*

"No!" Gareth cried, shaking his head, and then pandemonium broke loose as Lucien spurred Armageddon right up the shallow stairs onto the stage, the crowd shouting and roaring behind him. The referees were yelling. Snelling was hollering. The crowd swelled in a mighty human tide toward the ropes, Campbell came charging down on Gareth like a lion on a kill, and Gareth knew then that if he didn't do something, he was going to die.

Lunging to his feet, he braced himself, took a deep breath, and stopped the Butcher with a single blow between the eyes. Campbell dropped like a stone. The crowd went insane. And Gareth staggered away, reeling off the ropes and mustering all his strength in a desperate bid to stay on his feet as the referee began the slow count for his opponent....

"Twenty-eight . . . twenty-nine . . . thirty." He grabbed Gareth's bleeding fist and thrust it high. *"The winner!"*

And then the screaming throngs were rushing the stage, the Den members were vaulting in over the ropes, and Lucien, his face thunderous, was heading straight to where Gareth, sporting a silly little grin, stood swaying dizzily.

"Guess what, Luce . . . I'm a landowner now!"

He blinked as a slight form brushed past his brother and came running across the stage, skirts flying, tears streaming down her face.

"Juliet?" he managed, in stunned disbelief.

And as Gareth's tenuous hold on consciousness finally broke, it was she who caught him and, holding him until Lucien could pick him up and lift him over his shoulder, silently followed the brothers back across the stage to where Armageddon waited—leaving Sir Roger Foxcote, and the constable, to approach a suddenly quaking Snelling.

"You, my man, are under arrest."

# 34

**I**f Campbell hadn't nearly murdered his brother, Lucien swore he would've done so himself.

It had taken Gareth almost two hours to regain consciousness after he'd gone down that final time, and as a grim-faced Lucien had put his senseless sibling aboard Armageddon and brought him back to Swanthorpe with hundreds of cheering, reveling people following in their wake, he had thought for sure he'd soon be mourning a second brother.

Victory, exhaustion, and a concussion had made for a powerful sedative. But late that night—after the doctor had set his broken arm, and while Juliet was sitting on the bed holding cold compresses to his swollen face—Gareth finally opened his eyes, his return to consciousness greeted by dizziness, blurred vision, and bouts of severe nausea.

"Serves you right," Lucien growled. He took the cloth from Juliet and hurled it at his brother's bare chest. "Put this against your head, and it won't hurt so bad."

But Gareth, looking dazedly up at Juliet, wasn't paying him any attention. Instead, he was staring at his wife as though she was the dearest thing he had ever beheld, as though he had never expected to see her again. Which, Lucien reflected dryly, was not so unlikely a supposition. He had arrived at the dower house just after six to find his brother already gone to the fight—and his new sister-in-law packing her trunk and sobbing her eyes out.

Crying females did not amuse him. Soppy tales of prideful husbands did not faze him. And her angry protests did not deter him when, after precisely two minutes of listening to that idiotic nonsense, he plucked Charlotte from her arms and thrust her into the stunned Sir Hugh's, bodily threw Juliet over his shoulder and, striding back outside to where Armageddon waited, personally brought her to the fight himself—where her bristling defiance had turned to heartbroken misery as she'd seen Gareth taking a beating from the Butcher and realized just what her husband was doing for her.

Not for himself—but for her and Charlotte.

Now, as Lucien stood there watching their nauseating display of love and forgiveness, he felt compelled to vent his spleen.

"All right, that's enough of this damned sickly-sweet foolishness," he growled, stalking to the bed and glaring down at his brother. "You listen to me, and you listen well, Gareth. Your fighting days are over. And if I *ever* hear of you taking on a champion pugilist again—"

Gareth waved him off. "Give me some credit, would you? After all, I *did* beat the fellow."

Lucien tightened his jaw. So he had. He'd also won himself a lucrative estate, exposed Snelling for the murdering swindler he was, and won the hearts of the people of Abingdon with his courage against the Butcher.

Earlier, while waiting for Gareth to come to his senses, Juliet had told Lucien everything she knew. Her story had been confirmed by Fox, who had stopped by after having applied a certain amount of . . . duress to Snelling to get a confession not only from him, but also from Woodford, Creedon, and even Angus "the Butcher" Campbell—who admitted that Snelling had promised him an additional two hundred pounds if he killed his opponent during the fight.

Enhanced by testimonies from the widowed Mrs. Fleming, the chemist in Oxford, and even a sober Bull O'Rourke, it was not hard to put together a frightening picture.

Snelling, it appeared, had assembled a stable of tough, seasoned fighters who were among the best in England and pitted them against each other every Friday night. When he'd seen Gareth fight Joe Lumford that evening at Mrs. Bottomley's, Snelling had come up with a scheme that would make him a staggering amount of money. As Gareth was an unknown newcomer, there was little reason for the vast crowds who came to watch the fights to think he could hold his own against the likes of Nails Fleming, Bull O'Rourke, or Angus "the Butcher" Campbell—much less beat them. And they had bet their money accordingly. With each fight, Snelling had matched Gareth against a man who was heavily favored to trounce him. Then, all Snelling had to do was put *his* money on Gareth, slip just enough laudanum to the favorite to subtly dull his reflexes, and take home a fortune.

Unfortunately, an innocent man had died because of it. But Nails's death would not go unavenged. The next trip Snelling made would be his last, for at this very moment, the brilliant Fox was pulling out all the stops to ensure that Snelling and his henchman would hang for Nails's murder.

*And for plotting to kill my brother*, Lucien thought, savagely.

Thank God for his trusty informer, who was not quite as brainless as everyone believed. If Chilcot had not sent word to him, he would never have reached Abingdon in time.

Not that it would've mattered. As things turned out, his brother had done just fine without him.

Lucien was still scowling as he helped Juliet prop Gareth's shoulders up on the pillows to ease his throbbing head. Amazingly, she was not angry with him for dragging her to the fight in such a rough and undignified way—not that he cared one way or another whether she was or not. She had seen him cursing Snelling to eternal hell while the doctor had set Gareth's arm. She had seen him fretting, swearing, and pacing as he'd waited impatiently for his brother to come to. Oh, she saw right through him, had done so from the start, and knew him exactly for what he was: an overprotective older brother whose fear for the sibling he loved had switched to angry relief the moment Gareth had opened those guileless blue eyes of his.

Lucien grabbed up the candlestick beside the bed. "You ought to count yourself damned lucky that you're not dead," he growled, holding the candle over Gareth's face and leaning down to stare into his eyes.

Gareth swatted him away. "What the devil are you doing?"

"Nothing."

"The doctor told us to watch your pupils," Juliet explained. "If they're different sizes, it could mean you have brain damage."

Gareth only laughed.

"Nothing wrong with *you*," Lucien muttered, straightening up. He slammed the candlestick back on the nighttable so hard that it dented the wood.

"Yes, well, stay out of my face and there'll be nothing wrong with *you*, either," Gareth returned with mock threat, sighing happily as Juliet pulled the covers up over his arms. Lucien saw another of those nauseatingly sweet, sickeningly tender gazes pass between them. Faintly disgusted, he rolled his eyes and turned away.

Leave it to the Wild One to stumble into a killer's scheme and emerge with one of the finest estates in Berkshire. He was lucky he wasn't dead.

*But by God, I am proud of him.*

Proud, yes. But furious. And what still had him particularly incensed was the fact that Gareth had known what Snelling was doing, but hadn't summoned him until it was nearly too late. Then Snelling's man had intercepted his message. *Christ.* Had Snelling found out any earlier that Gareth had been on to him, Gareth—like Charles—might be lying in a grave with a bullet in him. Lucien cursed between his teeth, even as he silently admired his brother for his courage and cleverness.

"Luce?"

Lucien, hiding that admiration beneath a black scowl, stared down at him.

"You still haven't told me how you got Crusader back."

"Fox saw him at Tattersall's and promptly bought him back for you. Now, go to sleep. Get some rest. I want you to heal up so I can beat the living daylights out of you, myself."

"I dare you to try it," Gareth whispered, with a weak grin. "I'm a champion now, you know."

Lucien stared down at him. And then he shook his head, no longer able to prevent a little smile from touching his severe and unforgiving mouth. "So you are," he said softly. "So you are."

Gareth raised one eyebrow in surprise.

Lucien added, "Believe it or not, you've fulfilled my expectations and become the man I always thought you could be." His smile deepened. "You've grown up, little brother. I'm proud of you."

And with that he turned on his heel and left the couple staring after him in stunned shock.

\* \* \*

The room was quiet, dimly lit by two candles; pulled up near the bed, in her cradle, Charlotte gave a tiny sigh as she dreamed.

Juliet waited until the duke's footsteps faded, then looked down at her husband.

"Well, well. Monsters do have hearts, after all," she mused, grinning. And then, as she caressed his lips with her fingertip: "Gareth?"

"Yes, my love?"

"Just one thing. If you ever *do* do anything like this again, Lucien won't have the chance to kill you because I'm going to get to you first."

He laughed, curved his good arm around her neck, and, ignoring her feeble protests, pulled her down, kissing her so soundly that her head was soon as dizzy as his.

She snuggled up beside him, and he drew her right up next to him. They lay facing each other on one pillow, his fingers lightly caressing her breast.

"I love you, Gareth."

"Ah, Juliet, I love you, too. I cannot tell you what it meant to me to see you running across the stage toward me tonight . . . to know that you had not left me, after all." He swallowed hard, his eyes dark with the force of his gratitude, his love. "My greatest victory this evening was not defeating the Butcher; it was waking up and finding you here, with me."

"Oh, Gareth . . . can you ever forgive me for doubting you?"

"I will forgive you anything, my love. Now, go snuff out the candles and get back down here under the covers with me, would you?" He found her nipple with his thumb and, with a wicked little grin, played with it until it peaked. "This bed is too big and lonely without you."

# Epilogue

I t was three weeks before Christmas. Lucien, who'd lingered at breakfast after the others had made their excuses, was sipping his coffee and contemplating how to straighten out Andrew—as he had so cleverly straightened out Gareth—when a footman brought in a silver platter bearing the morning post and presented it to His Grace.

He went through it with his usual lack of interest. Nothing out of the ordinary, here. Bills, investment opportunities, loan requests from friends and charities, invitations to social events, and ah!—his brows rose in interest—two letters. He tossed the other post aside and slit the seal on the first one. It was from Gareth and Juliet, full of recent news: about Charlotte, who was now walking; about Gareth, who'd recently been elected the local Member of Parliament; about Juliet, who was expecting their second child. The letter ended with an invitation for the whole family to spend Christmas at Swanthorpe.

The duke leaned back, thoughtfully stroking his chin. Outside, it was one of those rare days in an English winter when the sun, low in the sky and still weak, had managed to burn through the clouds and turn the sky the color of bluebells.

Christmas at Swanthorpe. He smiled. Hell, why not?

He folded the letter, basking in the satisfied glow he always got when he considered his part in bringing Gareth and Juliet together. Another grand machination with a fruitful outcome.

Of course.

The Wild One all squared away. *Time to get to work on Andrew, the Defiant One.*

Ah, yes. Now *there* would be a challenge....

Still grinning, he picked up the other letter, bearing the postmark of some town in America he had never heard of. The writing on the front looked oddly familiar. Frowning, Lucien turned the letter over, broke the seal—and began to read:

> *October 28, 1776*
>
> *My dear brother, Lucien ...*

*What?!* Lucien came halfway out of his chair, nearly upsetting the table. "My God! *He's alive!*"

He cursed his eyes for their inability to travel as fast as his excitement as he raced through the rest of the letter:

> *... I do not quite know how to begin this letter, especially knowing what you must believe—and what you will think of me after you have read it through. I hope to God my family has not wept for me, as I do not deserve your tears, your concern, not even your forgiveness. I have much to say, and much to explain as regards my absence and the unhappy fact that everyone seems to have believed me dead—but I dare say that a letter is not the place to do it, and there are things I would speak to you about only when I am back in England with my family.*
>
> *To that end, I will be taking passage home in two weeks, and hope to be with you all for Christmas.*

*Please discard all memories of the man you once knew me to be; illness and circumstance have made me but a shadow of my former self, and you should not expect too highly of me when next we meet.*

*I look forward to seeing you all soon. May God bless and keep you.*

*Charles*

Lucien sat there for a moment, stunned. Then, the letter clenched in his hand, he strode hurriedly from the room, bellowing for Nerissa and Andrew.

Work on the Defiant One, it seemed, would just have to wait.

The Beloved One was coming home.

# Author's Note

**I** hope you've enjoyed meeting Juliet and her dashing Wild One, whose story is the first in my de Montforte Brothers series. We can only wonder what the enigmatic Lucien has planned for poor Charles—who has been rather broken by his experiences in America. I dare say the duke will have his hands full; the Beloved One may require his brother's manipulating interference even more than Gareth did!

Those intimately familiar with England may wonder about the strange geographical placement of Abingdon-on-Thames in this book. In the mid-1970s, county boundaries were shifted, and Abingdon—once the County Town of Berkshire—became part of Oxfordshire, where it remains today.

I enjoyed giving Juliet and Gareth a home in this town which is very dear to my own heart. My husband and I were married in Abingdon, where we have made many lovely friends and memories. Swanthorpe Manor is set in the meadow beside the River Thames where my dog, Roscoe, and I went for our morning walks, and many of the landmarks mentioned in this book—St. Nicholas's Church, East St. Helen's Street, the Mill Stream, Abbey Meadow, the Market Place, even the County Hall where Gareth won both a fight and a home for his family—are well worth a visit for anyone traveling in the heart of England.

For more about my books, visit my web page at: http://members.aol.com/dharmon2—where you can see covers, read my newsletter, and even vote for your favorite "Harmon Hero." You can also write to me; either by e-mail at *Dharmon2@aol.com*, or old-fashioned "snail mail" c/o Danelle Harmon, P.O. Box 6091, Newburyport, MA, 01950. I love hearing from my readers.

Wishing you all the best,

*Danelle Harmon*

Dear Reader,

If you've just finished this Avon romance title and are looking for more of the best in romantic fiction, then be on the watch for these upcoming romance titles—available at your favorite bookstore!

*Affaire de Coeur* says Genell Dellin is " . . . one of the best writers of ethnic romances starring Native Americans." And her latest, AFTER THE THUNDER, is Native American romance filled with sensuality and emotion. When a young Shaman falls for a scandalous young woman he must decide if he will fulfill the needs of the spirit—or the body.

For lovers of Scotland settings, don't miss the luscious A ROSE IN SCOTLAND by Joan Overfield. When a desperate young woman marries the handsome, brooding Laird of Lochhaven, she expects nothing more than a marriage of convenience. But what begins as duty turns into something much more.

Maureen McKade's A DIME NOVEL HERO is a must-read for those who like their heroes tough and their settings western. This tender romance about a woman who writes dime novels, her adopted son and the man she's turned into an unwilling hero—and who is unknowingly the boy's father—is sure to touch your heart.

Contemporary romance fans are sure to love SIMPLY IRRESISTIBLE by debut author Rachel Gibson. A sassy charm school graduate is on the run—from her own wedding. She's rescued by a sexy guest but never dreams that, nine months later, she'll have a little bundle of joy—proof of their whirlwind romance. And when he barges back into her life, complications ensue—and romance is rekindled.

Remember, look to Avon Books for the very best in romance!

Sincerely,
Lucia Macro
Avon Books

AEL 1197